THE DARKNESS WITHIN

RACHEL GIES

© Copyright 2008 Fairburn Publishing Corporation

First Edition

All rights reserved. Reproduction in whole or part of any portion in any form without permission of the publisher is prohibited.

P.O. Box 1164
St. Charles, IL 60175
fairburn22@aol.com
(630) 513-6070

ISBN: 978-0-9709960-2-2

Library of Congress: 2007942076

Printed in the United States of America

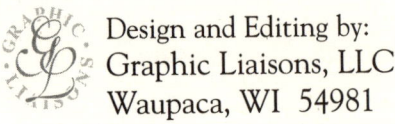

Design and Editing by:
Graphic Liaisons, LLC
Waupaca, WI 54981

Detailing and Research by:

DEDICATION

To Larry, my beloved husband, who has always stood beside me. To my children and wonderful grandchildren, the lights in my life.
Love,
Amoo/Oma

If you fear the life hereafter,
You don't believe in God.

If you don't believe in God,
Why fear the life hereafter?

—Larry Gies Sr.

PROLOGUE

Standing quietly in the shadows of the garage—the beast waited: watching for the approach of the two people on this earth who were to be removed. Backing up slightly it merged with the darkness—not wanting to be spotted. This would free them, it thought, just before a shooting pain encompassed its brain. A clammy hand moved to rub slowly across a worried brow. Not now—it was finally time to finish this.

The pain subsided momentarily answering the feverish command. Slowly drops of perspiration gathered before escaping in rivulets off the bridge of its nose. The figures neared—they could be heard arguing. The woman's high-pitched voice echoed through the air as the man's deep, but slurred speech, dominated the bickering.

The beast tensed, barely able to make out what was being said. But what was transpiring between the couple was all too familiar. The face contorted into a cynical twist. Of course! That bastard was drunk, as usual.

The world had no idea of the evil, self-serving man who hid behind the socially prominent businessman. The mansion and Mercedes were a small payoff for the sins this man had committed in the name of business. He had used and abused for the last time, it was time for him to pay.

The plans for this evening had been a dominant force in its brain for months. Nothing would go wrong. It had all been planned carefully. The brakes would give out on old River Road near Morton's Curve, there was no way anyone could make it around the cliffs without brakes. They would die—both of them! They deserved to go together! Rubbing sweaty palms in anticipation it muttered, "They will die!" clenching its teeth fiercely. So many would be freed when this devil has left the earth.

They got into the car and both car doors slammed shut simultaneously. The man behind the wheel backed out of the long drive. The police would immediately think George's drunk driving caused the accident. It was a well-known fact that George had a penchant for getting behind the wheel after one too many.

Too bad, so sad, it thought, chuckling quietly. The car disappeared ahead. The beast would follow them and watch—just to be sure. There would be no clues and the plan would be complete.

Not too close. Not that they would notice—obviously, they were still fighting as usual. The fight probably started long before they left the house. She got off on it, why else would she have tolerated it for so long?

Following close enough to see the red gleam of the tail lights ahead, it only wished to see their faces the moment they discovered their imminent demise. Soon, soon, the misery would end. Finally, the drunk would get what he deserved and he would have to answer for his disgusting and unforgivable history, with her right beside him as she always was—knowing, but unapologetic!

It was amazing how steady George kept the car on the narrow road. The bastard actually drove better drunk than sober … *Ah, but, slow down—here it comes.*

The brake lights glowed as the driver began to weave across the winding road. Tires screeched and the smell of rubber burning filled the silent night air as he took the sharp turns around the hilltop at a dangerous speed.

Back off, not too close! Hands clenched the steering wheel tightly. The beating of its evil heart vibrated in its ears as if following a rolling drumbeat in the night. It could feel the blood rushing through beastly veins. The tongue moistened cracked, dry lips.

Desperate to control the out-of-control vehicle around the cliff's rocky curve, George Coleman turned too fast causing the car to rise off two wheels and suddenly disappear over the edge and into the night.

A crazy excitement empowered the beast like some kind of weird high. It had been so easy. The planet was finally rid of the rank poison that had affected so many lives. Maybe … no, definitely, this should have been done sooner, a long time ago. So many people would have been spared.

But there were no regrets now as the beast got out to peer over the edge. Quickly it returned to the vehicle and sped away from the scene. *The world is better off without them*, it thought. Taking one last look into the rearview mirror the stench of burning metal and gas enveloped it. Breathing the pollution deep into its animalistic lungs the beast thought to itself *as if the dead would have one last say before descending into the bowels of hell. May you rot in hell George Coleman— you and your bitch wife!* The echoes of uncontrollable laughter reverberated off the still, silent cliffs.

ACKNOWLEDGMENTS

My sincere thanks to Camin Potts of Graphic Liaisons, LLC for photography, design, and layout, Marcia Lorenzen for proofreading and editing, and to VJ Bardship Research and Development for their assistance in my writing endeavors. Thanks also to Jenny Vater and Jory Eaton.

Special thanks to my good friend Carol Bayer for helping me out, you've done so much more than take my picture! You're the best.

Thanks to the Animal Haven Zoo and its owners, Dawn and Jim Hofferber in Weyauwega, Wisconsin, and the lions and ligers who posed for our camera. Visit the zoo at www.go2weyauwega.com.

—*Rachel Gies*

ONE

Kate Coleman stared vacantly at the magnificent house in front of her as she held back the tears that were threatening to fall once more. Her topaz-colored eyes were red and swollen. The brisk wind whipping about her face pulled at her emotions and she bit her bottom lip to hold back the flood threatening to cloud her vision.

"This was home once." she said out loud, as if to convince herself of that actual fact. Even though her condo was only a few miles away, she and her parents were three strangers that rarely crossed paths. The well-manicured lawn and pristine flower garden belied the turmoil and unhappiness that was hidden behind the walls of the stunning estate. The time had come to make some decisions. The tragedy of last week could no longer be held at bay—she needed to move on.

The death of both parents in the fatal car accident had been a hard hitting reality for her as she made funeral arrangements and attended alone. Her brother, Nick, was off on assignment for his newspaper and was impossible to track down. He called in sporadically to let her know he was still alive, but this time was the longest she'd ever been without him. Odd though, she wasn't worried, she knew he'd be back, not for her parents, but for her.

The true miracle was that it hadn't happened sooner. Her father was a drunk. There! She admitted it! Her father had been a drunk—a mean drunk. It had been a fact of her family's life. A fact they had tried to keep hidden from the outside world.

Kate knew her parents rarely spent time together, but because it was an anniversary, they probably forced themselves to go out. Mom had been concerned with her image and Dad ... well— Dad had his own kind of entertainment. How ironic that her parents died on their wedding anniversary!

When the call came from the detective and was asked to identify the bodies she had been shocked. But if she was honest with herself she always knew the day would come. When the investigation had shown George Coleman was drunk at the time of the accident Kate could only summon feelings of relief, that the abuse was over, and sadness for the life that might have been. Identifying the badly-burned bodies had been difficult and she wished again that her brother had been available. A family friend, Dr. Norton, had accompanied her to the morgue. His steady shoulder and kind words had helped Kate through the ordeal.

"Nick, where are you?" she whispered. The newspaper had tried to reach him but so far had not met with any success. He had forwarded articles to the paper from France, and should be in Paris, but until he called in again the paper could not reach him. Nick was a somewhat renegade reporter—often going off on tangents other than his assignments. The paper tolerated his side jaunts because, on several occasions, his hide-and-seek methods of reporting had led the paper to breaking news and exclusive reports that boosted their circulation.

Sighing heavily, Kate fumbled for the house key. Her friend, Casey Waters, had dropped her off and was disappearing in reverse down the long drive. Kate was ready to check on the house. Casey insisted on going with her but she had an appointment in a half hour and Kate wouldn't wait. She wanted to be able to take her time in the vacant house and wasn't afraid to be alone. The monsters who once lived here were dead. But, the true friend that she was, Casey stubbornly tried to refused to accept Kate's logic.

"At least let me drop you off and I will be back as soon as I can. You don't need to be alone now, girl. It's my week to drive and drive I shall! Besides, you know the rule! Driver picks the diner!"

Casey had a never-ending craving for the spicy side of life—whether it was music, men, or food. While Kate liked authentic Mexican food as well as Casey—three nights in a row could be a bit much. But Casey was craving hot tamales and burritos at a record pace. Casey found comfort in food when things got stressful.

Resolutely she made her way to the front door, turning the key in the lock and fumbling for the light switch. The sudden brightness of the recessed lights burned her weary eyes stopping her just inside the doorway. But it was the scene before her that caused her to drop the keys. She didn't know what she was looking at, then slowly she realized it was her own image in shards of broken glass. In the foyer mirror looking back at her was a menagerie of her reflection in shattered glass, it was difficult to recognize that the image in the mirror was actually her. Breaking the hold it had on her she looked past the mirror. Overturned and broken furniture, smashed lamps, and a slashed sofa screamed of hatred. Quickly she turned to stop Casey only to see her car disappear around the corner.

Backing out of the doorway and shaking badly she fumbled desperately for the cell phone in her purse and dialed 911. It seemed an eternity before the responder came on the line.

"San Francisco 911, what is your emergency?"

"I want to report a break-in!" Kate whispered as she hurried down the front steps to get away from the house.

"Are you alone, Miss?" the responder asked.

"Yes. What should I do? Please help me." She didn't know where she was going and almost tripped over the hedges into the front lawn.

"Give me your name and address please, Miss," came the calm voice on the other end of the line.

"Kate Coleman, and I'm at my parents' home at 1237 Gateway Drive." She glanced up at the house numbers as if she may be wrong.

"Are you still in the house?"

"Yes, er, no ... I am at the house well, outside the house ..."

"All right, Miss Coleman, I want you to leave the residence and wait for the patrol car that is already on its way. Do you have a vehicle there?"

"Yes, my brother's car is parked in the driveway, but I don't know if its open."

"I'll wait while you try to get into the car and lock the doors. What type of car is it, Miss Coleman?"

She ran toward the car with the phone glued to her ear.

"A brown Chevy Malibu." She was in luck the driver's door was open. "I'm in!"

"All right, Miss Coleman. I have informed the officers and I'll stay on the line with you until they arrive. Is there any other information you can give me?"

"My parents died in an automobile accident last week on River Road not far from here. The house has been empty since then."

There was a pause at the other end, then a gentle, "I am very sorry for your loss, Miss Coleman. The police officers should be there in a minute and Detective Connery is right behind them."

As the operator finished Kate could see the flashing lights of the San Francisco squad car as it swung into the drive. She thanked the voice on the phone for the help as the officers motioned her to stay put and made their way into the residence with guns drawn. A sedan pulled up behind her and a tall, slender man emerged from the black 4-door. *This must be the detective,* Kate thought as she eyed a pair of unbelievably long legs and chiseled features. He shot her a look with cold, steel-blue eyes.

"Miss Coleman?" His smokey voice made her hold her breath.

Kate nodded and for some reason wanted to cry.

"Detective Flynn Connery. Please stay in your car while we check out the premises."

Kate couldn't take her eyes off the detective and admired his business-like stroll. Broad shoulders topped the "V" of his frame. There was definitely nothing "hard on the eyes" about this man. Mentally Kate shook herself. *What was wrong with her—ogling a man with all that is going on?* In a few long strides he made his way to the front door and disappeared inside.

Connery surveyed the violent disarray as he entered. He called out to the team already searching the premises. He could hear doors kicked open followed by the word "Clear" as the officers checked room after room. "Nobody's here—no sign of entry or exit." *Someone wasn't just looking for something, this is random damage as if someone just went nuts,* he thought as he surveyed the destroyed couch and broken lamps. He carefully made notes while dialing the precinct office to ask for a Crime Scene Investigator to be sent over. Considering the owners had just recently been killed in a car accident and that the Colemans had been a wealthy family the list of "who-dun-its" would be long. He cautiously made his way to the back of the house as the other officers made their way upstairs.

Connery was returning to the foyer when Officer Malone called from the second floor.

"Connery, you'd better get up here."

Connery made short work of the stairs. Malone was standing back against the hallway wall with his gun drawn while his partner, Sergeant Wilkes, checked the room. As Connery crossed the threshold into the bedroom Malone muttered, "This is some sick S.O.B."

There, lying on the bed, were two child-size dolls dressed up in oversized business-like clothing. Both had big red smiles painted on their faces. Connery had the same crawling feeling run down his spine that he had two years ago when he helped track down a serial killer in the same area. He learned to pay attention to that feeling. He searched the room for anything the experts might miss—the more eyes the better. He never trusted anyone to do their job if it had anything to do with his. Convinced the perpetrator set this scene up to scare the woman who found it he slowly backed out of the room. Still searching floor to ceiling for anything out of the ordinary, he made his way to the frightened woman outside.

"Miss Coleman?"

Kate nodded.

"You don't actually live here do you?"

Kate nodded, then shook her head "Yes, no, uhm, what I mean is, this is my parents' home but they just died in a car accident last week, I have a condo up the road ... why?"

"You'll need to stay out of the house while we investigate thoroughly."

"Why? What happened inside?" Kate asked anxiously.

"Do you know anyone who would want to hurt you—or your family?"

Well, my parents are dead, but that was an accident, wasn't it? she thought as she found herself mesmerized by the pale-blue glint of the detective's eyes, peering down at her. The tousled brown hair added to his rugged good looks.

"No. I didn't think so, until now. Why?"

Detective Connery explained the scene that was obviously meant for her to find in the bedroom upstairs.

Kate's eyes widened in fear, "Why would someone do this?" she asked, bewildered. "It was meant for me to find, wasn't it? ... No one lives here anymore, since ..."

"That's what we're going to find out Miss Coleman. In the meantime I have a CSI on the way. Do you have someone you can stay with tonight?"

"Yes, my condo is over on DuPont. B-but my roommate dropped me off and was going to pick me up after her appointment ... I just had to ... I wanted to ..."

"I can escort you home. Why don't you see if you can find her, let her know what's going on. We can go over our findings tomorrow. You're obviously in a state of shock, this is a lot to absorb."

Kate nodded in agreement as she pulled out her cell phone and dialed the familiar number, hoping that Casey would answer. She heard Casey's voice, "Casey, it's Kate ... someone broke into my parent's house and the police are here. Can you come and get me?"

The detective could see the relief on her oval-shaped face and knew that she was in good hands with her friend. Against his will he felt drawn to the woman in the car. Her amazing eyes and caramel-colored hair complimented her skin, making her look soft and dreamlike. Her long, elegant fingers tapped absently on the car door as she finished her conversation. *Hmmm, No ring, but K.C. is probably her boyfriend.* Mentally he gave himself a shake. *What is the matter with me? I am on a case! I never mixed business with pleasure! I learned a long time ago, the cold, hard facts of police work. Commitment and romance does not stand up to late hours of obsessive investigation.*

"My Casey, er, uh my friend, will come and get me Detective. She'll be here soon." Kate was still shaking.

"Okay. Would you mind meeting here tomorrow to help identify anything missing? The CSI will be here as well."

"Yes, I have to know if anything was taken and why this happened. I get off work at four. It takes about twenty minutes to get here."

"Fine, we'll meet here by 4:30. You can walk through the house and see if you notice anything missing. In the meantime, try to think about who might want to hurt you or your family."

They waited in silence for Casey to arrive. Occasionally, Detective Connery would ask a question and Kate would try her best to answer honestly. But her mind was spinning. She felt personally attacked and bruised emotionally. What she really wanted was to rest and to feel safe and warm. She was suddenly very tired.

Casey finally arrived in her little Toyota. Connery breathed an involuntary sigh of relief to see she was a friend of the female persuasion. He escorted Kate to the car, gallantly opening her door for her before imparting one last word of caution. "Be careful ladies. Don't hesitate to call if something seems amiss or, Miss Coleman, if something comes to mind. Here is my card. I am always available." He closed the door gently and watched as they backed out of the driveway.

Casey pummeled Kate with questions as she headed her car back the way she had come. Kate explained the scene and they both reluctantly agreed that this must be related to her parents' death. Her father was bound to have pissed someone off as the owner of a major oil distributing company. They didn't know much about his business, but they knew he had been a shrewd business man and wasn't liked much. Besides, who would want to hurt or scare Kate? But with her parents already dead, what would they have to gain?

Casey chattered rapidly about nothing trying to change the mood. Kate welcomed the distraction, and before she knew it Casey had her at ease and involved in conversation. She forgot for a moment that someone may be after her, or worse yet, her parents' accident wasn't an accident. As she tried to forget the day's events, thoughts were replaced with a dull ache behind her eyes.

"Here we are," Casey interjected happily.

Kate groaned as she recognized where they were: The Hot Tamale, Casey's favorite Mexican restaurant. "You've got to be kidding me, Casey! You think my stomach can handle food right now?"

"Hey, I'm driving and I think a margarita will calm us both! What's the rule?"

Kate moaned but had to smile, "Driver picks the diner."

And both women climbed out of the car smiling, linking arms as they made their way inside. The cheery noise of the busy restaurant and the aroma of spicy food soon had Kate and Casey forgetting their worries.

I am very lucky to have such a friend, Kate thought to herself, not for the first time. Casey may not be a fashion model, in her torn jeans, pony tail, and gym shoes, but her unique ability to turn clouds into sunshine was priceless.

Later that night Kate tried to get some sleep and fight off thoughts of what kind of message someone was trying to send her. Her thoughts turning to Jason. She wasn't sure how long he'd been gone and so much had happened. She was seeing a successful surgeon at the same hospital where she and Casey worked in the Claims Department. Dr. Jason Mueller had jumped at the chance to join an elite team of surgeons in Africa on a mission to further medical awareness in the north African countries. They had discussed his leaving and Kate had been supportive of the trip, realizing that it was a great opportunity for him. The mission would also look impressive on his curriculum vittae once he decided to leave the hospital to join an independent practice.

The night before his departure Jason's proposal was ill-timed. "Marry me Kate, please, I love you."

She put him off telling him she needed time to think, giving him the reason that she wasn't ready to assume the position of a doctor's wife in high society. She thought this trip would be the opportunity she needed to put some distance between them. He was much too serious for her. She had seen the love shining in his eyes and wondered why she couldn't return it. Her dysfunctional family had done a real number on her and trusting others didn't come easy. She doubted if love would, either. If she couldn't love him it wouldn't be fair to string him along. Could she settle for a man who obviously adored her, or should she wait for the man that could set off fireworks? Is there such a man out there? With that thought in mind she fell into a fitful sleep.

The foggy scene confused the small girl. The muffled moaning continued as she made her way into the pink room. Her mother lay with her face buried in the oversized bed pillow.

"Mommy why are you crying? Please don't cry!" the small girl pleaded. Then she gasped in horror as her mother turned over to expose a swollen black eye and big bloody lip. Desperately the small girl tried to comfort her. Her little hands patted her mother's back and stroked her soft hair.

"Why do you let Daddy hurt you?" the small child questioned.

"Enough, Kate, shut-up! It's how our marriage works.

He gets what he wants and so do I," her mother sputtered.

The children had cringed when their father opened another bottle, but their mother was right there, pouring his drinks. The kids had learned to run, to hide, and to stay quiet. Why didn't she?

"Why don't you run and hide, Mommy? Can we leave him and go somewhere, anywhere else?"

Grace looked at her daughter wearily. "Keep your interfering mouth shut! Do you hear me? Leave? Why would I leave? Where would I go? Do you want to live out of a car? I couldn't find another man who could provide us with all of the things your father's money does—beautiful clothes, jewelry, a huge house. Where do you think this all comes from? Do you think I'm stupid? I'd never give all this up! No matter what it costs me—bruises heal. Diamonds are forever."

THE DARK BEAST INSIDE THE HOST SLEPT PEACEFULLY NOW. FOR THE TIME BEING THE VENGEANCE ON THE CLIFF HAD APPEASED ITS THIRST FOR JUSTICE.

THE HOST RELAXED, ENJOYING THE SILENCE AND THE FREEDOM FROM THE PAIN OF THE POUNDING HEADACHE. FOR NOW THE HOST COULD RETURN TO A NORMAL LIFE.

BUT DEEP INSIDE THE HOST KNEW THIS WAS ONLY A REPRIEVE. THE BEAST WOULD AWAKEN ONCE AGAIN, HUNGRY AND FURIOUS. WHEN THAT HAPPENED IT WOULD NEED TO FEED ITS HUNGER AND SOOTHE ITS FURY.

AS THE HOST THOUGHT OF HOME, THERE WAS HOPE THAT THIS WOULD, AT LAST, BE THE FINAL VENGEANCE DEMANDED BY THE BEAST.

COULD A BEGINNING BE THE END?

TWO

Kate slowly made her way through the ransacked interior, trying to distance herself from the damage and view the contents with a detached calm. She scanned the rooms carefully for any evidence of robbery, but she could not detect anything was missing.

Mechanically, she made her way upstairs to her parent's rooms. She had not entered her mother's bedroom since the day she had tried to comfort her as a little girl. The expensive paintings and wall hangings that had justified her mother's life choices were still hanging in the same places. The room smelled stuffy even though she knew that Mary Selina, the housekeeper, had been there just a few days before the break-in. The pink walls were a dull peachy color now. The closet was open and her mother's clothes were ripped off hangers.

Kate's heart lurched at the thought of releasing Mary. But until she knew what would happen with the estate she would keep Mary on as long as possible. Kate wondered if it was safe for the housekeeper to be in the house alone after the break-in. She was sure Mary would want to stay on. She had been with them for as long as Kate could remember. Kate realized she should have the detective talk to Mary. She left the room to lean over the hall banister and tell him so as he stood below in the downstairs stairwell.

Later she could contemplate whether she should keep the estate or sell the property. Nothing would be done until Nick returned from assignment. This must be a joint decision. Although, she couldn't imagine that they would want to keep the place—it wasn't as if the house held any memories of happy family times. Kate shook her head, bringing her back to the task at hand.

She let out a sigh as she took another look around her mother's bedroom. From the expensive French furniture to the impressionist paintings the room spoke of taste and elegance. But Kate had never cared for her mother's taste in decorating. Closing the door she made her way down the hallway to Nick's room.

The bed still wore the same well-used bedspread that it always had when Nick lived at home. Her mother's decorating stopped at the children's rooms. Without her brother's presence the room felt cold and empty. Nick's battered Teddy Bear sat on the shelf as if guarding the books that had been Nick's escape from reality. Again, Kate could not see that anything was missing. His room seemed to be left untouched.

Entering the hall, Kate made her way to the room that had been hers during her life in this house. The door was open and she prepared herself for the sight of the child-size dolls on the bed. She was so thankful the Detective had warned her in advance of the morbid scene. Fingerprint dust left a sticky black residue all over the dresser and shelves. The bed covers were draped awkwardly at the end of the bed where they had been left by the CSI team as they checked the dolls and bedding for clues to the intrusion. Even the mattress had been slashed. The closet doors hung open giving view of ransacked clothes and dislodged shoes—as if someone had been looking for something. The room spun. Inside she was going faster than she appeared outside. *How can I not take this personally and what the hell does it mean?* Her head screamed with questions. The feeling of being violated was quickly being replaced by anger.

Detective Connery paced restlessly in the main room downstairs, waiting for Miss Coleman to finish her perusal of the rooms. He felt a cold breath of air on the back of his neck and a tingling sensation traveled down his spine. He sprang to action racing upstairs to find Kate staring blankly at a wall.

"Are you all right Miss Coleman?" the Detective asked.

A deep breath was released from her parted lips drawing his attention to the perfection of their shape. *Those lips were meant for …* he quickly pushed the thought from his mind. *Get a grip Connery—she's a case!* He mentally kicked himself. He never got involved on a case. "Bad form," his father would say.

"It just seems so scary that someone would go to so much trouble and not take anything. Granted there isn't much of value in this room, or Nick's, but some of the paintings in my mother's room are quite valuable and her jewelry is all there."

"So you don't think anything is missing?" Connery asked.

"Not yet. I've yet to go through my father's room just across from mine." Her skin crawled. To have said that out loud sounded awful to her. Memories clouded her vision. His room was right across from hers. She made her way beginning to shake.

"Why don't I come with you?" Connery couldn't dismiss the shiver that had swept over him earlier. Through the years in police work he had learned to take the warning for what it was—an Irish sixth sense. A warning from the little people, his father had called it. With that feeling his dad would set out a saucer of cream to keep in the little folk's good graces—superstitious Irishman! But the one time his father had disregarded the sense of foreboding had been his last. Killed in the line of duty protecting his partner who had been huddled over a child, he used his own body to shield them both from the flying bullets of a gang assault.

Connery still remembered the look on his father's face as he had walked out the door that night. His father had known he would not be returning. He had reeled at his death then, but now, after his own experience on the force, he understood. His father had weighed the cost—two lives for one—and had known he could not live with himself if he didn't do what he did. He was a hero and so was his partner. Who was he to say his father had made the wrong choice? He missed him every day but he was proud of his old man.

Kate had made her way to her father's room. Connery followed her into the room, leaning casually against the door frame as she moved from the bedroom to the large master bath. She seemed puzzled and he moved to her side.

"Something missing?"

Nothing seemed to be missing, but it was torn apart. The closets were rifled through and clothes in a heap on the floor, just as her mothers were, but cuff links and rings were still there. Her young life played before her eyes like a movie stuck in fast forward and suddenly stopped in a dark closet.

Her puzzled frown made Connery ask, "Did you remember something?"

"No, uh, I was just wondering if Mary had noticed anything strange."

"Isn't she the housekeeper?"

"Yes, that's right."

"I spoke with her today and she remembers nothing out of the ordinary."

"I hate to say this Detective, but I wonder if this might have something to do with my brother. He's a reporter, you know, and often works on news stories that lead to arrests. Perhaps this was meant as a warning for Nick? To scare me—to get to Nick? I don't know, it just doesn't make sense to me and I am wondering if it would mean anything to him, like a warning or something?"

"Have you been able to get in contact with him yet?"

"No, I left word at the newspaper but it isn't unusual for Nick to be out of contact, months at a time. They did promise to inform him of our parents' accident. Hopefully he will return."

The detective found that last comment very odd. "You don't think he will?"

Kate looked him in the eye before taking a deep breath and began: "Ours was not a happy home or a blessed childhood—no matter how it looks. Bad things happened within these walls. I hope Nick will return to help me—he was always there for me. I know he wouldn't want me to be going through any of this alone. But I honestly wouldn't blame him if he didn't rush back."

Her pale face looked so sad and vulnerable. *God, she was gorgeous!* Her long fingers were clasped together as if the action could hold madness and despair at bay. Losing both parents must have been devastating, even if it was an unhappy home. Then to have to make all the arrangements alone must have been unimaginable. Briefly he wished he was an available option to help lighten her grief.

He glanced at his watch, noting the hour.

"It's already past 6 p.m.—I'm going to have to get back to the station. Are you okay to drive?"

"A little shaky, but I just want to get out of here. I don't feel comfortable being here alone right now, so I will follow you out."

"That's understandable, Miss Coleman. You won't be alone tonight will you? I mean, your friend will be with you, right? You will be in good company?"

Kate laughed. "Casey could charm the rattles off a snake and have him laughing while she did. Frankly Detective Connery that is just what I need right now!"

"Well then let's be on our way. I'll see to having someone patrol the area regularly tonight and if you think of anything, please don't hesitate to call, you have my card."

The twenty minutes to the condo went fast. The silence was a welcome relief and Kate relished the insight of the Detective to recommend company. *My, he was a looker!* His broad shoulders seemed to stretch forever under the jacket that concealed his revolver. His big strong hands had been gentle as they helped her into her car and Kate had to admit that his chiseled jaw and full lips almost had her licking her own lips in anticipation. *Geez! What was wrong with her?* She'd never been so strongly attracted to any man she had just met like she was with this one. Was it all physical or is she so emotional right now that she needed a man to lean on? Or was she finally realizing there was more out there than the comfort of familiarity? *I wonder if he is attracted to me, too?* she thought. She realized his squad car was next to hers at the red light and she tried not to look over at him. If she had turned she would have seen the hot glint of Connery's eyes on her all of her questions would have gone flying out the window.

The nagging dance music of her cell phone brought Kate to a dazed wakefulness. Groping blindly for the offending phone, her groggy "Hello?" brought an anxious, "Kate, are you all right?" from the caller on the other end.

"Nick?"—the fractional pause before the voice answered reminded Kate that her brother was halfway around the world and satellite communications could be maddeningly slow on the uptake.

"Are you okay? What's going on? My editor told me to contact you a.s.a.p. ... Kate, about Mom and Dad ... did you? ..."

"I'm fine, Nick," *at least physically,* Kate thought. "It's true, Mom and Dad were killed last week in an automobile accident. Their car flew off River Road and they crashed into the cliffs." She decided not to mention the break-in and the possibility that the accident wasn't an accident. She would fill him in later, face-to-face.

There was a silent pause on the other end and she wasn't sure if it was that long distance split-second phone lag. "Nick, are you still there?"

"Yeah, Kate, I'm here. I just can't believe it but I can, you know what I mean?"

"I know, it's crazy, but they're both gone."

Another long pause as they both regressed into their own memories. Neither had to speak a word to communicate.

"Kate, I'm on the way. I'm coming into LaGuardia Airport in an hour. I'll catch the first flight to Frisco. How are you holding up?"

"Okay, I guess—wishing you were here to lean on."

"Sorry, Kate, I am so sorry." The sadness in her brother's voice brought to mind the many other times he had tried to comfort her.

"Really, Nick, it's okay. Call me when you get in and I'll come pick you up."

"Right, Sis. I'll see real you soon. Stay safe."

Kate smiled at their childhood parting. "You stay safe, too, brother," she whispered into the phone—even though Nick was already gone.

Nick motioned for the stewardess.

"Something I can help you with, Sir?"

"I'd like a scotch and water, please."

"Are you all right, Sir?" The woman had noticed his pale complexion and shaking hands.

"My parents were killed in a car accident."

"I'm sorry for your loss, Sir. Be right back with your drink."

Nick rubbed his head. He could feel the beginning of a nagging headache. Bitch of a time for a migraine! God, Kate must have been at her wits' end without him. What the hell happened? She must have been beside herself, having to prepare all of their funeral arrangements and everything else. He wondered if their attorneys would handle contacting family members. They'd never even met half of them. Nick imagined the funeral to be crowded with "yes men" and business acquaintances. Soon he'd be back at her side to help sort out this mess.

The stewardess returned and Nick slugged down the drink and asked for another. The next few hours were going to take forever.

Kate sat up as the old bell alarm in Casey's room rang. *Geez, why did she keep that old ringer alarm clock? That thing could jump start a car with its noise!*

"Do you want the shower first, Kate?"

"No, go ahead Casey—I'll make coffee." Kate heard the water start in the shower indicating Casey had heard her. She sighed as she thought about the day ahead.

Someday she was going to get herself a different job. The thought of dealing with the anger and desperation of medical claims was beginning to wear on her. Casey worked in the same department and some days having her in the next cubicle kept Kate from giving in to the desperation that could be heard over her phone line.

Last week, for instance, the man, whose wife was dying from cancer, had almost brought her to the point of quitting her job. Kate understood the desperation some of her callers felt and she honestly tried to help them find avenues of recourse through the hospital payment plan, or their insurance. But sometimes there just weren't any good answers. The man was going to lose his wife as well as his house. Understandably he was upset. When the factory where he had worked closed he lost his insurance coverage—leaving the couple with nothing. Thank God, his children were grown and on their own. Kate had felt her own heart breaking at their last meeting when she had tried to help him come up with some kind of payment plan. Finally she had reluctantly suggested bankruptcy, then the state would be responsible for his wife's medical bills. The man had been outraged—he was used to paying his own way and the thought of taking state aid or charity, had been too much for him to bear. He had walked out swearing that she wouldn't understand until it happened to her. It was almost like a curse the way he said it glaring and pointing at her as he backed out of her cubicle.

Kate's roommate, Casey, had actually gotten Kate the job. Casey majored in administrative insurance. Casey knew the medical jargon and was sympathetic to her client's needs. She was satisfied with her job. Kate saw that she was actually helping people and making a difference. As a visual communications major, Kate realized her field was very competitive and had a hard time finding and keeping a job. While she continued to look for work she asked Casey to put in a good word for her in the Insurance Claims Department. And here she was, several years later, "making a difference". But the job proved otherwise.

When she first accepted the position Kate thought she could help people who really needed it. Lately, however, there seemed to be more and more patients who simply didn't have the insurance or the financial means to pay the mounting medical expenses. Many didn't come in for help until it was too late—like this man. Which she totally understood, the man was having to watch his wife die a slow painful death as cancer took her from the inside. There was nothing he could do to help her. There was no time to deal with insurance companies when precious time with his wife could end any moment. There really wasn't anything anyone could do about the rising cost of health care until the insurance companies took some responsibility for the poor coverage that had seemed to change overnight—everywhere. Then of course, it all comes back to what hospitals have to charge to make up for what insurance doesn't pay. Shaking her head to clear the hopeless thoughts Kate went back to searching for breakfast.

Casey was finished in the bathroom and Kate proceeded to get ready for work herself. Fortunately the ten-minute drive to the hospital left time for Starbucks.

Stepping out of the elevator onto the third floor, an orderly named, Tim Matthews, stopped Kate to tell her that the surgery department had heard from Jason's team in Africa and that she should stop by to read the latest update. Kate waved her thanks as she continued on her way.

At her desk Kate began organizing the stack of new claims that always seemed to materialize overnight. Quickly, she scanned through them delegating the forms that should go to insurance companies from those she would need to provide with financing schedules. Sensitive to the mental state of those clients who would have problems with making payments, she first made notations as to where, or how, the claimants might receive help. She cheerfully called people when she found help available and gave them the information, or offered to forward their claims. Fortunately for some the hospital had some caring and generous patrons who regularly helped those less fortunate. But clients had to meet the donors' criteria to be considered and there were always those who didn't—they were the harder ones for Kate to help. Sympathetically, she offered to set up minimum payment plans that were basically "the payment in good faith clause" outlined in the hospital's procedures manual. It wasn't much, but she thought she was doing her share of helping others and slaying each dragon for them as they crossed her desk.

By break time she had made a small dent in the stack. She activated her voice mail before making her way to the break room. Several "work friends" were seated around a table off to one side. Kate found herself a snack before joining them.

They were talking about someone who had called the night before and threatened to kill one of their doctors. Eventually it had been tracked to some crank with a grudge against the "Don Juan" of 4th floor surgery. Not even a doctor, but someone posing as one.

"He probably got too cozy with some guy's wife, again," shot Felix. "Wouldn't be the first time Majors got busted with a patient."

"Better be his last," said Jenny from the pharmacy. "How long are we going to have to put up with that guy anyway? He thinks he is God's gift to women and patients are always falling for him."

"The hospital can't afford to have that kind of a scandal get around. We'd lose funding from several of our regular donors if they knew," stated Kate, "and we all know we can't afford that!"

There were several murmured agreements before the topic changed ironically to the good-looking new orderly. Kate found herself sitting longer than she should if she was going to get the news on Jason's team and all too soon it was time to return to work. Coffee cups were tossed at the receptacle and someone shouted, "Nothing but net!" as they left the room.

Detective Flynn Connery pulled up to his apartment after 9 p.m., cursing the paperwork that seemed to increase daily on his desk. He realized that documentation was becoming a large part of being a "private eye" and he resigned himself to the dregs of black coffee and eyestrain the paperwork required. But he wished someone could explain to him how the paperwork increased faster than the hours in his shift. He made his way down the poorly-lit hallway vowing to read his landlord the riot act for not replacing the burned out bulbs in the hall fixtures. Just once, he'd like to come home and not wonder what waited around the dark corners. The key slid in smoothly opening the locked door. The lights of the city were visible through the window shades calling him to the large living room where he stared tiredly out onto the bay. This view always lightened his soul. His favorite dark brown oversized chair beckoned to him. Gratefully he sank into it watching the glimmering water reflecting the city in all its glory. The soft brush against his legs had him tightening his abdomen in readiness, just in time to provide a landing zone for the large tomcat.

"Hey there Sam, how you doin' fella?" Flynn stroked battle-scarred ears and slid his hand along the cat's back. Sam worked his paws carefully into the man's stomach responding with a soft purr. Before long the cat jumped off landing heavily on the floor and emitted a distressed, "Meow," as he glided toward the kitchen.

"Hungry, you furry bugger?"

Sam turned his head staring at Flynn with eerie, yellow eyes before continuing toward the kitchen.

Flynn heaved his frame up from the chair to follow along. "Well, what would you like tonight?" he questioned. "Let's see—we have tuna, tuna, and tuna. How about tuna?" Flynn quickly opened the can and placed Sam's portion on a plate and sat the plate on the floor. "Now what shall I have? Let's see—tuna, tuna, or tuna. Guess it's tuna tonight. You know, Sam, I really have got to go shopping. You're getting way too fat on this diet and my taste buds could use a change in the menu."

Opening the fridge He grabbed a beer and popped the top, then took both the bottle and the sandwich with him on his way back to his seat. Settled once more his mind began to replay the events of the day.

Before long the tom was back, jumping lightly into the familiar lap. Petting Sam, Flynn's thoughts turned to Kate Coleman. *God, she was a beauty!* Her classic lines and caramel-colored hair framed a face he had difficulty erasing from his memory. He let her vision float through his thoughts while turning over the events that had introduced her into his life. Why was he so fascinated with this woman? Granted, she was a looker. Her innocent look tugged at his male protective instincts. But, he'd dated stunning women before, enough to know looks could be deceiving. So what made her different? He'd done some research on her family—rich types at first glance. Further digging had revealed numerous hospital visits when she was young, as well as shady business dealings by her father. The finances of the family were firmly in the black—leaving him to wonder why she chose to work in the Insurance Claims Department at the hospital.

He couldn't help it, but his mind kept insisting on wondering what her lips would taste like and how warm they would feel against his. He forced her image out of his mind and back to the case.

It worried him that someone would break in and not take anything. If the burglar had absconded with some bit of jewelry, or other valuable, it would indicate the problem was probably over. But this criminal mind was playing with Miss Coleman. The guy would be back. According to a criminal psychologist he had consulted in the past, the warped mind of a perpetrator like this could escalate to torturous play. The man or woman had a grudge—a cat-and-mouse game may have only just begun. Miss Coleman was the target of a very disturbed person.

The CSI would consult CODIS for any known criminal mind fitting the profile. This CODIS program usually could link serial crimes to each other from local, state, and national databases of DNA profiles from convicted offenders, unsolved crime scene evidence, and missing persons. But Connery was skeptical, how much could turn up without prints or DNA? The team had gone over the house with a fine-tooth comb and they'd come up with nothing. They could rule out the parents, and Flynn couldn't imagine Kate doing this to herself. The brother had been thoroughly checked, he was on assignment in France. Even the housekeeper had an alibi. *Damn! This job was so much easier when the bad guys were crack addicts who sold stolen goods to the pawn shop.*

Tomorrow he would head over to the Coleman Oil Distributing Company and check into the staff. The break-in had to be related to the parents. Then he planned on visiting the hospital to see what the scoop was on Miss Coleman. Did she have any enemies at her place of employment? Her boyfriend worked in surgery—Connery would check into him, too.

He resumed stroking the heavyweight in his lap. Ironic how the tables had turned with this cat! Here, he had thought he was rescuing the tomcat the night he found him battered and bloody on his steps. Sam snarled when Flynn picked him up and Flynn snarled back. At times Flynn was sure the tough old tom had rescued him. He had returned home battered and torn from his job a few times and that damn cat always knew when to land gently in his lap or keep his distance. Right now the warm weight and Sam's purring was comforting—lulling Flynn into peaceful dreams. Peaceful dreams of caramel-colored hair, topaz eyes, and long fingers.

THREE

Flynn Connery stood bleary-eyed in front of the coffee maker as the drip, drip, drip, broke the silence in the apartment. Even Sam knew better than to approach before the man had his first gulp of java. He drank slowly, mindful of the temperature of the brew, waiting for the caffeine to jump-start his system. With a sigh of pleasure his mood lightened and his system began to function. Bread was dropped into the toaster and Sam appeared to wind around his legs in a plea for his own breakfast. The two males shared the toast and peanut butter before Flynn got ready for the job.

On his way to work he mentally listed the things he had to do. He was always thorough in his quest for answers. Sometimes a different slant on the questions provided the missing information. The notes from the Colemans' accident were still in a file on his desk. He had not been satisfied with the obvious—accidental death and drunken driving. He and the CSI team were still investigating.

Once at his desk he scanned his notes before heading to the Captain's office. Captain Tanner was a heavy-set man with shrewd, knowledgeable eyes. Though not a very large man he was quick—both of mind and body. A man you could depend on and one that backed his men and women. Connery took a seat and brought the Captain up to date on the investigation and his theories.

"Well, looks like you've got some leg work ahead of you, Connery. Take Bell with you when you go."

"Yes, Sir."

Darien Bell was a detective on the force who had worked in the Department a couple of years. Before that he'd been a patrolman in Sacramento. The man was bright and had a mind that some called "crazy" because his thought process was so radically different from the normal detective's approach. However, this gave Bell a totally different outlook which, a couple of times, had helped the Department wrap up a stubborn case. Connery heard it mentioned more than once that it was a good thing Bell was on their side since he would have made a maddening criminal mind. Bell's looks were deceiving, his appearance was more like a computer nerd than a police officer. This had often helped him get information from his suspects because they made the assumption, judging by his looks, that he wasn't very street smart.

Connery stopped and got Bell on his way out and filled him in on the way to the car. Bell skimmed over Connery's notes on the ride to Coleman Oil Distributing.

The building was impressive, but then it should be. This one company was responsible for sixty percent of the oil distribution on the West Coast. Any man who had that big of a business had to have some enemies. The very thought sent their minds spinning. *This could be huge!*

The two men formulated their plan of attack. Bell would question the men at the plant and Connery would follow up in the office. He wouldn't admit it, but he knew he had a way with the ladies. Maybe it was his comforting demeanor.

The Detectives made their rounds, asking questions and interviewing different people. Even though many of the employees hadn't liked the alcoholic who was their boss, the two investigators were stumped when it came to new leads. It was pretty obvious they'd have to start at the top of the ladder, with the decision makers, to find some answers.

Back in the car on the way to the hospital to question Miss Coleman's co-workers they reviewed what they had found.

"Do you suppose this might be some foreign vendetta against the family? If the old man ticked off some Middle East oil lord, or his son wrote some story that exposed an underground drug ring, and someone might be after the whole family. And, I hate to say this Connery, but the macabre dolls in the bed is something a drug dealer might pull to terrorize the family after killing the parents."

"We'll need to go through the company files and see who they have outbid, or undersold, recently. And we had better talk to Nick Coleman the minute he gets back in the States. I'll call Miss Coleman and the newspaper to see if they have any information on his return."

At the hospital the two detectives made the rounds talking to Kate's co-workers. All had a high opinion of the young woman. Her work ethics were highly admired by her superiors and her co-workers found her friendly and helpful. But, as the men continued their questioning, the incident of a husband of one of the patients and the threats he had delivered came to the forefront of several conversations.

"Kate tried every avenue the hospital has and a few outside of our payment plans to try to help the man, but he just refused to see the effort she had made on his behalf. I truly doubt if the threats are real, or even directed at Kate, specifically. The man just had to release his frustration with the system," confided Kate's superior, Mrs. Boe. "It happens," shrugged the woman. "We can't take it personally."

"Well, maybe somebody should," replied Connery. "The Colemans are dead and their residence has been more than ransacked. It was obviously done to terrorize the family. I'd like the name of that guy and his address, or do I need to get a search warrant?"

Mrs. Boe was in a quandary. Patient privilege and all—so she finally called the Administrative Legal Department for advice. The hospital would require a warrant before releasing the name of the man who had made the threat.

"Fine," growled Connery as he whipped out his cell phone and speed-dialed his favorite judge.

Mrs. Boe gasped in surprise as she recognized the judge's name and the fact that Connery was transferred directly to speak with him.

Connery explained the situation and with a curt nod of his head he flipped the cell phone shut. "Bell, head over to the courthouse. The warrant should be ready by the time you get there." Connery tossed his partner the keys to the car before turning to give Mrs. Boe a sarcastic grin. "Pays to have friends in high places."

With the information on the patient they required from the hospital, Connery and Bell would find the man for questioning.

The Detectives' next stop was the newspaper where Nick Coleman worked as a lead investigative reporter. They were ushered into the publisher's office by a long-legged brunette who had Bell's head turning to follow her every move.

"What can I do for you gentlemen?" queried the publisher.

"I'm Detective Connery and this is my partner Detective Bell. We're hoping you can tell us when you expect Nick Coleman."

"Jack Wells," he raised his eyebrows, "and just what do you want with my lead reporter, Detective?"

"We have reason to believe Nick, and maybe his sister, may be in some danger. Sorry, can't give you the details." Connery's tight smile quickly put him on equal footing with the publisher, for he knew how to play this game. "It's possible that your lead reporter has stirred up someone's interest lately."

"That's why Coleman is our lead reporter. He is always stirring up interest. It's the type of reporting that wins him and this paper national recognition."

"National recognition, indeed. It would be a sorry state of affairs if his latest nosing around got him killed before the story got printed."

Mr. Wells furrowed his brow before he broke the silence that had settled on the room. "Tell you what Detective, I'll be sure to have Nick call you as soon as I hear from him. The paper doesn't keep close tabs on the man's whereabouts. Difficult to track him down, you know."

"So, I take it Coleman has had his life threatened on occasion? What's he working on now?"

"Detective, you seem to be an intelligent man. I'm sure you looked into Nick's background before you came here, so let's cut to the chase. You know he's the reporter that broke the scandal on a customs' drug case two years ago. Some very high-powered men were arrested and indicted. The trial of one of them is coming up on appeal in thirty days. As for what he is working on at this moment, I couldn't tell you—I don't know. If I could find him I would try but as it is, I'll have to wait for him to check in. I'll have him call you if he does."

"Thank you, Mr. Wells, and by all means give the man a warning next time you talk to him. The criminal behind this threat seems to be very real and very disturbed."

As the two exited the building Bell stated, "Didn't get anywhere with that."

"Maybe—maybe not. If Coleman does call in at least the paper can give him the heads up—forewarned is forearmed."

"Connery, I'd like to go back and look at the records at

Coleman Oil Distributing."

"Any specific reason?"

"Yeah, maybe. A thought came to mind when Wells mentioned that customs' drug bust."

"Care to let me in on this Bell?"

"I'd rather see if I come up with anything first."

"Alright. I'm sure I can find something to stick my nose into while you're turning papers."

Several hours later at Coleman Oil, Bell interrupted Connery's snooze with a sharp dig in the ribs. Connery came to sudden wakefulness with gun drawn and eyes focused on his partner.

"Geez, man, trying to give me heart failure?" Bell exclaimed as the breath he'd suddenly been holding escaped.

"Sorry, survival reaction."

"I can see that—remind me to never sneak up on you again! Anyway Connery, I think I may have a lead. Look here at this shipping manifest."

"Yeah?"

"Here, look at the cargo weight at the point of departure. Then again, here, at the San Francisco dock when the ship was unloaded. The equipment and barrels of crude oil have a different weight from when the ship left port in Russia."

"Could it be an error in the translation or a typo?"

"Possibly, but in the last nine months I have found three such errors. Not from the same port of departure, but all in the Russian market. Might be something—or might be nothing, but it pays to dig some more."

Nick followed the other passengers off the American Airlines jumbo jet all the way to Customs. Backpack slung over his shoulder, he dug into his pocket to remove his passport and press credentials. In these days of terrorism and drugs anyone was suspect. His IDs in hand, along with his press pass he hoped this wouldn't take long. If he could manage to get through Customs quickly, he might be able to catch the red-eye to San Francisco. If not, well, he'd be spending the night in the "Big Apple".

He was in luck! Not only did the Customs official accept his papers, the man recognized him for a story that had been published when Nick had blown the Customs scandal in the docks of New York and San Francisco. Waving to the official, Nick sprinted toward Gate 5B to catch the red-eye home. Again, things were going his way. There were seats still available, and flipping out his American Express card, Nick quickly purchased his ticket and headed for the loading gate muttering to himself, "never leave home without it!".

Safely seated and belted in he took out his pocket notebook. The world around him might find technology the only way to go but he still wrote his notes in his own secret code with pen and paper. His writing would put a doctor's to shame! If someone was going to try to decipher his notes they'd have to get past his handwriting before trying to figure out the seemingly random combination of letters and numbers that made up his code. A computer whiz might break down a computer code—but his notes? Well, it had been tried before with no success.

As usual, Lady Luck had helped Nick stumble onto the subject for his next lead story. Few people knew of the slave trade running between Russia and the United States and no one wanted to admit that such a medieval practice still existed. Tie that into the fact that Nick had evidence the Russian Mafia was behind the trade on the west coast, and most reporters would throw up a big "hands off" sign. But Nick had never been daunted by bad guys, the bigger the better. Since his father had been one Nick had learned to stand up for himself and the ones he loved—damn the consequences. He had also learned to be sneaky, quiet, and safe. But most importantly, he had learned to cover his tracks. His contacts had learned over the years that he was good on his word. He would never divulge his sources—even when commanded by the courts, and the fact that he was privy to his family money allowed him to pay his sources well and keep them loyal.

Now his leads pointed to his father's business being involved with his latest story. Nick had wondered how it was that Coleman Oil was always the top bidder, whether purchasing oil or selling it. If the evidence could be found in company records he would have to go to the police. He hated being involved in his own story, however no amount of fame and glory could replace his wish to keep Kate safe. Personally, he could take care of himself, but he had been protecting

Kate since they were kids. For Nick, protecting Kate was worth any cost. She was his only family and always had been—even more so than his parents who'd given them both life but also threatened to take it away on a daily basis.

It was ironic that the men who had made his father rich could have been the ones to have taken his life. *Should I warn Kate?* He needed some hard evidence before upsetting her world. Nick leaned back—resting as the plane made its way to the Golden Gate City. *Man! I am glad to be home!* No matter where he traveled he always had a renewed sense of appreciation for the country he called "Home". More people needed to get out of their tight-woven little worlds— there was nothing like a glimpse of someone else's life to make you appreciate what you had. Maybe he would write a piece to that effect.

Turning that idea over in his mind he drifted off for some much needed sleep.

Dr. Jason Mueller was beat. *No,* he thought, *bone weary would better describe my feeling of exhaustion and defeat. Why did I agree to this hell?* When the opportunity to accompany the world-famous team in north Africa was offered to him he had been literally floored. A second-year resident surgeon on the road to success, he never thought he'd be noticed by such a prestigious team. But the horror of the third world was wearing on him. Frankly, he didn't know if he could make it another two months.

The dirt and filth was never ending. Water was a commodity some would kill for. The drugs the team carried with them were worth a fortune on the black market, and a civil war was brewing. He was tired of being dirty, hot, and bug bitten. Tired of sickness and death. Tired of being tired. He wanted a hot bath, a hot meal, and a bottle of anything. Most of all, he wanted Kate in his arms—telling him how much she missed him.

Why hadn't she written? Granted the mail service was unreliable, at best, but there had been no word from her at all. Last week when the team had up-linked to the hospital through the satellite she had been unavailable. What was going on? She wouldn't date another man, would she? Had she moved on while I'm here trying to help mankind in this dirt and poverty? Of course not! I am on the fast track to fame, good-looking, and I make enough to keep her in the style to which she was accustomed. I never understood why she doesn't use her family money to better her standing at the hospital. But then Kate had always been one to consider her future. She was probably just being careful. One never knew what the market might do. But, then again, didn't most women want their man to provide for them? Of course they did! And now I can do that! I just have to get back to her before Africa does me in.

A lion roared in the distance, sending a shiver of dread down his spine. The locals told stories of the lions turning into man-eaters when the sun scorched the earth killing all the wildlife. Everyone else in the team took the lions as a matter of circumstance. They were part and parcel of Africa—not something to dread, and as common as wild dogs in Mexico. But lately Jason had been dreaming of being stalked by the lions of the plains. The nightmares interfered with his sleep—keeping him up till the sun began to shine over the horizon. Then he'd get back to sleep and it would be time for the team to begin their rounds. They would start early in the morning to make as much progress as possible before the heat rose to unbearable temperatures. The rest of the team had begun to notice his sleep deprivation and several times the team leader, Dr. Hunt, had inquired as to Jason's health. Of course, he had vehemently protested that he was fine—not wanting to appear inadequate or weak. Although, if Hunt sent him home against his objections—his curriculum vitae would still be glowing and he'd be done with Africa for good and ready to reap the benefits of his time spent here in hell! By the end of the week they would be heading into the city to replenish their supplies and take a short break. He could make it until then and perhaps contact Kate and get the reassurance he so badly needed. With that thought in his head and the sun beginning to dissolve into the horizon Jason fell into a fitful sleep.

THE BEAST AWOKE AND STRETCHED
DISTURBED BY THE SCENT OF ANOTHER.

THE SCENT MOVED AWAY AND THE BEAST
RESUMED ITS SLEEP CURLING INTO
A TIGHT BALL WITHIN THE HOST.

IT BECAME A SMALL, BLACK SPECK IN
THE CORNER OF THE MIND, BLENDING
IN WITH HAZY MEMORIES OF CHILDHOOD
AND FORGOTTEN DREAMS IT
DISAPPEARED INTO THE DARKNESS
ONCE AGAIN.

FOUR

Kate finally drug herself up to the surgery department before leaving work for the day. There was a message from Jason's team but it contained nothing of a personal nature. She wondered why she even bothered. The facts were becoming startlingly clear. She didn't love Jason—perhaps she never had. She needed to end it with him but would have to wait for him to return. They both deserved better than to settle for a relationship that wasn't based on love. Kate wondered if she would have realized this in time to correct it if she hadn't met the dashing Detective Connery. Her pulse quickened again at the thought of him. *My God, the man makes me wish for an empty elevator that I would stop and keep him stranded in for hours! Had he ever done it in an elevator?* she wondered. *My God, Kate, get your mind out of the gutter. I don't even know if he's interested,* she chastised herself. Her body hummed when he was around. She couldn't keep her mind out of the gutter! Maybe part of her problem was the suggestive wordplay between Felix and Jenny. Those two could heat up a polar ice cap!

Kate stood in the hospital lobby waiting for Casey to appear. The day was done and she wanted Casey's offbeat humor and a hot dinner—even if it was going to be Mexican, again. At first she didn't connect the vibrating next to her hand with the cell phone, then its melody began to play. She reached into her pocket to retrieve the phone and flipped open the cover.

"Hello."

"Kate, it's Nick. Still want to pick me up?"

"Of course! When will you be getting in?"

"My flight should land in about 20 minutes. Will that work for you?"

"Sure, Nick. Casey and I will be there to meet you."

"What's the matter Kate?" came Nick's worried reply. Nick could always tell when something was wrong.

"I'll explain when I see you."

"Okay, Sis. I'll be coming in through Gate 6B. I'll meet you in the bar. Then maybe the two best looking ladies in Frisco will let me take them to dinner," Nick replied trying to ease the tension he heard in his sister's voice.

"Well … I suppose we could be persuaded. But you should be forewarned that Casey is on one of her famous food forays. Spicy is what's in this week."

"Muy Bien. See you shortly—love you, Kate, adiós."

"You too, Nick." She smiled, she didn't even say it had to be Mexican food and he knew. Kate returned her phone to her pocket as Casey hurried around the corner. "Hey, girlfriend—change of plans."

"What? Did hot and sexy ask you to dinner?" Casey quipped, meaning the detective.

Kate laughed. "No. Tall and tired is coming into the airport and needs a lift. Nick promised to buy us dinner if we'd pick him up."

Casey rolled her eyes. "Well, any man is better than no man, as long as he's buying."

The two women laughed. Kate was thankful that Nick and Casey got along and accepted each other's weird sense of humors and idiosyncrasies. Though Nick usually had women falling over him Casey had never been interested in him and that allowed the three of them to remain friends through good times and bad. The situation would have been very uncomfortable if Kate's roommate and best friend was dating her brother. The two quickly made their way to Casey's car and headed for the freeway leading to the airport.

"How long was Nick gone this time?" quizzed Casey.

"Let's see—about a month I think. And no, I don't know what he's working on. Frankly, Casey, I don't want to know. It scares me—the stuff he does to uncover a story."

"I hear you, Kate. I worry about him and he's not even my brother. But you have to admit the man works hard to make the world a better place. Not too many people want to take on the things Nick investigates."

Kate stared moodily out the window wondering if Nick would ever slow down. She didn't feel it was her place to ask him—her brother was driven to expose the wrongs of the world. She was scared. Not just because of what had happened to their parents, or the house, but because of a deep-down feeling that told her, her world was about to fall apart. Shaking her head she tried to turn her thoughts back to her crazy friend and the conversation. She knew Casey was trying to lighten her worries. Before she knew it they had entered the pick-up zone at the airport.

Kate headed to the bar to grab some seats while Casey parked the car. If Nick's plane was on time they wouldn't have long to wait. Casey arrived in just a few minutes and chose a lemon water for her cocktail as she was the "designated driver" for the evening. A voice over the loudspeaker stated that flight 562 from New York would be unloading at gate 6B in ten minutes. Casey had just sat her water down when a tall, dark-haired, unshaven, and rumpled man slid into the seat next to them.

"I simply must claim this seat," he uttered with exhausted delight. "Never should two glorious women, such as yourselves, be left alone without an escort!" he proclaimed with a wickedly, sexy grin.

Casey immediately jumped in, "And, pray tell, just what do you have to offer two such discerning women as ourselves? I see a scruffy, down-on-his-luck schemer."

"Scruffy, perhaps Mademoiselle, but never down-on-my-luck as long as I have your company. Why your witty tongue and charming manner could lead a man astray."

Casey batted her eyelashes.

"Geez! You two either get a room or take me home."

"Still the play-it-safe girl, eh Sis?"

"Welcome home, brother dear. Glad to see you, too."

Nick rose—giving first Kate and then Casey a warm hug. "So glad to see you girls still have some caution when it comes to strange men. Do you really think I look scruffy? I hear that it's all the rage in the city for picking up the hot chicks!"

"Come on, Bozo. It's time to Hot Tamale me," Casey replied with a twinkle in her eye. "The Hot Tamale has a new special and it's sure to burn your socks off. Dare you to try it!"

Nick cast his glance Kate's way and noticed the shaking of her head—but he plunged on anyway. "You're on Casey! Someday you're going to meet the man that can out hot your tamale tastes—then what are you going to do?"

"God hasn't made the man that can match my tastes, but if he did—guess I'd have to stick my ring on him, walk him down the aisle, and lock him in my kitchen!"

The three laughed as they headed out of the airport to the parking lot. Kate slid into the driver's seat before startling Casey with her comment. "Umm … let's see … think I'm in the mood for French tonight. I'm driving—so it's my pick." The surprised look on Casey's face was priceless.

"Not fair, Kate! My car, my keys, and I had the water! You know he doesn't do French! It's so … blah!"

"Aww Kate, come on, I was just in Paris!"

Kate laughed at Casey's woe-be-gone face as she shifted the car into drive and headed out of the parking lot, and turned back toward the condo. A heavy sigh of relief could be heard in the back—they all knew Kate's favorite French restaurant was in the other direction!

As they passed along the expressway Kate filled Nick in on the happenings of the last few days. She could tell by his quick glances in her direction that he was worried.

"Nick, what's up?"

"I may have stumbled onto something that followed me home, Kate. Do you really trust this Detective Connery?"

"Yes, I do. He seems very good at his job and is very concerned."

"Got that detective's number Kate? I think I should give him a call."

"Sure, Nick, It's in my cell phone."

"I'll call him after dinner." As they made their way down the final miles to the Hot Tamale Nick spun tales of the Paris lights and characters he met on this last trip to Europe. Reaching the parking lot Kate slid the car into a parking spot near the doorway—noticing that there was quite a crowd for the middle of the week. The three friends linked arms as they made their way inside to come face to face with Romeo, the manager of el restaurante.

"Buenos Días, Miss Waters! What a pleasure to see you and Miss Coleman again so soon! Was it your turn to drive?" They all laughed, drawing the attention of two men in a nearby table.

"Speak of the devil Connery—isn't that Miss Coleman? And it sounds like she knows the owner …" Bell asked motioning toward the door.

Connery turned to look—hardly believing his luck. The people he wanted to talk to—practically falling into his lap! The angry client from the hospital, Mike Henderson who'd threatened Kate, had been employed here at the Hot Tamale. He and Bell were following up on a lead from the Jobs' Opportunity Office where he was sent when the factory closed. Was it a coincidence Miss Coleman and her friend ate here regularly, or had the man been stalking the women for later retribution?

According to the manager, Mike Henderson had been a prompt, hard worker, but suddenly quit—just didn't show up for work one day. Romeo had conceded that while it wasn't looking good for his bookkeeper to be so slack, he had allowed the wavier of address for the man. Mike Henderson had confided in him that he had lost his home and was living hand to mouth. Romeo had given him a job based on his gut feeling and the man had not let him down until the day he didn't show.

"Shall we invite them over Connery? We have enough room and they wouldn't have to wait for a table."

Connery nodded in agreement as he rose from the table to make his way over to the group.

"Excuse me, but if Miss Coleman and her friends would care to join me and my partner they wouldn't have to wait for a table," he offered to Romeo.

"That would be sooo lovely Detective," Casey offered gleefully. "You have a partner, ishemarried?" Casey said it so fast it sounded like one word.

"Darien Bell is his name and no, he isn't. We have the table in the corner there. This way ladies, and gentleman."

Grasping her heart and batting her eyes Casey replied in her best southern accent, "Why sir, I had thought that all the gentlemen had been lost in that awful civil war. My heart is just aflutter at the prospect of being in such a man's company!"

Connery didn't know quite what to make of Casey's theatrical talents. But just then Nick stepped up and tapped him on the shoulder whispering, "Nick, Nick Coleman. Ya'll know that those awful carpetbaggers done drove all the men out of the country, and the ladies have only the schemers and down-on-their-lucks to chose from nowadays!"

Kate was trying hard to control her laughter—as was Romeo. Connery was rescued from the impending theatrical scene when Kate grasped his arm leading him away from the others. "You have to ignore them or jump into their game if you are going to survive their company, Detective. This is my brother Nick who we just picked up at the airport."

Connery smiled at her upturned face. "I imagine those two can do a lot to relieve the stress of the day."

"Yes, they can and they do."

Connery shook Nick's hand, "Nice to meet you Nick, Detective Flynn Connery, just call me Connery, everyone else does."

Kate continued, "Whenever Nick is in town you can find us here. And with Casey's constant cravings it's almost a second home."

Connery made a mental note to pursue that comment. Her eyes had turned sad and thoughtful.

"Are you in need of a second home, Miss Coleman?"

"Everyone needs a place where they are accepted for who they are, Detective. Some people find it with family—and some people find it with strangers who become like family."

Bell rose as they reached the table offering his hand as introductions were made and motioning to Casey for a seat next to him.

"Oh my," Casey couldn't get any more out. "You guys haven't ordered yet?" she mustered.

"No, ma'am. I've been trying to convince Connery to jump ship and try something different for a change, something hot and spicy, but I feel I have failed once again." Then in an indonesian accent, he said, "He is a bland man, very bland."

Casey caught it right away having been a fan of Jerry Seinfeld since "day one". She was definitely liking this Bell guy.

"I like to leave a restaurant with my taste buds still intact, thank you," Connery muttered.

Kate's laugh was light and musical. "I'm with you, Connery.

However, Casey and Nick will try anything. 'Hot' is Casey's middle name, Detective Bell. The three of you can have a face-off in a 'Casey Waters' Challenge'."

Still true to his southern character, Nick bowed to allow Kate to choose her seat and then he was undermined by Bell—who pulled out the chair on his other side with a gallant flourish.

With a deep northern accent he mannerly addressed Casey, "I will have you know, Miss Waters, that there are men from the North who do heartily enlist the grace of proper manners when they are in the presence of true ladies. At first glance I could tell these gentlemen were not up to your standards and I would gallantly offer my services as your escort. I assure you Miss, you will be in capable hands."

Casey smiled, batting her eyes. "Oh my, Mama did say never to trust a Northerner, for surely they did not have a lady's best interest at heart."

"I remind you, Sir, the ladies are under my protection. You must come through me to reach them," Nick stated looking stern and menacing.

Bell sized up the competition and then surprised them all with his reply, "How about a pitcher of beer on me? Will that get me through your defenses, Mr. Coleman?"

"Done," Nick countered and waving at the waiter hollered, "Hey José, beer here and he's buying!" The table broke into laughter with the men roaring loudly and the ladies trying to maintain some semblance of order. But, when the patrons in the restaurant started to applaud they lost all composure. Their innocent private game had been taken for one of Casey and Nick's ongoing theatrics at the Hot Tamale. The applause settled down—allowing them the luxury to study the menu and sip their drinks.

During a lull in the conversation Nick caught Connery's attention. "I need to talk with you—can we meet sometime tomorrow?"

"Sure, you name the time and place, Coleman."

"Call me Nick. How about 9 a.m. at Starbucks on Main."

"Works for me—and Nick … "

"What?"

"Be careful and stick close to your sister and her friend.

Something nasty is coming down."

Nick muttered under his breath, "Don't I know it."

Connery raised an eyebrow at the comment but kept silent at the look thrown his way by Nick.

The reporter was worried and from what Connery knew about Nick Coleman that didn't happen easily. The reporter was a closed-mouth investigator, so if he was worried the threat to him and his family must be real.

When the waiter arrived to take their orders they were ready. Casey waggled her eyebrows at Bell and Nick and issued her challenge. "I'll have the new Hot Tamale special, José. But I'm not sure if my escorts are up to the challenge!"

Nick jumped in—ordering the special with little regard to José's warning.

Bell looked thoughtful—and then ordered the special as he sized up Casey.

His look reminded Kate of the tiger getting ready to eat the impala. Had Casey finally met someone that could match her tit for tat? Both she and Connery had better sense.

Connery, politely, let Kate order next. She chose the house specialty salad—a meal in itself with all the flavor of its south-of-the-border background, without the kick. Connery ordered the Nachos Grande meal—another of Kate's favorites. Seems they had something in common.

The men kept the conversation light while the group waited to eat. Casey added her unique sense of humor and soon they were all laughing away the day's stress. Soon they were launched into a "what if" game, designed to allow the participants to gather knowledge about one another in a light-hearted way, the questions could be answered thoughtfully—or imaginatively.

Casey started the second round with a standard question. "If you were stranded on a desert island, who, or what, would you want along?"

Kate knew Nick's answer before he even started to speak. A reporter to the bone, his reply was always the same to this question.

"A hot story and a paper to print it!"

"Geez, Nick get a life!" Casey replied. "Couldn't you come up with something more original for a change?"

"Sorry to burst your bubble, Casey, but the story changes every time!" Nick replied with a wink.

Casey just rolled her eyes.

"Detective Connery?"

"Call me Connery, please. I'd take Sam and anything but tuna." The puzzled looks from the group made him chuckle with a little embarrassment. "Looks like explanations are in order. Sam is my best friend and we've both been eating too much tuna lately!"

Bell muttered, "Sam is his tomcat and the man doesn't buy anything but tuna."

"Hey, it's nutritious, quick, and easy—and you can eat it right out of the can!" Connery shot back. "Anyway, it's Sam's favorite."

The women groaned but Nick agreed with him.

"Your turn, Kate," Casey stated.

Kate thought carefully. Should she play it safe—or should she shoot for the moon? Taking a deep breath she jumped in with both feet. "Aged wine, mellow food, and a hot San Fran detective." She laughed as she looked at Casey's stunned face—and then stuck her tongue out at her friend, causing everyone to break into a laugh.

Casey jumped in next. "Hot food, hot man, and hot sss … sun!" The men roared with laughter for they had all been expecting another avenue of thought from Casey, which was intended.

Bell was last. The silence hung thickly over the table as they waited for his answer.

Even Connery was anxious to know more about the guy. What did he really know about his partner, outside of the job? He knew he could trust Bell with his back and not much else really seemed to matter.

Just when he thought Bell wouldn't answer the man uttered in his most proper northern gentlemanly dialogue, "Why, of course, a gentleman would have all he needed with a lovely companion versed in the gentle ways of the South."

Casey groaned, but Bell continued switching to a pirate's drawl, "However, me hearties, I'd not settle for less than a fast ship flying the Jolly Roger with which to make me escape!"

They all roared again. Never having expected that out of the reserved Darien Bell.

Casey was the first to recover—fluttering her hand like a fan.

"Why, Sir, I do believe you a rogue in disguise!"

Just then their meal arrived. Conversation took a back seat to the task of feeding themselves and eyeing each others' entrées. Kate and Connery sat back and watched anxiously as the three dug into the Hot Tamale special (a.k.a. The Casey Waters Challenge). Kate had no worries about Casey. There wasn't a spicy meal that could do her in—but already Nick was making a valiant effort to stay hydrated. Bell looked calm, cool, and collected. It wasn't long before Nick flagged down José for beer and salt—the only sure way to smolder the fire. Casey and Bell continued on. Romeo stopped to inquire if there was anything they needed. Casey's endurance was legendary at the Hot Tamale, but never before had the staff seen another "gringo" equal to Casey at the task of demolishing spicy food. Both Bell and Casey finished off the main course in high style.

When José came to clear the plates, astonishment showed on his face as Bell ordered a serving of their hot and spicy tortillas to finish off the meal.

"Care to join me, Miss Waters?"

The attraction in Casey's gaze was apparent to everyone at the table. "Why, Mr. Bell, I might just have to join you for life!"

"About time someone made an honest woman outa her!" Nick half covered his mouth as if to keep Casey from hearing it.

Bell's mouth dropped open as Kate pointed at him and laughed. "The hot sauce didn't even have you turning *that* red!"

FIVE

The desert heat had actually fried his brain—Jason was sure of it. Thank God, they were off for the city tonight when it would be cool without the hot sun beating down on them. His head was pounding and rational thoughts were becoming more difficult. Everyone noticed. And his stupid slip-ups were getting more life threatening. During surgery he almost left something inside a patient as he tried to suture up too quickly. The looks and annoying questions persisted. Then the team leader, Dr. Hunt, pulled him off the surgery floor and insisted that Jason accompany him back to his office. Jason's feet dragged as he followed.

"Jason, please come in and have a seat." The man handed him a bottle of the water that was such a precious commodity. "We'll be leaving within the hour for the city. I'd like you to pack what you have and prepare to return to the States."

"I am not finished here, you can't do this—this is important to me!" Jason's voice rose but he wondered if it sounded half as fake to Hunt as it did for him to hear himself say it.

"Jason, calm down. Let me reassure you I have the highest regard for your work and will provide you with excellent references. However, I'm having you admitted to the hospital for testing when we get to the city." Hunt raised his hand to stop Jason from a rebuttal. "Jason, you are exhibiting symptoms of the advanced stage of African sleeping sickness. I believe you may have been bitten by the tsetse fly. Although this area has not had massive outbreaks of the disease, there are incidents of the illness and you, sir, are exhibiting some of its classic symptoms. I want you tested as soon as we get to the city. The sooner we determine if you are affected the sooner we can begin treatment for your recovery. As you know, the cure is time consuming and must begin immediately. That's why, if you are positive, I'm getting you on the first flight back to the States. Your help has been invaluable—but your health must come first."

At first Jason was confused and then elation began to set in. No more heat! No more roaring lions! He was going home—home to his sweet Kate. Home to the sanity of the hospital and his cushy life. Why, everything made sense now! Of course he wasn't a weak man; he had an illness that was draining all his strength. This was why he couldn't function! As Hunt said, he would be missed but his continued health was the first concern, the team didn't want to lose his talent and skills but what they had seen from him lately fell short.

Jason envisioned the welcome home Kate would bestow upon him. She would be at his bedside throughout the treatment. She would coddle him and cater to his every whim. He'd have Hunt place the call to her. The seriousness of the illness would have her running to meet him at his plane—everyone knew he was a hard-working and dedicated surgeon. Of course, Kate would want them to marry immediately so she might take charge of his care, but perhaps he should dissuade her until his health improved. Yes, that was what he would do—this plan would cast a better light on their soon-to-be marriage. People would come to witness the magnificence of their union and remark on how lucky Kate was to have snagged such a rich and distinguished surgeon!

When Hunt had finally ceased his ramblings, Jason made for his tent and packed the few items he had. Long before the rest of the team was packed he was waiting in the Land Rover.

The ride seemed to go on forever. He could feel the lions pacing just out of sight. Waiting, watching. When the brilliant orange sun finally began to drop below the horizon the intermittent roars and coughs of the lions could be heard echoing across the African plains. The tiredness that had grasped Jason so tightly began to peel away like the dried outer skin of an onion. He felt fresh, new, and alert. Though no one else seemed concerned, Jason often would catch the fleeting shadow of the stalking felines as the Land Rover made its way toward the city. Since no one else seemed anxious, for now, Jason followed their lead. Soon he would be home and the lions would have to hunt for fresh, new prey. What did he care if it was someone he had known—as long as it wasn't him!

When Dr. Hunt settled the Land Rover next to the curb near

the entrance of the hospital Jason heaved a sigh of relief. The lions could not follow him here. Already their lusty growls were fading from his mind giving him sweet release.

Hunt accompanied him into the hospital to introduce him to Dr. Naaromai, one of the leading specialists in the African sleeping sickness.

"Of course," Naaromai spoke in his thick African accent, "we will have to perform Dr. Jason Mueller's tests immediately. This is very serious. First we shall draw your blood to see if we can detect the parasite in your blood or lymph nodes. If we do we will next need to perform a lumbar puncture to determine if you have reached the second stage of the illness." The African surgeon shook his head in regret for the procedure of which he spoke was extremely painful.

Jason heard the man from a distance, not really grounded in the facts of the upcoming tests. Of course, he knew the hell he was soon to undergo! But Jason knew that he would be fine eventually, wasn't he one of the brightest in his field? There was no way that God would pull such an evil trick as to send him home to his sweet Kate only to take him away from her once things were back on track.

"I will arrange for the testing to begin immediately. Time is our enemy," spoke Dr. Naaromai. "Please feel free to make what arrangements you need in the meantime." The African hurried out to assemble his team for the tests.

Dr. Hunt was worried at Jason's calm reaction at such disturbing news, that in itself may be a red flag. He did understand what he was up against. They were all well aware of the many dangers they faced here. "Jason, you are in good hands."

"I'll be fine, Dr. Hunt, thank you for your concern. However, I would really like to call my fiancée and explain all of this to her." Jason lied, she hadn't said yes to his proposal yet, but he was sure she would be his fiancée as soon as he got back. She must have missed him so much, his dear, sweet Kate.

Ah, thought Hunt, *a man in love*. So, Jason was worried about her reaction and so the facts had yet to sink into his own subconscious. "Perhaps you would like me to speak to your fiancée and explain the circumstances to her?" The kind doctor offered.

Jason's attention snapped to! Exactly what he had hoped for. The doctor could break the sad news to her while he would play the brave, suffering surgeon who tried to save the world but returned with a life-threatening illness instead. Kate would fall right into his arms.

"If you don't mind that might be best, however, Dr. Hunt, I have to speak to her before the testing begins."

Hunt nodded his agreement as Jason gave Hunt the number of Kate's cell phone and then waited quietly while the other doctor began the process of dialing Kate.

Kate's phone was ringing insistently—waking her from the most delicious dream of a white sandy beach, wine, and a maddeningly familiar face feeding her tuna while a large tomcat rubbed against her naked belly. Groggily she sat up and reached for the phone. "This is Kate."

"Miss Coleman, this is Dr. Hunt from the World Health Organization in Africa. I'm calling on behalf of Dr. Jason Mueller."

"Is something wrong with Jason?" Even though Kate had decided to refuse Jason's proposal, she would not want him to be in any type of misfortune.

"Miss Coleman, Jason has possibly contracted African sleeping sickness. We will begin testing as soon as possible. I don't know if you are familiar with this illness, but the tests are extremely painful and time consuming. If it is determined he has contracted the disease, he will be rushed back to the States for medical treatment."

Kate was momentarily speechless. Jason with a sleeping sickness? What does this mean? She couldn't break it off with him now could she? *Of course you can*, spoke her little voice. *Why lead him on to believe there is a future with you just because he's sick? The split will only be that much harder later.* Of course, her voice was right; there was no good reason to lead Jason to believe they had a future just because he was in dire straits now.

"I'm very sorry to hear that, Dr. Hunt. May I speak with him, please?"

"Of course." The phone was silent and Kate could hear a door closing on the other end.

"Kate, now you shouldn't worry sweetheart. I'll be fine—I just know I will. You can't do anything for me there and worrying doesn't help. I am in good hands here. Now tell me, why I haven't heard from you?" Jason was going to milk this for everything it was worth! Guilt could be a great equalizer.

  Kate was put off by his remark. *How dare he! It wasn't as if he was sending her love letters from Africa!* "For your information, Jason, my parents were recently killed in a car accident and the police think it could have been murder. Then someone broke into the house and left a scene in my old bedroom. Now someone may be after both Nick and me. I'm sorry that you are having difficulties with your illness—but I am having difficulties of my own. In fact, I think it may be safer for you if we don't see each other when you get back to the States. Certainly with your illness you should not be subjected to anything that might further compromise your health. I'm sure your family will be glad that you will be coming home and they will see to your needs. I truly wish you the best of luck Jason. Goodbye."

  The phone went dead leaving Jason staring at the silent device. *What the hell was that?* A rapidly building feeling of hatred raged in his gut and his heart felt as if it was torn apart. *How dare she, brush me off like that! Did she even hear what I am about to go through? Wait till I get back! Why I'll have her eating out of my hand in no time. She would be so sorry. It was too bad she was having trouble at home (Did she just say her parents were killed? They never even got along!) that was no reason to be such a short-tempered bitch! I will get better just to make her regret! She will be mine for the rest of her life and it would take that long to make up for her behavior. I have never failed to get what I want. Kate isn't going to get away this easy! Obviously, she was confused, but I will straighten her out when I get home.*

THE BEAST STRUGGLED TO RISE. THE HOST WAS RIPE FOR THE TAKING, BUT SO CONCERNED WITH OTHER EVENTS THAT THE PATHWAY WAS BLOCKED, FORCING THE BEAST TO PACE THE CONFINES OF THE CAGE THAT KEPT IT LOCKED INSIDE.

IMPATIENTLY, THE BEAST SEARCHED FOR A SIGN OF WEAKNESS. HOWEVER, NONE COULD BE FOUND. THE BEAST RETREATED. ITS CHANCE WOULD COME! SOON. VERY SOON. A SOFT COUGH ESCAPED ITS THROAT, REACHING SUBCONSCIOUSLY TO THE HOST.

PATIENCE! EVERY GREAT HUNTER LEARNS THE TEST OF PATIENCE. AND THE BEAST WAS A GREAT HUNTER, ENDURING FOR YEARS UNTIL A CHANCE WOULD COME TO ESCAPE. IT COULD WAIT. EVENTUALLY THE BEAST WOULD FIND ITS WAY OUT.

IT ALWAYS DID!

SIX

Nick was already seated at a corner table near the back of Starbucks when Connery and Bell arrived. After the two men had ordered, Connery joined Nick while Bell positioned himself on a stool, which gave him an unobstructed view of the door. Nick's first impression of the detective was borne out in the care he and his partner took to ensure everyone's safety. After the conversation of last night and the few details Nick had shared, Connery's actions showed how seriously he took Nick's fears.

"What've you got, Coleman?"

"Get right to the point don't you, Connery?"

"Time's wasting—this guy already has a lead on us and I don't favor it getting any larger."

"You sure it's the same guy? My father was an SOB to the core. Could be more than one guy who might like to even the score."

"Sure—anything's possible at this point," replied the detective.

"Okay, well, while I was working on some leads into the slavery ring that operates from Russia to right here in San Francisco I ran across the mention of our father's company—and not just once. It seems that Coleman Oil Distributing Company may have been involved in the transportation on a worldwide scale. Knowing my father, I'm pretty sure he knew about the trafficking and the use of his tankers. I haven't checked the books yet, but I will."

"No need. The department has seized the files from the company and we're already onto that lead. Any name in particular that I should pay attention to?"

"Trovoishek. Watch for him—or any mention of Perek, a small village near the sea."

"Any chance someone was onto you?" Connery asked.

"Probably. Some pretty strange things happened while I was in Europe."

"Such as?" Connery raised an eyebrow.

"A couple of times I came back to my room to find things slightly out of place. Could have been the maid service, but I've stayed in this hotel before and never had anything happen. A few things went missing—nothing of importance, just odd. Almost like someone wanted to make me nervous."

"What type of things?"

"A favorite pen, a notepad, a pair of socks—just weird stuff."

"Did you ever notice whether you were being followed?" questioned the detective.

"I learned to watch my back a long time ago, Connery. If I hadn't I'd be dead. But yeah, I've had that shiver run down my back—like scraping fingernails across a blackboard."

Connery slowly nodded.

"Well, a couple of times that shiver got real intense. So I scrapped my lead and made damn sure I wasn't followed."

"Been there, Nick. That feeling might have saved your life. Your lead have any contacts here in the United States?"

"Yeah, could be. The damndest thing was when that shiver got real intense I could have sworn I heard the growl of a big cat—like a lion. Weird, huh?" Nick didn't want to mention anything else, he just met the man and he was a detective.

"Definitely. Any zoo nearby? Maybe the cat you heard was in the distance?"

"Not unless they built a zoo near the Louvre, or in a back alley in Russia."

Connery jotted some quick notes before steering Nick to another subject.

"What do you know about your sister's boyfriend, Jason?"

"He is a first-rate surgeon at the hospital. Gossip says he's on the fast track to fame and fortune. Comes from old family money. Personally, I never cared for the man. Too smug and holier-than-thou for me. But he was good to Kate."

"Was?"

"Jason called last night. Seems the guy has African sleeping sickness. He called Kate to let her know and evidently pissed her off real good."

Connery raised an eyebrow.

"Kate told the bugger to buzz off. 'Sorry for your condition, but best we not see each other anymore. I've got enough going on. Call on your family to take care of you'."

"Any chance that the boyfriend could be behind this? Trying to keep her close to him?" Connery couldn't imagine Kate being so rude, but he didn't know what exactly was said.

"It would be a little hard to do all that from Africa, don't you think?"

"Stranger things have been known to happen. The man has money so he has the means to hire someone to do his dirty work and if he's the vindictive type, well ... lions are pretty common in Africa. Maybe he taped the growling and had the person tailing you play the sound to make you slowly loose your mind. I always say—'when the alibi is too neat you should dig deeper'."

"As much as I don't care for the man I can't see him going to such lengths—but then I'm only a lowly reporter."

Connery rolled his eyes. *Right, only a lowly reporter. The man was known for breaking some of the biggest scandals in the country. Probably knew as much, or more, about the criminal element in the area than the cops did.*

"Stay on your guard, Nick. I have a feeling this is about to bust wide open. I'll have a unit watch the condo." Connery paused before continuing. "You know it would make our job a lot easier if you and Kate could stay together. Got any ideas?"

"Actually, I do. Kate and I need to go through things at the house. How about we stay there? We have the new security system and even with the break-in, I would feel safer with her there because of the added security. I hate to think of anyone getting into her condo."

"Sounds good. Let's see if you can get the lady to agree. One more thing before you go. Don't suppose that you might give me any more of the information you got while you were out of the country?"

Nick gave the detective a man-to-man look. Casually shrugging his shoulder he responded, "Not here—or now. It's something big Connery, and I'm really afraid I've brought this down on Kate."

"Why don't Bell and I meet you and your sister at the house? Say about seven this evening? We can use the excuse of going over the security at the house while you and I discuss your concerns."

"Sure, I'll pick Kate up from work and meet you there."

"Keep sharp, Nick. Whether it's your perpetrator, or mine, the man has a devious criminal mind. Don't take any chances." Connery downed his last swig of coffee and strolled over to pick up his partner before leaving Starbucks.

Nick ordered another espresso and stared out the window as he pondered what he knew, what he guessed, and the shadows of "what ifs" in his mind. He hadn't thought he was so close to the top level of the slavery ring running children into the United States. Nothing his contacts in Europe had given him had led him to sense one person was in charge of it all. Had he been wrong? Everyone knew that many of the black market leaders were men who at one time had been at the top of the Communist ladder. Such powerful men never took lightly their fall from the privilege and wealth that had once been theirs. Most of the names Nick had come across had been bottom feeders, or a middleman—or so he thought. Had he stumbled onto a lead to the top—or had he thwarted someone's plans on the way to the top? Nick had many back alleys and underground sources that might provide him with more concrete leads. He could dig up one of his old contacts and set him on finding out more information.

Or—was Connery on the right track with Jason? Personally Nick hadn't liked him from day one. All his survival instincts went on alert when he was around—even though he had nothing on which to base those feelings. Nick was sure Connery was looking into Jason's background, but it wouldn't hurt to see what a nosy reporter might find.

Right now he had to get Kate to agree to move back into the family home. Nick shuddered at the thought! The house was never a happy home and his mother's decorating style had been geared toward showing off her position and wealth rather than making it a loving home for her family. He shook his head, chasing the memories back into the shadows. He was fine, and Kate was fine, and if he had anything to say about it things would stay that way. Despite their parents and their childhood secrets they had both grown into talented and well-adjusted adults. No one was going to take that from them!

Finishing his drink, he left the coffeehouse and flagged a cab to the curb. He directed the driver to the hospital. If he hurried he could catch Kate on her break. They could discuss the move and then, hopefully, they'd have time to pick up her things before heading out to the house tonight. If there was some weirdo out there looking to eliminate his family, the guy would have a few surprises when, and if, he returned.

Connery noticed Casey's car parked in the driveway. Nick and Kate were waiting on the front steps along with Casey. Connery wondered what Casey was doing there but then remembered that the girls carpooled to work. Nick's car was parked in the same place as it had been on the night of the first call of intrusion.

"Evening everyone," Connery greeted the three pleasantly before noticing that Nick had a scowl on his face. "What's the matter Nick? Did you have to eat Mexican again?"

The girls laughed, but Nick's scowl only deepened. "You tell him," he motioned toward the girls.

Kate tossed back her hair before replying. "Casey is moving in with us—and before you go all macho like my brother let me point out that Casey has been seen with us everywhere for the past several days. If someone is stalking us, Casey could also be a target. I am not leaving her alone."

Bell closed in on the group adding his own reasoning. "The ladies have a point. This criminal might go after Casey just to get a reaction. If the ladies stick together—it might be in our favor."

The reason Connery appreciated Bell on this case was for his unusual insight into the criminal mind. If Bell was thinking the same thing it could be there was something to the idea. Connery expelled a deep breath before addressing the others. "Let's go in and discuss this."

"Sorry, detective, we can't," answered Nick. "We're waiting for the security guy to come with the new PIN numbers for the system. I called after our meeting to have them do a complete check and change all the PINs before we moved in. Didn't want to take a chance that the new numbers might fall into the wrong hands—so the main man is bringing them out as we speak."

"What kind of security does the house have?"

"There are security locks on the windows and doors and floodlights are located above the doors. The gate can be opened by remote and if the alarms go off, the relay informs the police immediately. Not a whole lot considering what we might be up against, but at least it's a start," said Nick.

"What about the garage? We'll want security there also and cameras mounted at all exits."

"I already talked to the security team about it. They'll start tomorrow," Nick answered.

The group turned at the sound of a truck coming up the drive. It carried the name PRIME Security on the side. A tall, distinguished man exited the driver's side. "Nick Coleman?"

"That would be me. Matt Donovan?"

"In the flesh."

The two shook hands as Connery sized up the older man. PRIME was well known for their excellent work. They were fast and thorough. Donovan was good at pointing out added features to increase security, as well as keeping the costs from skyrocketing. The company was a mixture of old and new, using the best they could find as well as the old tried-and-true methods.

Donovan turned over the pass codes for the alarm system and the gate. He diligently watched as both Nick and Kate repeated the sequence several times flawlessly before giving his approval. They entered the house making sure everything was in order before the men excused themselves to take a look around outside. Donovan, true to his reputation, pointed out several ways to increase the security around the exterior. Connery chuckled at Nick's raised eyebrows when dogs were brought up.

"Uhhh, no way man!" came Nick's vehement reply.

"At least stop to consider the idea first," interjected Connery. "I know it sounds like a lot of havoc—but I've seen what a couple of guards dogs can do."

Kate and Casey joined them outside in time to catch the tail end of the dog idea.

"Yeah, I like dogs as well as the next guy—but Kate was attacked by one when she was a child and she never really got over it. She doesn't need to live with something she's afraid of."

Kate was silent and Casey pointed to the scar on Kate's arm.

Connery stored the information for later use while Donovan scratched his head in concentration.

"What do you think of birds, Nick?" Donovan asked.

"Birds?!"

"Yes, some breeds of geese, guinea fowl, or peafowl can be great alarm systems."

"Your kidding, right?" Kate interjected.

"No, not at all. Why, I've seen a couple of hissing geese chase off coyotes of both the two- and four-legged variety. It is almost impossible to scare a goose off."

Casey laughed at the idea, "Next you're gonna tell us peacocks can fight off our perpetrator!"

"Actually peacocks are very territorial. They will put up a fuss at any stranger who dares to come around. On the plus side, the peacocks are beautiful birds. They like to fly, so to start with you have to clip the flight feathers to keep them home." Donovan definitely had their attention so he went on: "Geese won't fly and they become very tolerant and downright friendly to the people they know—but they are more messy than the other birds. Guinea fowl can get annoying with their constant chatter—but they aren't very big and they are fairly easy to come by in this area. Not pretty to look at, but the ruccuss they'd cause would be heard inside a vault during a loud storm. It would be something your perpetrator wouldn't be looking for, definitely throw a kink in his plan."

He studied the three friends whose chastising smiles turned to raised eyebrows that reflected thoughts of consideration.

"Well, why don't you talk it over and let me know. I can access any of them fairly easily."

Nick agreed to consider the watch-bird idea. Personally, he didn't see Kate going for it. Their mother had never allowed pets—too messy. He didn't see it working out, simply because no one was ever around, and if they had animals—that meant a caretaker. He just couldn't imagine using birds for what he was thinking they might be up against.

At the back of the property Donovan recommended something along the fence, "This is your most vulnerable area. It can't be seen directly from the house and once they're over the fence, they're in. A thorn-bearing vine for the rock wall would be preferred but they all agreed they didn't have time for it to strengthen and mature. Their option was barbed wire hidden smartly along the wall. "Won't bother your birds—but it can damage a human's skin pretty seriously. And if they can get past that, the laser beam alarms along the house will alert the police and let you know inside the house as well."

Nick nodded his approval and the group continued on with Donovan making a list of the devices agreed upon. They ended up at the front of the house again.

Kate was against the birds but agreed to think about it and Donovan would return as soon as possible with a crew to get started on the high-tech end of things.

As Donovan was headed down the drive Connery turned to Kate, "You need to remember that for all intents and purposes this is a war. A war that could get you killed, Miss Coleman. Donovan is the best there is and you should take every suggestion seriously. Birds would be easy to live with, they don't require the care of a couple of dogs and they can always be returned if it doesn't work for you."

Kate nodded as she and Casey made their way back into the house. Faded pictures of her father holding a large, ugly dog flashed through her mind before she resolutely shut the door of memory.

Nick motioned Connery and Bell toward the garden. The three men strolled casually along the wall, as if examining the perimeter. Connery waited patiently for Nick to start.

"I thought I hit a dead end in Europe with my story Connery, but as I play back my conversation with informants I'm beginning to wonder. I thought Trovoishek was a middleman. Now I'm not so sure. His family has diplomatic immunity, which might allow him to cover his tracks. They're investors in a few Russian shipping lines. I think we need to check Coleman Oil's shipping records for contacts with Slavec Blue Shipping. I'm going to contact some colleagues in Russia and France. Perhaps they can shed some light on this."

Connery and Bell agreed to go through the Coleman shipping records in the morning.

Connery voiced his next concern. "Hey Nick, see what you can dig up on Dr. Jason Mueller will you? My first attempts were blocked by blue money. Makes me wonder why."

"I'll see what dirt I can turn over for you."

The men returned to the house and seeing that Kate and Casey were safely settled in, Connery and Bell made their departure assuring them that a squad car would be parked just down the lane for the entire night.

The morning dawned bright and sunny instantly lightening Kate's mood. She hadn't been sure how she would sleep, being back in this house—but the night had passed peacefully. One look at her alarm clock told her there was no rush to get ready for work. It was still early and she quickly made the decision to have her breakfast out on the back terrace and enjoy the radiant flowers that were in full bloom. She hummed to herself as she got her breakfast ready. She would wake the other two late sleepers with the smell of scrambled eggs, toast, and coffee. As the coffee perked she stole a cup for herself and added it to her breakfast tray, rolling the cart toward the French doors she made for sunny fresh air. She unlocked the French doors leading outside. She closed her eyes as she stepped out, letting the sun bathe her face. Slowly, she opened her eyes to an eerie destruction. The massive patches of blooms were savagely destroyed! There were no flowers to be seen, only shredded ribbons of color and twisted stalks left standing bare—raped of their beauty before their time. Backing up indoors her eyes focused now on the glass panes in the French doors. The bottom half of the doors were smeared with mud. Kate backed up and turned to run, falling over the breakfast cart and righting herself just as quickly, all the while calling raggedly for Nick as she dialed the police demanding Detective Connery.

"I'm sorry, Miss Coleman, but Connery hasn't come in yet. It is quite early, you know."

Imbecile! Like she'd be calling at this hour of the morning if nothing was wrong! "Get him over here!" she screamed uncharacteristically. "There's been another incident at the Coleman Estate!" Kate slammed down the receiver as she heard Nick frantically calling her name followed by Casey's determined cadence of feet rushing down the stairs.

"Kate! Kate!"

"Over here." Nick quickly materialized in wrinkled jeans and shirtless. "What's wrong—are you okay?"

Kate motioned to the garden.

Nick took several slow steps forward as his jaw dropped.

Casey screamed. "OH MY GOD!"

A string of ragged curses fell from his lips as he processed the night's vandalism.

"Stay here. We don't want to mess up any evidence that might be out there. Casey, Kate, take a seat here at the counter. Might as well have some coffee while you wait. I'll take a quick look around just to make sure things are okay." From behind his back Nick withdrew a small, wicked-looking pistol that he expertly brought to readiness. Kate was shocked by the familiarness with which her brother handled the weapon and she determinedly resolved to question him about it later. It wasn't long before the blaring of sirens announced the arrival of the police. Nick stuck the weapon back in his waistband before answering the door to Bell's insistent ringing.

"Anyone hurt?" Bell asked.

"No, Bell, we're okay. Come take a look out back."

As Nick turned, the detective saw the gun in his waistband.

"That is some chuck of steel." Bell had to comment on it, if anything but to let Nick know he saw it.

"Of course, just a little protection, you know, my job and all."

The policeman followed Nick outside, scrutinized the area and quickly went back to the women seated at the counter. "Looks to me as if you had a wild animal destroy your landscaping last night!"

Connery arrived followed by the CSI team. The detectives started a floor-to-floor search of the house. It wasn't long before they were back with a grim look on their faces. "Come with us," Connery stated. He led them up the stairway to their mother's room. From the doorway Kate viewed the appalling scene that made her realize immediately they were not alone last night. The hair on the back of her neck stood up and she suddenly felt violated. Her mother's bed was covered with more shredded blooms. The riotous color made the pale creams and pinks of the room seem dreary in comparison. How could flowers appear so violent? Such a passive-aggressive act ... with flowers. But a threat none the less.

Another shudder ran down Kate's back when she realized the intruder was right here, just down the hall from her room. Connery turned her gently away from the sight and led her to her own room. Thinking he was guiding her toward a chair she began to protest. She would not be able to sit down and relax. Instead they stopped in her doorway, here the scene was different. The shear curtains that had hung on the long windows forever lay across the pillows of her bed— shredded and torn. There was mud everywhere that seemed to have come in on the curtains as if the intruder dragged everything from the garden upstairs on the long drapes.

    But ... she slept here last night ... she was just here ... this must have just taken place ... while she was downstairs. How long had she been up? Was the intruder still in the house? Again, what were they trying to say? Flowers didn't scare her, but, someone being this close, in their home while they were in it, that scared her to death! Only then she noticed the edges of the curtains were dripping crimson droplets onto the white rug below and she felt her knees give out.

SEVEN

Back at the office, Bell and Connery continued their investigation online. For some reason Connery didn't want to admit, the idea of someone being after Nick wasn't sitting right. Resolutely he forced the notion to leave his mind as he returned to the task at hand. He would follow through with Nick's lead as it was bound to go somewhere. The Interpol file he was scanning contained background on the Russian Mafia. Pieter Trovoishek was one man the Interpol had been tracking for years, yet the file held no evidence to indicate the head of the Mafia, this name was repeated more than any.

"Bell, you still got that contact in the CIA?"

"Sure. What are you thinking?"

"This Trovoishek character seems to have Interpol bothered as well as us. Think you can find anything?"

"I'll give a call and see what I can do." Bell paused before continuing, "Would that be a Pieter Trovoishek?"

"Yeah, how did you know?"

"There was a reference to a Pieter T. in the books at Coleman Oil—from Russia."

"Couldn't be a coincidence." Both detectives knew there was no such thing as a coincidence in their world.

"I'll see what I can come up with. Anything from the lab?"

"Same as last time. No DNA, no fingerprints, no evidence left behind. This guy's not an idiot."

Connery returned to his computer screen intent on his own line of investigation. The references to Pieter T. began to show a pattern. Payments seemed to be going to Pieter T. after the captain of the out-going vessel received a lightweight delivery. The weights recorded with those deliveries led him to believe it might be a "designer" drug deal because kilos were too light to be associated with any major drug deal. Then one glaring difference jumped off the screen: T=267Φ/30M.

What the hell was that? Then from some other reality Connery's brain latched onto the T=, and linked it to the research his sister had been doing on the Connery family tree. There was no way to miss the script used with that T=! In his family tree that symbol meant a twin. His brain refused to release the idea until he began to take another look at the data. Could the numbers be weights of individual passengers—or even more sinister could it be the weights of children? The underground child slavery ring was here in the Bay Area—right under his nose!

This had been the focus of Nick's research in Europe and would definitely link all the items together. If he was on the right track they had found the connecting link between the death of the Coleman parents, the break-in at the Coleman home, and the strange occurrences Nick had encountered! Connery rested his elbows on the edge of his desk as he began to reread the records from Coleman Oil.

Kate responded to the flashing of her call button on the phone, quickly picking it up, "This is Kate. How may I help you?"

"Kate you have a call on line two. The woman sounds rather upset."

"Thank you. I'll take it." Kate drew a quick breath before punching the flashing button. "This is Kate, how may I help you?"

"I can't believe what a cold-hearted bitch you've become Kate Coleman!" The voice immediately sounded familiar, but Kate was too busy digesting the words to make the connection immediately. "The nerve you have to abandon Jason in the midst of his current medical condition! A woman of any worth would have flown to his side to comfort him in the trials he is to endure! Do you have any idea how utterly painful the treatment is for African sleeping sickness? It kills me to think Jason wanted to take you as his wife! Why he would ever consider lowering himself to the likes of you is beyond me!"

"Abigail, I don't believe that now is the time, or place, for this conversation. Are you aware that you called me at work?"

"You will get yours Kate Coleman—and I WILL see to it! Good riddance!" The receiver slammed down on the other end making Kate jump.

Kate cringed, shaking her head at the irate intervention of Jason's mother. More and more she was realizing her breakup with Jason was for the best. She sighed wearily. There were times when she had the chance to regret her decision to break up with Jason. The repeated phone calls from Jason himself while he was suffering in Africa with the disease had left her feeling guilty. The toxic treatments had been explained to her at length earlier by Dr. Hunt. The derivative form of arsenic known as melarsoprol was extremely painful. Since its introduction in 1949 the drug had become less effective, although Jason was responding to the treatments. It was Jason's fanatical ravings over the phone that took a toll on her peace of mind. He seemed fixated on the fact that they would marry when he returned. She had tried to explain her feelings for him and the circumstances that had her jumping at shadows, but the man was set on his own dreams and his macabre sense of reality. She didn't think Jason would harm her. The doctor in Africa had said this bizarre sense of reality was part of the side effects of both the drug and the disease. But Jason's calls were beginning to scare her. Yesterday he had ranted and raved about lions roaring and that Kate must save him.

Now, after the call from Abigail, Kate was determined to keep her distance. She had never been comfortable around Jason's mother and this was another reason to sever all ties.

When Jason had informed Kate he would be back in the States shortly she had found her lip curling upward in disgust. How was she to hold him at arm's length when he was back at the hospital? Hopefully, once he was healthy, honesty would prevail and the man would realize the futility of his advances and he would move on with his life. She was definitely going to talk to Nick about this obsessed freak and his overbearing mother. If only for her own sanity. Nick knew her better than anyone. They were cut from the same cloth and a team since she could remember. Just the thought of sharing her problems with Nick made her feel better. He seemed so charming and gentlemanly to outward appearance—yet Kate knew that Nick was a dangerous adversary when backed into a corner. Memories from her childhood threatened to spill into the here and now. Determined she focused on the one that had always made her smile.

The memory played in her mind like a movie. She was backed up against a locker with a gaggle of mean-spirited girls surrounding her. She was threatened and trapped. Then, out of the blue, Nick was forcing his way through the column of girls reaching out his hand to her. She reached for his fingers as one girl dove to intercept the gesture he flattened her with one punch that could have taken down a linebacker. Perhaps a little much, but Nick's strength came from somewhere deep within.

The shocked look on the girl's face as her bottom hit the cool tile floor was priceless—as was her brother's parting remark. "I really think you should take more ballet lessons, Melissa. You seem rather graceless to me." Laughter from the spectators had caused the ringleader's face to blush in front of her peers. The girls parted and allowed Nick to escort Kate to the safety of her classroom. She smiled at the memory. *My, Kate thought, I'm so nasty getting such pleasure out of an incident from high school!* Nobody ever bothered her again, and to this day, Kate was convinced that without her brother to save her, she would not have made it this far. What they endured in their own home was so much worse than what school kids were capable of. However, she couldn't help the warm feeling that encompassed her, knowing that she had her brother for a guardian angel. She knew he would do anything to protect her.

Glancing at the clock Kate finished her paperwork quickly before heading to the cafeteria for a quick break and returned shortly with a granola bar and a mocha latté.

That's strange, Kate thought as she returned to her desk, *I could have sworn the computer was on when I left.* Shaking her head as she rebooted the hard drive, she decided she must have been so distracted by the call from Abigail that she had shut down instead of locking her station. Patiently, she waited for the computer to come up and made a list of priorities for the afternoon. When she glanced up to look at her screen she let out a gasp! On a blood red screen was a video of a huge lion in the process of tearing a man into pieces. The blood and gore were so graphic it had to be real, as was the man's agonized look as he begged the camera for help. Kate began to shake and frantically fought for her voice as the lion moved veraciously, tearing at the man's limbs.

"FELIX! Come here!" she managed in a high crackly voice.

Felix appeared and took one look at the horror facing them on the screen and quickly shut it down then dialed for security.

THE BEAST RUMBLED JOYOUSLY!

FEAR WAS ITS FAVORITE MEAL. LIKE ALL CATS, IT ENJOYED PLAYING WITH ITS PREY.

FEAR WOULD PUT THE BEAST IN CONTROL. THEN IT WOULD ELIMINATE THE CONTENDERS. MEANWHILE, IT WAS SWEET TO CURL CONTENTLY IN ITS LAIR PEERING OUT AT THE HAVOC IT HAD INITIATED.

THE HOST WAS UNAWARE OF THE EVENTS THAT HAD BEEN SET IN MOTION AND THAT SUITED THE BEAST JUST FINE.

EIGHT

Nothing! Connery was seething with frustration! The crime scene crew had gone over Kate's office with a fine-tooth comb, twice—and nothing! No prints, no fibers, no DNA! Their computer technician was still attempting to trace the route that had been used to load the revolting carnage.

Bell turned to his partner, "Connery, they've tracked down the point of origin for the screen saver."

"Well?"

"You're not going to like this—it was sent from the boyfriend's office. And we all know he isn't scheduled to be back in the United States for several days yet."

"Okay, but maybe the mother did it. She threatened Kate this morning."

"I doubt that Abigail Mueller would lower herself to computer terrorism," Bell replied.

"Doesn't mean that blue money couldn't have hired someone to scare Kate. Let's pay the lady a visit."

The ride to the Mueller Estate was filled with conjectures about the fiend behind the crimes. Bell was trying to figure out the message being sent. What did it all mean? The dolls, the flowers, the computer scene. Someone was close, too close.

Connery was filled with the dread that one of these times they'd be too slow and someone would get hurt. So far it seemed like someone was just toying with them. Just the thought of Kate being hurt sent a sharp pang through his heart, and he was forced to admit to himself that he was becoming emotionally involved in this case.

"I am starting to think maybe this is someone with a personal score to settle against Kate Coleman herself."

"Could be Connery, but who—the boyfriend in Africa, the poor bastard who lost his wife without insurance, or the prissy high-society meddling mother who wouldn't even dirty her pretty little fingers with any of this. I'm still betting on it being someone Nick Coleman has stirred up. Come on—he is involved in drug busts, a slavery ring, he has unveiled worldwide enemies of the U.S., not to mention that dear old Dad was involved in some shady business of his own. I think Nick knows a lot more than he lets on. Targeting the sister would certainly get a bigger result than going after the man himself. And he certainly deals with the type of people who would actually terrorize like this. Besides, you don't really think Mrs. Mueller is behind this do you?"

"No, I don't. But, I haven't met the boyfriend either and it won't hurt to question the lady. If anything she'll think twice about threatening someone again or at least send a message to her son."

"You obviously haven't had many dealings with the crème de la crème have you Connery? Intimidation and threats are second nature for them—giving and getting."

"Firsthand knowledge, Bell?" Connery glanced at his partner but Bell was already a million miles away judging by the look on his face as he stared ahead. Sometimes Connery was glad he didn't know more about the man.

Connery swung the sedan into the estate driveway, parking near the main entrance. The detectives rang the bell and when the maid answered the door, Connery snapped out his badge giving her no time to think. "Detectives Connery and Bell to see Mrs. Mueller. We'll just wait here in the foyer while you announce us." Connery masterfully pushed his way inside the home before the startled maid could respond.

"I don't think …"

Connery interrupted her abruptly, "Please let Mrs. Mueller know we are waiting."

The maid could see the detectives weren't going to budge and so she hurried off to announce their presence.

Once she was out of sight Bell congratulated Connery on his masterful presence. "Well, that was something to see, Connery. I guess I was mistaken, you have dealt with this type before."

"On occasion, Bell. I've always found that if you presume to have the right, they believe you do."

A butler returned to announce that the lady of the house would be down shortly. "Would you gentleman please follow me to the terrace?"

Connery nodded and Bell whispered to his partner as they followed the man outside, "Scared her—she brought out the reinforcements!"

"Butler, Schmutler," Connery countered. Played this game before, too!" Thoughts intruded of his ex-wife. Learning how to deal with her family had been a lesson in survival. Connery should have known when she took her family's side that it wasn't meant to last, but, love could be blind.

"Would you care for refreshments while you wait, gentlemen?" From the tone of the butler's voice it was clear the offer wasn't sincere.

"Thank you. I believe I'd like an Earl Grey tea. Bell, here, takes milk and lemon with his."

The butler's eyebrows rose at the order, both from the presumption that Connery would order him about and the desired brew! Clearly confused as to what kind of detectives were sitting on his employer's terrace, the butler hurried off to see to the tea and his employer.

"How did you know I took milk and lemon in my tea Connery?"

"Do you?"

"I do now. Nice touch. Totally threw him off guard."

"My point exactly." The two men sat quietly while the tea was served and were just helping themselves to a scone when Mrs. Mueller sallied onto the terrace. The tall, stately matron of the estate was a commanding presence. But Connery wasn't impressed. He had often found that kind of presence was all just a cover for a mean-hearted, petty person.

The men set down their cups and rose in the lady's presence.

"Good morning, gentlemen. Whatever could I have done to warrant two detectives on my doorstep?" She took a seat facing them as they followed suit.

Connery began. "We are here to confirm a phone conversation you were involved in with Miss Kate Coleman this morning at approximately 9:15. Do you deny that you were threatening in the alleged conversation? I believe your exact words were …" Connery flipped open his notes rapidly scanning through them before continuing, "… I can't believe what a cold-hearted bitch you've become Kate Coleman! The nerve you have to abandon Jason in the midst of his current medical condition. You will get yours Kate Coleman I will to see it!" Connery glanced at Abigail Mueller, looking directly into her eyes.

The older woman was furious—although she was trying hard not to show it.

"How dare you come here and accuse me of such a thing!"

"Mrs. Mueller, are you aware that the hospital records all calls coming into the Insurance Claims Department?" Bell interjected.

The woman huffed under her breath before replying. "Yes, I made that call. You have no idea what my son has been going through and to have that little tramp drop him at the first sign of trouble."

"Come now, Mrs. Mueller. Did you know Miss Coleman's parents just died in a car accident, and there have been threats to both her and her brother?" He wouldn't call it murder just yet.

"Why, I knew there had been a car accident and they had both been killed—but why would someone threaten her and her brother? Do you think the Colemans were murdered? No!"

"The forensics evidence hasn't come in to prove the Colemans might have had help crashing off the bluffs. There have been several strange occurrences at the Coleman Estate and they all point to a killer stalking the family. Perhaps Miss Coleman was trying to protect your son, in his weakened medical condition, from becoming another pawn in this game with a killer." Connery could see that the wind was fast leaving the lady's sails. "We'll need to know where you were from the time you made the call until our arrival. And do you have a computer? If so we'll need to see it. Do we need a warrant, or will you cooperate?"

"I'll make a list of my activities for this morning. My husband has a computer in his office. I never touch the thing myself. You had best talk to him for access to the machine."

Bell nodded, whipping out his cell phone. "I'll contact Mr. Mueller." She gave him the number. He dialed as he walked back into the house.

"One more thing, Mrs. Mueller, do you know your son's computer password at the hospital?"

"Why would I ever bother with something like that?"

"Someone sent Miss Coleman a rather graphic and nasty screen saver not long after your conversation this morning. You don't know anything about that?"

"Of course not! I already told you that I don't use those things."

"We'll need to check your computer."

"As I said, Detective, you'll have to check with my husband. It is his machine."

"When is your son due back in the States, Mrs. Mueller?"

"Certainly you don't think Jason had anything to do with this Detective! Why the poor man has been fighting for his life with that awful African disease!"

Connery gave her his stoniest gaze and waited.

Finally Abigail snorted a deep breath before replying, "Jason is flying into Kennedy on Thursday. We'll be picking him up in a private jet to bring him back home. You are truly out of your mind Detective if you think that Jason had anything to do with this!!"

"A good detective follows every lead, Ma'am."

Bell returned shaking his head. "Mr. Mueller has declined to comply with our request." Abigail's frown began to tilt until Bell questioned his partner, "Want to call your friendly judge now?"

"Not at this moment, Bell."

"Then if you gentlemen are done, I'll ask you to leave."

"Of course, Ma'am." Connery gave her a scrutinizing gaze before turning to leave.

Once in the car the two detectives hashed over their information as they made their way back to the station. Once again, a dead end loomed in sight.

"We've got to turn up something, Bell. Criminals make mistakes. We are missing something."

"I'm going to get word out to some of my snitches on the street, Connery. I doubt I'll get anything back but it's the only avenue we haven't tried."

Connery nodded in agreement. Who knew—maybe the street

would turn up some lead they were missing?

Back at the office Bell finished up his report while Connery went to bring the Captain up to speed on their progress—or lack of it.

"Got any ideas, Captain? Bell and I are fast running out of them. I hate feeling like we have to wait for his next move."

"Did you think to break down each incident individually? Maybe it isn't one man you're looking for—but several? Remember how we caught the different guys in the Simson's murders?"

Connery nodded. Several people had vendettas against Mr. Coleman. Had they, by chance, started their path to revenge at the same time?

"Bell and I are going to make a run out to the Coleman Estate to check things out."

The Captain nodded his approval. Connery and Bell were a couple of his best—somehow, someway, they would find a chink in this case.

When they arrived at the gate it was locked and the new state-of-the-art remote camera watched their every move. Connery pressed the button and before long a Spanish accent came over the speaker, asking them to identify themselves.

"Detectives Connery and Bell."

"Please show your identification to the camera." Whoever manned the controls had been well trained. IDs were shown and then the camera zoomed out to get a look at both of the men.

"You may proceed Detectives."

As the car slowly made its way up the drive Connery was pleased to see the security team was busy working. Donovan was unloading a large pair of honking geese from a trailer. As the two birds were finally freed the male spread his wings flapping them nosily as he sauntered off after his mate. Connery and Bell watched as the pair joined several other geese out back near a newly-installed pond. Kate stood hesitantly nearby with a death grip on a loaf of bread as Donovan quickly stepped over to her.

"Now, Miss Coleman, tear that bread up and toss some out to them. Won't be long, and they'll eat right out of your hand."

"They're so big!"

"Well, the whole idea is to scare people off. These African Geese are loud and noisy around strangers or trespassers and they have a nasty twist if cornered. That big pair I just released are Frank and Fran. The smaller white ones are Tufted Romans. The Romans used them as sentries posted to keep watch along their walls and gates. They are faster to sound an alarm than the Africans, but not generally as noisy. Those Africans will take on just about anything that trespasses. I've seen them take on coyotes and dogs without breaking their stride. When they friendly up to you, you'll be surprised how much you'll enjoy them."

Kate looked doubtful.

"Feed them here and before long they'll figure out that the driveway is neutral territory. Call me if you have any problems at all."

Matt Donovan turned to the detective. "Good to see you Connery. Any luck?"

Connery shook his head. "Not much to speak of. We're going at it from another angle."

"Well, my team should be finished up here by Friday."

"That's good to know Donovan. The ex-boyfriend is returning on Thursday."

Donovan nodded his understanding. Connery watched Kate as she shakily attempted to feed the geese meandering about the backyard. He made his way over to help her. Standing close to her side he gently unpeeled her fingers from the smashed bread.

"The secret is to show them that you belong here as much as they do." He salvaged the bread, separating it into pieces and gently tossing it in the flock's direction. The birds eyed him suspiciously before one brave bird pecked at the offering. A gleeful honk escaped as it greedily gobbled up the treat. The others began to follow suit and soon the birds began to move in on the feeders.

"There's nothing to be afraid of, just toss them the bread and remember to breathe, Kate."

Kate turned to voice her thanks. Soft breath collided with masculine lips. She closed her eyes leaning into the moment and Connery gently breached the distance closing his mouth over her incredibly soft lips. Coming home—he felt like he had finally come home. They sank into the feeling—exploring the corners of each other's lips, soft breath meeting questing tongues. The mood deepened until a startled yelp made Connery withdraw to look into the forbidding gaze of a curious goose in search of more bread. Kate laughed—handing him more food, and the two finished off the loaf. Gradually the birds resumed the exploration of their new home. Connery gazed into Kate's eyes before taking, perhaps, the biggest gamble of his life. *This was wrong! She was a case! She was vulnerable and scared, but his heart roared, pushing him to test the waters one more time.* Before he could follow through, Kate leaned into him and resumed where they were interrupted. Her kiss roamed his mouth, heating his blood. He pulled her close to him deepening the kiss.

A choked coughing brought him back to reality. Bell was watching with a grin on his face. "We've been invited to dinner. I take it that's a 'Yes'?"

NINE

Jason was tired. *No*, he thought, *tired isn't even close to how I feel after the damnable treatment for this disease. Nothing in life could be as painful as the relentless treatment I have suffered through for this God-forsaken African sleeping sickness.* His veins still burned from the caustic drug injected to fight the parasitic disease. He was still angered by the slurred speech the disease had left behind. His doctors in Africa thought that with therapy and time he might regain his normal speech. *Of course, I will!* He was still on the fast track and nothing was going to stop him. He settled back in his seat. Kate would come around. Once he returned and was back in the hospital she would see the error of her ways. Mel Halloway, his traveling companion for the trip watched him closely. He was another doctor on the African mission, who had volunteered to return with Jason when the doctors had frowned upon his being alone on the flight. Mel would be returning to Africa after his sister's wedding. Jason thought he was an idiot of high account. *Who, in their right mind, would return to that hell of poverty and sand?* His thoughts turned to how to win over Kate as he drifted into a fitful sleep. Even now, when he was more or less free of the tiny parasite in his bloodstream, the lion still roared in his sleep.

"Hey Connery!" shouted O'Reilly from across the room. "Found your suspect!"

"Which one, O'Reilly?"

"That guy you were looking for—Henderson? We found him. He's cooling his heels in Room 4."

Bell and Connery exchanged glances. "Where did you find him?"

O'Reilly smiled knowingly. "The man walked back into the the restaurant to see if he could get his job back. Picked him up half an hour ago."

"Thanks—let's go Bell!" The two men made their way into the interrogation room where they found an irate man rocking in his chair.

"Will somebody tell me what's going on? I already made arrangements with the creditors so they shouldn't be pulling this crap."

"This has nothing to do with your creditors, Mr. Henderson. I'm Detective Connery and this is my partner, Detective Bell. We'd like to ask you some questions about your conversation with Miss Kate Coleman."

"Who?"

"Kate Coleman, your Claims Assistant at the hospital. Seems you threatened her over the phone several weeks ago."

"That's what this is about? What did she do—file a complaint?"

"Not that simple, sir. Seems someone is stalking her and you did threaten the lady."

"I can't believe this! My wife dies from inoperable cancer, I loose my job, the insurance won't pay the bills, the hospital is foreclosing on everything, and now I'm accused of stalking some hospital employee whose name I can't even remember?!"

Bell and Connery exchanged glances. The man didn't seem the type. "Then why did you take a job at the Hot Tamale? It's the favorite dining place of the lady in question."

"Hey, look Detectives. I'll admit I was really upset about my wife's death and the ensuing problems. But, honestly, I didn't even know the lady ate there. The manager gave me a job with decent pay and a place to sleep when I had nothing. That's why I took the job."

Bell interjected, "Then why did you leave without notice?"

"This may sound corny, Detectives, but I got a call from a Marine buddy of mine for a reunion of the 104th. At the time it seemed like a good idea to take a break—get my head back together. I am sorry I didn't give notice, I just had to get outa here, ya' know what I mean?"

"Can you prove you were at this reunion and the date you returned?"

"Sure Detective. I'll give you the number and some contacts."

The man paused, "You know, it was the best decision I ever made besides to marry Belle. Sunk into my brain that life wasn't so bad. Belle and me, we had thirty-five years together before the cancer ate her brain. I've got myself some beautiful kids that care about their old man, and friends that hang tight. Belle wouldn't have wanted to go on the way she was. I can see that now. But it still irks that I'm going to lose everything for taking care of my wife. There's just no way I would hurt that lady at the hospital over this. It wasn't her fault. Just had to let off some steam, you know?"

"You sit tight while we check out your story, Mr. Henderson." Connery looked at the names and dates Henderson had written down. If his story was true, and he'd eat his hat if it wasn't, there was no way Henderson had been involved in the Coleman case. Fort Worth, Texas, wasn't that long a drive for a man on the run from something, and Marines were truthful men. They wouldn't cover up—even for an old comrade in arms.

An hour later Henderson was released and removed from the list of suspects.

"Well, at least now we know where not to look," Bell said.

"Yeah, but we're still spinning our wheels. Let's go get coffee. I need a break."

"We could stop at the hospital to let Miss Coleman know she was right about Henderson. It might ease her mind."

Connery frowned at his partner. There would be no living with Bell after being caught in the garden with Kate. "Razzing my butt about getting involved with a case?"

"Nah, Connery—wouldn't do that to you!" Bell laughed.

"Huh! Now I am suspicious!"

When Kate and Casey arrived in the break room they were surprised to find the two detectives waiting for them. "Thought you ladies might enjoy some real coffee for a change, and since we're the bearers of good news …"

"What kind of good news?" Casey asked.

"We managed to locate Mr. Henderson. Your instincts were on the money Kate. It wasn't him. He was just letting out his frustrations, and you happened to be in the way. He's back working at the Hot Tamale, so don't freak if you see him there, okay?"

Kate nodded, sipping her mocha latté enthusiastically. *Poor Mr. Henderson. But where did Connery get those eyes? I could lose myself in them. His kisses weren't bad either!*

"Why, Miss Coleman, you're blushing! What is going on in that pretty little head of yours?" Connery teased.

"I'm not sure I want to say," she teased back.

Connery's look of surprise made her laugh, something, she realized that had been few and far between with Jason. Kate had always remained the prim and proper lady with Jason. He had always been reserved—concerned about his reputation and image, while Connery encouraged her to go a little crazy—to step outside of the shell she had always lived within. She dreaded the thought of Jason returning to the hospital. Hopefully, he wouldn't make a scene. She couldn't imagine that he would. Doing so would be bad form and beneath his status—yet, he could be quite manipulative and forceful. After all she had never accepted his proposal. Abigail would probably be thrilled to find a more acceptable daughter-in-law. Kate and Abigail Mueller had never seen eye to eye on much of anything and Kate could actually breathe easier knowing she wouldn't have to socialize with the Muellers any longer.

The conversation was lighthearted as the four bantered and kidded each other. Kate realized that it had been months since she had felt this good. Perhaps Connery was the reason. Nothing else in her life had changed for the better. Was it possible that one man could have such an effect on her?

Break time was up and Casey gathered up the empty cups as they headed back to work.

Kate still sat staring into space as the three walked away from the table.

"Kate? Yoo hoo, ground control to Kate Coleman!" Casey's voice brought her attention back to the cafeteria and she blushed as she looked up at her friends who were staring at her.

Bell's phone began to ring.

"Come on Kate, we gotta get back," Casey said.

Kate's eyes large, she slowly came back from somewhere dark, a million miles away.

"Bell here."

Connery noticed his frown and then picked up the pace to

keep up with Bell as he made for the parking garage.

"I'll check in with you later." Connery shouted back to the girls. "What?" Connery demanded of Bell.

"That was the port authorities. They just made a raid dockside. You'll never guess what they found."

"Don't play 'Twenty Questions' with me now partner," Connery growled.

"They opened a cargo compartment of a Coleman ship when the numbers were off on their weight."

"Yeah, so what did they find?"

Bell gave him a piercing gaze. "Children. It was full of children. Boys and girls of all ages with no papers, no luggage. Looks like we found our connection between Coleman Oil and the Russian Mafia. Child slavery."

TEN

Connery and Bell stood to one side watching the port authorities and the Coast Guard remove children from the Coleman Oil ship, *Rusiana*, where they had been confined in the ship's hold. Connery had seen some gruesome things in his years on the force, but this? They were children. Pathetically dirty, obviously starving, terrified children! The Coast Guard had an interpreter en route. Where and whatever they had come from must have been awful. The Captain was arrested and the crew held for questioning. There was no way anyone was getting out of this mess unscathed. Bell was going over the log with the Coast Guard Captain. The port of departure was Russia—what Nick Coleman had been hinting at had led them to this bust. Were the Colemans actually innocent of underground child slavery? His heart clenched at the thought. Could George Coleman's shady business dealings be able to continue with him in the grave? Was it a setup to incriminate Coleman Oil Distributing Company? Connery's thoughts whirled around the possibilities. He'd bet his heart that Kate wasn't involved—he already had!

This was going to be an all-nighter. By the time the interpreter finished with the children dawn would be on the horizon. Connery stretched his neck trying to smooth out some of the kinks from the hours spent with Bell dissecting the shipping manifest for the umpteenth time.

Exasperated, Connery slammed shut the books. "Let's go over to Coleman Oil and see what we can find out about this ship. Nothing in here is making any sense to me."

"I've got a better idea. Let's both go home and grab a couple hours of sleep. We'll go back to the office and go over those records we subpoenaed from the company in the a.m.. Seems to me I remember a ship's port of departure list."

"Let's go. Fresh eyes'll catch something we're not."

Connery painfully made his way up to his apartment. *Gotta get after that landlord. You wouldn't think one light bulb would be that hard to replace.*

Sam met him at the door. Winding himself around Connery's legs until the man was in danger of being tripped. "All right, you old hawk bait." Connery snuggled the cat to his chest, rubbing his ears until the volume of the cat's purrs drowned out the pounding of Connery's head. "Let's see what we have for breakfast, hmm?"

The cheery yellow note on his refrigerator could only be from one person—

> Flynn,
> It's been ages since you've dropped in for dinner. I suppose you've been working long hours AGAIN! Sam says it's been tuna, tuna, and more tuna lately. Really brother dear! Mom worries that you're wasting away. Even a cat needs a break!
>
> Enjoy—love you dearly!
> Beth

Connery was almost too excited to open the refrigerator. Previous experience told him that all his favorites (and Sam's) would be here—ready for reheating and maximum enjoyment. He wasn't disappointed. Tidy containers were labeled with meals and cooking instructions for the bachelor. Lasagna, beef tips with noodles and gravy, Mom's fry bread, and Beth's tortellini salad screamed EAT ME!

Sam began to yowl at the delay.

"Alright buddy, lasagna it is."

Sam jumped up to the counter against all the rules to encourage Connery to hurry, hurry! And today Connery didn't have the heart to force the tomcat down. They were both starving and dinner was calling—or breakfast, depending on how you looked at it. After second helpings the two bachelors retired to their favorite chair. Connery slouched down into Sam's favorite nesting pose, and Sam clambered up kneading his human in delight, as he shifted into position. Finally, the tom settled and with a contented burp he slipped into sleep. Connery's last thought was that as much as he appreciated the cat's affection he wished it were someone else snuggling up to him.

The plane slipped into the unloading bay without a problem and Jason departed with heartfelt thanks. His walk was slow and painful as he made his way into the lobby of the airport. Immediately, he saw his parents. Slowly he made his way through the press of people toward them. As he neared, the expression on his mother's face turned from joyful expectancy to dread and anger.

"Oh, my God, Jason look at you! You're so thin and ..."

Jason grimaced in anger. "Pale and crippled, Mother?" His speech slurred slightly as he gave way to his anger.

"You never mind, Jason, I've called in the best in the world and we'll have you back to normal in no time at all," his mother replied.

His father rested a helping hand under his arm before questioning, "Would you like a wheelchair, son?"

"NO! I'm better and I can walk!"

"Of course, you're getting better dear. Now that you're back in the states you'll recover much faster."

"Have you seen Kate, Mother?"

Abigail exchanged a worried glance with her husband. "We've talked dear. She is quite adamant about keeping her distance, she is apparently being stalked by some criminal threatening her life and her brother's. Good riddance, I say. You're too good for her Jason. Honestly, I don't know what you ever saw in that selfish little twit. A Detective Connery stopped by to ask us to stay away from the family." That was not quite the truth, but Jason didn't need to know the truth.

"Well, dear, it seems there have been several attempts to frighten and hurt both Kate and that brother of hers. The police have warned us to stay away until they catch the perpetrator, for fear that he might come after us to hurt the Coleman family. And Jason dear, Kate's parents were murdered. Perhaps it would be best for now if we followed the detective's directions."

"Whoa, Mother, did you just say murdered?"

Jason paused to digest the information from his mother. *Wait,*

I vaguely remember Kate spouting some nonsense about her parents being killed in an accident but I imagined they were driving intoxicated again. I did not take her warning to stay away seriously. Who would want to hurt my dear Kate? But, if the police were warning my family to stay away there must be something to it. So Kate was concerned for my safety, her distance was only to protect me! So, she does still care! It must be so hard for her to put me at arm's length. I will wait only until I am back at the hospital where our bumping into each other will look work related. That would also give me time to heal.

He hated weakness and he was weak and tired all the time. He detested the erratic thoughts and obsessions that played about in his head. Therapy and finishing the drug regime would have him back to being himself earlier than they predicted. Things would be going his way soon.

The Mueller family slowly continued their progress through the airport until they reached the boarding area for their sleek private jet that would return them to the west coast. A specialist and equipment to monitor Jason's progress were already on board, they would make him comfortable on the flight. Abigail regaled him with stories of the events and social gossip he missed while he was gone, until he asked for relief to rest.

THE GREAT BEAST LICKED ITS PAWS IN SATISFACTION.

IT WOULD WAIT IN QUIET ANTICIPATION FOR THE SCREAMS TO RIP THROUGH THE NIGHT AS ITS LATEST ADVENTURE WAS DISCOVERED.

IT WAS TIME TO START HERDING THE PREY INTO A GROUP WHERE THEY COULD BE PICKED OFF ONE BY ONE.

OF COURSE, IT WILL LEAVE ONE FOR LAST AND IF WORTHY, PERHAPS IT WOULD HAVE A MATE.

ELEVEN

Nick cussed loudly at the sight of the damage. Red paint ran down the windshields and front ends of both his and Casey's cars. Giant paw prints tattooed the windshields and hoods as if some wild beast had walked on the vehicles with bloody paws. Against his instinct to protect the finish on his seventies Malibu and wash the mess off, he pivoted and made his way back into the house. By now the number of police headquarters was on speed dial. He left a message for Detectives Connery and Bell to stop by as soon as possible, before heading upstairs to warn the ladies about the latest vandalism. If it didn't piss him off so badly (someone messing with his vintage car) Nick could almost find this amusing, if that was possible. How were these huge paw prints created?

Casey wasn't so amused. "If I find the SOB who did this to my car there won't be enough of him left for the police to identify!"

"Come on Casey. It's not too bad," Kate consoled, she was really worried that this had something to do with her since her car was spared.

"Next time those geese honk, Nick, I swear you're getting up to investigate every nook and cranny of this estate—not just the back gardens!"

"Well excuse me, Miss Waters, but when we discovered the neighbor's cat sulking in the bushes we figured we had found what all the honking was about!"

Kate tried to smother a laugh, but it escaped.

"See, even Kate can laugh about this one Casey. Try to relax."

"Well, yeah, Kate's car was left untouched!" She motioned toward Kate's glistening silver Escort.

Casey rolled her eyes and went back into the house and reappeared with a loaf of bread. Ripping pieces off to feed the stately pair of Roman Tufted geese Casey clucked and clicked and soon had them venturing onto the driveway toward her and the food.

"Hey, Donovan said to feed them over here—'neutral territory'!" Nick shouted.

"I want them guarding my car. If I have to feed them a whole bakery of bread they are going to learn to love my car!"

Nick and Kate laughed at her antics as the birds began to infringe on Casey's space. Soon the geese had her backing away from her car as they pursued her along the line of the driveway toward the back entrance to the kitchen. "Bread gone!" Casey cried, waving her hands in dismissal until the disgusted birds meandered off in search of whatever geese go in search of.

A royal blue '68 Camaro pulled into the driveway. Kate and Casey's eyes grew big as Bell exited the car. They hadn't seen his Camaro. Nick emitted a low whistle of appreciation for the detective's choice of transportation. The car was in mint condition.

"Nice wheels, man!"

"He may be old, he may be a geek, but the man's car is oh, so sweet!" recited Bell about himself.

Connery just shook his head, "Oh yeah, he's a geek alright," the others laughed.

"So what's going on?" Connery asked.

Nick pointed to the cars parked in the drive. "Someone had fun last night and as much as it looks like we have a giant putty tat, I seriously doubt it."

The detectives sauntered over to the cars. They examined the area. Bell put in the call for a CSI.

"What do you think Bell?"

"Smells like tempera paint to me. Whoever did this at least had the decency to use something that wouldn't hurt the paint jobs. You can be thankful for that."

"Thankful my ass," Casey muttered as Connery's phone rang. After a short conversation he hung up. "Seems we have a false alarm folks. A couple of kids were caught down the street this morning painting another car. Sounds like a harmless prank, but we'll check it out. We've definitely got them on trespassing and damaging property if you want to press charges. In the meantime, we can drop you at work. We still want the team to give all three cars a once over."

Casey and Kate left to grab their things as Nick talked with the detectives. "Think I'll call in and work at home today. When the team is done I can clean up the cars before the ladies return."

The detectives dropped Casey and Kate at work then headed to the station to question the teenage boys about their recent car painting escapade.

The boys were old enough to know that, while they were in trouble, they were under age and pretty safe from doing any jail time. It was obvious they had been down this road before so they wouldn't talk. Connery surprised the boys with allegations of vandalism and break-ins possibly all tying in with the murder of Mr. and Mrs. George Coleman. The tough-boy image soon disappeared. They admitted to the vandalism of the neighbors' cars, but were adamant that they had not entered the Coleman grounds. Bell believed them.

The other painted cars had the boys' prints all over the vehicles. But they were still waiting for the results on Casey and Nick's. In the meantime, the boys were left to stew.

Lawyers and parents arrived in full force. The lawyers were pricey and the parents were irate. The Detectives maintained their stoical presence under fire, alluding to the fact that what the boys had done put them under suspicion for the recent vandalism and break-ins. Things quieted down after that. Connery thought to himself that if the parents had been this concerned with where their children had been this wouldn't have happened. *This is what you get when you have too much money and not enough to do with your time*, he thought.

While they waited for the lab results, Connery and Bell began the task of searching the Coleman Oil records for any mention of the ship *Rusiana*. Bell located the roster of ships importing oil with their ports of origin. The *Rusiana's* origin was the Russian port city of Vladivostk. The busy port had ships moving in and out on a regular basis. Considering that Russia held the eighth largest oil and natural gas reserves in the world, there was a large population for the slavers to choose from among the working poor or orphaned. The mere thought of what the future might have held for the occupants of the ship, had they not discovered its cargo, chilled everyone involved.

Bell's phone broke the noisy concentration of the office. "Lab called. They want us down there right away."

The lab was as cool as it was sterile and Marco was waiting with the results. "What do you want first? The bad news—or the bad news?"

"What were the results on the paint?" Connery queried.

"Doesn't match your teenage pranksters. The boys were using a water base Crayola while the Coleman cars were a water base tempera. Both sold just about anywhere that carries school supplies."

"Two different paint pranks in one night?" replied Bell.

"What else have you got?" Connery asked.

"Nothing. No prints, no DNA, no trace. Wish I had better news, guys."

Connery shrugged his shoulders. "Hey, I'd be more surprised if you did find something. We're just going to have to find a different route to catch this guy. These pranks are getting old, something's gotta give."

Let's work the *Rusiana* slave ring as a case of its own. We'll follow our leads and see if it even takes us to Kate, Nick, and Casey."

"Works for me, Connery. It's a sure bet that we can't do any worse than we are now. Should we inform Nick about the incident on the *Rusiana*?"

"My instincts tell me that he might be helpful in this case. I'd like to keep him out of it on the basis that there is someone after him and his family ... ."

"But?"

"But, he knew more than we did about Coleman Oil's involvement in the slavery ring. That reporter has contacts and leads we could use." Bell nodded in agreement.

Jason arrived at the hospital Friday morning and headed for the executive offices. The hospital's chief of staff had left word that he would appreciate Jason stopping by when he had a chance. Jason wondered what was on the man's mind but imagined, since it was his first day back, it would be to sing him praises for risking his life to save so many others. He was ushered in as soon as he arrived.

"Jason, it's good to have you back."

"Thank you, Dr. Marks. I can't tell you how good it is to be back. Although I am distressed that my tour with the World Health

Organization had to be cut short."

"I just wanted you to stop in so that I could reassure you that there will be a position available here at the hospital no matter what the outcome may be from your bout with African sleeping sickness."

Jason scowled. "I will make a full recovery, Dr. Marks. I am determined."

"Of course you are Jason! Your determination and resolve are some of your outstanding credentials as a surgeon. However, if a full recovery outdistances you, there will be a position here for you. We don't want to loose you. Your fine surgical skills can be put to use outside of the operating room if necessary."

Jason fumed inwardly at the man's gall. He would recover and Kate would be his! He excused himself from his superior's office and headed to Therapy to schedule his appointments. Then he would drop by his office before seeing Kate.

Several hours later he stopped outside Kate's cubicle, noticing she was in conversation with someone. He made his way closer until he could overhear the conversation.

"Kate be careful. We have reason to believe there might be more than one person after you and Nick."

He must be that detective Mother has been talking about, Jason thought to himself. He listened intently bent on hearing the rest of the conversation.

"Bell and I are headed over to the house to inform Nick of some new developments. Maybe he can shed some light on the latest one."

"Why don't you and Bell stay for dinner?"

"I'd love to but we'll have to see how things go. I don't know where Bell is right now, but I'm sure he'd appreciate a home-cooked meal as much as I would. Thank you for the invitation. We'd like to check out the security system now that Donovan is finished and once we've seen Nick you may be home, so let's talk then."

"I'll look forward to seeing you then Detective." Using his title she was flirting with him. He realized this as their eyes met.

Jason made his way around Kate's cubicle and stopped quick. Kate seemed to be expressing more than appreciation for the job the man was doing. He watched, unnoticed, as the tall man left the office area and headed for the elevator. Then he made his way to Kate's cubicle.

"Hey Baby, miss me?" Jason noticed the becoming blush that tinted her cheeks. Then he noticed her eyes. Her beautiful topaz eyes had never sparkled like that for him. As her eyes focused on him the sparkle faded.

"What are you doing here, Jason?"

"That's a rather cold greeting after everything we have meant to each other, Katie Bear."

She cringed at the nickname. Her ire began to rise. More and more she saw the false front and overbearing personality of her father in Jason. It angered her. No longer would she put herself under the domineering control of a male. Flynn Connery never talked down to her as if she were a little girl. Jason's image began to shrink next to the detective's. Connery was truly concerned for her, unlike Jason who she could now see was only concerned if her behavior threatened his reputation.

"I thought I made it clear on the phone that I didn't think we should see each other anymore, Jason."

"I understand that you were trying to protect me, Kate, but we're bound to bump into each other here at the hospital. It'll only be a matter of time before we can resume our relationship."

"There isn't a relationship, Jason. I told you that I couldn't accept your proposal. That hasn't changed—and it won't. Just move on Jason."

Jason's temperature began to rise. "Like you've moved on with that cop?"

Kate refused to dignify his question by responding to it. "Jason, I have work to do and I'm sure that you do, too. I wish you a speedy recovery. Now please, leave me alone."

Jason turned slowly making his way down the hallway. *I'm not giving up so easily, Kate,* he thought to himself. *You're mine now and forever. You were mine before Africa and you'll be mine again. I'm not about to let some stinking Detective come between us and the relationship I have so carefully planned for us. I will have you.*

Jason remembered the look in her eyes after the Detective left. Once he reached the empty elevator he spoke aloud. "You're not taking my woman away from me, you hear? I didn't suffer through the horrors of Africa to have some working-class cop scoop up my woman while I'm out saving the world. Kate is MINE!"

The distant roar of a lion echoed in his mind and Jason nervously turned to look over his shoulder before hurrying off the elevator.

TWELVE

Connery and Bell were frustrated. The Russian children would not talk to the Coast Guard interpreter. In their country the police and uniforms were still feared and these kids were terrified. If they knew something they weren't giving it away. There had to be a way to break through the wall the kids had erected. But how? Then it hit him. Perhaps Nick Coleman could help. Even in Russia the man was known for his honesty and confidential dealings with his contacts. If Bell's contact was to be believed the kids had probably heard of Nick. Plus, Connery knew Nick spoke flawless Russian. It was worth a try.

Connery fiddled with his coffee cup as he waited on hold for the newspaper to put him through to Nick. The way his luck was going today the reporter would have left the office and be off on some trail of his own. But luck was with Connery today.

"Nick Coleman here."

"Nick, this is Flynn Connery. I'm hoping you may be able to help us out." Connery explained their situation with the Russian children and asked Nick if he would meet with the kids and try to get them to talk.

"Sure, be glad to help out Connery, but first I need to run back to the estate. I think I forgot to reset the code on the entrance gates before I left this morning. I don't want the girls to walk into any surprises later. Give me the address and I'll meet you there, in say ... an hour?"

"That will be fine. Bell and I will be there at 3:30." Connery gave Nick the address and directions and Nick assured him that he'd meet them there.

"Lab called," Bell interjected, "they might have something on that hideous screensaver that was on Kate's computer."

The men rapidly made their way down to the lab to find Marco grinning at them.

"You look rather pleased with yourself," Bell volunteered.

"I've found the source of your screensaver—although I don't know that it will do you much good. It looks like the graphics were downloaded from a website called "MANEATERS". The site deals with reports and graphics of animals that have been known to hunt, kill, and eat humans. It includes bears, tigers, lions, panthers, etc. Whoever your computer freak is he downloaded the photos from the site and then doctored the pics to get his graphic details. He also enhanced the graphics to make the finished product seem more real than the original photos. This guy is good. Somewhere in his background the interest in art or graphics might show up."

"Thanks Marco. Now if we just had a suspect!" Connery shot back sarcastically.

"Hey, I can only work with what you give me," Marco replied.

"Don't mind him Marco. He's just testy because so far this guy has managed to outsmart us," Bell answered.

"Wait a minute, Marco. You said this is a guy. Do you really know this is a male?" Connery questioned.

"Well, studies show seventy percent of the graphic detailing of this nature comes from males—so the odds are pretty good," Marco finished.

"Let us know if anything else shows up."

"You're the first one I'll call, Connery."

At precisely 3:30 p.m. Connery and Bell arrived at the house where the Russian children were being quartered. There was no sign of Nick's brown Malibu. They waited patiently until Connery checked his watch again to find that while he and Bell had been going over the case's facts the hands had crept to 4:15. Now he began to worry. Every dealing he'd had with Nick the man had been on time. From what he knew the reporter wouldn't be late.

"Bell, ring the estate and see if Nick's there. I'm calling his editor; I've got a bad feeling about this." Connery dialed the paper and after being forwarded to the editor he voiced his concern.

"Afraid I can't help you Detective. Nick left about 2:30. He didn't say where he was going."

"Shit! Bell drive!" Connery cut the connection to the newspaper and dialed the station. "This is Connery we have a possible situation at the Coleman Estate. Backup is requested and proceed with caution. Nick Coleman is not responding to his phone and this was his last known destination."

For once Connery wished he was driving—he was not a good passenger. But Bell didn't let him down—pushing the souped-up Camaro into hyper speed; they flew through the San Francisco streets with the siren blaring, becoming airborne over one of the city's famous hills. If they didn't get themselves killed on the way they might just beat the uniforms to the Coleman home. Had Nick been right? Had he left the estate gates unlocked? Or had their criminal forced his way inside before Nick returned?

As they rounded the last corner Connery almost swallowed his tongue. He would later swear Bell took the corner on two wheels.

"Shit," he muttered to his partner, "you missed your calling. NASCAR here we come!"

The car skidded to a halt just as O'Reilly came out the door radioing for an ambulance.

"It's bad Connery, somebody really worked him over good. He's breathing, but geez ... if you didn't know it was Nick Coleman you would never be able to guess."

"This bastard isn't getting away this time. Close off this area and seal the estate! I'm going in! O'Reilly, get some officers to check the perimeter." Connery rushed into the home to find O'Reilly's partner performing first aid on Nick. The frothy pink bubbles from his mouth spoke volumes. Busted ribs and a punctured lung for sure. Looked like his nose was broken, too. Connery knelt by the injured man.

"Nick, it's Connery. We've got you. You hang in there. The ambulance is on the way."

One battered eye opened and his bloodied swollen lips parted. No words came out but Connery understood.

"Don't worry! I'm not going to let anything happen to Kate. I'll personally make sure of it." From over Connery's shoulder Bell verified the statement.

"I've got Kate covered Nick, officers are already on the way to the hospital to guard the ladies. They're safe."

Nick's eye fluttered shut as the paramedics began their fast and efficient work. They quickly did what they could to stabilize Nick before heading off to the hospital. Bell and Connery followed at a more sedate pace than when they had arrived.

"Somebody is going to pay for this," Connery growled.

"In spades," came an answering reply from his partner. "With that much blood there has to be DNA at the scene. This time we'll get a break."

"We have to have round-the-clock protection for Nick. As long as he can identify the perpetrator his life isn't worth spit."

"Donovan's got contacts, Connery. I bet he could come up with someone to work security for the family," Bell paused, "cause you know that the department will have to pull our men if this guy doesn't show soon."

"Yeah, the facts of the public servant. I'll check with Kate and then give Donovan a call. Till then …"

"We're not going anywhere," Connery finished Bell's sentence for him. The worst case scenario had befallen the two detectives. They had both become personally involved with this case.

The beeping of Connery's phone broke the tense atmosphere of the car.

"What?!"

"Connery, this is Wells from the newspaper. Is Nick alright?"

"He's on his way to the hospital right now. He doesn't look good."

"I'm worried about him. I just got a phone call with a message for Nick. The voice on the other end was strained."

Connery perked up—paying strict attention to the editor as he continued.

"The message is that if Nick doesn't want to end up dead he'd better keep his nose out of Ligria's business." The editor paused, "Connery do you know what a Ligria is?"

"Am I supposed to?"

"A Ligria is a cross between a lion and a tiger. More commonly know as a liger. Usually an outcast from both species, they become crazy-fierce in the wild and will viciously attack anything, even their own and not just for food. Just for the fun of it. And, oh yeah, it just happens to be the name of the Russian mob boss involved in shipping with Coleman Oil that Nick was investigating." Wells sounded too scared for a man in his position.

"Nick's gotten himself in deep this time hasn't he?"

"On more than one continent. Doesn't get much deeper than this. Watch him, and watch yourself."

"I'll do that."

Connery thanked the man for his call and then relayed the information to Bell.

"Well, I guess you could say we yanked somebody's tail last night."

"I'm about ready to do more than yank when I find this bastard. We're about to become the great white hunters, Bell."

"Where do you want to start?"

"After we see Nick I want you to get back in touch with your contact at the CIA. I'm going to see if Interpol has anything on Ligria.

Connery and Bell joined Kate and Casey in the waiting room of the emergency ward. Connery's respect for Kate rose as he witnessed her calm, collected demeanor. The doctor was relating what they knew of Nick's injuries. Kate listened quietly, asking few questions, and then picked up the release papers for her brother. Bell went to sit with the ladies as Connery walked down the hallway with the doctor asking his own questions.

"How bad, Doc?"

The man looked him up and down and made his decision by answering Connery. "Four broken ribs, a punctured lung, broken clavicle, contusions of the chest and kidneys, broken nose, and that's just the beginning. I'm sorry Detective, but I have to get to surgery."

"The department is placing guards on Nick Coleman. There will be one stationed outside the operating room and several about the hospital. We'll try to stay out of your way."

The doctor nodded as he continued down the hall. Connery made his way back to the waiting room where Bell had filled Kate and Casey in on the details at the Coleman Estate.

"Kate has agreed to contact Donovan. Do you want to call?" Bell inquired of Connery.

"Sure, I've had dealings with the man before." Connery made

the call, getting through to the PRIME Security's main office. "Please inform Matt Donovan there is an emergency at the Coleman residence and I need him to return my call immediately." Connery gave his number to Donovan's secretary.

Flynn watched Kate wondering how to give comfort to someone, you were just beginning to know, in a situation like this. As he pondered how to help her, Kate's hand crept to his and her fingers intertwined with his. Flynn tightened the grip until his large hand comfortably enclosed hers. Its warmth and strength sending a clear message to her.

Kate was warmed by the silent message. He would stay. He would be by her side and be her strength. She smiled a small, sad smile in his direction before being interrupted by the ringing of Connery's phone.

"Connery here."

"This is Donovan. What's up?"

"Nick Coleman was attacked and beaten at the house this afternoon. We're at the hospital right now. Can you round up some private bodyguards for the family, or at least someone to be at the house?"

"Sure. Let me get back to you."

"Yeah, Bell and I have it covered until then. Thanks Donovan."

Connery looked at his companion. "He'll be all right Kate. Nick is tough and he's been in tougher situations before I'm sure. And we'll get this guy."

"I know you will, Flynn. It's just that I thought all these horrors were done with after the cars, and my parents."

Flynn gazed at her with a puzzled look.

With a deep breath Kate let go of the family secret. "We were beaten as children, Flynn. My father was extremely abusive and this isn't the first time I've sat in the emergency room praying for Nick. He always took the brunt of the physical abuse protecting me."

Flynn pulled her close—not caring who might see. Both Coleman children had turned their lives around and become productive, caring people. He was amazed that Kate would tell him this, but thankful she had enough trust in him to do so. He would be careful not to destroy that trust.

ITS CONFINES WERE TIGHT AND THE BEAST RUMBLED FURIOUSLY. IT WANTED OUT!

IT PACED IN ITS CAGE, SEARCHING FOR A WEAKNESS, NONE COULD BE FOUND.
MAYHEM WOULD EXPLODE WHEN IT GOT OUT!

IT WANTED TO FEED. IT WANTED TO FEEL THE TERROR OF ITS PREY WHEN CORNERED, FINDING THERE WAS NOWHERE TO RUN, AND THEN AN OPENING. THE BEAST WOULD ALLOW THE PREY TO RUN ONE MORE TIME, GIVING HOPE FOR ESCAPE, BEFORE TRAPPING IT.

MIGHTY JAWS WOULD CLOSE, RENDERING THE FLESH. IT COULD ALMOST FEEL THE SWEET BLOOD RUNNING INTO ITS MOUTH, COATING ITS TONGUE.

IT ROARED FURIOUSLY, THE SOUND ECHOING THROUGH THE HOST. THE BEAST FELT A MOMENT OF SATISFACTION AS IT FELT THE HOST SHUDDER IN RESPONSE.

LICKING ITS PAW THE BEAST RETURNED TO LAY IN WAIT. WATCHING AND WAITING FOR THE MOMENT WHEN THE HOST WOULD LET DOWN ITS GUARD.

THIRTEEN

Jason was fuming. He'd been home more than a week and Kate was still refusing to see him. She was seeing far too much of that detective! It seemed to Jason that the detective was at Kate's side every time he turned around. The sparkle in her eyes and her easy laugh when Connery was near did nothing to improve Jason's temperament. His mother was confident he deserved a better woman than Kate Coleman—but Jason wanted Kate! Something would have to be done, and soon.

He had made a point of appearing regularly at the room where Nick Coleman was recuperating from the tough surgeries he had undergone. Each time, the cop on duty had turned him away. Jason had smoothly declared his understanding until that private bodyguard had appeared—more of Connery's meddling! The new man had no need for the goodwill of the Mueller family and had pointedly informed Jason to stay away from the room, or prepare to deal with him. Silently the rage and frustration simmered inside. *Honestly—as if I'd hurt Nick! I only want Kate to know I am concerned, and now, that bastard Connery, convinced Kate to hire another bodyguard! This was almost like having a giant bad-tempered mongrel dog guarding my bone. (You never know when the animal will turn on you.)* Yes, something would have to be done!

The phone rang, breaking Jason's train of thought. "Jason Mueller."

"Jason, this is Mel Halloway. I've got a four-hour layover before heading back to Africa and I wondered if you would like to get together for dinner to help me kill some time."

There was nothing Jason wanted less than to spend the evening with someone who would remind him of Africa and the lions—but then he changed his mind. Mel would be the perfect foil to his mother's match-making dinner at the Country Club tonight!

"I certainly would, Mel. Say, there's a big shindig at my country club tonight and Mother is insisting that I make an appearance. What do you say to coming with me? The movers and shakers of the city can see two world-class doctors just back from Africa. We'll shake hands, make some contacts and have a fine meal—then we can escape to a more comfortable setting, if you wish."

There was a pause on the other end of the line. "I guess that would be fine."

Jason imagined the other man counting his pennies. "Mel, you're a life saver. You can help me fend off all the unmarried females tonight—in fact, I'll be so grateful that I'll pick up the tab." There was argument on the other end, but Jason insisted and finally Mel gave in. Jason gave Mel the directions to his condo and then proceeded to get ready for the evening.

Mel arrived right on time, picked up Jason, and had no problem following Jason's directions to the country club. The valet took the car as the two men made their way inside.

Abigail rushed to greet Jason and then turned to his guest.

"Mother, let me introduce Mel Halloway. Mel was in Africa with me and accompanied me on the return trip. He has a layover until his flight leaves, so I invited him to join us for dinner."

"Well, it's nice to meet you Mel. Thank you so much for accompanying Jason home. Now, I really must introduce you to our friends. Come along gentleman."

Mel followed obediently on Jason's heels as Abigail broke the ice. Soon Mel was chatting amicably with a couple of San Fran's well-to-do and explaining the mission in Africa. Jason, true to the social phenomena that he was in this circle, encouraged his colleague by adding comments every now and then. When the bell sounded for dinner Mel found himself guiding Mrs. Follmer to the table as they continued their discussion. Jason distanced himself until he found Sheila Wainright. He deftly crowded out her escort to accompany her to the table.

"Sheila, it's been such a long time."

"Hasn't it just, Jason—and I prefer to keep it that way."

"Why Sheila you can't tell me that Adam can keep you happy in bed."

"He's a close second—and the best part is I don't have to worry about finding him in bed with my best friend."

"Oh, come now dear—are you still fretting over that?"

"I hate to break the news to you Jason, but you don't consume that big a of part in my life. Now, can we find some other dinner conversation or am I going to have to cause a scene by changing partners?"

"I promise I'll be good—at least for now."

Sheila pointedly turned to converse with the person to her left. Jason didn't appreciate the snub.

Bitch, he snarled to himself. *She isn't that well stacked that I'd waste any more time on her! Why, her family had made their money in manufacturing. She really couldn't even be considered a true blue-blood!* Dinner finally ended and Jason politely made farewells for himself and Mel before summoning the valet to bring the car around.

"Are you sure you don't want to stick around Jason? They seem like such nice people."

"NO, I've had enough of that type for tonight. Let's go find some real people."

Mel gave him a puzzled look before sliding behind the wheel of the car. "Do you have some place in mind?"

"Let's head toward the airport. There's a jazz club near there."

Mel obediently merged the car into traffic on the freeway that led to the airport. As they drove, Mel glanced cautiously toward his companion. Jason had always seemed reserved in Africa, but now, well frankly, he was giving him the creeps. There seemed to be a sinister wave of rage pulsating from the man. Mel wondered if he dared ditch Jason once they reached this club. He couldn't get enough distance between them.

"Take this next exit," Jason directed.

Mel piloted the car swiftly down the ramp following Jason's navigating. Mel's uneasiness grew as the club turned out to be a high-class strip joint, and continued as Jason quickly exited the car. Mel opened his door and stepped out of the car—but left the engine running. "Jason, I don't think this is such a good idea." The face that turned back to him caused Mel to shrink inside himself—predatory and malicious, the eyes glinting with fury.

"Afraid to have some fun, Mel? Might be your last chance."

"Uh, no thanks Jason, I really can't afford to be late for my flight."

The laugh that answered him chilled his bones. "Well, then, by all means run along Mel."

Mel quickly entered the car and made his way back toward the freeway. A tinge of guilt stabbed at him as he thought of leaving Jason there with no way home, but his sense of survival pushed it aside. After all the man was perfectly capable of calling a cab.

Jason entered the Top Hat and was pleased to see there was a fairly small crowd. Good. He could watch at his leisure and then decide whom to take home. The shiny poles and sinuous ladies jump-started his blood. He watched carefully—unaware that he, also, was the object of a fixed stare. Zoia, one of the barmaids, was tingling with the opportunity that had just walked in the door. Imagine Jason Mueller, of THE Muellers, in *her* club! What a catch he would be for a girl! And, with that thought she set herself to the task of tempting the man with her charms.

"What's your pleasure, sir?" Her soft purr tickled Jason's ears, but he was too busy surveying the ladies gliding along the poles to take much stock in the lady at his elbow.

"Bourbon spritz."

Zoia took his order to the bar, watching as the bartender filled the glass. Her skimpy uniform didn't leave much to the imagination. As she sauntered back to his table she made her way to the front side, blocking his gaze of the runway. Leaning over seductively, she slid his drink within reach of his fingertips. "That will be six bucks, please."

Jason let his gaze settle on the dark-haired female in front of him. His eyes slid over her figure before looking at her face. Glorious dark hair tumbled over her shoulders and fell down her back, while dark glowing eyes hinted at wishes that might be granted. Perhaps this one would do, he thought as he slid a twenty toward the lady in front of him. "Keep my glass filled and there might be a reward in it for you."

"I hope it's a BIG one," she purred as she departed for the bar with her fanny swaying enticing him as she went.

Watching the seductive sway of the female gliding down the golden pole, Jason missed the predatory gaze that was sizing him up.

Zoia noted each intake of breath filing the catalyst away to be used later. If she could just get one chance with this fish she'd haul him in hook, line, and sinker. The night passed, as the onlookers began to thin and the girls wound down preparing to close shop and go home. Zoia watched as Jason slowly swirled the ice in his glass. Making her way to his side she softly asked, "One for the road?"

Jason turned his attention to the attentive barmaid. No longer focused on the stage he took a long look at the lady at his side. Small, on the petite side, she had an interesting face with high cheek bones and dark, sexy eyes—not too brazen, but they hinted at pleasures to come. The dark mane of hair that had originally caught his attention was indeed sexy. His eyes moved up and down her body—finally resting on her mouth, *not bad.*

"Could you call me a taxi, Miss?"

"Zoia. Do you live far?"

"I've got a condo near the hospital."

"It will probably take a while for a cab to get here, sir."

"Jason. Jason Mueller."

Zoia couldn't believe her luck! The Mueller name was well known in the circle of gossipy girls at the club. The society page was always the topic of conversation with hopes that one day one of them might get the chance to snatch a real man with money. IF she just played her cards right … .

"I've heard of you! You're the doctor who went overseas to help those poor people without medical help!" She saw his eyes darken immediately—could she salvage her blunder? "That was so noble of you! To help those poor people and leave everything you know—why I'd never be able to do that!"

Her practiced wide-eyed innocent gaze caught Jason off guard. Finally, someone who appreciated everything he had sacrificed and given up! "Thank you—it was somewhat of a hardship."

"Oh, you're just being modest! Well, I'd better call you that cab."

"Zoia, I don't suppose you would want to go get some coffee, or breakfast, with me? I realize we haven't met under the best of circumstances but I would love to have your company for a while."

She could have leapt with joy! She was going to get her chance. "Well, if we take a cab and go someplace where there are some people—I'd like to get to know you."

Jason smiled—a careful girl, but now he had her! "That would be just fine. A lady can't be too careful these days. Why don't you pick a place where you would be comfortable—if you make the arrangements, I'll pay the bill."

Be careful, Zoia, she thought to herself, *don't make him think you're after his money.*

"Tell you what Jason, I'll let you pay for the cab, but I'll buy my own coffee. After all, we're just getting to know each other."

Jason was impressed—perhaps she wouldn't be such an easy lay after all. He enjoyed a challenge. "That works for me."

During the cab ride Jason prodded her with questions. He was surprised to learn that she spoke three languages fluently and had worked as an interpreter. "So how did you come to work at the gentlemens' club?"

"This may sound silly to you, but I got tired of men masking their attempts to get me in bed. I decided if I had to put up with all that nonsense I might as well work at a club where at least everyone was up front about their intentions. And it might surprise you to know that I make better money at the club than I did working as an interpreter on the docks."

Jason sat back in the seat. This one had just thrown him a curveball. She wasn't the slut he thought—but from the look in her eyes he'd bet she had picked up enough tricks to keep him entertained. This was a relationship he was going to take some care with. It wouldn't pay to lose her too early in the game.

The diner Zoia had chosen was brightly lit with scattered customers. Not too crowded, but the kind of place where people noticed you when you came in. Smart girl. During breakfast Jason was further impressed that she could manage an intelligent conversation. She was up on current events both in the city and the world. Her movements were graceful and her manners weren't bad. There was nothing he hated more than a woman who ate like a pig.

The sun was beginning to rise as they finished. The waitress returned with the check, which Zoia asked her to separate between them—a girl of her word.

"Well, Jason, it's been really nice talking with you, but I've got to get home."

"Will you be all right?"

Her light laughter caught his attention making him wish for more. "Sure, I just live down the street." Her eyes laughed at him kindly.

Jason could appreciate her choice of diners even more. "Zoia, could I call you?"

She smiled before dragging on her coat. "You know where to find me, Jason."

He frowned, and she realized her mistake.

"Jason, if you truly want to see me again, drop by the club. I don't need any more promises of phone calls that never come."

Dark eyes softened and Jason was caught. He watched her until she turned the corner and was out of sight before calling a cab to drive him home. He'd be back at the club tonight!

FOURTEEN

Zoia sighed. She had obviously blown it. The hands on the brilliant neon clock over the bar read 10:01—Jason wasn't coming. When was she going to learn that there was only one thing a man wanted and if he didn't get it, he was gone? But then, if he got it he was gone too—so what was the difference? She wouldn't have felt any better if he laid her and then ditched her, so why was she feeling so down? Was it because he had actually seemed to like her? She cursed herself for getting her hopes up. She hadn't even lied to him! Translating down at the docks had been her job several years back, and yes, she was fluent in Russian, Greek, and Spanish—thanks to her parents. *Oh well, back to slinging drinks!*

As she delivered drinks a hand grabbed her ass and was abruptly removed. She turned to see Jason forcing the grabber to his knees.

"Just because she serves drinks doesn't give you liberties. Understand?" he growled.

The poor man on the floor nodded quickly and Jason released his hold. Zoia smiled brightly at him and Jason took a seat.

"You're going to cost me my tips," she smiled lightly.

Jason read her pleasant surprise at his actions and smiled back. "I'll make it up to you."

As the night unfolded Jason watched Zoia with predatory patience. He could appreciate her deft handling of both the drinks and the customers. As the hands on the clock made their rounds he found himself watching her more than the other women on stage. She had style and grace. She moved quickly and lightly through the jungle of tables and customers. She was observant of her customers wishes without being intrusive, taking care not to block their view of the stage. Long legs complemented graceful arms, starting a hunger in his groin. She wasn't as classy as Kate—considering where she worked, but she was gorgeous and would do until he would get Kate back.

The club finally closed its doors to the outside world and Jason waited as Zoia changed into street clothes and then he escorted her to his Bentley.

"Wow!" The appreciative stroke she bestowed on the car caused him to grin—this one had possibilities. The ride back to the condo was quiet. She was tired and it was obvious.

"I shouldn't have come, Jason."

"What's wrong?"

"I'm not sure I should do this—I really don't know you very well, and … well, I'm beat."

"I'll take care of you, Zoia." His tone was authoritative and she knew if she refused him now she would lose him for sure. Well, she knew how to play this game!

"Are you sure, Jason? You really don't need a girl like me in your life."

"What are you saying?"

"Well, I'm not exactly the type you usually associate with. What if someone sees us? Won't you be embarrassed to be seen with a barmaid from a gentlemen's club?" Her eyes filled with emotion.

Jason was taken in by her seemingly caring concern. The somewhat tarnished and gold-digging barmaid from the seedier side of town was snagging the playboy from the high-society set.

"I'm not embarrassed to be seen with you Zoia. Let me worry about how my acquaintances behave." His tone was stony and she realized that his possessiveness could work in her favor. *Am I finally going to achieve my deepest dreams? Money, wealth, and position can be mine if I play the game carefully.*

With those thoughts running through her head she settled back to enjoy the ride, gazing out at the skyline of San Francisco. There was a twinge of dawn in the east as the Bentley pulled up to an exclusive complex of snazzy condos. Even at this hour there was an attendant to park the car for Jason, leaving him free to guide Zoia toward the entrance. For the first time Zoia noticed a slight waver in his step. He hadn't consumed very much alcohol—was something else wrong? But as he guided her to the entrance the thought vanished as she caught sight of the lobby. Her awe and appreciation did not go unnoticed by her companion.

Finally, he had found a woman who could appreciate everything he might give her. Sultry looks combined with devoted attention might be just what was needed to draw Kate's attention back to him. He could have some fun exposing Zoia to the other side of life, while cultivating the response he wanted in Kate. That cop would be out of her life when Kate saw another woman was willing to take her place in his affections. Yes, everything would work out just fine.

The door to his condo swung open with a silent click as he disarmed the security system before ushering her inside the foyer. The immaculate residence was flashy in its simplicity. Windows set high in the vaulted ceiling let in the showering beams of morning light. The rich pale carpet intensified the look of the contrasting masculine deep-cherry furniture and burgundy accents of the room. This was obviously a man's room, and a man who preferred to dominate those around him.

He took Zoia's coat and hung it carefully in the foyer. She slipped off her shoes before entering the living room. He noted her manners again with appreciation—most women wouldn't have thought to be so careful. In his experience the women in his life didn't care if they tracked street dirt into his domicile, or if it might revolt him.

Zoia turned back to face him. "Jason this is beautiful!" Her luxurious hair swirled about her hips as she turned back to survey the room, causing his libido to kick into a higher gear.

What he would do with that mane of dark silk! He could almost feel it sliding against his bare stomach—the ends trailing lower and lower. Forcibly, he controlled his breathing. Best not to proceed too quickly—he wanted her in his bed, willing and hot.

"Let me show you around." Jason cupped her elbow steering her through the living room and on to the kitchen. Dark granite countertops contrasted nicely with the pale slate floor. Everything was state of the art.

"Do you cook?" she asked, hoping she wouldn't offend her companion.

"Some. But not enough to make use of all this. Do you?"

"I like to cook. Maybe I could cook for you sometime. Do you like Greek food?"

"I've never really tried Greek."

"Let me be your first, I mean, I have some really great dishes I love to cook—my father was Greek."

"Well maybe you'll have to indoctrinate me sometime," he mumbled softly as he moved behind her wrapping his arms about her waist and burying his head in the rich fall of her hair. "I love your hair." The words rumbled against the nape of her neck as he rolled his face into the thick locks. He felt her relax, leaning back against his chest. Jason indulged for a few seconds before pulling back and turning her to face him.

"Come with me."

Silently, Zoia followed him back through the living room to a set of double doors, which Jason threw open with a flourish. Inside was the most awesome bathroom she had ever seen. Her breath caught in her throat at the one-of-a-kind stained glass windows surrounding the Jacuzzi that was set squarely in the center of the five-cornered room. Skylights twinkled as the first fingers of dawn's light were captured in the beveled edges of the room's glass. Fresco tiles meandered about the walls drawing the eye to the large mural decorating the one wall without a window. The scene on the wall was sexual. Lovers entwined in the most exotic positions. She recognized it from the Karma Sutra. If he was familiar with the Karma Sutra then she knew she'd have to be ready to give herself up to just about anything. Her gasp brought Jason closer, pressing his body tight against her from behind, his hands roaming all over her.

"I want to do that with you Zoia. Your hair will fall about us and we will feel its sensual slide as I take you over and over again." His arms tightened dangerously around her. "You'll never forget the feel of me inside of you. You've never had anyone like me. Let me pleasure you Zoia."

To another woman his statement and the way he said it may have brought fear, but the artwork of the couples and promises that lie ahead created a heat deep inside her that was beginning to spread and she felt like she was ripening. Her breath became shallow, a signal for him that she was getting excited.

Jason took note as he pulled her deeper into his body so there was no mistake about the large bulge stroking inside the crease of her buttocks. They took on a slow rhythm as the mood intensified.

"I've never done anything on that wall."

Animal possessiveness flooded Jason's veins. "A woman never forgets her first time." The ferocity in his voice made her blood and most tender of parts pulsate.

She was maneuvered to a sable rug. Deft hands slipped open the buttons on her shirt, leaving the front to gape open. The blouse was torn off in an animal-like manner. He pinched her nipples causing them to stand at attention. He slid down to her feet and kissed each toe, then sucked one into his mouth, she almost screamed.

He peeled off her jeans to find her naked underneath. "You *are* a naughty girl," he whispered. Zoia heard buttons and his zipper as he quickly disrobed. His gentle teasing turned into an all consuming furious quest as he explored her with both his mouth and hands. He pressed himself against her and she felt him searching against her buttocks. Excitement ran through her nerve endings. She was so wet she couldn't wait much longer and began to pant. Jason quickly peeled a condom from its foil wrapper and lubed himself up with KY Jelly that he had at the ready. He turned her around again and rubbed himself up against her. Using his fingers to test her readiness he drove her insane with desire and the friction caused her to cream even more. She was too hot to care. The sweat that beaded along her spine helped his body slide along hers and he buried his face in her hair as they picked up a rhythm again. Quickly, before she had time to protest he parted her smooth buttocks and edged himself into her. Mixed signals flashed through Zoia's muscles. Discomfort, followed by a fullness she never felt before made her gasp. His progress was relentless, but strangely welcome. When he was finally fully within her he stopped—allowing her some time to breath. As she relaxed he began to pull out and push back in slowly, then more aggressively. Her nerve endings began to pulse as she became accustomed to this unorthodox entry. The strangeness was forgotten as her excitement built. A soft hand circled to the front, stimulating her far too sensitive areas but she was already there. As her excitement built his strokes became more forceful. Her body was demanding a finish to this torment. She pushed against him and he took this as a signal to increase the pace. They were both panting heavily. With a final plunge so deep inside her he sent her over the edge as he met her in one great explosion. Their pulses joined together and he bit her neck possessively before withdrawing. Her knees collapsed, tumbling them both into a mound on the rug. She heard him cleaning himself, but she was too exhausted to follow suit. She could not believe that she would have enjoyed anything like that.

Jason snuck up behind her "Mmmm, again?" His hot breath on her neck gave her goosebumps and she giggled. Effortlessly she was lifted in his arms and taken gently to the Jacuzzi. Carefully she was set in the tub, then Jason joined her. The heat was intoxicating. Her eyelids drooped. Leaning carefully into her partner Zoia barely whispered, "My bones are going to drift away—and then I'll drown in pure and simple bliss."

"Then I'd better get you into my bed." He toweled her dry with amazing soft and fluffy white Egyptian cotton towels and guided her into the massive bedroom and into his bed. Right now he could do anything to her, she was beyond caring and still riding the waves of sexual bliss. Watching her drift off to sleep he almost thought the peace of the moment would find him. But just as he lay down beside her the looming vision of a roaring lion floated in his mind. Startled, he bolted upright. Would he never have any peace from the awful memories of Africa? Would the dementia and horrifying visions of this disease follow him forever? Even the peace of sexual fulfillment could not ward off the wakefulness that still followed into the morning hours.

Sleep forgotten, he made his way to the kitchen. Coffee was set to brew as he sifted through the mail and medical journals lying on the table. A vision of Kate flitted through his mind and he wondered how she would look lying naked in his bed. He knew she could erase the horrors of Africa from his mind and he became more certain than ever that he would do anything to win her back.

FIFTEEN

Nick punched the remote for the hundredth time searching for something—anything that might keep his interest. He had never made a good patient. The man standing guard at his door drew his interest. Some "heavy" hired by his sister to watch his back. Nick couldn't have been any less pleased when Kate had informed him of her decision to hire a bodyguard. But, he had to admit that watching the man head off Jason's inquiries had given him a rare pleasure. He was glad she had dumped the man, truth be told—he had a grudging admiration for her attraction to the detective, Flynn Connery. The man seemed decent enough, honest and straightforward. For the first time in his memory Nick had seen Kate loose her reserve with a man. Connery had given her back her laughter and smile. Something Nick had only seen fleetingly through their adult lives. Trust didn't come easily after their childhood. Connery had gained Kate's trust. Unlike their father. Nick shook his head dispelling the thoughts that threatened to emerge. *Bad idea*, he thought as his head began to throb anew.

What was the guard's name? Darrin? Dick? No—that wasn't right. Dirk? Yes that was it! "Dirk! Get in here!"

"Something wrong, sir?" The big guy filled his doorway!

"Yeah. To start with call me Nick. Second—I'm bored out of my brain. Think you can solve that problem?"

Dirk eyed the sorry-looking case in the hospital bed. *Man, after a week he still looked like pulverized meat.* The file on Nick Coleman read like an adventure story: world-class reporter, controversial news-breaking stories, underground informants. No wonder the man was bored. His orders were to keep the man safe. Dirk knew from experience that bored men were stupid men—taking chances they shouldn't.

"Well, doesn't look like you're even ready for the Book of the Month Club just yet."

Nick frowned before breaking out in a pained laugh. "Oh God! I needed that! How about some conversation then?"

Before replying Dirk cast about the room before picking a chair and relocating it in line with the entrance to the door. Then he took a seat out of sight. "So what's your pleasure?"

"I find I am utterly bored with myself so let's talk about you."

The guard frowned before starting. "Well, there are some things I can't tell you 'cause then I'd have to kill you."

"Been there and done that—just recently. So let's skip that part. What made you want to be a big, bad bodyguard for little ol' me?"

"The company got a call and I was available."

"So," Nick went on, "what makes you so big and bad? Besides your size—that is." At six foot eight inches the man towered over almost everyone he encountered.

"I was in the special forces. Did very bad deeds for very bad people," Dirk made a ferrous face reminding Nick of the times Kate had tried to make the characters in a story come alive with different voices and faces.

"Yeah, yeah—move on. Heard that one before and I've played with the big, bad guys. They don't make me tremble in my boots."

Dirk smiled. He liked this guy. "After the service there didn't seem to be too many opportunities for men with—shall we say, my skills? Cop, mercenary, or bodyguard were my choices. I'm too righteous for a mercenary and I like my hot car too much to be a cop so … here I am."

"Pays good, huh?"

"Let's just say it's right nigh impossible to bribe one of our crew. Too many perks. Makes us good at our job and trustworthy to boot."

"Nice to know you're not going to stab me in the back."

The conversation continued until a knock at the door had Dirk evaporating into a lethal shadow.

"Dirk? It's Connery."

The big man didn't relax until the detective stepped through the door. "Everybody okay?"

"Yeah, we're fine Connery," Nick replied. "Dirk was just relieving my boredom before I was forced to do something stupid."

Connery gave the big man a nod of appreciation.

"I'll wait outside."

"Stick around Dirk. No need for me to tell the story twice."

Nick was all attention. "You found something?!"

"You could say that. Forensics found some hair and DNA that isn't yours. Looks like you might have landed a lucky blow there Nick."

Nick rolled his blood red eyes, the broken blood vessels were slow to heal and it made him look so much worse.

"The lab is running it through CODIS right now. Your editor has also had some interesting phone calls about how you should manage your health. He's agreed to let us bug his phone at the newspaper since it's the only line the calls come in on. Have you remembered anything new about who jumped you?"

"Not really Connery. They were there when I got to the house. I was grabbed from behind—I think there were three or four of them. Russian, I'd think."

"What gives you that idea?"

Nick carefully shook his head. "Couldn't tell you why—I just have this gut feeling."

"Nick were you gathering information on Ligria?" Connery watched as Nick's face went cold.

"What makes you ask that?"

"News on the streets is there's a man in town who is on the rampage over something—or someone. Give you three guesses who and what that is, and the first two don't count. Come on Nick, spill it. We need to know what we are up against to keep you and Kate safe."

"Why? What happened to Kate?"

"Her admirer made another visit and I'm not so sure it's not your new friends."

"Tell me what happened!"

"The morning you got jumped there was a voice message left for Kate at the hospital. Someone used a computer program to leave the message so the lab couldn't filter out the distortion to get to his voice."

"What did it say?"

"The beast is watching." Connery watched as Nick went pale then he continued, "The message left for you from Wells was for you to stay away from Ligria. Nick!" Connery's sharp tone focused Nick's attention back on the detective. "What do you know?"

Nick visibly gathered himself before replying. "While I was in Paris this summer there were a couple of killings. Really bloody—and each one was left with the message, 'The beast is watching'. The Paris officials reported they had a serial killer on the loose, the killings were savage, like some type of beastly animal ripped its prey apart. But just as suddenly as it started the killings stopped."

Connery shook his head. *Could this really be the same killer? Some sicko traveling the globe killing as he went? What's the motive? Why would this be related?*

"I'm going to need everything you've got on Ligria, and don't give me that reporter bullshit. You are going to be honest with everything you know before you or your sister end up dead. Do you understand me?"

Just then a nurse came in with a wheelchair for Nick, "Sorry Detective, this will have to wait until tomorrow, Mr. Coleman has to come with me."

Nick nodded. "Tomorrow then. Everything's in my head so come with plenty of time, a sharp #2 and paper."

"I'll be back with Bell. Dirk, call your office and ask your boss for another 'big and bad'."

Nick watched as Connery left the room with deadly intent in his eyes.

Dirk could be heard to say, "Geez, I'd hate to be the guy that pissed him off."

Nick silently agreed.

Bell waited anxiously at the Old Times Bookstore for their new translator. Word had come from the port authorities that the translator who had helped them on the bust resigned after being threatened by an unknown assailant. Nick still wanted to help but there was no way he was able to go anywhere. Bell had come in this morning with the name of a woman from the area who had resigned a few years earlier. Bell had her name and number and had gone in search of her, hoping to persuade her to help him out. When Connery returned from the hospital Bell informed him that they had an appointment to meet the new translator at the bookstore. Her fee had been high—which meant she was good.

Connery pulled up to the curb and made his way inside. The cozy atmosphere enticed one to grab a book, sit in a comfy chair, and read away while sipping a fragrant beverage. As arranged, Bell grabbed *Angels and Demons* then he sat to wait in a large armchair with the book where she would see it. Connery garnered a cup of java, a magazine, and perched on a stool at the counter. Then they waited.

Around the corner of a tall bookshelf sauntered a striking young woman, Bell's eyes narrowed as she approached, her eyes on his book.

"Have you read the sequel?" she queried.

"I'm waiting for the movie," he replied. "Would you care to join me in a cup of coffee?"

She nodded in agreement, sitting on the edge of the neighboring chair while Bell commandeered the beverages.

Bell studied the woman as they sipped the hot brew, rehashing the information that had accompanied her photo from the District Attorney. She had been "cleared" when they saw her employment had been at the Bay docks. Because of her fluency in Greek, Russian, and Spanish the department had often required her services from the company supplying translators at the docks. The report had commended her language skills and her work ethic. Then the employment had ended abruptly about three years earlier with no apparent reason. Bell was suspicious. Why would anyone leave a translating position to wait tables at a gentlemen's club? Could she be trusted?

She was the first to end the silence. "What do you want?"

"I thought that the DA made that clear. My partner and I need a translator who hasn't been 'made'. You were recommended."

She snorted in contempt. "Try again Detective. I burnt all bridges when I left the docks. There is no way the DA would recommend me for anything. What's the story?"

Bell considered before answering. He and Connery needed her cooperation. Finally he answered, "They did recommend you.

Some high profile people are being threatened by someone who may be an international killer. We just found a cargo hold full of Russian kids who were being sold into an underground slavery ring in the city. You can imagine who would buy foreign children who don't speak the language from the black market can't you? Interested or not?"

Zoia leaned forward into the conversation. This explained the call and the sum offered for her cooperation. Some scumbag was rattling the international cage. This might be interesting—as long as she was kept out of the picture. "I want complete anonymity, and tell your contacts that the price has just doubled! If I'm going to stick my neck into this—it has to be worth my while!"

"We can do that." Bell's tone was harsh. "When can you start?"

Zoia glanced at Connery. "Your partner?"

"Yeah."

"Tomorrow. Give me the address and tell the watchdogs I'll be there at nine. You two come about an hour later."

"It doesn't work that way."

"It does if you want me to do this. I don't want anyone thinking we're working together—and the kids aren't going to talk with you two around. Where they come from you're the bad guys. I'll break the ice and see if I can get someone to loosen up. If you come with a list of questions—I'll get you answers. Deal?"

Bell glanced at Connery, who just shrugged. It was Bell's call and his contact. Right now Connery was just back up.

"Alright." Bell gave her the information and as abruptly as she appeared—the woman was gone.

Connery walked over and lowered himself into the still-warm seat of the over-sized chair. "Well?"

"Well, we've got our translator. We're to meet her at the house at ten tomorrow morning—she'll go in at nine to see if she can get anyone to talk."

"So, what's the problem?"

"Something feels … off."

"Then we better keep our guard up, partner. Now are you going to pay for that book—or put it back on the shelf?"

Zoia took the bus home, getting off a stop earlier than normal before walking the rest of the way to her apartment. Life was funny. Just when you thought things couldn't get any more interesting ...

Her thoughts strayed to the time she had worked at the docks. She made a lot of enemies in the DEA with her accusations and complaints against those in power. Who would have ever thought they would crawl back to her for help? Well, nothing said a girl couldn't get a little payback. They would get her help and she would do a damn good job. But, they were going to pay! And—if she found something really interesting they were going to owe her big time. Yes indeed, life could be grand!

The off feeling Bell had at the bookstore had now encompassed Connery as well. The two were still feeling on edge. Information from Interpol had cast some light on the enigma of Ligria and Trovoishek. The more Connery found out—the more they realized how dangerous the game had become. They were not dealing with just any criminal. Interpol reported they had evidence showing Trovoishek was directly involved with as many as a dozen murders in Europe and Russia. He was slick, smart, and deadly. No one crossed him and lived. Ligria, however, took pride in hiring the gun and not firing the gun.

Promptly at eight the next morning, Connery and Bell appeared in Nick's hospital room.

"Show time!" Nick smiled ruefully.

"Cut the crap, Nick," Connery growled.

"Well, aren't we in a fine mood this morning! Did you lose a crook, or do you need a 'Kate fix'?"

Bell coughed to cover his laugh. It was becoming obvious that Connery had a thing for Miss Coleman. His surly attitude wasn't helped by the fact that she had been working as late as they were. Kate and Casey had been given strict instructions to stay at the hospital until Connery or Bell arrived to pick them up. Connery wasn't taking any chances with their welfare. Their ride home would be in the company of men trained to detect danger. They made sure there would be no surprises waiting for them in the darkened house when the ladies came home.

With little prompting, Nick began to expand on the documentary of his travels and the information he had obtained.

As the story unfolded Connery sensed a growing dread and began facing the fact that many of Nick's contacts with his sources coincided with the brutal murders in Paris. It seemed Nick had been linked to his informants. Connery became even more convinced that he finally had at least the identification of his perpetrator. To know they were dealing with one man was somewhat of a relief—even if he was the most dangerous of men. Nick had to know what was happening. Kate and Casey were in grave danger, Trovoishek was known for the destruction of his enemies and their entire families. *Could Coleman Oil be an enemy or Nick Coleman?*

Connery's cell phone started to beep. The caller ID confirmed the call was coming from the station so he quickly stepped to one side of the room to take the call.

Bell watched as his partner's face turned to stone—all emotion drained from his partner's expression.

"Nick, I'm sorry, but we've got to go. Your editor was just found dead in the parking garage of the newspaper."

Nick was at a total loss for words but the detectives were already gone. In a minute, colorful language followed them down the hall once Nick found his voice.

When they arrived at the garage the patrolmen had already taped off the area and the forensics team was collecting evidence. Connery and Bell waited impatiently for them to finish as they talked to the security guard who had discovered the gruesome scene. The editor's hands and tongue were cut off—a clear warning to anyone else that talking, or printing information, about Ligria was a peril worth one's life. Trovoishek was efficient (if it was indeed Trovoishek). The newspaper had called security to track down the editor only ten minutes after he had left the building. When he didn't answer his cell phone security had immediately searched the building and found Mr. Wells in the garage, but the killer had already disappeared. Trovoishek was loose in their city—who would be next?!

As the forensics team finished with the body and made it ready for transport to the morgue Connery asked, "Find anything?"

"Actually, we did—some kind of hair. We'll call you when we know more."

Connery was hopeful—but also doubtful. This killer didn't

leave any DNA or prints. He had wanted them to find this—there was something they were supposed to know!

With nothing more to be accomplished at the scene they made their way up to the editor's office. The secretary quickly let them in and then reverently backed out of the room. Bell sat down at the computer while Connery began to go through the paperwork on the desk. The hum of the computer told Connery that Bell had accessed the hard drive and was scanning through the files.

"Let me know when you've pulled up the e-mail. Remember he said he'd had threats? Maybe there is something there."

Bell grunted his compliance. Then, "Shit!"

Connery turned to see what appeared to be the face of a man, morphed with a lion's. The macabre animal was laughing as it teased two men with badges for faces. They were being played, and exactly where the killer wanted them, two steps behind!

SIXTEEN

Bell called the lab for the computer expert to be sent over to the editor's office. There had to be a way to trace the computer images being sent to the intended victims and their families. Before the age of computers things had sure been much easier. Typewriters and letters were a snap to trace compared to cyber space.

The buzzing of Bell's cell phone caused both men to focus with interest on the object. The ID flashed the number of the forensic lab. Bell snapped open the phone with a flash, "Yeah. Got it. Right away," left Connery chomping at the bit.

"So?"

"Lab got the results on that hair found at the Coleman residence after Nick's attack. Problem is every time they try for an ID they get red flagged. We need to get over there."

They quickly sealed off the editor's office and made their way to Bell's Camaro. The shiny-blue machine purred as they made their way back to the station.

The lab tech was waiting when they arrived. "Your DNA came back from the Coleman break-in. I ran it through CODIS and we've got results! The hair sample belongs to a Pieter Trovoishek—a known Russian Mafia muscle. He's wanted in Europe as well as the U.S. for extortion and criminal assault. Last known residence was Paris. The other sample is red flagged by Interpol. I don't have the clearance to get any more information—think you guys would have any luck?"

Connery glanced at his partner and Bell shrugged before replying, "I can try. But I think that my source is about to dry up."

"I'll put out an APB on Ligria. Maybe we'll get lucky and he is still here in the states. Meanwhile, let's go talk to the Captain. Maybe he can get us some info before we have to go to your source one more time."

"Connery, why don't we try the DEA? We already have them involved with the children. They might be able to rattle the cage as well as anyone."

"Sounds like a plan. Let's see how much DEA really wants this guy." The call was put in, but their contact unavailable. The detectives decided to begin a run down on Trovoishek.

Cruising the lower side of the city Connery kept his eyes peeled for one of the snitches he and Bell regularly used. Bell pulled curbside when he spotted Lola, their snitch's girlfriend. Connery called the streetwalker over to the car. Trying to look like they were in search of cheap female company they quickly told her to have Richie call them, then acted like she charged too much. Connery slipped a twenty into her palm before they left. "There's more where that came from for Richie when he calls."

They continued cruising and watching the streets. Bell pulled into an alley where several males were congregating. He shut down the engine and exited the car with Connery following and wondering what his partner was up to.

"Yo—Slider."

"Hey, Carbman—what's with the stiff?"

Connery frowned at the interchange—what made him look like a cop?

"Need some 411. Zeke around?"

"I seen him a couple a days ago. He was looking for a hit, probably spaced by now."

"If he comes by let him know I'm waiting for him to call?"

"Sure enough. Hey dog, I'm looking at some new wheels. Do a brotha' a solid and once over 'em for me?"

"Might be tough for the next few weeks—but leave a message and I'll get back." Bell turned and headed back for the car with Connery following, amused.

"What was all that about?"

Inside the car Bell glanced at his partner while shifting into reverse and barreling out of the alley. "Boys like toys. They like to race—and I like to tinker. Sometimes we help each other out. None of them has ever been involved in anything serious—I'm sorta like a big brother to 'em. No harm done."

"Let's head over to the hospital and see what else Nick has on Trovoishek and Ligria."

As Bell turned the Camaro back east toward the hospital he recognized Richie, lounging against the alley wall of his favorite bar, The Keeper. In a classic Dukes of Hazard move Bell cranked the wheel sending the car spinning into a 180 and sliding to a stop right in front of the snitch. Before Richie could think to run Connery jumped out and cornered him against the building.

"So—what you been up to lately, Richie?"

"N-nothing Connery. Keeping my uh, my nose clean." The snitch wiped the back of his hand subconsciously across his nose. "You got no reason to bust me."

Connery grinned, "Well now, Richie, old friend, just trying to get reacquainted—it's been a long time." He was obviously strung out.

"Not long enough, Connery. You gonna haul my ass in?"

"Naa ... nothing that dramatic, Richie. We're just looking for some info and, of course, we thought of you since you always seem to have the low-down on the neighborhood."

Richie caught the scent of a payoff and warmed visibly.

"No need to manhandle the messenger, Detective, you know I always got time for you."

Connery released the man since it was obvious he wasn't going to run. "We're looking to find out if any high-paid Russians have entered our fair city over the last couple of weeks. Two, maybe more. They're the dangerous kind, so keep your head low on this one. One might be going by the name of Ligria. And Richie, see if you can find out if anyone has a grudge against Nick Coleman, the reporter."

"Okay Connery," Richie weaseled, "but this one'll cost you. Still contact you at the same place?"

"Leave a message. We'll meet you at the Dockside Diner if you come up with anything." Connery stepped back allowing Richie an exit path down the side street.

"Man, I always want to wash after we've talked with that slime ball," Bell sneered.

"Know the feeling. Worst part of it is that dear old Richie would stab you in the back if it would get him a nickel more. I always meet him in populated places."

With the message on its way along the grapevine the two detectives once more sped toward the hospital and Nick Coleman. Connery glanced at his watch and noticed time was getting away from them. "Let's pop up to Kate's office and let the girls know to meet us in Nick's room. We're never going to be on time for their pickup otherwise." They entered the elevator and punched the number for the girls' floor. Exiting with a decidedly lighter step, Connery wove through the space dividers until he reached Kate's work area. Bright eyes met his and a jolt of electricity jumped between them.

"Detective," Kate eyed him slowly, up and down.

"Miss Coleman. Bell and I are just headed up to see Nick. Would you and Casey mind meeting us there?"

"Not a problem Detective. Shall we say in about an hour?"

"Take your time." Connery gave her a wink as he turned to leave.

Dirk was manning the entrance—watchful and ready. He moved silently aside as the two reached the door. As they entered, the sight of Nick Coleman stilled them. For the first time in their acquaintance they saw the man quiet and sober. Worry riddled his brow.

"Nick?" Connery disturbed the silence.

"It's my fault—my fault that Wells is dead! He was protecting my story and it got him killed." Nick was in obvious shock.

"You can't blame yourself, Nick, don't let his death be in vain. Help us catch this monster."

Nick sighed wearily. "What do you want to know?"

"Everything."

Settling himself more comfortably, Nick drew a breath before beginning. "About a year ago, when I was researching the Senate scandal, I ran across information on a child slavery ring headquartered here in San Francisco. At the time I didn't know what to do so I did nothing. Yes its been eating at my conscious, but I was afraid to get involved. Then I stumbled across another lead, so I decided to do a little digging. Before I knew it I'd dug a pretty big hole. The slavery was controlled by the Russian Mafia, who were using U.S. shipping lines to smuggle children. My Dad's ships, Coleman Oil's. While I was in France covering another story one of my informants confirmed that they were also operating there—specifically, Paris. The more I tried to stay away from it, the closer I got to being involved. I began to seriously pursue the story. One name kept cropping up."

"Your Father's?"

"No, Trovoishek. A couple of names were associated with it, I could never pin down just who was in charge, but I did believe him to be dangerous, of course, running a slavery ring in this day and age."

"Ever heard of Ligria?"

"Yes, he was a Russian linked to several strong-arm tactics in Paris. But everyone knew Trovoishek worked for him. They could never get enough info on either one to commit. They bought off or killed anyone who would talk. Interpol was very touchy about my digging."

"We think these guys put you here."

"I hate to say this but it wouldn't surprise me Connery." Nick rubbed a finger along the line of stitches on his forehead while he continued his story. "I never meant for anyone to get hurt, and I didn't think my following a story would be a threat to Kate. Can you guys stop this before anyone else gets hurt?" Nick asked desperately.

By the time Kate and Casey arrived they had it all figured out. Nick had the answers all along. Why did he wait so long with it?

Connery and Bell waited patiently while Kate and Casey consoled Nick. Kate was able to brighten his spirits by informing him he was being released the next day, and she would pick him up after work. As they left him, Nick managed to smile weakly.

Approaching the parking lot Kate spoke first, "Well, Detectives, I still owe you some lasagna and I have everything ready to go. Are you free tonight?"

"Free as a bird," Connery said.

"I would be honored," Bell said, bowing and taking Casey's hand in his.

Connery said, "Casey, your keys. I'll drive Kate in your car and you ride with Bell back to the estate."

"Oh, come on Flynn, aren't you being overly cautious?" Casey teased.

"Casey," Connery watched Kate out of the corner of his eye, "Nick's editor was murdered today." Their gasps of alarm stopped all protest.

The ride was quiet until they pulled into the estate gates. Donovan's watch geese were in full alarm. From the back wall they could hear hissing and loud honks, accompanied by several curses. Connery drew his gun and motioned for Kate to stay in the car.

Bell opened the car door to run out and Connery whispered, "Stay with the ladies, Bell!"

Then Connery took off racing silently toward the back. He hugged the wall of the house carefully peering around the corner. The geese had someone pinned against the wall and they were showing no mercy. Long necks were darting to peck at the intruder, while massive wings beat both the air and the man. Every time the man grabbed for one of the birds, the other one advanced furiously defending its mate. At forty pounds a piece, the geese packed quite a wallop. Gun ready, Connery advanced watching both the man and the geese carefully. Donovan had said the geese would recognize the residents of the house as tolerated intruders, but he didn't really explain how they would hold off a stranger. Now he knew.

"Keep still and put your hands were I can see them," Connery spoke slowly.

"Bloody hell! Call these monsters off!"

"Not until I can see your hands."

Slowly, the intruder extended his hands—showing he had nothing in them but a 35 mm camera.

Connery called Bell on his cell in front of the house, "Bell, bring the ladies, see if Kate knows this man."

When Kate rounded the corner behind Bell she was scared, then she saw he was just a photographer and she couldn't contain her laughter. Casey's amused giggle soon followed. "The stock just rose on those geese!" she cried.

"Come on mate, call off those damn birds!"

"Kate, see if you can get them to back off."

"Frank—Fran, come goose!" Casey handed Kate the bread they kept in a container near the wall. Kate shredded the pieces advancing toward the geese until she had their attention. Then she tossed them a tidbit. "Good geese! Come on Frank—come Fran." With one last peck and a hiss the two birds waddled toward Kate's offering. The effect was marred by their greedy gobbling of their favorite treat. Kate continued to lead them toward their pool, teasing them with bread as they went. When they were finally soothed and in the water, Kate made her way back to the others.

Connery had jerked the man upright and cuffed him roughly as Bell read him his rights.

"Hey, not so rough!"

"Who are you and what are you doing here?" Connery growled.

"Jake Mills. I'm a reporter. ID is in my pocket."

Connery pulled the man's wallet free and flipped it open to reveal that the intruder was indeed who he said he was.

"Works for that rag *Globe Investigations*."

"Are you sure he doesn't work for the *Intruder*? That's not a newspaper," Casey vented. "They're just a bunch of lying peeping toms posing as reporters!"

"Hey, I've got the right to work, freedom of speech and all!"

"Not here you don't," Bell replied.

"What are you gonna do?"

"Well, so nice of you to ask …" Bell replied, "… how about charging you with trespassing. This is a crime scene and you just returned to it. We could figure you to be our stalker. Then there's the murder … Seems like maybe we've got one of our assailants, huh Connery?"

"Yup. Assault, attempted murder at least. You're going to be tied up for a while my man."

"Hey! I didn't do anything but look for a story, I didn't even get any pictures."

"Tell it to the uniforms. I bet we can lock you up for several days at least, and I'm sure Miss Coleman will be pressing charges. Life is going to get very miserable for you, Jake Mills, you just missed your deadline."

"Bell, call in the uniforms to escort our suspect downtown."

"Can you really do that?" Kate whispered to Connery. "You don't honestly think he is mixed up in this do you?"

"Yes, I can and no, I don't. But it will give him and all the others something to think about the next time they try this kind of a stunt."

"I think Frank and Frannie already took care of that," Kate replied with a laugh. As the men made their way toward the drive, the two geese exited their pool and charged toward the men with necks stretched out, hissing and flapping their wings. They completely ignored Bell and made a beeline for the reporter.

"Keep them away from me! God damn birds are a menace!"

Laughter followed Mills as he was handed over to the two officers who had responded to the call to take him downtown.

Flynn turned back to Kate, watching her eyes twinkle brightly over the protective gander and his goose. "Well, at least now we know that Donovan knew what he was talking about with these birds," he said as Kate's eyes met his.

"Quite." Kate smiled as the sparks were flying between them.

Heaven help me, Flynn thought. *This was not a good idea*. His heart was pounding so hard it was impossible to hear the voice in his head telling him to stop.

Kate looked up at him and pressed her body against his. She felt so excited to have someone risk their life to protect hers. Nick had always done that for her. This was surprisingly turning her on more than she ever knew.

I don't know what's going on, or how any of this is going to end, but I think I owe it to myself to see where this can go. Maybe this is a Godsend? Kate told herself, always flexible.

"Come on, my great protector. Let's make that lasagna."

SEVENTEEN

As he sipped hot coffee Sam was twining between Flynn's legs. Last night's dinner with Kate had been a cool breeze releasing the tension of the past few weeks. He and Bell helped Casey and Kate cook her famous lasagna and simple pudding pie for dessert. The food was excellent—the company even better. *God help me, but this is one case that I not going to be able to keep on a professional level. There is something with this woman that I cannot ignore.* From the look in her eyes last night she knew it, too. They were plunging fast into the brink. It was sweet torture waiting and anticipating moments connecting with a kiss or a touch. Sam, tired of being ignored, unsheathed his claws and gave his roommate a stab.

"Yeow, Sam! What's with the claws?" Flynn frowned at the cat's disgusted stare. A placated "merrr" rumbled from the feline's throat as Flynn reached down to pet him. The empty dish still sitting on the countertop brought a meek grin to Flynn's face.

"Sorry, old man," Connery apologized as he filled the dish with leftover lasagna, and then added a splash of cream as a peace offering before placing the dish in front of the tom's nose. Sam gave the man a doleful stare before digging into his favorite treat. A purr grew until it almost became a growl—all was forgiven.

Connery finished his coffee before giving the cat a last pet and then headed out the door. He was picking up Bell and they were to meet the interpreter at the safe house at ten. Hopefully, she could work some magic with the Russian kids. Whether they would gain any viable leads from them was anybody's guess.

The detectives arrived outside the safe house and proceeded around to the back door where a grizzled former Marine checked their IDs before ushering them in. The translator was waiting.

"I don't think these children will be of much help, Detectives. Most of them come from different areas and they were all approached by different people. Here are my notes."

Connery and Bell scanned the neat notations. The information seemed to confirm the woman's statement but Connery's gut told him the connection was there—they just weren't seeing it.

"Do you think the kids would talk with us in the room? It would be easier to ask questions that way. We might pick up on something no one else would."

Zoia shrugged, "I can ask. But you have to remember where these kids came from—you are the bad guys back home." She left to deliver the request while Bell and Connery went over their notes from Nick. Shortly she returned with an agreement. There was one request from the kids; the detectives had to agree to do their best to help keep them in the States. None of them wanted to return to their homeland, they were already living on the streets there and they knew if anyone found out they talked, they were as good as dead.

"We can put in a good word for them—but we honestly don't have much to say in that department," replied Connery.

"Surely your DEA contacts could pull some strings for you, no?" Zoia questioned.

Bell had to admire the woman's guts—but he didn't like the sneaky look that accompanied her statement. "We can only ask," Bell replied and Connery nodded his agreement.

"Very well, let's get to it."

The children were positioned around the kitchen reminding the officers of a bunch of perched, frightened birds. Bell noticed that several had eyes constantly moving as if looking for an escape. He was sure they had been abused and restrained before. He thought to himself that sometimes the lessons life chose to teach us were not of the friendliest nature. These young people looked as if they had been raised in the streets where only the strongest, or smartest, survive.

"Okay Zoia, let's start again with the same info. Place of birth, where they were picked up—not only the city, and the person doing the contacting, please." All of the children barely looked the age of sixteen. Connery chose the oldest looking boy first.

Zoia relayed the requests and would translate for each of the seventeen young people in the room. Connery and Bell took notes—

listening carefully to the tones and observing the body language of the Russian children, orphaned by their country.

Almost halfway through a red flag went up. "Wait! Back up—ask him again?"

Zoia threw a puzzled look, but agreed.

Bell had caught it, too. This kid and Nick had both been to the same back street alley, in the same city. That was just too much coincidence for the detectives.

"Hang on a sec," Connery thumbed through his notes from Nick—looking for the date to go with the location. "Ask him if he remembers the date, day and month, when he was approached."

Zoia complied. The boy shook his head as he tried to remember. The exact date was a mystery, but the month was the same and finally the date was narrowed down to within a couple of days from when Nick had been in that same alley.

"Ask him if he remembers seeing, or hearing, an American man?" Bell asked.

Zoia once again translated. The little boy thought—shaking his head about seeing an American around that time. But then he remembered that one of the other kids had been excited about a pay-off. He remembered because the other boy was planning on getting a hot meal with his money.

That was it! There was no way this could be a coincidence. Nick was related to this boy somehow, in some way, and this was what had gotten him marked by the Russian Mafia.

"Ask him if he knows what happened to the other boy."

"Щидт идррэпэd тф уфця ғяiэпd?"

The child shook his head and shrugged—giving Zoia an indiscriminate answer.

"He doesn't know, he left that evening to get on the ship."

"Tell him thank you. I guess we are lucky to have this much. Officer O'Reilly will be here in a minute with the pizza." The detectives stood, making their way out to the sitting room with Zoia following.

"Anything else, gentlemen?"

"I don't think so—not for today anyway. Thanks for your help."

She nodded and then quietly left the room.

"That woman makes my skin crawl—something is not quite right with her," Bell offered.

"Yeah, I got that same feeling."

Connery turned his car toward the hospital—they needed to see Nick immediately. With the information coming together they wanted to confirm with Nick about the timing and his Russian informant. As they turned into the hospital parking lot Kate was exiting her car.

"Nick is being released" she said.

"How about Bell and I take him home? We need to talk to him and I will know you are safe at work."

"Honestly Flynn, you worry way too much!"

"Please Kate …"

"All right, but you owe me big time—and don't be manhandling my brother!"

Kate accompanied them into the hospital where she ran headfirst into Jason.

"Why Kate, it's so nice to see you! I heard Nick was being released and thought I'd come down to wish him well." He chose to ignore the two detectives accompanying her.

"That's considerate of you Jason, but quite unnecessary, since we are no longer dating," and with that she kept walking away from him toward Nick's room with Bell and Connery.

Jason followed, watching her with angry eyes.

Connery took a step back behind them adding his presence to her slight stature and interrupting Jason's view. His nonverbal warning was perfectly clear—*back off, she's mine.*

Jason didn't like the implication. Kate was his and would always be his! No mere street cop was getting between him and what he wanted. But, there was no need to antagonize the cop. There would be another time for that.

"Just trying to show that there are no hard feelings Katie Bear. My, you act like you're the only woman on earth! It's not like I can't find another woman!" he was starting to get loud as if she weren't just ignoring him, more like she didn't hear him. He followed her down the hall.

"So, have you?" Connery questioned falling in beside Jason.

Jason bristled and then thought—*what the hell?* "As a matter of fact, I have met someone. Perhaps I'll introduce you at the hospital's charity ball this weekend. I assume you will be there in place of your parents, Kate?" Then he turned smartly on his heel and headed down another hallway.

"Exit, stage left," said Bell. "That guy drives me nuts, are you sure we can't arrest him?"

Connery shook his head. He wasn't fooled, Jason Mueller still had it bad for Kate Coleman.

"Let's get Nick out of here," Kate volunteered. As she signed the paperwork releasing her brother the two detectives made their way to Nick's room. He was arguing with the nurse about riding in the wheelchair. Dirk stood to one side waiting with a grin on his face.

"Coleman, shut up and get in the chair before I have Dirk toss you over his shoulder and carry you out."

As if the surprised look on Nick's face wasn't enough, like a little boy he slowly slunk into the wheelchair as the nurse gathered up his things and thrust them into Connery's hands. Cocking her head toward Dirk she said, "That one already informed me that he wasn't carrying Mr. Coleman's bag—so you're elected."

"I thought Kate was picking me up."

"She's taking care of the paperwork. Then we're escorting you home. We need to talk again. Dirk, would you follow in your car?"

"Sure, I guess if he's riding with a cop he should be safe."

When they arrived at the Coleman Estate Dirk stood watch by the cars while Connery and Bell made a quick, but thorough, scan of the house and grounds before allowing Nick out of the car. Once they were all settled on the patio with their drinks Connery broke the silence.

"We may have found a connection between you and the kids from the ship, Nick. One of the boys was picked up in the same alley, in the city of Volsonvad, at the same time you met there with one of your sources. He heard one of the other boys talking about a big payoff for leaking information. What do you think?"

"My source certainly was no boy. In fact my source was female." A wistful look had entered Nick's eyes as he recounted the exchange with his contact. The look on his face led Connery to believe the woman was more than just a contact.

"She'd use the street kids as lookouts. She would give them enough for a hot meal out of what I paid her. It worked well for everyone."

"Is there any way to find out if she is still there?"

"What are you saying Connery?"

"What if Trovoishek got wind of a snitch, same time he was arranging for the kids to be smuggled out of the country—finds out you're the guy paying for the information. You're way too close to a lucrative operation that goes south because of you snooping around. He jumps to conclusions chin deep when the shipment is busted here just after you've returned to the States. So the guy decides to take care of you and yours—warnings, even murder."

"A lot of that makes sense Connery, but what about all the stuff happening to Kate before the shipment got busted? And if my parents' deaths are related. My Dad was involved."

"Maybe they were trying to warn you off by scaring Kate. Maybe he figured that threatening her would be a red flag for you to back off. He probably didn't even know who your parents were at the time. If that was his M.O. you wouldn't be here now. Then the bust, things began to escalate and people ended up dead."

"I don't know Connery. Something's not right. If he was trying to warn me by scaring my sister with what seemed to be pranks, it wasn't clear enough for me to figure out it was him trying to tell me to back off. So, how are you going to find Trovoishek and put a stop to him and his organization? Or do you think busting that one shipment has stopped him?"

"Still working on that one. At least we have an angle to work with. Can you try to get in contact with your source in Russia, if she is still there, and find out what she knows?"

"I have to try, if I can find her, she may know if Trovoishek still has a business after you busted the *Rusiana* full of kids." Nick was sounding more alive than he had in days.

"We'd really like to know how pissed off this Trovoishek is before we start pissing him off more." Bell said.

EIGHTEEN

The evening sun glowed a brilliant gold as Jason watched Zoia twirl before him in a midnight blue strapless gown he had purchased for her. The view was stunning. The woman was beautiful. The color set off her complexion perfectly, while the design hinted of the delights beneath. *When Kate sees Zoia on my arm she will be filled with jealousy. Yes, the thought of Zoia and I together will absolutely kill her. Soon, Kate will be back in my life. And Zoia will remain in my bed.*

"Well, what do you think?" Zoia asked.

"You are stunning," Jason replied. He liked the way she had managed her long hair. A fancy braid held it up away from her face, while the ends tickled her shoulders causing his fingers to want to touch. He wondered how she managed the feat of containing all its long glory but still allowing the strands to entice a man. "There's only one thing missing." The disappointment on her face was heartwarming. The woman wanted to please him. Jason offered a long black-velvet box.

When she opened it she was stunned. Inside rested a filigree necklace of fine twined black wire and dark blue stones. Earrings that matched nestled inside the box, too. A second box contained a matching bracelet, turned in the style of a slave bracelet, a ring was attached to the bracelet with a delicate black twined chain that matched the workmanship in the necklace. "Jason, it's lovely!"

"So are you. It will complement your beauty perfectly." He was pleased to see the relatively inexpensive jewels had not disappointed her. She was much too new to warrant precious stones.

"Did you know this style is derived from an eighteenth century Russian design that was very popular among royalty? Thank you so much Jason."

Her warm smile caused the blood to heat up between his legs

and he wished there was time before the hospital charity ball. He sighed, reminding himself that good things are worth waiting for. "I'm glad you're pleased. I'll fasten this for you."

Quickly Zoia removed the earrings and necklace she had on, and then lifted her hair for his ease.

Jason buried his nose in her glorious hair before releasing her to help her fasten the bracelet. "I love the way you have your hair. How do you do that?"

"Perhaps I'll let you figure it out later." She smiled coyly at him.

Jason wrapped the black cape about her shoulders before escorting her out the door.

At the Carlton, the valet stood mouth open—entranced by the vision climbing out of the car.

Jason was pleased by the reaction to his creation, but no mere servant should be so rude. "Close your mouth, boy!" he whispered angrily to the young man. Quickly the boy snapped his mouth shut as Jason tossed him the keys. Jason was pleased to see Zoia retained the lady-like demur ignoring the awestruck young man to focus her attention on her escort. They proceeded inside where Jason took stock of the people who had already arrived. A liveried waiter offered champagne. Jason watched Zoia sip the champagne delicately and the action of her swallowing drew his eyes to her lovely throat. He guided her inside to the main hall where people from the richer walks of life mingled and played. So far he hadn't seen Kate. *Well, there's Nick, resting against the wall martini in one hand, chatting with another reporter, while his hired dog stands close by.* Jason knew she would be here with Nick. Their parents were very generous donors and never missed a ball. Nick and Kate were required to attend since they turned eighteen. Their father probably insisted they continue their attendance to all fundraisers in his will. It wasn't that George Coleman cared about the hospital, he cared about tax write-offs and his wife's position in society. Jason continued to work the crowd with Zoia on his arm. She played the mystery woman very well. She skillfully sidestepped questions about herself—giving answers that intentionally left people wanting more, but not quite sure how to ask.

"Sorry, Senator Calsworth. I see my mother waving to me and you know how mothers are …"

"Miss Zartoni and Mr. Mueller, perhaps we can chat again."

As they made their way toward Jason's mother, he added a warning. "My mother is a master snoop, Zoia. Watch what you say."

"I'll be careful, Jason."

"Mother, I'd like to introduce Zoia Zartoni. Zoia, my mother, Abigail Mueller."

"Mrs. Mueller, a pleasure to meet you."

Abigail scrutinized the sensuous woman on her son's arm. The straight carriage and proud demeanor spoke of breeding. Her speech was slightly accented, but Abigail couldn't quite put her finger on its origin. "Nice to meet you, dear. And, you are from where?"

Jason made to run interference, but the tightening of Zoia's hand on his arm forestalled him. She had handled the senator with ease; perhaps she could handle his mother, also.

"I've grown up in the Bay area, Madam."

"But you are originally from?"

"My ancestry is Russian and Greek, Mrs. Mueller."

Abigail was an expert at fielding questions. Immediately she recognized another master of the game. She would not get any more than this girl was willing to give. Abigail studied her carefully—noting the calculating gaze and relaxed stance. Fine cheekbones and exotic eyes stared back, taking Abigail's measure. Elegant hands deftly held the crystal champagne stem with a practiced ease. Zoia was someone to reckon with, she could be an opponent—or an ally. Abigail couldn't decide which right now, but immediately she had a disgruntled respect for her. Something she had never had for that Coleman girl. "That must have something to do with your lovely accent. Are you fluent in either language, dear?"

"Both, Madam."

"Ah—well, you are certainly lovely enough to grace my dear son's arm. Please enjoy yourselves. Run along now, Jason. I'm sure you have better things to do than entertain your mother."

Jason led Zoia off—mentally shaking his head. Never, never had his mother approved of any female he had escorted before. His admiration for Zoia heightened. He had definitely picked the right woman this time!

Flynn readjusted the ivory shawl over Kate's shoulders before they descended the steps into the ball.

"I hate these things! It's nothing but a contest for those who have more, and those who are trying to get more. People staring at you and talking behind your back all hiding behind the word charity!"

"Relax Kate. You're not alone, and I promise I won't leave your side." Flynn reassured her, as once again, he drank in the exquisite woman at his side. In the short time they had known each other Flynn had become very aware of Kate's growing confidence in herself and her actions. The woman was blooming in his presence. Buoyed by his attention and confidence in himself, hers was growing quickly allowing her personality and presence to shine. The chocolate velvet gown was stunning on Kate's lithe figure. Modest in the front with long sleeves that were gathered every few inches to provide a form-fitting sleeve—the back plunged daringly to the small of her back, revealing a gorgeous backbone that invited a man to press his palm there. The shimmering caramel hues of her hair complemented the gown to perfection. No one else could have carried it off with such style. Occasionally, a polished toe nail could be seen from beneath the hem of the gown as she floated across the red carpet to the door. She had put her hair up tonight, fastening it in place with some kind of shimmering pearl drops that perfectly matched the pearl drop earrings and necklace that completed the ensemble. She reminded him of some slim goddess from ancient times as they proceeded inside. The golden light of the ballroom only served to accent her beauty. Flynn pressed his fingers a little more firmly into her side as he led her down the stairs into the ballroom, giving her added assurance of his presence. He paused for a moment to let her get her bearings before spotting Nick at the north wall.

"There's Nick. Let's go over and say 'hi'."

Flynn made note of the eyes turning as they made their way across the room.

Hostile eyes were watching the couple, too. Jason knew the moment Kate entered the room. She was impeccable! Her beauty seemed to dim the rest of the room in comparison. He snarled as he noticed that Connery was holding her close. The cop would have to go!

Jason thought his emotions were under control, but Zoia noticed the awestruck rapture directed at the woman entering and the rage directed toward her escort. So, she had competition did she? Zoia surveyed the other woman's apparel. There was no way she was going to lose Jason! Something would have to be done!

"Hello, Nick. You seem to be handling this fairly well," Connery winked at the reporter.

Nick grinned. "A whole lot better than my sister. She just hates crowds. Me, I find them interesting. You can learn so much about people at one of these things—without ever talking to anyone."

"Such as?"

"Well, for instance, if looks could kill you'd both be dead!"

"Huh?"

"There is a stunning dark-haired beauty over there throwing daggers at my sister and the man whose arm is supporting her has just skinned you alive."

"What are you talking about?"

"Jason Mueller and his companion. Take a look."

Connery turned, meeting Jason's eyes across the room. The hate was palatable and it was directed at him. The stunning beauty next to him looked somewhat familiar. It took him a minute to realize that it was the interpreter. "Wow!" It was the only word he could come up with. She was dazzling! And her dagger eyes were all over Kate. This might turn out to be a very interesting evening.

"Don't look now love," Connery spoke to Kate, "but your ex's new girl is ready to scratch your eyes out."

"What? I have never even met that woman."

"That's easy to see, sis. The man she is with is drooling over you. The green-eyed cat called jealousy has consumed her. Let's go over and say 'hi'."

"Are you nuts, Nick?"

"Not at all Kate. These things are always dealt with best out in the open. Aren't you even a little curious as to whom that woman is? God! She is something else!"

Kate looked up into Flynn's eyes to see them twinkling with merriment—but the steel muscles in his forearm told her he was

THE DARKNESS WITHIN   **165**

anything but relaxed.

"Oh, all right. Maybe I can soothe my competition, now that I'm no longer in the running."

Flynn smiled proudly at Kate. "That's my girl. Don't run from a challenge Kate. Stand your ground and look your enemy square in the eye. That way at least you know which direction they are coming from."

The three made their way across the room with Dirk following nonchalantly behind.

Nick broke the silence. "Hello there, beautiful. Just who are you and how do I get to know you?"

Zoia couldn't help smiling at the glib remark made by the dashing man—but she turned her eyes to her date instead. She was not going to lose her chance with Jason for one complimentary remark by a handsome man.

"This is Zoia Zartoni. Zoia, this smart mouth is Nick Coleman, his sister Kate Coleman, and Detective Connery."

"Miss Coleman, gentlemen—a pleasure I'm sure."

Kate offered her hand to Zoia. "I'm so glad to meet you, Zoia. It's a great comfort to know that Jason has met someone. I hope the two of you will be very happy together."

Jason's mouth tightened as Connery's eyes twinkled. He was happy to know Kate was finally feeling confident enough to stand up for herself. He saw the questioning look in Zoia's eyes and simply smiled. He would not be giving away the lady's past, or present, to Mueller or his date. As far as Connery was concerned they deserved each other.

"Nick, you look like you need to sit down. If you'll excuse us please." Connery steered Nick and Kate away from Mueller toward a table where Nick could take a break and they could talk.

"Well, Zoia seems very devoted to Jason. I hope they will be happy."

"Don't bet on it Kate," Connery cautioned. "You need to be careful, I'm not so sure Jason has given up on you yet."

"What makes you say that?"

"Just call it a cop's intuition." The steely edge of his voice gave her pause.

As the night progressed Jason kept one eye on Kate. Zoia was charming and engaging. She could hold her own with his peers as Kate had never been willing to do. The woman was an asset and even Jason could see that. So why was he so obsessed with Kate?

"Will you be all right if I leave you for a moment, dear?" Jason asked Zoia.

"Of course, Jason." Zoia ran her fingers discreetly down his coat sleeve.

"Back shortly then."

Her eyes followed Jason as he made his way down the hallway.

The orchestra struck up a waltz and Flynn led Kate to the floor for one last dance before taking her home. She smiled up at him admiring the cut of his dress shirt. He was a rebel at heart. Instead of the classical shirt and tie, the man was decked out in one of those collarless dress shirts worn so well by cowboys. The stylish black snap buttons contrasted smartly with his trousers and the longer than average cut of his coat. He might be dressed to kill, but it was in his very own style—no one else's.

Kate looked at him again and realized with startling clarity that she was falling in love with the man! Her stomach dropped as the past fast forwarded through her mind. The anger, the abuse, and the lies. Then with a gentle stoke of his fingers across her palm, Flynn made everything beautiful and real. Perhaps the fear she had always harbored of being twisted and broken was only that—fear. Flynn made her feel whole and clean—perhaps there was a future for her with this man. She smiled up at him as he twirled her across the floor, guiding her expertly through the crowd of dancers. Not once did he hesitate, not once did she brush against another dancer. Could he steer her through life as easily? Her heart increased its pace as she threw caution to the wind and finally, after years of fear, jumped with both feet into the pool of his love.

Flynn saw the difference in her immediately. His smile lit up the room for her as he held her close, sheltering her in his arms.

Breathless after the dance, Kate excused herself to find her way to the ladies lounge. It was crowded, but Kate instantly recognized Zoia in the throng. Thinking to put the other woman at ease, Kate made her way to her.

"Are you enjoying the ball, Zoia?"

Cold black eyes turned her way. "I was."

Kate was caught off guard by the steely blast from the other woman.

"Jason is mine! I will not tolerate your interference!" Zoia whispered fervently. "Stay out of my way."

Kate was shellshocked as Zoia exited the room. *My,* she thought to herself, *they deserve each other! As if I'd want anything to do with that cad!* Kate made her way back and put the encounter out of her mind.

"Nick, you look beat. Why don't you head home?"

"What? And miss all the fun?"

"What fun? Have Dirk take you home," Connery suggested.

"We're leaving, too, Nick. I think Kate has made enough of an appearance tonight. We'll follow you back to the estate."

"Well, when you put it that way, okay." Dirk appeared as if by magic. "I've already called for your wheels. Why don't you hand me your keys and I'll have yours brought around too, Connery."

Flynn dug out the keys and handed them to Dirk. Before long he was back. "We're ready to roll. Do you want us to wait?"

"No mine should be up shortly. We'll meet you back at the estate," Flynn answered.

Flynn and Kate made their way to the entrance hall where Flynn retrieved Kate's shawl from the attendant.

"This seems to be taking an awful long time, don't you think Flynn?" Kate mentioned as they waited for the car.

"Too long. I wonder what's up?"

Just then the head valet returned. "I'm sorry, sir, but some ill-minded person has slashed the tires on your vehicle. I have already taken the privilege of calling the police."

"I am the police! That's just great!" Connery dug out his cell phone. "Dirk, someone has slashed the tires on my car. This might be a set up—don't go to the estate. Take Nick to my place. Bell and Casey are already there. Once the estate has been checked out we'll bring them home."

"Sorry, Kate. Looks like the evening isn't going to end early after all."

"Good. That means I get to spend more time with you!" She looped her arm around his waist moving in close. The last thing she wanted to do after a night like this was be alone.

"Do you think this is a good idea? People are going to talk. The princess and the cop thing."

"I don't care. I'm happy and warm. Do you mind?"

"Mind? I've got the best girl at the party on my arm. Turn on the lights and let the cameras roll."

Kate laughed lightly. "Will this get you in trouble at work? I mean our getting involved?"

"Probably, but I've never been one for following the rules. Right now I'm glad you're here and I don't care who knows."

Angry sets of eyes watched from behind the bright lights, recognizing the silhouettes in the drive. Carefully they backed into the crowd when the police cars arrived to investigate the detective's car. There would be another time—very soon!

NINETEEN

Sam was one very pissed-off cat! A stranger in his house? The nerve! He made no bones about letting Flynn know. The yowling feline met him at the door and sank his claws into Flynn's pants attempting to climb up his leg.

"Hey! Enough of that Sam! Get a grip man." He grabbed the ornery cat by the back of the neck and set him firmly on the floor. "Mind your manners—or I'll have to lock you in the bathroom."

"Poor fella," Kate purred, "has your space been invaded? Let's find you some supper, huh? C'mere kitty, kitty."

Flynn was in the motion of rescuing Kate's hand from one nasty alley cat—only to stop in mid-flight. The feisty feline was purring! Purring at a stranger? Sam followed Kate to the kitchen, where she scoped out the fridge before choosing a dish for the cat. "Hey, I was going to have that for breakfast!" Connery yelped.

"I'll cook you something else for breakfast."

His eyes widened at the innuendo.

"Here Sam—do you like lasagna as much as your roommate?"

The cat twined between her legs then graciously accepted her offering after giving Flynn a disgusted look.

"I have never seen him do that. Hell, he doesn't even like me."

Kate laughed. "Any woman knows that the way to sooth a savage beast is to feed him." Kate pulled a strawberry from behind her back and dangled it in front of his nose. "Did you actually buy strawberries?" she whispered accusingly.

"Noooo, my sister dropped off a care package of home-cooked meals if you must know."

"Mmmmm, do you like strawberries?" Kate was taking a stab at being sexy with food and it looked like it was working as she dragged the berry across her parted lips. His eyes followed. She popped it into her mouth and kissed him, pushing half of it into his mouth.

Casey and Bell entered the kitchen followed by Dirk.

"Am I ever glad you're finally here!" Casey interjected. "That cat is a menace. He's been throwing a fit ever since we arrived."

It took a minute for the detective to recover and remember there were others in his apartment tonight.

He cleared his throat, "Sam doesn't take well to strangers. He's suspicious of people he doesn't know."

"Get that from his roommate, does he?" questioned Bell.

"Comes with being a cop, why are you guys still here?"

"What? You said to stay here!" Bell pointed at him.

"I didn't mean all night." Connery was kidding. A little.

Casey was already trying to drag Kate into the living room begging for details about the dance like a teenager's little sister.

Flynn suddenly noticed how small his apartment was with six people in the kitchen. All at once the realization of just how small his world had become hit home. *When was the last time someone had stopped by—I haven't had any friends over since Bell's first visit.* He glanced at Kate. *But damn the interruption just now. I liked where that was going,* he thought, watching her laughing mouth and the swing of her hair as she pulled it down. She had opened his world to people and feelings again.

He motioned to Bell and the two men made their way into the hall. Connery explained what had happened at the ball with Mueller and his girlfriend watching as Bell's gears turned over all the information.

"I don't think this is coincidence—but it doesn't feel like the Russian Mafia, either," Bell interjected.

"Exactly what I thought. Was I off the wall sending everyone here? Maybe they would have been fine at the estate."

Bell shrugged, "Better safe than sorry."

"I'm going to get out of this monkey suit."

Bell refocused his attention on the rest of the group. It looked like both he and his partner had forgotten the first rule in police work. Do not to get involved in a relationship on a case.

Bell watched Casey. She was a different kind of beautiful; her figure was a little round and she was a little short, but the life and exuberance that surrounded her had punched him in the gut the first time they met. That crazy sense of drama mixed with her humor and that laugh had taken him down hard.

Casey felt his stare and turned her eyes to his and Bell smiled, wiggling his eyebrows at her. Her laugh was full-bodied and music to his ears. *There was no way I will allow anything to harm his lady.* He turned the thought over in his mind. It was time he took the plunge—*would she be his lady?* He wanted this to be something that would last and with Casey he thought it would.

A low beeping brought everyone's attention to the pager on Dirk's belt. He glanced at the small electronic device and announced, "The alarm's been tripped at the estate."

"Connery!" Bell hollered, "Let's go! Dirk, you and Nick stay here with the girls."

Connery came on the run still pulling a dark T-shirt over his head. "What's up?"

"The alarms have been tripped at the estate. I'll drive."

Connery gathered up his shoes as both men headed for the door. "Does Nick know how to use a gun?"

"Yeah, why?"

Connery looked Dirk square in the eye. "There's a shotgun in the bedroom closet in the bottom of the trunk. Ammo's in the dresser, bottom drawer. Don't let anything happen to them," he looked toward the ladies. Then he was gone. Soon the rumble of Bell's Camaro could be heard as it roared down the street.

The shrill beeping of Connery's phone broke the silence of the ride. With less than four blocks between them and the apartment tensions was rising fast.

"Connery here, whadaya got?"

"Already on the road—should be there in 15 minutes. Okay."

"That was dispatch," he said to Bell. "Coleman's neighbors called in a complaint about the racket the geese were making. A patrol car was sent out and they found the gate lock was broken so they called for backup."

Bell shifted into a higher gear and Connery held on.

Shit! He was regretting that he wasn't the one driving. "How about we get there in one piece?"

Bell slid to a stop in front of the estate's entrance gate. A squad car was parked behind a PRIME Security SUV along the road. Just inside the fence the cops and security team waited.

"Malloy, take your partner and proceed up the drive."

Connery recognized one of the PRIME Security employees. "Reese, have your guys cover the perimeter. Bell and I will take the back."

Weapons drawn, slinking from cover to cover, the men made their way toward the residence. Bell and Connery flanked each other, moving to the backyard toward the patio and kitchen entrance.

The geese could be heard honking and hissing but less erratic, almost like they were calming down. Connery took it as a sign the intruder was no longer in the area. Carefully, he moved forward, checking the doors and windows while Bell moved toward the alarm box.

"Bell?"

"Alarms have been tampered with—looks like a professional job, but he didn't find the backup."

The two continued toward the kitchen door, radioing their next step.

The front door was still locked, but a security man produced the extra key and swung wide the front door. "Looks and feels empty, Connery," Reese radioed back.

"Same here—I'm going to figure out what's got the geese so upset. Make your way through the house."

Bell kept one eye on the door as Connery carefully moved on toward the big pair of geese. The male beat his wings, hissing as Connery moved forward.

"Easy, big guy. What's got you so upset, huh?" The two fowl moved off slowly allowing Connery to see what was irritating the pair. Near the pond, headless and bloody, lay several decapitated chickens. The fresh blood still dripped from their necks.

"Found something," Bell stated as he carefully held up a bloody butcher knife in his gloved fingers. "Some kinda chicken massacre took place back here. Nasty."

"Maybe a message that was interrupted."

Bell bagged the knife and proceeded to the car.

The security guard, Reese, approached Connery, "Everything

seems to be intact in here Detective. Something scared him, or them, off. They should be caught on video. My crew can stick around to take care of the alarm system and the gate. Want us to wait until your team is finished?"

"Thanks, Reese. We'll get forensics out to dust everything. Maybe we'll get lucky. Something's gotta show up on those cameras."

Twenty four hours later, the tapes reportedly showed nothing but black. Someone knew they were there and further investigation at the estate proved it. Black velvet clothes were thrown over the security cameras. Smart, simple, aggravating as hell that they didn't think to look at them when they were there. Connery couldn't stand to admit it, but he felt like the weakest link.

DARK THOUGHTS TWIRLED.
COMPETITORS MUST BE
ELIMINATED.

NAILS FLEXED AS THOUGHTS OF
ELIMINATION DOVE THROUGH THE
MIND.

A CALL FROM ANOTHER ROOM
DISTURBED THE SHADOWY PLAN.

IT WOULD BE. TIME SOON. IT
HAD WAITED TOO LONG WITH ITS
ANGER EATING AWAY AT IT. IT
WAS TIME TO BE FREE.

TWENTY

The days that followed were quiet. Kate and Casey quickly fell into a routine. They would drive to work, followed by a PRIME Security employee. Dirk remained with Nick at the estate since Nick was still having difficulty getting around. In the evenings either Bell or Connery would escort the ladies home when they were available. But Kate wasn't feeling very safe and secure. She felt as if she were waiting for the dam to burst. Shadows seemed to follow her wherever she went. Shadows on the walls and hushed curses—she wondered if she was going insane. Afraid to mention them to anyone, she found her work was beginning to suffer. It seemed the muted whispers were at their worst in the hospital. Even though she was surrounded by people she felt isolated and trapped in a whispering world of fear. Nick and Casey shared plenty of conversations and laughs, but Kate was usually uninvolved. Their silly antics were getting old—how could anyone joke around at a time like this? They should be as scared and worried as she was about the killer's next move. She was worried that people were forgetting that Wells and her parents' deaths were probably related—just giving warnings and pulling pranks with them didn't mean it couldn't still become a killer again.

Connery and Bell had been MIA, busy chasing down leads on the Russian hit men. The detective's visits with Kate and Casey were brief. Casey and Nick were getting pretty flirty but then, Casey was always flirty with everyone. She had looked at Kate questioningly several times—but Kate kept her lips firmly locked about her fears. Nick finally brought her worst nightmares out into the open after dinner once they were alone.

"Can I tell you a secret, Kate?"

"Sure Nick, what are you, eight years old? Tell me, I won't tell anyone," and she crossed her heart with her right hand.

"Seriously Kate—I think I'm falling for Casey," he paused, seeing the look of disgust on Kate's face. Then he began to ramble. "I always liked her, you know that, but you said she was off limits because she was your friend and I'm never here anyway and it would ruin everything. But seeing her with Bell …"

"No, Nick, uh-uh. Leave her alone. She is happy with Bell, and that's gross, I mean, you are my brother and she is like a sister! Don't even think about it!"

"Hate to mention this Kate, but you look like hell. Are you sleeping at all, or up with nightmares again?" He switched modes so quickly she started to choke on a piece of meat.

Casey pounded her on the back. She must have entered the room behind Kate, how much did she hear? When her vision and throat cleared Nick's face was locked in concentration on his sister.

Resolutely, Kate began, "I think I'm losing my mind, guys. I hear whispered voices cursing me all the time. I can't get away from it—and it's worse at the hospital."

Nick was silent for a moment before rising and walking to the phone and dialing. "This is Nick Coleman. Would you inform Detective Connery that he needs to stop by the Coleman Estate when he gets off duty tonight? Thank you."

"Nick, you shouldn't have done that! What am I going to tell him? That I'm going mad?"

"Your right sis, I should've called a shrink!" Nick reached across the table and gathered her hands in his. "Kate, if this mad man could break into your computer at the hospital and leave no trace, what makes you think he didn't hide a device in your office to haunt you?"

Casey agreed, "Yeah, Kate, just let Connery check it out. If he doesn't find anything, then we'll call the shrink!" She broke the mood and made everyone laugh again. With fears out in the open Kate was able to give Nick several examples of the little things that were driving her mad. The shadowy figures in the hallways and the whispered threats that were driving her to insomnia. She kept the headaches and the flashbacks to herself.

By the time Connery and Bell arrived she already felt much better but then she had to explain it all over again.

"Is there anything else of importance you didn't think you should mention? Don't hold anymore back, Kate."

"Well, maybe—just that I have been having really bad migraines like Nick. They started way back before my parents' accident though."

"Seriously Kate, you have to be honest with me. I am on your side. I know you have had bad experiences with people you have trusted, but you can trust me, us, you can trust us."

Kate smiled outside, but inside, she didn't even know if she could trust herself.

Instead of calling the precinct Connery made a call to Matt Donovan and they agreed to meet later that night at Kate's office.

"Why did you call Donovan?" Nick asked.

"PRIME Security has more advanced electronics than the department does. The department would probably call them anyway. If something is there, they will find it. Then we'll call in the forensics team."

"You really think they'll find something?" Kate was worried they wouldn't find anything, which would mean it was all in her head.

"We'll find whatever it is—you're not crazy! I believe you Kate. We've got to go. We've got a lead on Trovoishek and we need to check it out before we lose him again. Nick, we'll call when we know something."

At an upscale restaurant specializing in East Asian cuisine, the detectives found Richie, the snitch, waiting. He was lurking in the alley trying to look innocent when Bell parked the car.

"What gives, Richie?"

"Trovoishek went in 'bout 20 minutes ago with two high-class stiffs. Ain't seen him come out yet. Where's my dough?"

"You'll get paid when we find the man. Here's half your squatter's fee." Connery said as he handed him a folded bill.

"Hey! Give Connery! I ain't sticking around for this!"

"If your tip's legit you'll get the rest. You know the rules." With that Connery turned his back and made his way inside the restaurant. Bell kept his eye on Richie as he backed through the doors.

They were met by a maitre' de, who was not accustomed to being confronted. But, Connery's cold demeanor and badge convinced him to point the way to the man they were seeking. "Give us that empty table next to Mr. Trovoishek and we'll try to not disturb the rest of the place. Play games with us and we'll turn this restaurant into a barroom brawl like you've never seen. Understand?"

The man led them to the requested table and then sent a waiter with menus.

Pretending to study the cuisine, Connery kept his ears on the conversation at the next table. The mixture of English and Russian was hard to follow.

Bell was studying the other occupants and when the waiter arrived he ordered a bottle of wine and hors d'oeuvres. They would at least look like customers.

The restaurant was busy but was designed in such a way that it didn't seem crowded. How to get their man was the question. Should they try to approach as he left—or would it be better to surprise him at the table? The same thought was running through both of their minds. Connery sent a questioning gaze in Bell's direction and Bell shrugged his shoulders.

Some fancy dish with a cream sauce appeared on their table, along with a bottle of red wine. Connery glanced at Bell, "Do I want to know?"

Bell shook his head.

Connery picked up the dainty fork that had arrived with the food and began to disassemble the offering on the plate. He was sure if he knew what it was he wouldn't be able to eat it—but surprisingly enough, the taste was exotic and spicy. As they were halfway through their dish one of Trovoishek's cohorts excused himself, and then as if luck was finally on their side, the other companion made his way to another table to visit.

No time like the present! Bell made his way around Trovoishek's table as if heading for the men's room, while Connery stepped to the front of the table. The surprise on Trovoishek's face as he recognized the feel of Bell's Beretta in his back gave Connery an instant of joy.

Connery leaned over and whispered, "Nice and easy, Trovoishek. My friend has an itchy finger, and personally, I don't care if we deliver you dead or alive. We're going to walk out of here nice and easy—as if we're old friends. Keep the conversation in English so my friend doesn't get nervous, you know what I mean. Now, let's go."

Once they made the exit Connery quickly handcuffed their

prize and Bell kept the Beretta snugged up close to the man's ribs.

Connery carefully patted the man down, relieving him of a taser, guillotine wire, and a knife from his boot.

They steered the man to Bell's car and quickly forced him into the cramped trunk while no one was looking. Then Connery called their DEA contact.

There was no way they were putting this killer in the Bay City lockup. The Feds could hold him much easier and tighter. They agreed to meet at the nearest government building to exchange the merchandise; with the understanding they would have access for questioning and all the records on the prisoner. Normally, they didn't get on well with the Feds, but in this case they had worked as a well-oiled team. It was time for them to trust the DEA agents as they had trusted Bell and Connery earlier.

The hour was approaching to meet with Donovan at the hospital. Cruising along the highway Connery wondered if now they might get a break. He didn't imagine that Trovoishek would cooperate, but maybe the Feds had some weight they could throw at the man.

Once the Claims Department was closed the Assistant Manager called PRIME Securities who in turn paged Mr. Donovan. Donovan and the detectives were waiting at the elevator to Kate's floor with other high-tech personnel.

"Keep it quiet, once we get up there, in case of bugs. Connery, I'd like you and Bell to position yourselves at the elevator to keep anyone off the floor who might wander up. We'll see what we can find."

In the hallway outside the office Donovan's team set up their gear. Computers with wireless access were up-linked to help with the surveillance. Men moved quietly along the hallway with listening devices that would rival military equipment. After pacing the hallway twice, the team focused on the entrance to the office area. Donovan produced a key set that quickly opened the door.

Connery waited impatiently. He didn't doubt Kate. After everything that had happened so far he knew in his gut that she wasn't hearing ghosts. Or, at least, not ghosts of her imagination.

Bell watched over the shoulder of the female computer tech scanning the readouts.

After 15 minutes Donovan reappeared. He walked quietly

over and handed Connery a written note. The others whispered into mouthpieces attached to headgear.

> *We've got something.*
> *Just can't pin it down yet.*
> *We're definitely getting an audio feed.*

One of the techs returned, whispering quietly, "Boss, we think it's locked into her computer and only shows up when she boots the thing up. We're going to turn the other computers on and see what happens. We'll need the passwords." Connery handed him the paper with the passwords Kate's boss had collected for them. He returned to guard duty at the elevator. The buzz of computers could be heard faintly through the doorway. As the passwords of the two stations were punched in the tech whispered. "Gotcha!"

With the audio feed located, their mission was complete.

"We placed a buffer on the audio so Miss Coleman doesn't hear the feed and we've got a trace hooked on for backfeed. We'll know more tomorrow. We will leave it this way until we are able to trace its origin."

Quietly, the group made their way back to the parking lot.

"Connery, this guy is good and extremely high-tech. This is some of the newest surveillance equipment out there. Nobody's even able to get it yet. Your bad guy must be very well connected. Be careful."

"Thanks Donovan, but I'm not surprised."

TWENTY ONE

Bell and Connery waited impatiently in the lobby of the DEA office. Even though they had turned Ligria over to their DEA contact there was no way they were going to stand there and twiddle their thumbs waiting for someone else to break their case. After Connery threatened to cause a nasty scene, one of the agents they had worked with appeared.

"What the hell do you think you're doing Connery?" the agent growled.

"We're both working on this case—remember? Don't get all narcissistic on us now! I'm sure there is room in your observation room for two more cops. Don't forget who brought him in."

The agent took a look at the detectives and realized they were two guys who weren't taking no for an answer. "All right—follow me."

Heads turned as the three men made their way down to where detainees were held. The possibility of someone getting in here to sabotage their prisoner was much less likely than in the local law enforcement center, which was why Connery and Bell had turned Ligria over to the Feds. The three entered the room quietly—listening intently to the questioning in the adjoining room. Ligria seemed comfortable and relaxed. That wasn't a good sign! Ten minutes into the interview Connery was feeling frustrated. The Russian was acting like he didn't speak English and the translator was spinning his wheels. Ligria looked straight at the two-way glass and smiled. Connery fumed. There had to be something on this guy they could use to get him to talk. Then the door of the questioning room opened to reveal a smart-looking woman with dark hair.

The DEA agent leaned into Connery and muttered, "Here we go, I love this part …"

The questioning agent was smugly introducing Ligria to the woman. "Mr. Ligria, meet Captain Montiav, she's with Israeli intelligence. Seems the two of you have much to talk about. In fact, our government has agreed to release you into the custody of Israeli intelligence. You'll be leaving shortly—have a nice trip!" With that the agent stood, nodded to the interpreter, and left the questioning room.

The woman sat down, propped her feet up on another chair and looked intensely at Ligria. Not a word was spoken.

"You don't look Israeli," Ligria muttered.

The woman's eyes never left his face. After a lengthy pause she spoke, "Masada is very good at blending in."

The impact of her words could be seen on the Russian's face. Masada! The Israeli intelligence death squad! They had taken down numerous threats to the state of Israel. Most terrorists learned since Munich that this was one force you did not want to piss off! No matter what, they always got their man—and they usually didn't take prisoners.

"So a tiny woman like you will escort this big man back to Israel, yes?" Ligria's attempt to seem bold and unafraid struck deaf ears.

The agent neither moved, nor spoke. Just leaned back and gazed at him, then she spoke. "My brother was on the freighter *Novia*."

A man of Ligria's background could understand this! Before him sat a Masada agent with a personal vendetta against him and a job he was connected to. He would never reach Israel alive, but worse than death would be the torture tactics Masada was known for! Perhaps it was better to cooperate with the Americans it would be easier to escape from them. They were not as deadly as Masada.

"I will talk to the American agent. Bring him back in."

"No."

Connery glanced at the agents in the observation room. One turned to him and smiled. "Works every time! None of these bad guys are so tough that they aren't afraid of Masada. And Captain Montiav is on loan to us from Israel. She's very good, isn't she? We'll let him sweat for a while and then we'll give him another chance. Still want to stick around—or can we meet later to discuss our findings?"

"Give us a call when you get something. Looks like you guys

have it under control."

"Connery," the DEA agent called as they left the room, "I wouldn't have forgotten you. I appreciate your help—I will call."

Connery nodded.

Bell's pager beeped as they left the federal building. He glanced at the screen and then turned to his partner. "Your car is ready. Should I drop you off?"

"Yeah, I'll meet you back at the station afterward."

The drive to the mechanic's was quiet. Connery exited Bell's Camaro and entered the office. "Hey Mel, heard my car was ready."

"Just giving her a last spit shine. Somebody sure had a hard-on for you to slice all four, huh?"

"Goes with the job." Connery paid the bill, picked up his keys, and made for his sedan.

Back at the station with the car parked and locked he went inside. The next step was to contact PRIME. Hopefully they had made some progress on the electronic equipment from the hospital.

When Connery reached his desk there was a message from Donovan. The electronics producer had been located and they were following up on the purchaser.

PRIME had reached a dead end on who was receiving the feed from the computer. It seemed to loop through the hospital system and fizzle out. Apparently the white noise had been set up only to intimidate Kate. The other computers had no access to the loop. Another dead end.

Abigail Mueller sat across the table from Zoia—watching the girl with admiration. She had sent her investigator to do some serious digging on the woman's background—and while her present occupation was not what Abigail would have wished for—she made her son happy and Abigail would have fun playing with her for a while. The woman had taste and breeding. Her lineage could be traced to both Greek and ancient Russian royalty. Pity she spent her time dealing with perverts.

"You have quite an ancestry and background Zoia. I am most impressed with your current, hmmm, how shall I say it, occupational skills?"

A flutter of the fork was the only sign of Zoia's stress. "What exactly are you trying to say Mrs. Mueller?" The eyes were cold and the voice was guarded. She didn't appreciated the personal intrusion.

"What I'm saying dear, is, despite your present occupation I feel you suit my son to a "T", and we must work together to bring him into hand."

Zoia's surprise was evident. Her Cosmo shook as she raised it to her lips. A long, slow sip gave her time to collect her thoughts. "You know—and you don't care where I work?"

"Of course I care! It certainly isn't appropriate for my future daughter-in-law to serve drinks at a gentlemen's club! However, your education and background make up for that, in a way. I like that you are still able to be a translator. I will accept you for my son's sake. I'm saying—let's work together and get him over that Kate girl! However, if Jason finds out we are working together he'll drop you—just to irritate me." Now it was Abigail's turn to pause for a sip of her Manhattan.

"I doubt that he is even the least bit interested in Kate anymore, I have been keeping him, hmmm, how shall I put it? ... pretty busy," Zoia purred. "What did you have in mind Mrs. Mueller?" Now this was interesting. These rich people took themselves so seriously, yet they were all so silly.

"You leave that to me, dear. When I need your involvement I shall contact you, that is if you want in ..." and putting her elbows on the table she leaned forward flipping her wrists and raising her palms up glancing around as if referring to her own special world of class, high society, and of course, money.

Zoia raised one eyebrow and her drink in a toast of acceptance and Abigail met her glass with a clink of her own.

After lunch the women went their separate ways.

"I swear a little "red-pen munchkin" has run off with all of my red pens again!" Casey dramatically complained to the girls in the office. Giggles were heard from the gang— Casey was well known for loosing her pens only to find them later right where she left them. In the meantime she would regale them all with stories of the munchkins before heading to supply to requisition enough for the whole floor, once again.

"Casey, I'll go get you those pens. Gibson is probably tired of seeing your face in his supply room," Kate volunteered. "I'll grab us some drinks on the way back, okay?"

Dramatically rolling her eyes with her hand over her heart Casey responded, "You have simply saved my good name Kate! I shall be forever in your debt."

Kate's phone rang.

"Ahhh, saved by the bell, eh, Kate? It's okay, I'll go get my own pens and your coffee, princess." With laughter and giggles following her Casey left for the elevator and punched the number for the supply room floor.

Once there she greeted the giant man behind the desk, "Hi Gibson. Got any red pens left?"

"Lose yer pens again, Casey?"

"Yeah, I swear I'm getting worse—this is the third time this week!"

Gibson drew out an empty box from under his desk with bold black writing that said, "CASEY'S PENS".

"We are on the lookout. Just go on back and help yourself, I know I will get them back sooner or later."

Casey laughed. "You are SO bad! Why I awta … " she said it like Popeye as she pummeled him with soft playful punches.

"Hey, I'm off on my break so pull the door closed when you leave, okay?"

"Sure thing buddy." Shaking her head with mirth Casey made her way back to the closet labeled office supplies. Switching on the light she made her way through the shelving and located the pens in question. Picking up a couple of boxes she returned to the door and tried to turn the knob—it was locked!

Again, Casey tried the knob giving the door a jiggle—but to no avail. It wouldn't budge. She hollered for Gibson.

"Well, isn't this just fine and dandy!" she huffed "Stuck in a closet! Gibson should be back in about 15 minutes so I'll just sit tight—everything will be okay." Casey paced back and forth, trying to think positive thoughts and not how this could be in any way related to the break-ins and terrorizing that had been going on.

Just then there was a flash and the light went out.

Nick was finished with his checkup and decided to drop in on Casey and Kate. Maybe they could all go for dinner if the girls weren't going to be working too late. He wouldn't mind hanging around. He entered the office and found Kate but Casey's desk was empty. "Hey Kate, where's Casey?"

Kate frowned, "She went down to the supply room to get some things. Why?" She had told him to leave Casey alone.

"Just thought maybe you girls might want to hit the Hot Tamale on the way home." He held his hands up to ward her off.

"Oh, sounds good. I'm sure she'll want to. She should be back any minute."

"Supply is on the first floor, right? Maybe I'll head down there and surprise her."

"She was going to stop and get coffee on her way back."

"OK, I'll just park my tired body here in this chair and wait." After fifteen minutes passed and there was no sign of Casey Nick started to get antsy.

"Kate, I'm going to see if I can find her."

"Geez Nick, you in heat?" She rolled her eyes.

"No, thank you very much, I just don't like the feel of this. Can a friend worry?"

Nick entered the elevator and pushed the button for the cafeteria. Maybe she had gotten waylaid there. But there was no sign of Casey. He continued down to the supply room. There was no one at the desk. That was strange. That big guy—whatever his name was, was always here.

"Casey?" he called. It was silly, he told himself, but he was more than worried, he was scared. "Casey?" he called again, louder. Listening intently his eyes darted about taking in details. From under the supply closet door he saw a red puddle growing larger. Moving slowly so as not to be surprised he made his way to the supply closet.

"Casey?"

He paled as he pushed past the door and saw the clerk on the floor. Gibson, that was his name! There was blood everywhere but the man was unconscious. "Gibson, stay with me Gibson!" He fell to his knees and tipped the unconscious man's head back to apply CPR. His head fell back like a rag doll and Connery realized his throat was slashed, ear to ear.

He located his cell phone with his free hand and called Bell. Shortly an EMT arrived with security and a policeman. The only sign of Casey were the smashed boxes of red pens on the floor.

TWENTY TWO

After spending precious time on a hopeless search, the hospital notified Detective Flynn Connery regarding the disappearance of Casey Waters. There was no sign of her anywhere in, or around, the hospital.

Nick held Kate through involuntary shivers—her terrors that had been held at bay with the thinnest of threads were threatening to surface. He tried to comfort her—but this was her best friend, his friend, who was missing. *Not Casey, Please God, NOT CASEY!*

Connery appeared and pulled Nick aside to take Kate in his arms. His warm masculine calm and soft words, "Don't worry Kate—she'll be just fine," did nothing to vanquish her demons.

"Go do your job, Flynn. FIND CASEY! I'm okay. Nick and Dirk are here. I want you to find her—YOU HAVE TO FIND HER!" Her voice started in a whisper and ended through clenched teeth as if it helped her to appear in control.

With a squeeze of her fingers Connery went to join the officers searching for Casey.

As Connery checked with the others on the first floor, Bell appeared around a corner with a grim set to his mouth and watery eyes. He couldn't speak.

Connery's questioning gaze was answered by a tilt of Bell's head. He followed his partner to a small hallway and a service elevator which they took into the basement. As they stepped out Bell pointed to blood near the handle of the hospital incinerator. They snapped their gloves on and Bell cautiously opened the large incinerator door for Connery to peer inside. Bell turned away, he could not look. As he did something caught his eye. Behind the incinerator, was the crumpled form of a woman. His woman.

"Casey!"

Quickly, the detectives flew into action! Bell squeezed

through the opening to be closer to her lifeless form. He checked vitals, then shouted up at Connery "She's still with us! SHE'S ALIVE!" Casey was unconscious. Her head was bleeding profusely. Bell pulled his shirt off and held it against the pulsing broken spot where her hair was all matted in a coagulating pool of blood.

Thank you, God. Connery finally released the breath he had been holding. "Bell, get out of there so the doctors can get to work." They were already surrounded and worked together to save Casey as fast as they could.

A group of hospital employees crowded in the hallway. Connery drew the department head aside—and gave him the news.

"We need this area sealed off. It's going to be awhile before we're done. We have a victim here who must be moved."

As the emergency team took over, Bell was asked to step away. The crowd was inching in closer and closer, making it impossible for Bell to step back and the EMTs were too close together to do their job effectively.

That's when Bell lost it and ran at the concerned coworkers. "Back up! Back the FUCK UP! People, give some space! You are all in the way!—Get away! Go away! GO!" He waved his arms frantically at the shocked crowd "MOVE!"

The code red was announced " ... and please remember, our patients' health is our number one goal. Business must resume." The crowd slowly disappeared as Casey was rushed to Emergency on a stretcher. Bell turned his attention to the forensics team. Needing something to do he began helping the officers string the yellow tape across hallways and elevators—declaring for all to see that a crime had been committed here.

Hours of waiting outside the emergency room, turned into what seemed to be years. Nick walked with Connery and Kate to the cafeteria to get a change of scenery and see what light they could shed on the incident. Bell oversaw the long, tedious process of logging the crime scene. They were focusing on the positive, she was alive, poor Gibson, one blow to the head ... Bell would have to go and see Gibson's family. God, how he hated that part!

He knew in his gut this was related to the Coleman's case. The attempt on Casey's life had been foiled due to Gibson and then

Nick's timely entrance—but at what cost? And why Casey? Were they trying to get to Kate?

Connery, Kate, Dirk, and Nick were joined by several of the girls' friends and coworkers. People stopped by for good news and when there was none, they didn't know how to leave. It was becoming awkward. The girls' boss approached Detective Connery.

"Detective, this is too much to comprehend. Casey was such a ray of sunshine. She didn't have a mean bone in her body. Why, and how, could anyone do something like this to such a good person?"

Connery bit his lower lip. He knew she worked in Claims and was sure she heard her share of heartaches. When its someone you know ... he thought he knew the answer but he wasn't ready to discuss it. The perpetrator had been after Nick or Kate. Casey and Gibson had just been in the way. It was a miracle Nick had thought to go looking for Casey. There was no telling what might have happened to her. It seemed to Connery that while Gibson was on his break, he left Casey alone. The killer (*yes, he was ready to call the perpetrator a killer*) was with Casey when Gibson came back. Gibson got killed, but if he hadn't ... then again, something must have stopped the killer at the incinerator. Could it have been Nick looking for Casey?

"Let's get these people back to their jobs so we can do ours."

"Certainly, sir. Everyone! Please return to your work stations." The woman tried to gently herd her employees along—but they stalled in the hallway.

"What happened to Gibson? Is he going to be okay?" several people wanted to know. He was probably very popular, being in charge of the supplies. Connery knew they would get nowhere until these people knew the truth.

"May I have everyone's attention please? I'm Detective Connery. Mr. Gibson suffered a severe head injury and did not make it. We are, at present, trying to determine the circumstances. I would suggest you return to your desks—keep your eyes open for anything suspicious, and keep tabs on each other until we figure out what is going on here."

Amongst disgruntled rumblings and fearful whispers the group began to dissipate.

SOMEWHERE DARK AND HIDDEN THE BEAST LICKED ITS PAWS IN DISAPPOINTMENT.

THE HUNT WAS UNSUCCESSFUL.
IT WAS STILL HUNGRY.

THE HOST STILL UNAWARE.

THE BEAST WAS SPENT.

THE TIME WAS FAST APPROACHING WHEN IT WOULD BE FREE TO HUNT AT ITS LEISURE.

FOR NOW IT COULD AFFORD TO LET THE HOST BELIEVE THAT IT WAS ON ITS OWN, AND IN CONTROL.

TWENTY THREE

Connery studied the police report. A single well-aimed blow to the back of his head had killed Gibson. "Blunt force trauma" read the results. A comment from the CSI read that either someone was "extremely lucky—or very knowledgeable", the blow had been placed where it would do the quickest deadly trauma with the least amount of force. That meant the slashing of his throat was just for fun. Casey suffered the same head wound, "very knowledgeable" was what was sticking with Connery. Luck didn't have much to do with it. He had two victims with the same head trauma, but one was dead and the other was just hanging on.

He glanced at his watch. Connery wanted to catch this bastard more than anything. He wondered how he could protect Kate. There was nothing he could do now for Casey, that was up to the doctors and the "Big Guy" in charge. Yesterday they'd made Kate go home, but today she insisted on staying. She was useless at home, she said, and she wanted to stay close to Casey. She brought her coffee in the morning for when she woke up, checked on her at every break, and read the paper to her at lunch. She felt responsible. She might as well be lying in the bed next to Casey. She couldn't think straight, couldn't concentrate, she didn't even make eye contact anymore. Nick seemed different, too. The reporter was quiet and brooding since the trauma at the hospital. "Bad memories," muttered Connery. The beating Nick had taken didn't alter his spirit, but the terror in his sister's eyes did. The house they had grown up in was the stuff horror movies were made of and they seemed to pull together and withdraw like scared children when faced with a trauma. To have their best friend in the hospital maybe because of something they did, or were related to, was too much for them to handle. They both were disappearing into themselves.

The doctor had explained that Casey was in a coma due to blunt force trauma by one well-place blow to the back of her head. They would not be able to tell what kind of damage she sustained until the swelling of her brain went down.

"After forty eight hours, if the swelling hasn't gone down, the physicians will drill burr holes to release the pressure of the swelling of her brain. The pressure will go down immediately, but the medications will keep her in a coma for a few days until she is weaned off of them. There are many complications but we are hoping for the best."

This was not what anyone wanted to hear. Kate broke down at the news. She expected Casey to wake up any minute and this, this was not in the plan.

Connery picked up the next set of papers. Once more the crime lab had little to work with—no fingerprints, no DNA—and they had yet to locate the murder weapon.

"Let's go back and view the hospital surveillance tapes again Connery," Bell suggested.

Connery eyed Bell speculatively. "Why? What do you think we missed?"

"Missed? We haven't found anything at all yet! How could this happen in a hospital with extra security posted and surveillance cameras everywhere and we can't find anything?" Then Bell froze, "Wait! What if Casey saw the killer? What if she knew the killer? What if we know the killer and we are seeing 'em on the tapes but we don't realize it? We keep thinking Ligria is behind this. What if we're wrong? What if this is a personal vendetta and someone in the hospital is involved? We need to re-check those tapes."

"Hello, dear."

Jason raised his eyes from the report he was reading to see his mother standing in the doorway.

"Hello, Mother. What do you want now?"

Abigail frowned at his tone. Pouting like a little girl, her reply sounded hurt. "I'm sorry to disturb you." She turned to leave. "I should have called I suppose, but sometimes a mother just wants to see her son."

"Mother, come back here, I apologize for my tone, to what do I owe this honor?"

"The committee was just finishing up with the fundraising details from the ball. We finished earlier than expected so I thought, perhaps I could persuade you to have coffee with me."

Jason looked at his report. Ever since his return from Africa he had been banned from surgery. The occasional tremors and fogginess of mind had crippled his surgical career. Not that consultation wasn't a challenging position—but damn it! He had a gift with the knife and he wanted to return to his chosen field!

"Why not. Let's get out of here. I need a break!"

"You've read my mind, dear. How about the little place over on the square? You know the one I mean?"

"Yes. Shall we walk?"

"As you wish, are you all right Jason?"

He read the concern in her eyes. "Yes, Mother, I've just been sitting too long going over this consultation and I need to stretch my legs." He held out his arm, escorting Abigail from the office and heading toward the elevator.

Once out of the hospital and on their way, Abigail began, "Jason, dear, the Governor has sent an invitation to your father for a party he's throwing. He'd like you to come."

"I'm sure the Governor has no interest in me."

"Quite the contrary, dear. He specifically asked if you could join us."

Jason eyed her. "What's this party for?"

"The Governor is putting together a medical panel for one thing or another. You'll have to read the invitation for yourself. I'm simply the messenger today."

Jason thought carefully. The Governor is interested in me for a medical panel? Depending on the circumstances this might be interesting. "All right, I'll stop by to check it out."

"Thank you, dear," Abigail paused before continuing. "If you would like, you could come by for dinner this evening, and bring that lovely lady you escorted to the ball."

Jason watched his mother carefully. Was she up to her matchmaking again? But she showed only a mild interest in his reaction.

"Her name is Zoia, Mother. Do you like her? That would be one for the books!"

Abigail chose her words carefully. "Well, you don't seem to

like any of my choices. I just want you to be happy, dear. She seemed quite cultured—and lovely to look at. If she makes you happy …"

He smiled, his mother almost sounded sincere. So, this was what had brought her to his office! He knew she dreamed of him settling down and producing a new generation of Muellers. Perhaps it would be advantageous to let his mother pin her hopes on Zoia. He smiled to himself. What would she think of her occupation if she knew?

"I'll check with Zoia and see if she is available."

"That would be fine, dear," Abigail smiled, too.

Coffee had been surprisingly pleasant. Without his mother badgering him to meet this lady—or that lady, Jason had found the time enjoyable. He'd try to get hold of Zoia when he returned to the office to see if she was free for dinner. If she would keep his mother at bay perhaps it was time to take the next step. Although, most of the crowd he associated with did not frequent the Top Hat Club, he couldn't take the risk of anyone recognizing Zoia as being employed there. Yes, it was time for her to get out of that club.

"Hello?" The voice on the other end of the phone was sleepy.

"Morning sunshine! Did I wake you?"

"You can wake me anytime, Jason. What time is it?"

"Closing in on one o'clock Zoia."

"So, what's the reason for this call, sir?" Her voice teased him with memories and Jason let himself imagine her hands doing the same with him in bed. The image was delightful.

"Are you working tonight?"

"Hmm—it's Thursday? Not tonight. Why?"

"Are you up to having dinner with my parents?"

"I suppose—what time?"

"Seven. But I'll be by at five."

"See you then." The phone clicked softly.

Jason smiled at the slight irritation he felt at Zoia ending the call. He didn't like not getting the last word. But her soft sleepiness was sexy, as was her devil-may-care attitude. Now the problem would be to wait until five o'clock. He picked up the consultation papers once more—studying them intently. Shortly he began to jot notes in the margins as the words regained his concentration.

The stunned look on Jason's face put Zoia's fears at ease. She had carefully thought out what she would wear to dinner with his parents, and it seemed to have paid off.

He was awed! The sight of Zoia in dark bejeweled jeans was inspiring. Long legs were set off to a tee by the strappy leather heels. Gold toe rings were tastefully displayed—drawing attention to the pale pink toenails. As his eyes worked their way back up, they encountered a delicate gold ankle chain just peeking out from the hem of the jeans, and a delicate matching chain belt draped across her hips. A fine linen shirt of the palest pink adorned her torso. To top it off, she had worn her hair tied loosely with a matching ribbon. Everything about her from her head to her toes screamed 'magnificence'! Jason had never seen anyone look so expensive in jeans and a simple shirt.

"Wow!"

Zoia smiled, "Will I pass?" They both knew the answer. "Come in Jason." She thought she knew what was coming and she wanted Jason to have no regrets. "Sit down. May I get you something to drink?"

"Nothing—thank you." Jason took her hand and pulled her to the couch before continuing. "Zoia, I know we haven't been seeing each other long, but (he had thought this over carefully as to how to get what he wanted) I really hate the idea of you working at the Top Hat." He rushed on, "Not the job itself—but the fact that you have to contend with men who think everything is for sale. The thought of another man's hands on you drives me to distraction! Will you move in with me?"

She smiled playfully before replying. "So, Dr. Mueller, you want me to be a 'kept woman', what will I do for fun?"

Jason was taken aback—he hadn't thought she would take it like that. "I didn't mean that you couldn't work—or become involved with something. I just really want you out of the Top Hat."

"Jason, let's be honest, okay? You also don't want anyone you know to see me working there, right? It would be embarrassing. So, if I agree to give up the Top Hat what do you think I should do? I won't be reliant on you for my income."

"I'm sure we can come up with something we both would find

acceptable. I have connections—even outside the family. I'm sure we can find you a position you would enjoy with pay probably better than you earn at the club. Let's say you move in with me and I will help you find something to do. Would that work?"

Zoia could see that he was serious. To refuse she would risk offending him, or worse, making him walk out of her life. Jason Mueller got what he wanted! But so did she! "I'd like to think about it Jason." She'd be an absolute fool to pass up the opportunity and she knew it, but she wasn't about to loose her big fish to something that might be temporary.

"How about you let me know before we get to my parent's?"

"What? Kinda short notice, don't you think?" Zoia teased.

"Alright. Take some time, but not much, the sooner you get out of that club, the better."

"Shall we get going? You're going to want to stop at the condo first, right?"

"What for?"

"I just assumed you would want to change before going."

"I did change," Jason replied.

Zoia decided she might mention it now, since he was trying to change her, "Jason, you need to learn to relax. Change into something more comfortable and let the world pass you by for a change. It can really be quite fun!" She gave him her best smile. "Why don't you try it?"

He wanted her and if this would help get her to move in—he could play the game. "Alright."

She gathered her jacket and purse before they made their way to his car. "Jason, do you even own a pair of jeans?"

His silence answered her question.

"Come on—you're going shopping!" There was no holding her back. She directed him to a posh, upscale shop where she cajoled him into trying on jeans until he found a pair that suited him. Next, was a fine Indian raw silk shirt of the softest green and her enthusiasm soon infected Jason. He drew the line at his shoes and Zoia, laughing, let him be. "I love to shop here—it's pricey so I don't come often, but everything is so unique and finely made that it lasts forever and I look like …"

"A million dollars?!" Jason interrupted.

"Yes, now let's get you showered and dressed for the big night with Mama," she said in her sexy Greek accent. A quick hug and she was on her way to the cash register with Jason in tow.

He found his shoulders relaxing as her cheery mood engulfed him. At the register he noticed a handbag like the one she carried. His eyes widened at the tag. She did have a taste for the expensive! He realized that Zoia might have fine things she had obviously needed to save to get them. The girl had control—and was money savvy. His admiration for her grew.

At the condo Zoia passed through the rooms, studying them and the man who lived there. The only objects decorating his office walls were awards and commendations. But that kind of stuff belonged here. There was one family photo with Jason and Kate and his parents taken at some ceremony. She resisted the urge to destroy it. He may resent her moving too quickly if she already started to change things. She must read him carefully before her next step. When Jason rejoined her she was staring out the large window overlooking the bay. She turned to find him standing uncomfortably in his new clothes. She smiled, giving him a once over that no man could misinterpret. He relaxed.

"You look good enough to eat—and I might just have to." She leaned close and nibbled on his ear, trailing down to his neck bone with her tongue and she took a little bite.

Jason's blood thickened "Enough of that woman, we cannot be late to my mother's," he growled.

"Really, Jason, you do look yummy." She licked her lips.

Suddenly she looked serious. "I've decided I'll move into the condo with you if you really want me to." Before he answered she held up her hand. "Hear me out first, Jason. I'd like to bring some of my things to your condo—so it feels like my home, too. AND you're going to have to go shopping with me and on walks. Can you do that?"

"That doesn't seem like too much to ask."

"Okay, when do you want me?"

"Right now! But what about your job."

"Okay. If we leave now we can stop on the way to dinner and take care of that. How's that for commitment under pressure?"

He nodded his approval.

Zoia sat quietly in the passenger seat, eyes shut. Jason glanced at her from time to time. The Top Hat owner hadn't been happy or pleasant. She stood up to him and held firm to get her last paycheck on the spot. Jason wanted to haul her out of there and then return to punch the man out. Zoia made him promise before they went in to let her handle it. Now she seemed to have withdrawn from the world.

"Zoia, are you alright? We'll be there soon."

Her eyes opened. "I'm fine—just trading skins."

At Jason's puzzled look she explained.

"My father always used that phrase. When he had to do some unpleasant task he would sit quietly when finished and trade skins into something more pleasant. I always found it comforting to think of him as changing from a tiger to a kitten."

Jason tried the mental image. He could definitely see Zoia as the tiger in the club—but a kitten? Never! She was more like a sleek jungle cat that only answered on her own terms.

"A panther."

"What?"

"A panther—I can't see you as a kitten. You're more like a sleek jungle cat, a black panther."

She smiled at his analogy. If Jason was comparing her to a panther, he had some insight into her personality already. She would come at his beck and call—but only on her own terms.

After parking in the circle drive, Jason came around to open her door and escorted her up the steps and into the main hall.

His mother came out of the parlor. "Jason, I'm so glad you're here! Zoia, welcome to our home."

"Thank you, Mrs. Mueller."

Abigail noticed the change in Jason. *She had never seen her son in jeans! This must be Zoia's doing. Although I have to admit—he does look relaxed. Could clothes do that to a man—or was it the woman?*

"Well, come this way. I have cocktails set up on the patio. Jason, your father is in his study. Would you ask him to join us?"

"Zoia, what would you like?"

"A glass of red wine would be nice."

Abigail watched Jason leave and then returned to Zoia. "Here dear, would you care for a tour of the gardens?"

The two women made their way into the brightly-hued flowers scattered about the grassy lawn. By the time the men arrived they had made their way back to the patio. Abigail was dying to find out if Jason was going to accept the Governor's invitation, but she resolutely kept her impatience to herself—all in good time.

They progressed through dinner and when Jason and Zoia rose to leave Abigail graciously ushered them to the door. "It was very nice to see you again, Zoia. Jason, please bring her back again."

"Thank you, Mother."

"Abigail, the meal was very nice. Thank you for inviting me."

As the two made their way to the car Abigail closed the door firmly and floated back to her husband.

"And?"

"He's coming to the party. Do you know that girl from somewhere?"

"Well, Jason brought her to the ball—don't you remember?"

"Of course, I do Abigail. I just wondered where we knew her from."

"We don't dear. Jason found her all on his own." Abigail trailed off onto another subject but her husband was far away, trying to recall why his son's girlfriend looked so familiar.

The car ride back toward the city was quiet. "I hope my mother didn't badger you too much."

"Not at all Jason. She was very pleasant."

Jason found that highly unlikely, but as Zoia had proven at the ball, she could handle his mother.

"I've been invited to attend a party at the Governor's mansion in three weeks. Will you come with me?"

"Of course I will, if you truly want me to. We might have to go shopping again!" Zoia smiled at him and he returned her smile as the blood in his veins heated—matching the fire in her eyes.

TWENTY FOUR

With the lead Donovan had given them, Bell and Connery were on their way to question the man who had sold the electronic equipment involved with the "bugging" at the hospital. It seemed like backtracking, but everything leads somewhere. Since the audio was looped into the system, the supplier was their only hope. The technology had originally been "Army issue", but had fast been absorbed by the private techno industry. The detectives hoped to get a lead that would connect the technology to the man behind the action.

The Camaro pulled to a stop before the store front. Bell noted the high-tech cameras as Connery scanned the sidewalk and streets. Inside, the store was dimly lit—as if to keep its secrets from the world. Connery headed toward the bulky man behind the counter. He flashed his badge.

"Understand you sold some pretty high-end equipment lately. Some audio equipment—small, lightweight, relays into a laptop."

"Sure. I remember the stuff. It was a new customer, though. Never seen him before—or since. Paid in large bills and packed it in a gray duffel—then left in a black SUV."

"Can you describe him?"

The man scratched his head. "Mmmm—six foot, light-brown hair, gray eyes. He wore jeans and a black jacket. Didn't get the license—didn't think I'd need it. Thought he was a professional."

"Why do you say that?"

"He knew exactly what he wanted, and he didn't waste any time. Might have been a local—but I'm not sure."

"Hey, you're pretty good at this!"

The storekeeper grinned. "Semper fi. Marine Sergeant for

twenty years. Old habits die hard, Detective."

Figuring they had all they would get the detectives made their way out of the store. As they exited the store a bright glint was the only warning given. The sharp report of a high-powered rifle was heard as a bullet smacked into the brick building missing Connery's head. Bell was already running for the Camaro, gun drawn. The ping of metal on metal had him cursing as a bullet ricocheted off his chrome bumper.

"High noon across the street," Bell hollered to Connery.

Connery nodded as he rapidly fired his Beretta in that direction. Bell shimmied through the open window to reach the radio and call for backup.

Another shot—then silence. Connery tentatively raised his gun, then his head for another look. When there was no answering shot the two men raced across the street and into the building where the shots had come from, making their way up to the roof. The only sign of the sniper was the brass shell casings littering the roof. Bell carefully gathered up the brass—slipping them into an envelope.

Back at the car they radioed headquarters calling off the wild rush for backup. They were informed a team was en route and would cover the area.

"We must be on to something!" Connery stated.

"Yeah, and this is all really getting on my nerves. Damn!" Bell swore as he took stock of his bumper. "That's going to take at least one paycheck."

"Sorry partner—but better the bumper than us."

"Got that right. With us incapacitated, who'd watch our girls?"

"Our girls?" Connery was confused.

"What's that mean? You quit seeing Kate?"

"No, I didn't realize you and Casey were really, uh, for sure ... and I haven't seen Kate alone since Casey ..."

"You're right, I haven't had a chance to actually tell Casey how I feel, but I will as soon as she comes back to me. And don't worry about Kate, she has been uptight about Casey lately. Doesn't like to leave her. I feel the same but work keeps me busy, my God, if I had to go to that hospital every day for work like Kate does it would kill me every minute. I would be right where Kate is—in that chair next to Casey. I really miss her Connery. I didn't realize it, but I am addicted to Casey Waters. She has to pull through this 'cause I don't know what I'll do if she doesn't."

"Don't worry partner, this is almost over." Connery believed what he said, he had to, and he was going to make sure it was true.

Kate had bitten off all of her fingernails and was working on the skin around them when the doctor came through the double doors. It seemed he walked in slow motion straight to her. They had paged Kate and Casey's parents. Kate was the first to arrive. She held her breath. She couldn't believe he was out here already. Was that good? That couldn't be good ... maybe Casey's all better now, maybe she can go home. Kate could take her home today, they'd play hooky tomorrow and spend the whole day on the couch ...

"Miss Coleman?"

Kate's eyes refocused on the doctor.

"We did all that we can to relieve the pressure on your friend's brain. Now we'll have to take it day by day to see how much swelling her brain has sustained before we can tell how much permanent damage there is."

"Will she be okay?" Kate wasn't listening, it wasn't good news. She wouldn't listen to anything but good news.

"The pressure has gone down. But the medications keeping her stable now will also help keep her in a coma while her body tries to repair itself. She'll still be in this state for a few days. Miss Coleman, the human body is in a constant state of repair. We can count on that. We will not know if her quality of life will ever be the same, she may loose her short-term memory, she may loose her speech. We do not know how much of her motor skills she will regain. She has a long road to recovery. You must prepare yourself and her family. We will start to wean her off the medication during the next few days. Then perhaps, we will have a better idea of what kind of therapy will help her regain what she is capable of."

Kate's head spun. This was not happening. She understood that they had to drill into Casey's head, and she numbly accepted that. She thought with the pressure back to normal, Casey would be, too. It seemed there should be something they could do to speed up all this waiting. How could they work on another patient until they fixed her friend? How could they go home, to their families night after night, and not finish what they started? Casey couldn't go home. Why weren't they doing more?

With nothing more to say the doctor squeezed her hand and walked away.

That's it? Wait and see? They had kicked Kate out of the hospital every night; "Go home, Kate, there is nothing you can do. Get some sleep and pray for your friend."

Sleep, yeah right, sleep. Kate was unable to sleep. She'd lay awake worrying and reliving her last few minutes, then days, then life with Casey since the first time they met. Which brought her back to grade school, and then home to her parents, then the nightmares started all over again, reliving the horrible childhood she knew all to well. Nick would stop their father from sneaking into Kate's room for "a visit". He was so drunk he didn't know what room he was in. At least that's what he said. Then he'd get so mad when she refused his petting. So mad. It was her fault, he said. He'd attack Kate for even looking at him the wrong way but Nick would stop him. Nick would stop him every time. And then he would start on Nick. All she could do was watch as Nick took the beatings while yelling at Kate to stay back, or run and hide. Back into the corner of the dark closet, way back where her father couldn't reach her. Where she could barely hear Nick begging for him to stop. Just like she begged him to stop. "Please, no. Please stop!" She'd hold her ears to block out his cries, plug them till they bled. And she'd pray for it to end and she'd wait, wait for a miracle, wait for Jesus to come and save them and take them to a gentle world where everything was white. But it would be Nick who came to get her, usually the next morning, after he was all cleaned up. Then they wouldn't talk about it. If she tried he would stop her with a game of distraction. They would become the strongest most ferocious thing they could think of (usually the same thing). They would take on the bravest hearts of the King and Queen of the jungle. They would rip their predators to shreds and they would take turns saving each other from the feared hunter. It wasn't just pretend to them. They were lions!

But why wouldn't Jesus save them? How could Jesus love them and leave them there with this awful man? If there was a God how could he allow this man to prosper and his children to suffer?

No, prayer never helped them then, why would it help her now?

Casey came to. Her eyes were heavy and dry, she moved her hand to rub them. Nothing. She couldn't move. How long was she asleep? She was sore and stiff. *Her eyelids were so heavy they wouldn't open. She tried to move her arm again. Nothing. She felt her heart quicken, something was wrong. Her legs, she didn't feel her legs. She didn't feel anything. Again, she tried to open her eyes. Nothing. She tried to scream, nothing. She had to get up, where was she? She couldn't move her head. She knew she could figure out where she was if she could open her eyes. Something felt familiar but she couldn't carry the thought through to the answer. Everything was in pieces. Why can't I move?* Suddenly a jagged pain cut through her head.

Her mind raced back to the last thing she could remember. *The Hot Tamale, Bell, Kate, Nick, and Connery. Dinner, home, sleep, then work. Driving in with Kate, stopping for coffee, at her desk in the hospital. Okay, now, what? Pens? Oh yes, I didn't have any red pens again. Kate offered, but I like to visit Gibson, he always laughed at my jokes. I went down to supply, saw Gibson, then he was gone. I was alone in the dark ... in the dark? Alone? What, why? And then nothing. Nothing? How can my memory just stop? Back up again, elevator, Gibson, pens ... nothing.* She was tired, she was so tired. Maybe later she would try again and there would be more. Her head hurt. Now she must sleep. It was all she could do. She was so tired.

THE BEAST WATCHED ITS PREY CLOSELY.

IT IS NOT OVER.

WHEN WE ARE ALONE AGAIN I WILL TAKE
CARE OF YOU.

I AM IN CONTROL.

ONCE YOU UNDERSTAND THAT,
WE CAN WORK TOGETHER.

YOU NEED ME!

TWENTY FIVE

Zoia carefully smoothed the garment bag over the gown Jason had purchased for her to wear to the Governor's ball. Once again she gave herself a mental pat on the back for snagging this man. His wallet seemed to have no limits and he wasn't opposed to spending it on nice things. She was a little surprised with his choice of gowns. It was very stylish. A deep, dark purple—almost black, with a fine lace netting covering the gown. Very fitted through the bodice and torso, the skirt flared out with stitched insets extending to several inches above her knees. She loved it! The filigree necklace and earrings she had worn to the hospital ball were an elegant addition. Yet, he insisted she be seen in something new. Even the tiniest detail in accessories had been part of the purchase—from handbag to shoes to a fine silver anklet, he had insisted she have it all.

Once more she ran her hand down the dress bag before turning to Jason's tuxedo. With a little flirting she had managed to modernize his formal wear. He still sported the formal white shirt, but she had talked him into dark purple studs. Zoia wondered what Abigail would think. Carefully she packed everything and laid the garment bags on the bed. Then, on second thought, she moved them to a chair—they may need the bed. When Jason arrived home from the hospital she would be ready for anything.

They were traveling to Sacramento for the weekend in the family limo with his parents. Jason had to insure the garments would arrive in pristine condition and since his African trip he really didn't like flying, traveling with his parents was a high price to pay. Zoia frowned when she thought of Africa. The last couple of days Jason had seemed … occupied and jumpy. Almost as if he thought someone was following him. Hopefully he would shake that feeling this weekend. She would have to make sure she brought the flask.

Carefully she placed the file with her latest job on the entry table. Once again her gift for languages had seen to her future. An acquaintance had recommended her to the university to translate some documents they had acquired for the history department. It was something she could work on during the drive to Sacramento—she wanted Jason's parents to see she was successful. 'A woman with an income was always looked upon with more favor than a kept woman', her father always said. Everything in her life was actually falling into place. A doctor, a beautiful home, and a career. Still, she was waiting for the other proverbial shoe to drop.

Hearing the click of the latch Zoia turned to see Jason entering. He looked haunted. What was going on with him? She knew he hated questions so she went to him with a smile—taking his coat to hang it up for him. And turning to fetch him a glass of wine.

"I'm glad you're home Jason. My first day in our home was so lonely."

Unfocused eyes blinked. "I need to pack."

"I've taken care of most of that for you. We've time before we leave, why don't you relax?" She tried to get him to sit down.

Finally his eyes latched onto her. "Well, then …" he grabbed her roughly, pulling her close.

She didn't resist. She liked him when he got this way. Slipping her hands inside his shirt she nibbled on his ear whispering, "The shower?"

He picked her up, she wrapped her legs around him. His mouth found hers and as they consumed each other she urgently worked off his tie and unbuttoned his shirt as he carried her down the long hallway and threw her on the bed.

A call from Abigail saying they were just pulling up to the condo had them hurrying to finish. Zoia laughed as she pulled on the blouse he had just ripped off her.

He turned, looking for his pants and she threw him a pair of jeans. He frowned and then, with a shrug, slipped them on.

She braided her long hair with cool efficiency. He stopped to admire her deft fingers moving rapidly through the silken strands. In seconds both were ready.

The ringing of the doorbell announced the arrival of the chauffeur to transfer their luggage to the limo. Zoia grabbed her file on the way out. Jason pulled the door shut softly—all thoughts of Africa were safely back in their sealed room in the corner of his mind.

Abigail frowned as the two young people entered the limo. Mouth tightly pressed closed to keep herself from commenting on their choice of traveling attire, she launched into the itinerary as soon as the door was closed.

"Tomorrow morning you boys have golf at eight, I expect that will be all day, then after drinks with the Rossmans at six we'll be off to dinner at eight with several of the senators. Then the ball, Saturday night!" Abigail ended in a sing-song voice.

Zoia could feel the tension mounting in Jason and she wondered how Abigail would react to her very own methods of tension relief. She slipped her hand into Jason's and slowly stroked his palm. Scooting closer, she circled Jason with her arm—Abigail's scowl came to focus on her.

"I don't think that's going to work for us, Abigail. Jason what do you think?"

He glanced at his mother's puckered face and realized that Zoia was willing to take his mother on and give him a way out from her constant need to manage his time and career.

"We'll meet you at the dinner at eight, Mother. Zoia and I have other plans for this afternoon. I'm sure the Rossmans will never miss us, as they are your friends, Mother, not mine."

Abigail was not happy. How dare they! But she could tell that now was not the time to begin a debate. As usual her husband, William, was absorbed in his journals. *No help there!* She sat back with a sigh.

"Very well, Jason. It is your future we are talking about."

"Yes it is Mother. Would you be so kind as to ask next time, since it is my life you are meddling in?"

Promptly at eight that evening Jason and Zoia entered the country club doors, ushered in by the maitre d'. Several senators were crowded around Mr. William Mueller listening intently to his words. While the man had little to say in his wife's ambitious presence, he was, by all standards, a brilliant lawyer. Even a congressman was listening intently to his opinion on the latest bills and other legislative agendas. Jason spied his mother off with the senators' wives. Zoia could, by any standards, hold her own. The woman by his side was stunning in the demur, yet flattering, red silk form-fitting dress. Dropping just below her knees her legs were displayed to full advantage. The only woman who had ever looked nearly as good as Kate. But Kate would never battle his mother. There was a bit of a viper in Zoia and he loved it!

They moved toward the couples congregating by the bar. As Jason introduced her he watched both mens' and womens' heads turned Zoia's way. When one brazen young stud asked what career she followed, her reply, "I'm a translator," took many by surprise. When the same young man asked who she translated for, Zoia's, "Ahh, if I told you that I'd have to kill you," reply brought laughter and amusement among the group. Suddenly, things were looking up for Jason. Everyone assumed she worked in some high-level government capacity and Jason wouldn't do anything to dissuade them.

As they made their way around the room Jason took stock of the powerful people present.

"Jason, is this really what you want or is your mother driving you into this?"

Zoia's quiet question annoyed him. "Why do you ask that?"

"I always assumed you loved being a surgeon."

"I do, but the hospital isn't cooperating since I got back and I won't be a consultant."

"Whatever makes you happy—as long as it's your idea." She dropped the subject when she noticed his scowl. "I suppose I should go say 'hello' to your mother. You don't have to come. I can handle myself just fine." Jason's scowl deepened. She caressed his shoulder in a calming gesture.

He followed her hand with his eyes. Kate had never been so caring in public. Zoia didn't seem to care who saw the small gestures. Now that he had the attention, Jason wasn't sure he liked it.

"Come rescue me before we go in for dinner," Zoia whispered as she headed off toward his mother's group. As she joined them she greeted Abigail. "Good evening Mrs. Mueller."

"Ms. Zartoni. Ladies, this is Jason's new friend Zoia Zartoni."

One nosy old biddy (Zoia had taken an instant dislike to from across the room) began to grill her. There would be no help from Abigail as she was still put out from the incident in the limo. Zoia put on her aloof, regal, Greek pose she learned from her mother and evaded the woman's probing questions like a pro.

Even through her disgruntlement, Abigail had to tip her hat to Zoia's artful dodge in the quest for personal information. The girl was good.

"I'm a translator, madam. At the moment I am not at liberty to reveal who my employer is. I speak over seven languages fluently and can read even more. How about you?"

Abigail could not help the chuckle that escaped her lips. She'd never seen Mrs. Johnson's claws so easily clipped. "Alright ladies, that's enough. Let's admit Zoia can hold her own and that's saying a lot with this group."

Others joined in the laughter, even Mrs. Johnson, and they moved on to other subjects.

Dinner with the senators seemed to have gone well. They had a better understanding of what was in store for them tomorrow at the Governor's ball. Jason sat relaxed in the hotel suite watching Zoia comb through her luxurious hair. He never tired of that hair! As he watched her the walls began to fade. He blinked, watching in denial as the tasteful wallpaper began to run together and merge into the grasses and brilliant sun of the African plains. No matter how hard he blinked—the scene would not fade. Tremors began to work their way through his body. Concentrating on Zoia's black strands, he tried to shake the feeling of dread that overcame him.

Zoia turned at his silence. The unfocused eyes were back and he was shaking uncontrollably. The look of horror on his face mobilized her into action. Her sudden movement made his eyes dart about the room as if looking for some unseen foe. She slowed, moving as if in slow motion she crawled off the bed and made her way to his side, her arms held out to him. His hands suddenly seized her hair, wrapping it around and around his fists. She called out his name but it did not register and Zoia turned to the only other power she had over him. Carefully she teased him with soft licks and bites until his fists softened in her hair. Slowly, the man returned to the temptation in front of him. She led him down the path of redemption, all the while promising herself she would find the answer to her questions—and soon. For one day she feared he would not return before violence first made its mark.

TWENTY SIX

"Hey Connery! Call on line 3!"

Connery punched the line. "Detective Connery."

"It's Nick—you better get over here."

"What happened? Is Kate all right?"

"Oh yeah, don't rush. Something interesting just showed up on my computer. Thought you'd better see it."

"We're on our way. Let's go Bell. We have another computer glitch at the Coleman's."

Both men grabbed their jackets before making their way to the car. At the estate a PRIME Security guard waved them through before Bell had even slowed down. Nick met them at the door.

"I got an interesting e-mail this morning. Take a look for yourself." Nick motioned toward the laptop sitting on the coffee table in the living room. As they approached Connery braced himself for what he was sure would be gruesome.

On the screen there was an opening to a cave. Then as the camera went into it, a faint light began to appear. The light revealed terrified people hiding in a corner of the cave. Ghostly white faces registering sheer terror. Then, a fast-moving blur fastened into one person's back and dragged them kicking and screaming into the darkness. Then, you could hear the crunching of bones before the screen went black and silent except for a few sporadic whimpers which were probably muffled screams. A roar erupted from the screen just when you thought it was over. Then it began all over again.

"God! What the hell was that?!" Connery grimaced.

"It doesn't stop there, the e-mail was sent from my editor's computer. Kind of makes your skin crawl, doesn't it? I thought your department had his computer since he was killed."

"We do," Connery snapped open his cell phone and dialed up

the lab. "This is Connery, do you have the computer from *The Times* editor? Yeah? Maybe you can tell me how Nick Coleman just got an e-mail from that computer? Good, do that!" He snapped the phone shut. "They're checking into it."

"It's not that difficult Connery," Bell interjected. "You can send time-released e-mails. Whoever is behind the e-mails probably set this up prior to the editor's murder."

"Well, that sure helps! Shit, what next? This guy could be sending this stuff from anywhere in the world and at any time."

Bell shrugged. One thing was certain—this perpetrator was computer savvy. They might be chasing their tails for months.

"I booted up the computer to check my e-mail," Nick continued. "I thought I might have something from one of my sources by now. I suppose you guys are going to want my computer?"

"Right now I think you're better off using it to help us gather information. We have your editor's computer to trace back to and hopefully we'll learn something on that end, that is if 'its not that difficult', like Bell says." Connery did not like looking stupid.

"Then I'll log in and see if anything came through from my contacts." Nick peered intently at the screen as he scanned through the list of messages waiting for him. "Bingo! I've got something from one of the street kids in Russia. I'll have to decode it first—you guys got time?"

Nick worked patiently while Connery paced and Bell gazed out the window. The geese were strolling along the property fence checking out the nooks and crannies for grubs and bugs. Bell chuckled to himself—remembering the story of Casey trying to train the two fowl to 'love her car'.

"Okay, I've got something. Says to go to the docks and look for the fishing boat *Angel Lace*. You're looking for one of the workers named Meko. Tell him that Halo sends best wishes. He'll get back to you." Nick looked up from the computer. "Looks like we're going for a ride."

"You're staying here Nick." Connery was adamant.

"And what makes you think that Meko will talk to a cop? He's going to be expecting a reporter—namely me. Besides, it's my contacts' lives on the line here! They've all been very loyal to me and that means something. You might not understand that—but I'm responsible for bringing them to Ligria's attention. I'm not going to put them in any more danger than I already have. You guys can watch from the car."

"It's too dangerous. You've barely recovered from the last hit."

Nick looked at the two cops intently. "This is my family they're trying to kill, and if you think for one moment I'm going to let you blow the only lead we have—you have thought wrong!"

Bell gazed at Nick keenly, "We can have Dirk cover the dock. We'll plan it for tomorrow when people are out and about, so we won't be so obvious. That gives us this afternoon to find the boat's berth and figure out her schedule."

"Okay," Connery glared at Nick, "but if you get hurt I'm going to kill you myself and save them the trouble! Got it?"

"Loud and clear, boss!" Nick kidded light heartedly, "and you get to explain it to the girls." Nick stopped, thinking he shouldn't have mentioned "the girls" in front of Bell.

Connery closed his eyes as he looked up. He was trying really hard not to mention Casey in front of Bell. *Geez! Why did he always get stuck with idiots?*

Nick wasn't really into worrying about Bell's feelings. He was waiting to tell Casey how he felt about her. The latest news they'd gotten from Kate on Casey wasn't so good. Nick knew she would be okay. It didn't make sense to loose her. He was sure she would come back to him. He just wasn't sure about how Bell felt. Right now, though, he knew he had to do something to stop the madness. He had to give them all he had and he would be the next one to put his life on the line if it meant protecting Kate and Casey.

The morning fog was still clinging to the board planks when Nick made his way down the dock watching for the *Angel Lace*. According to the harbor master she was still docked today for repairs on her radio. The crew should be somewhere close by. Dirk was casting his line off the pier to the left, not near enough to cause suspicion, but close enough if there was trouble. He could see Bell's blue Camaro parked at the hot dog stand. Dressed in his leather jacket, jeans and a T-shirt, Bell, (a.k.a. James Dean) was surrounded by motorheads looking under his hood. Connery lounged on a bench behind a paper, hot dog in hand. *Could they be more obvious?* Nick thought this was right out of a bad cop show. Now, to find Meko.

The *Angel Lace* was three berths down. Several of the crew were repairing nets while two were working on the radio. Nick hailed one of the crew members, "Permission to come aboard?"

"What you want drylander?" The voice was gruff and unfriendly. Nick looked at the guy. If you looked up "Russian" in the dictionary, you'd find this guy's picture.

"I've got a message for Meko."

"How you know Meko?"

"Nick Coleman. I'm a reporter and I've just returned from Russia. I was asked to deliver a message to Meko. Is he around?"

"Coleman. Big time reporter who busts bad guys. No bad guys here!"

The other crew members laughed. Nick stood his ground, waiting silently. He'd been in this situation before. Men like these couldn't be rushed. They'd answer his questions when they were good and ready.

"You gonna hang around all day Mr. Reporter?"

"Let me keep this simple so you can understand. I can stand here all day. I find big story hanging around. Like maybe, 'Russian Hit-Man Sneaks into the Country on a Fishing Boat,' or maybe 'Slavery Ring Discovered in San Francisco Bay by Reporter Hanging Around', get the idea?"

The man eyed him warily. "Meko!"

Then from below, "Ya?"

"Some guy here got message for you!"

Nick watched as a greasy head appeared from below the deck. The body attached to it was covered with oil and grime. He was probably the engine man.

"You? What you want?"

The man wiped his hands on a rag pulled from his pocket, then strode over to Nick.

"You got message for me?"

"From Halo, how about I buy you a cup of coffee?"

Meko eyed the burly firstmate, "I be back."

The two men strode up the dock and quickly Nick relayed the coded message from his contact. At the stand the two ordered coffee and dogs while information was exchanged.

"Thanks Coleman. Nice to know my nephew is alive. You see him?"

"Yes, I did. He has made himself a place in the information exchange. He delivers messages and is constantly moving so he is rarely in any danger. He gets a hot meal a day and a dry place to sleep."

Meko nodded. "Thank you for message."

"You're welcome. Your nephew was an excellent guide while I was there. I am glad I could return this small favor for him." Deciding that Meko could be trusted, Nick took the plunge. "If I wanted to get someone out of Russia quick-like, and quiet, could that be done?"

Meko eyed him warily. "What you have in mind?"

"I think one of my contacts might be under the glass—I need to get a warning out and get them out of Russia. Any ideas?"

"I can ask around. Maybe I'll have something for you tomorrow."

Nick watched as the man strode back toward his boat. Dirk was already at the SUV when Nick got there. Nick sat in the seat, leaning back, he closed his eyes. A mental picture of laughing eyes and sweet, pouty lips flashed across his mind. He resolved to check with Meko soon. Nothing must happen to his contact. The SUV pulled into traffic and headed back to the estate. The Camaro not far behind.

TWENTY SEVEN

Abigail stood with her mouth open watching as her son escorted Zoia into the ballroom at the governor's mansion. As much as it pained her to say it, the girl could leave her speechless. Her earlier aggravation at the pair evaporated like steam as she pondered the transformation of them. From jeans to satin! They were incredible even if she said so herself.

Zoia's deep-purple (almost black) gown sparkled ever so slightly in the light of the chandeliers. Ending just above her ankles with strappy silver heels the girl's legs seemed to never end. The intricate braid in her hair ended at the base of her neck, leaving the dark, silky hair to envelope her as if she wore a shawl. Every minute detail had been seen to! And Jason! My God, the girl must have had something to do with his choice of apparel, Abigail had never seen him in anything so breathtaking!

He wore a white silk shirt, tailored coat, and pants of a deep purple, almost black like Zoia's dress, obviously designed together just for them. It boasted a new stand-up-type collar that called for the narrow string of a formal tie. *The effect was powerful! My, what a pair they would make at the state capitol!* Heads were turning and the whispers were making her insides bubble with glee! As much as Zoia could twist her tail, the girl certainly knew how and when to shine. Now, if Jason would just hang on to her. Abigail knew he still fancied Kate. Why, she couldn't understand for there was no doubt in her mind that the people in attendance tonight would have eaten Kate Coleman for breakfast! Zoia would be eating them! Yes, this one had definite possibilities. And, she was driven, too. Not a bad combination if she could be cajoled to do things Abigail's way.

Abigail knew Jason never had aspirations for politics. Medicine had always been the drive in his life. Africa had changed that. The hospital would never allow him to operate again. With the possibility of a reoccurrence of the dementia from the sleeping sickness, the board would never take a chance that something might happen to cause a lawsuit against them. She believed Jason knew this. If he could come to terms with this new direction, he could be a powerful force. The family had the money and the connections to fuel a campaign if the candidate would run. She had always wanted to live in the capitol city, but William would not leave his law practice and no amount of enticement would drive him in this direction. Jason, however, was easier to manipulate—if she was careful.

She watched from across the room. Carefully noting who was curing favor with Jason and his sultry companion. Most were not of interest—but some she would take note to talk with later. She had tickled Jason's interest in coming because of the medical bills that were due to come up in the legislature, shortly. Many in the capitol knew of his recent foray to Africa, and his prowess in the operating room. Coupled with William's magic touch in the law business they were garnering interest in the room tonight for their expert knowledge. Mitchell, the representative from their district, was not running again. She had already peaked his interest in Jason. If things went well tonight, Mr. Mitchell would broach the subject of Jason running for his seat in November. With Mitchell's endorsement, Jason's chances of winning were astounding! If he would run. Again the big "IF". Abigail dare not push her son any further in that direction, lest he revolt. But Zoia might be able to give him a nudge—if the girl would cooperate.

Zoia parried questions and advances from the other males clustered around Jason, leaving no doubt in any man's mind where her affections lie. Jason had to admire her tact, for she managed to toss out rejection without hurting political feelings. She grew quiet when an elder statesman advanced on their group, turning her attention to him causing everyone else to do the same.

"Representative Mitchell, it is an honor to meet you, sir." Her voice glided over them like silken water. Mitchell smiled warmly.

"I don't know who you are, dear lady, but if Jason ever frees you—you must simply let me know."

Zoia smiled before replying, "You are very kind Representative Mitchell, but it is common knowledge that you are totally devoted to Mrs. Mitchell."

"Jason, you've landed one that is smart and beautiful. You are either very lucky, or in all kinds of trouble!"

Just then the call was made that they should be seated. The meal went smoothly. Jason relaxed in the presence of Mitchell, with Zoia at his side. Later in the evening as they were strolling along the causeway he paused. Zoia gazed at him questionably.

"Jason?"

"Did you hear that?"

"What?"

"Can't you hear the lion roaring?" He cast his eyes about the room frantically.

Zoia wasn't sure what was going on, however, the political sharks didn't need to see this. She quickly caught the eye of a passing waiter.

"Please find Mrs. Abigail Mueller and direct her to come here with all speed. Thank you." She subtly slipped him a fifty from her bag.

It wasn't long before Abigail arrived. Zoia motioned her over to the corner where she had steered Jason. The glassy stare and sweating brow was all the information Abigail needed.

"We have to get him out of here."

"How?"

"There is a back entrance off to your left. Follow the brick floor. I'll meet you out back with the limo."

Gently Zoia steered Jason along the hallway.

"What is going on?"

"Here Jason, this way."

"Do you hear the lion?"

"Follow me Jason, you'll be safe. Just come with me."

At the back entrance the limo was waiting. Zoia crawled in after Jason.

"I'll make your excuses. Shall we say that he was called to the hospital?"

"Fine, Abigail. But we still have to talk." Zoia gave her a steely look, and the older woman nodded in agreement.

"Lions! The lions are coming!" Jason muttered from the safety of the limo.

THE DARKNESS WITHIN

Connery flipped through the forensics file lying on his desk, noting the identification of the fingerprints and the DNA samples from the hospital murder. The team had dusted every doorknob and surface—but to date nothing was showing a clear path to the culprit. Prints lifted from the area included an uncountable number of hospital employees including Nick's and Kate's. Nothing that he didn't expect since they had all been searching for Casey. The coroner had yet to finish with Gibson's body. Hopefully there would be something when he was finished. Connery went over his notes again. Each incident was categorized not only by itself, but included in common items of interest. If all the recent incidents were related it was someone who had common knowledge not only of the hospital, but of the Coleman residence as well.

"Connery, we've got a lead! One of our local law enforcers has gone missing. The warrant for his bank account and apartment will be waiting at the courthouse."

Gathering the papers from the file, Connery stuffed them inside the file jacket before dropping it in his desk drawer and locking it. After shrugging into his jacket he retrieved his "piece" from his drawer and followed Bell down to the parking lot.

"Let's hit his bank first. Maybe we'll get lucky."

Bell nodded in agreement as he fired up the Camaro. "I alerted the airport authorities," Bell continued.

"What do we know about Madison?"

"He's a local enforcer, but crooked—anything for the right amount. Never heard of him taking on a contract before and he'd never kill another cop. Must have been some payoff to make him change his ways."

"Or he owed somebody big," Connery added.

Bell slid the Camaro into a spot in front of the courthouse as Connery went to retrieve the warrant. He was back in minutes with the warrant in hand.

They were shown into the bank manager's office. Connery snapped the warrant open as he asked to see the account activity for Madison. The bank manager frowned—but complied.

"As you can see, gentlemen, nothing unusual is showing up. Mr. Madison's account reflects his normal pattern of credits and withdrawals."

"What's this notation here mean?" Connery asked.

The bank manager frowned before bringing up another file. "It seems that Mr. Madison opened another account in the Bahamas. There was no transfer, however, from this account. Really, Detectives, this is not unusual. Many clients open an account in our branch before going on vacation to the Bahamas. Finances are easier to transact with less chance of loss by dealing with a branch office."

"Sure, but Mr. Madison's not the type to pull up stakes for a vacation in the sunny islands. Can you bring up the branch office's account?"

Frowning again, the manager complied.

Bell strolled back behind the desk to take a look over the manager's shoulder. "Seems like Mr. Madison had the branch office wire his money to a Cayman bank. No way we're going to get any cooperation there, Connery."

"How much did he transfer?"

"A hundred grand."

"Some vacation."

The beeping of Bell's cell phone interrupted the tense silence.

"Bell, here. Okay, we're on our way." Turning to Connery, Bell exclaimed. "That was the airport—time to fly!"

"Geez, Bell, I really hate you driving all the time. This job is dangerous enough without having to contend with your recklessness."

"What? You didn't join the force for fun and excitement?"

"To protect and serve."

"That doesn't mean you can't have some fun while you're at it, partner. Live a little will ya? What's the fun of having a hot car if you're not going to use it?"

"That's why I drive a sedan!"

The airport loomed into site allowing Connery to take a deep breath. Parking in the "No Parking Zone" and leaving his "Police" sticker on the dash, Bell exited the car right behind Connery. Pausing just long enough to go through security, the two detectives made their way to the airport security office—only to find their man had landed in the Bahamas only minutes before.

"Damn!" Connery fumed.

"Let's go get my computer. Seems to me we ought to be able to trace back to where Madison's hundred grand came from. Since the warrant gave us access to his account number, some fancy computer tweaking ought to give us a lead. Come on partner—we're not done yet!"

Back at the office Bell booted up his laptop. Bell had programs even the department didn't have. Many were probably designed by the man himself, as Connery knew from reading his background. Bell had been a computer geek before joining the force.

Punching in a few commands, Bell sat back to wait. The powerful machine was feeding Bell information in a language Connery could not comprehend.

"Gotcha! The hundred grand was transferred from another account in the Caymans, which came from an account in India, which traces back to the good old USA. Right here in San Fran! I can't get through the bank's security into that original account, but maybe we can get a judge to do us the favor. Want to see?"

"You bet. I'm getting real tired of this cat and mouse. For once I want to be the cat."

"I'd like to see the bank manager, please."

"Of course, Mrs. Mueller."

"Abigail, what a delight to see you! Do tell me that this is more than a business call."

"Jonathan, I'm afraid not. At least not today. Can we speak in your office?"

"Of course."

"I need to hide some recent purchases from my husband. I've planned something quite magnificent for his birthday and I'm afraid he's going to discover it when the bank statements come through for the quarter, which will be right before for his birthday. Do you think you can help me out?"

"Are you planning something that is going to outdo that 50th birthday celebration?"

"Ooo, you remember! You know I'll have to top that, Jonathan."

"I'll be looking forward to how you possibly could. I believe I can take care of this for you. Let's see. If we close the account and rename it into a dummy corporation, we can send the statement to your private lawyer—then it becomes client privilege. I'll change the name of the account and erase the memory of your name." After a few minutes passed Jonathan assured his visitor, "There, it's done—you should be set."

"Jonathan, you are such a dear—and so helpful, too. I must simply find some way to repay you for your kindness."

"Abigail, you know that isn't necessary."

Abigail just smiled, and the banker knew he was going to get his "Beemer" much sooner than he had planned.

Abigail was proud of herself. She had done so much for Jason. If he only knew. He'd always needed her, he would always need her. If he ever found out how much she sculpted his entire being, his career, that trip to Africa, and his future. He would be absolutely nothing if it weren't for her. It was the most fun she'd ever had, but now she didn't know how to stop.

And last night, what was that all about—this weakness? This crazy business? Could her own pawn deceive her with insanity? No, she reminded herself, it was just the African sleeping sickness. No big deal. But how was she going to control that? She thought back to how she buffered his little bouts through high school. It got harder being away from him while he was in college, but that was when she discovered the power of the almighty dollar. Yes, many people would do just about anything for money. Jason never even realized he never knew what competition was. She bought the competition. She had taken care of everything. Like he's really that brilliant. She was brilliant!

What was it that started her quest for power through Jason? Was it that she was in control of him from the start? Control that she would never have with her husband. Whatever it was, and why she did what she did, one thing was for sure—she couldn't stop now. Now she could pick her daughter-in-law. Kate was out of her control, but now that she was gone, even if Zoia wasn't the one, she had her opening. Once he realized he needed her to help him hide his sickness, she would gain more influence with the next one.

What would she do without Jason?

TWENTY EIGHT

Home again, Zoia stared out the window as she waited for the teakettle to whistle. Thoughts tumbled through her mind. *Can I really handle a relationship where I'm not the needy one, he is? Do I want to? The money, the wealth, all the finery would be gone if I abandoned Jason now. But how long could she deal with his delusions?* The sleeping sickness explained a lot of Jason's problems. She had to remind herself that it was temporary. Her eyes roamed about the condo taking in the grand view of the San Francisco skyline, the chandeliers and marble floors. Everything here spoke of style and wealth. Was she woman enough to take what she wanted and deal with Jason's periods of dementia as well? She stuck out her chin in defiance. Her father had not raised a weak or cowardly woman. She would stay in the game to the finish. The two of them could handle the few fits Jason would have until he recovered. She wanted this life and she would have it!

How best to handle Jason? He wouldn't want to know that she knew of his delusions, it would make him feel weak. That would not be a problem, she was a great pretender. But when he lost it at the ball and mumbled incoherently—what he mumbled was the problem. A problem of a whole different kind. It wasn't "Zoia" he said over and over, it was "Kate"! She would not have her man pining for another woman—even in his subconscious. Abigail didn't seem to have much of an opinion of Kate, either. Together they would end Jason's feelings for her—or eliminate the competition. A sultry smile covered Zoia's lips at the thought. History had shown Greek vengeance to be a terrible thing.

As Kate made her way down in the elevator, Casey was still her all-consuming obsession. She remembered the day they met in school. Casey was the ring leader in the group of popular girls, she made everyone laugh. But she had this passive-aggressive way about cutting people down without them knowing it until they thought about it later. Someone once said 'Casey could build you up with one hand, and tear you down with the other'. Kate knew all too well.

Casey had what Kate wanted, control. She was in control of herself, a crowd, any situation she could get through it and leave everyone in stitches. Back then, Kate was never in control. She did not know what control was. She thought her father was in control, as she got older, she realized, when he wasn't in control he turned into a monster. And she thought Nick was in control when he saved her, he just replaced her and spared her that monster's onslaught of verbal and physical abuse.

Kate wanted to be sure of herself. She wanted to smile. More than anything she wanted control. And Casey made her smile at least on the outside.

"Hey girl", Casey and her clan approached Kate, sitting alone at a lunch table. "Let me do you a favor and spare you some calories." Casey pushed her tray into the garbage. "You weren't really going to eat that were you?" The girls around her were all laughing.

"N-no." Kate stuttered. She didn't quite know what hit her.

Casey kept walking, ripping on kids as she passed with everyone laughing hysterically. Then she'd disappeared.

The attention from someone so popular and funny, even though it wasn't so nice, meant something to Kate. The next time Casey noticed her they were in gym class.

Kate was worried about being in the same group with a bully she remembered from 6th grade. "Why do you look so worried?" Casey asked her as she sprawled out on the floor, she cracking her neck. "It's only gym."

Kate was sitting on the gymnasium floor with her arms wrapped all the way around her folded knees. "I'm not, just need to avoid someone."

"Aww, come on, are you kidding? Stick with me kid," and she did. She was the butt of a lot of jokes from Casey but she knew Casey liked her. Casey trusted her to do all of her homework. They had a great system for cheating. In her own weird way, Kate thought she was taking care of Casey. She felt responsible for all of her grades.

The night of the Valentine's Day Dance, Casey called Kate.

"Kate? Girl, you busy with our science project?"

"No, I ah, I was getting ready for the dance."

Laughing, Casey said "Kate, how will we finish the project if we are both at the dance? You are so silly, get back to work. I'll keep the boys warm for you!" As she hung up she heard others laughing.

Someone beeped a horn and Kate realized she must have gotten off the elevator and was standing in the parking garage. Connery would have a fit if he knew she had parked down here. 'Not secure' he would say. Just then a gloved hand reached around her, and pulled her back into a stone wall of a man's chest! Thoughts raced through her head. *Oh God! Connery had been right!*

"Listen carefully мдпэИьКдЯ СЗСРтд (little sister), tell your brother to tread very carefully lest he loses what is dearest to him. Russia keeps her secrets. Do you understand мдпэИьКдЯ СЗСРтд?"

The man was gone as suddenly as he had appeared. Tears filling her eyes, Kate looked around her at the empty garage with trembling lips. Running to the car, she slid into the seat, locked the door, and tore out of the parking garage into the sunshine of the hospital parking lot. There wasn't any man around. Women, children, and one guy in a wheelchair. She put the car into park, leaving the engine idling before speed dialing Nick's cell phone.

"I'm okay. There doesn't seem to be anyone around. Yes, Nick, they warned me to warn you. Meet you at the Hot Tamale. Don't argue with me—it's a public place and the staff knows us. Just, be there, please?" In the background she could hear the raucous honking of the geese—irritated and territorial.

"Gotta go!" The line went dead.

Kate dialed Connery. Eternity stretched into forever before she heard him on the other end. "Flynn, please, something is wrong at the house can you go? I am worried about Nick. I'll wait at the restaurant."

"Bell something's wrong at the house!" Connery snapped his cell shut.

Two Margaritas later Kate's hands quit shaking. By the time

the guys arrived she was much calmer—having figured out her next move.

Nick and Dirk had Bell and Connery close on their heels when they entered. The waiter brought them to the table, taking their drink orders just as quickly.

"Well, Kate?"

"You first, what happened at the house?"

"Accidental star sighting," Bell answered.

"What?"

"Some tourist thought a movie star lived at the house and was trying to get in for a picture. The geese changed his mind!" The detectives burst out laughing.

When he could breathe again Connery continued. "You should have seen it! The guy bent over to shoo the geese away so the goose grabbed onto his ear. About the same time the gander decided to latch onto the guy's wife's posterior!" Connery was wiping tears from his eyes. "The funniest thing I've ever seen." He was wheezing with the effort to hold in the laughter.

Nick was trying to keep a straight face. "Then when they found out there weren't any stars on the property and that they were being charged with trespassing I thought I'd bust my gut! Their Minnesota accent did me in!"

Dirk interrupted, "The crowning moment was when they slipped in the goose shit."

Now they were all laughing. Kate was happy the men had relayed their story first. Why did laughter always seem to make everything better—for a little while anyway?

After relating the goose tale and recovering from the laughter, things sobered.

Kate relayed the message for Nick's ears.

He was somber instantly, and resolutely added, "That's it! I'm done! There's no way I'm taking any chances with Kate's life. The damn story can die! Casey's in a coma and my editor is dead maybe I am responsible for my parents' deaths."

Everyone was shocked silent by Nick's statement. He had never been known to quit anything. How much more was there to his story he wasn't telling them?

"Nick," Kate began.

"Stop Kate. If my story is causing all these threats, deaths, and endangering your safety, and Casey's life!?—It's not worth it. You're all I have—I won't lose you."

Turning to Connery he spoke quietly, "I'll give you everything I have to help you—I'm done!"

"Think about it Nick, this could mean your career," Connery looked into the other man's eyes seeing the truth. "You know what you're doing, Nick. A story is never worth a life—although, I doubt the DEA or Immigration will concede the case."

A silence fell over the table.

Kate cocked a brow trying to lighten the load in Casey's absence. "Do you suppose the surveillance cameras caught the goose attack? We could send it to 'America's Funniest Videos!'"

The guys laughed nervously not expecting that from Kate. They were all caught off guard but happy for the change in subject. She brought the mood back down and ordered another round of drinks, this time Tequila shots. Spirits rose and fear receded.

SOMEWHERE THE BEAST ROARED.

IT WAS TIME.

That night Bell employed his laptop while Connery interjected questions as Nick unlocked the files of his mind back at the estate. Connery was amazed at the amount of confidential information Nick had been holding back. The details were like fine photographs—neat, clear, and precise and the backup to prove it all tumbled forth. This wealth of information was going to lead to someone's downfall. This was definitely too big for two San Francisco detectives. Interpol and the DEA were definitely going to be taking over.

As Nick continued, it was becoming obvious to the detectives why Nick was such a threat. The people he threatened to expose must think everything Nick knew could explode all over the papers the minute he turned up dead. They would have killed him a long time ago. His little black book was only a mind jogger—not the *real* thing. Nick had been smart letting people think he had it all written down and it was ready to blow. A good way to protect himself! The little black book only made sense to him, so his adversaries needed the code he carried in his head to access the info. As long as Nick kept his mouth shut they didn't dare kill him. Who else might have a copy and know how to translate the seemingly gibberish writings? Or would he e-mail his print sources from the grave?

It was after two a.m. when the men left the estate. Bell fired up the Camaro and without consulting his partner headed to the section of town where a message could be delivered to the man in charge. They were setting themselves up as the "mice" in a life threatening game of "cat and mouse". If the mob wanted Nick's book they would have to deal through Bell and Connery.

The seedy bar sported blackened windows and neon signs with a large no-brain type guarding the door. Bell took an "in-your-face pose" matching his height against the bouncer's, which allowed Connery to flip his badge before the guy could alert the men inside.

"Now we're not here to cause any trouble, buddy. You're going to deliver a message to your boss so get it right! Tell your boss that Coleman doesn't have the book—Connery and Bell do. We're willing to parlay, but time is limited. He's got four hours to give us a call." As he finished, Bell stuffed his card in the man's shirt pocket. "Number's on the card—don't disappoint us!" Bell backed off and the two detectives got back in the car. Engine roaring they sped off into the night.

"Bell, this might be the dumbest move we've ever made."

"Probably. That's what happens when you get involved with the case. Nobody is going to threaten those two ladies again without some serious repercussions."

"So, let's assume we are both smart enough to be where they won't find us. Got any ideas?"

"Nope. I'm just driving—and heading out of town. Less eyes that way. We'll stay close, but not too close."

"Works for me. Drive!"

The sunrise was glowing through a fine mist over the bay when Bell's phone began to chime. The spot was beautiful and isolated this time of day. They had picked it randomly, just 40 minutes out of the city. As Bell flipped open the phone, Connery started his timer. They weren't giving anyone enough time to find their location.

"You listen! You want to talk, meet me at the The Bay Bull Car Rally at two o'clock. We are the blue Camaro with the muscle cars. Don't be late!" Bell flipped the phone shut.

"Well, we're set. The gates are closed until check in at nine a.m. That will give us plenty of time to scope things out. Want to grab some breakfast on the way?"

"Coffee for sure." For once finding reassurance in his partner's madcap driving and souped-up muscle car. They had the edge—if it came to a car race, anyway.

The Camaro slunk up to the gate purring like a contented feline. Bell presented his gate pass.

"Here's your packet, sir. Your dash plaque and program are also enclosed. This is the map of displays. The bad-ass cars are in the section I've circled. I see you've been here before so you know where to go, right?"

"Yes, I do. Thanks."

"You're welcome. Have a nice time."

Cruising slowly through the lanes identified with yellow tape, Bell wove through the field to his section. Connery recognized one of the kids from the alley. He was beaming and waving at Bell. "Who's the kid?"

Bell chuckled, *was he kidding?* "Whatever you do, don't call him that to his face! He's a 25-year-old car geek with a black belt and a marksman certificate in the Rangers. Insult him and you might end up dead!"

"You'd never figure that kid, I mean 'guy' was such a bad dude."

"Looks can be deceiving. I helped him with his engine. He finished it last week. Great looking Charger isn't it?"

"It sure is. Can it beat yours?"

Bell scowled. "You want to walk home tonight?"

Connery burst out laughing. "No way partner. I'm beginning to appreciate your hot rod and your NASCAR-style driving."

Bell backed in next to the Charger, letting the Camaro purr before shutting it off.

"Hey, Tommy. Looks awesome! Cool color!"

"Thanks, Bell. Took some time getting everything right, I like the results." He patted the lime green hood affectionately. "The guys are coming in with their cars now." Tommy looked closer at Bell. "What's up? You look like you haven't slept in a week."

"That feels about right," Connery chimed in.

"Who's the stiff?"

"Tommy, this is my partner, Flynn Connery. I'm trying to give the man an appreciation for the finer things in life."

Connery turned, hearing the rumble of power. Three more cars crawled toward them and then backed into line.

"Yo! Bell!"

"Mark! See you got the chrome done."

The slick black GTO looked as sleek and as deadly as a cougar. Its chrome reflected the sun so fiercely it hurt your eyes. A cherry-red Chevy SS slid into line followed by a lemon-yellow Impala that was pimped to the max. The guys exchanged high-fives before Bell caught their attention.

"You know those favors you guys always say you owe me? Well, I'm calling 'em in. Connery and I have some business this afternoon. I need you guys to watch for some Russians and keep an eye on the cars."

"No problem, Bell. We've got your back," Tommy spoke quietly more like the focused Ranger than a kid.

Connery breathed a sigh of relief. He was realizing Bell rode with a dangerous crowd and they were all good guys. When several Harley riders came up to say "hey" the fact solidified. All of 'em knew Bell and one got down to business looking for the mechanic who fixed Tony's bike.

"That's Bell," the SS driver replied.

"Think you've got time to tweak my hog?"

"It'll cost you," Bell replied.

"How much?"

"A favor."

"What kind?"

"Nothing illegal or too time consuming. Need my back watched later."

One of the gang turned to Connery. "Don't I know you?"

"I know you. Busted you for assault last year."

"You're the bastard!" The man reached for his boot, but the biker stopped him.

"What's going on?"

Bell interrupted innocently. "Connery's my partner. Still want your bike fixed?"

The biker eyed the two up and then seemed to make up his mind. "This favor can't go against code."

"No problem," Bell answered, "now, what's the trouble with the bike?"

While Bell tinkered on the bike, Connery stretched out in the shade between the two cars for a quick nap. His last thought was that he really needed to get to know his partner better.

Several hours later a cold thump on his belly had him awake and in fighting mode. He was on his feet, reaching for his gun before Tommy had time to finish his "Whoa! Brought something tall and cold. Bell thought you might like some."

Connery glanced down to see an iced-cold water bottle and a tray with a burger and fries. He rubbed his eyes, looked at his watch, and breathed a sigh of relief. It was pushing eleven a.m., still plenty of time.

"Where's Bell?"

Pointing two rows over to a metallic-gray Mustang, Tommy replied. "Tinkering. Bell never gets a break here. He's too well-known for his mechanical abilities here at the rallies. I'll watch the cars, if you want to go over."

Connery nodded, he downed the burger in four bites, then attacked the fries and drink.

When he reached the car, Bell called out, "Connery, find me a rag, will you?"

Rag in hand Connery approached the hood of the car and handed it to his partner he softly asked, "What's up?"

"Everything's set. My guys are watching for our friends and Mog's riders are going to watch our back." Seeing Connery's scowl, Bell grinned. "Relax Connery. Here it's my rules and a favor holds the weight of gold. Mog's boys all have some kind of record, so they know the score. Today the bad guys are on our side. So relax and enjoy."

"Geez! Sometimes you're a bit scary!"

"Yeah, ain't it grand?" Bell was wearing an ear-to-ear grin at surprising his partner, again. "I'm done here. I'm heading back to the Camaro for a nap. Take one of the guys with you as a guide—come back and wake me at noon."

With a half hour to spare, everything was all set at. Bell lounged against the car with a cold beer in one hand. The Harley gang was scattered loosely about—drifting in and out of the hog section. Bell's car cronies puttered and chewed the fat in and about cars. Connery, now decked out in a "Fast Cars, Fast Women" T-shirt and mirrored shades listened with one ear to the car talk and kept his eyes peeled. Their contact had to be here somewhere. He didn't believe they would wait till the last minute to show. Being the kind of thugs they were, they would want to scope out the area before closing in. Before long one of the biker crew sauntered over, looking over the car.

"Ten o'clock, gray pants, white button shirt. See him?"

"Got him. Thanks Marley." Connery watched as the big man made his way over to the Camaro. Connery, cloth in hand, strolled behind the Chevy parked next to Bell, and proceeded to wipe off the non-existent dust.

"Nice car. Too bad if something happened to it," the big man spoke with a decidedly European accent.

"Extremely bad for your health," Bell countered. "This baby has teeth and isn't afraid to use them."

"You American cops. You think you're so tough. You know nothing!"

"Look around, pal. What kind of cops do you know that have this kind of backup?" With a flip of his rag Connery stood up and the Harley boys closed in.

Marley drifted through the boys like smoke, coming face-to-face with the Russian. Raking his eyes up and down the big man Marley growled, "Bad news to mess with people I owe. Thought you would have learned that last time Polischek. You know it's been kind of dull lately. Hate to see anything happen to Bell here, but me and the hogs are just itching for some payback. Want to oblige?"

Connery could see the big Russian didn't want to back down

but he could also read the caution in his demeanor.

Turning back to Bell, "What is it you want?"

"My partner and I want you to leave the Colemans and their friends alone. No more threats, no more visits to the estate, and no more computer games."

"Why would I follow your instructions? What can you do to me?"

Connery leaned over the car. "Let's just say that you might get breathing room to get out of the country before all hell breaks loose. Tell Ligria that we've got the book. We want to know why he's after the Colemans. If anything happens, we won't wait to start busting up his operations. Interpol and DEA are already breathing down our necks for more info. You check in with your boss. We'll be here all day." With that Connery snapped his cloth sending flickering dust particles into the air. The hogs vaporized into the crowd and Bell smiled. The Russian drifted off.

Now it was time to wait.

The Rally was winding down with no sign of the Russian when Tommy broke into the conversation. "Hey, guys we're being invaded."

Coming down the lane were several tough-looking thugs and one man, who was obviously the boss. Mog's crew had seen them, too, and this time Mog himself drifted over to lean against the rear end of Bell's car.

"Detective Bell?"

"Ligria?"

"I'd hate to disappoint you. Let's just say I am his Vice President. Now, you have something I want. It would be in your best interest to hand it over."

"Well, my mom didn't raise no dummy, I've always been stubborn. Are you going to leave the Colemans alone?"

"I have no interest in the family if the brother will keep his nose out of my business. However, I would warn him to stay out of Russia. People aren't so understanding there."

"I can pass on the message."

"Where is the book?"

"One last question. Who is the computer terrorist?"

The man looked puzzled. "I have no idea what you are talking about."

Connery butted in. "You're going to deny your terror tactics?"

"My men are responsible for the visits at the house and the garage—but computers? No. I have always found old-school works much better and is harder to track. Are we now done?"

"How do we know we can trust you?"

"Gentlemen! I may be on the underside of your law, but my word has always been good. How do I know I can trust you? Enough, now the book!"

Bell glanced at Connery, who nodded. Bell flipped the book out and handed it to the Russian.

"Thank you, Detectives."

"Don't get too comfortable. We've played this game before."

"Ahh. You have another copy? I am disappointed gentlemen. Where is your honor?"

"Now, did we say we had another copy?"

"Nope."

He mumbled some Russian and then said "This is a dangerous game you play, Detectives."

"We didn't include the key for the code. You didn't really expect American cops to just let you ride off into the sunset, now did you?"

"Americans—so much drama! This is not a movie. You have no idea who you are messing with. Let's not meet again, gentlemen."

"We won't if you stay out of the U.S."

The Russians moved on as Connery watched them make their way to the entrance gate where a white limo waited.

"Think he's done?" Connery asked as he turned to Bell.

"Don't know. What bothers me is that if he wasn't behind the computer intimidation, who was? I think we've got another villain in the mix."

"Shit! Any ideas on where to start looking, Bell?"

"Yeah, just one, in the computer."

THE BEAST WAS ENJOYING A NEW FREEDOM.

IT WAS NICE TO BE IN CONTROL AGAIN.

SO MANY POSSIBILITIES.

ON ITS OWN IT WAS NO LONGER HELD BACK BY THE COMPASSION, GUILT TRIPS, AND FEAR OF THE HOST.

THE HOST SHOULD BE GRATEFUL FOR THE EMPOWERMENT OF THE BEAST.

TWENTY NINE

The hospital cafeteria was buzzing. It was lunchtime and Kate had avoided coming here without Casey. She missed her and there were bound to be too many questions from everyone else. Questions with no answers. She sampled the lunch on her tray. Felix and the others in line rambled on and on about something. They were there for the convenience and to take Kate's mind off Casey for a minute. By the time they got to a table, Kate's guard was down and they all had her laughing again. It was a fine line, if she didn't laugh, she was sure she'd cry.

From the entrance doors Jason watched glaring. *How dare she! Kate had never laughed like that with me! I will make her see that we were right for each other. She was meant to be the mother of my children, this was the plan.* Then his thoughts turned to Zoia. She was indeed exotic and daring. *No, I won't give her up, either. She will entertain me while Kate will grace my house.* His mind set on the best of both worlds, he sauntered into the cafeteria and made his way to her table.

Kate was the first to note his entrance and the others watched her smile fade. The eyes of that cheeky friend of hers, Felix, flashed fire.

"Good morning, Kate."

"Dr. Mueller."

Jason frowned at the stiff response. Playing the consummate actor, he put a smile on his face. "You look well."

"Jason, I thought we both had moved on. How is Zoia?"

Jason's blood began to boil—but he maintained a cool reserve. "I am trying to be friendly. After all, we do work in the same building."

"Please don't bother. You seem to have found a lovely woman who enjoys your company and I am perfectly happy with my life. Let's just go our separate ways."

Jason's face began to warm at her public put down. *How could she? There was no one who could know her like I did.* His fist clenched in anger. *No. I will not make a scene here in public! I am better bred than that!* So instead he gave her a curt nod and turned to leave.

A dark head, hidden from view, took in the scene. Zoia fumed. *Jason you are mine! That bitch obviously doesn't care for you like I do. Why do you keep humiliating yourself?!* Taking a deep breath she calmed her features before striding into the cafeteria to meet Jason.

"Jason," she purred as he looked up, finally noticing her.

"What are you doing here?"

She could sense his displeasure. "This came special delivery for you this morning. I thought it might be important, so I brought it over." She handed him the stiff envelope.

Trying to regain a semblance of calm, (he couldn't believe she was here—after he specifically told her not to bother him at work) he noticed the seal on the envelope. It was from the Governor! He began to cool as he saw the reason for her disobedience.

"Come on. We'll open this in my office." He gripped her elbow, escorting her out. Reaching his office Jason determinedly slit open the outer envelope exposing the embossed card within. He scanned the lettering in mild disbelief, then read the card again.

Zoia wandered off, giving him space. She ran her finger along the frames of his medical degrees, then admired the bronze statue on his desk. All the while her mind was turning. There must be something she could do to keep Kate away from Jason. She would *not* be giving him up! Perhaps she should consult with Abigail. If Jason thought she was involved with frightening Kate all would be lost. Abigail, on the other hand, Jason always thought of as interfering and planning her own agenda. Yes, she would talk to Abigail, let her do the dirty work. It wasn't worth risking her relationship with him.

Jason raised his eyes and pondered the sight of Zoia in his office. She was immaculately dressed in slender copper slacks and one of those silk blouses he loved in a soft cream. A large copper choker brought the eyes to her sexy clavicle as the blouse fell open. Both casual and elegant at the same time. "We've been invited for a weekend golf outing with the Governor. What do you think Zoia?"

"I believe this should be your decision, Jason. Do you want to attend? I'm sure the Governor couldn't possibly care less if I'm there or not." Her carefully schooled features did not give away her feelings.

"What's the matter with you? I thought you'd jump at the chance to spend another weekend with the Governor!"

"Jason," she softly countered, "I want what makes you happy. If you wish to attend, please do."

His anger quieted as he realized Zoia was trying to bow to his wishes. "Would you accompany me, please, Zoia?"

"As you wish."

Jason nodded at her reply, realizing that Zoia might be a great asset to his career if he wished to go into politics. Maybe he had it wrong. Maybe she would be his wife and Kate would be merely his plaything! Life was looking up.

After leaving Jason, Zoia met her lunch date at Carmichael's. Abigail was already waiting and was just finishing her first cocktail.

"I apologize for being late, Abigail, but something came up."

"Is Jason alright?"

"Yes, of course, but I'll let him tell you the news. While I was at the hospital I saw him talking with Kate Coleman. He is still infatuated with her. I hope she isn't going to be a problem."

"Let me worry about that dear, that little chit will never get anywhere near this family!"

"Good. I'm glad we've set our sights on the same goal, Abigail. Now, what sounds good for lunch?"

Abigail leaned back against the leather seat of the car, contemplating. Jason would need some help to get over the Coleman girl. Running into her at the hospital was not helping. With a press of her finger she raised the soundproof glass between herself and the chauffeur. Deliberately she picked up the cell phone and dialed the number of an old friend.

"Wallace Renfeld please. This is Abigail Mueller. Wallace how are you?!"

"Well, you know the family has always supported the hospital. Really, Wallace, it wasn't that much, but the children's wing is amazing, you are right about that. Well, yes, there is something you could help me with. There's a woman in the Claims Department who won't leave Jason alone. Oh, we've tried, but the girl just doesn't seem to understand that Jason isn't interested and has a lovely young lady friend. Yes, the one from the ball. Well, Miss Coleman seems to find excuses to run into Jason at the hospital and I believe that not only is it affecting her work, it may begin to affect Jason's. Do you really think you could help? Oh, that would be just wonderful, Wallace. Thank you so much. Buh-bye now!"

Abigail Mueller leaned back in self satisfaction. Her day was going so well! Things would work out just the way she planned.

Leaning over Kate's desk Mrs. Boe spoke softly. "Kate, when you finish this, please come into my office."

Kate gave her a puzzled smile before returning to her computer screen and the claim she was working on.

Taking a seat across from Mrs. Boe, Kate waited patiently—hands folded.

"I don't quite know how to tell you this, but you've been terminated." Mrs. Boe was having trouble meeting Kate's eyes.

"What?"

"We are eliminating your position, Kate. I guess there is no easy way to say it."

"What? Why?"

Mrs. Boe shuffled the papers on her desk. "Listen Kate. This isn't coming from me. I feel you do an exceptional job here. This comes from higher up. All I know is several personnel have received their walking papers. The only thing I see in common is that all of you have another source of income, so that you won't be floundering from this action. I know the administration has been talking of cutting back, and until today I thought it was all just that—talk. I'm sorry Kate, please have all your things cleared out immediately and give me the password for your computer." Mrs. Boe's eyes flitted back to her desk and Kate shakily rose to leave the office.

She tried to finished up what reports she could and left memos for the next person but was stopped by a security guard. Her few personal items fit easily into a box and as she snapped off the computer for the last time a mist covered her eyes. Was there something they knew that she didn't? How could they just do that?

She held herself together just long enough to get to her car. She cried on the way home and found her composure as she got out of the car and climbed the steps to the house. They were still living in it since the security was so souped up and right now it was nice to go home and know Nick would be there. She couldn't imagine having to go back to the condo without Casey there. She found Nick in her father's office on his laptop.

"Why are you home so early?" His smiled turned to a frown as she lost it and collapsed into his arms. She told him what happened between sobs.

Nick was shell shocked! "They can't do that! We'll get a lawyer! We'll sue the hospital! Just who do they think they are anyway, the boss or something?!"

"They are the boss, Nick. We have to let it go. Mrs. Boe was right. I don't need this job. I only took it because of Casey and now she's ..."

"What about Casey? You visit her every day on your breaks. And now they are down two people in claims? It makes no sense!"

"Don't get all riled up about this, Nick, please! I am trying to stay calm and you're getting me all upset again."

"Connery."
"Huh?"
"What's bothering you? You've been staring at that report for twenty minutes."
"Does it seem too easy to you, or am I just paranoid?"
"What are you talking about?"
"Ligria's guy. Seems like he gave up the chase way too easy for being some big-time Russian mob boss. We hand over the book, and the bad guys go bye-bye. Why would he have fallen for the book idea? Of course its a dummy. Why would a little book from a reporter be a threat to him? Did we act too soon? What about you?"

"Think he's feeling us out? Maybe he wasn't threatened by a note book and he just showed to check us out."

"Well, we didn't exactly tell all with that book of Nick's. We left out plenty of stuff. Maybe Ligria's planning on snatching Nick. And the more I think on it, I don't think that was Ligria."

"Think he sent his second in command, or something?"

"Wouldn't surprise me. Think the DEA got anything out of Trovoishek yet?"

"I'll find out."

Bell sat in the lab at police headquarters scanning the screen of Nick's editor's computer. As he traced the e-mail back to where it originated by breaking the computer back down to code he got a strange result.

"Connery you'd better get over here." He spoke loud enough for Connery to hear from his desk but quietly as he was on the phone with the DEA as he continued his magic. The final adjustment on the keyboard was being made as Connery appeared.

"Find something?"

"Something all right! The Lion podcast was sent from the editor's private network. So either it was Wells, but he's dead, and someone gained access to the editor's home computer—or someone sent a time released e-mail, like Nick received earlier. And when it was sent is something a bigger geek can figure out."

"Did we run background checks on the staff?"

"Yup, they all checked out. Come on Connery, once in a while it could be the obvious answer."

"Yeah, I guess its narrowing down."

Connery thought of his notes. "Computer knowledge, access to the editor and the Coleman Estate—still points at Nick or someone after Nick."

"We'll go to the board of directors, Kate. They can't take away your job like that!"

"Nick, let it go."

"What?! You loved that job."

"Yes, I did—but I've got a plan."

Nick gave her an exasperated stare.

"Really, I know what I want to do—and you're going to help me. Remember how Bell found the information about Ligria's ship in the Coleman shipping records? Well, I think it's high time the two of us took an interest in something that bears our name. If the company is hiding information and money for the Russian mob it's up to us to find out. Nick, with your nose for digging up information, and my attention to detail, I bet we could get to the bottom of this and straighten out the company."

"I'm sure Dad's cronies are going to appreciate that!"

"Frankly, as far as I'm concerned they can all take a flying leap! We own sixty-eight percent of the stock in that company. If they don't like it they can bail. Tomorrow morning we're going to work."

"What the hell, Kate," Nick shrugged one shoulder, "we might as well. You know damn well if we don't do it ourselves it would take anyone else a hell of a lot longer. And we can start tomorrow!" Nick raised his glass, "Here's to the next corporate managers of the Coleman Oil Distributing Company. May we live longer than its predecessors!"

"That's pretty morbid, Nick."

"Think so? I bet the old man is having a fit in hell as he watches us dig up dirt on his company. All those years of hiding secrets and we think we're gonna find some type of paper trail?" Nick took a deep gulp before setting down his glass. "Is it chilly in here—or is it just me?"

"Probably Dad sending you a warning," Kate snickered trying to lighten the mood, but Nick continued to have a worried look. Shortly thereafter a migraine was consuming him and he retreated into his own head, silent for a while.

THIRTY

Back from his trip and needing to locate his love, Jason was beginning to fume. He had checked the cafeteria, the lounge, and the claims office. Kate was nowhere to be found. *Damn she was a hard habit to break. Where could she be? Could she have called in sick?* Turning the corner he came face-to-face with Mrs. Boe, Kate's supervisor.

"Good morning, Mrs. Boe."

"Doctor Mueller."

"Have you seen Miss Coleman this morning?"

Mrs. Boe gave him an odd glance—then mentally shrugged. None of her business. "Miss Coleman is no longer with us, Doctor Mueller."

"What do you mean, she's dead?"

"No, not that. Miss Coleman's position at the hospital was terminated. My two best claims' people, gone!"

Jason moved on before she had finished. *Kate terminated?! Was the hospital doing that bad? What did she mean, she was missing two people? Of course, I'd forgotten, Kate's friend Casey was almost murdered, how could I have forgotten that? This place has been utter chaos since. How will I keep an eye on Kate if she is no longer employed at the hospital? This won't fit into my plans at all! No not at all!* His mind racing he slammed his office door. His mother rose from behind his desk to greet him.

"Not now Mother, I've work to do."

"My goodness, I know you have better manners than that, Jason!"

Taking a deep breath and mentally strangling her, Jason sat at his desk. "What is it Mother?"

"Well, the Historical Society has acquired some historical documents that seem to be written in Russian, and I was wondering if you would mind if I asked Zoia to translate them for us."

He studied his mother. Was she scheming to get closer to Zoia? With her it was hard to tell—although, this could be what it seemed.

"I suppose that she might enjoy helping out the Society. You can call her at the condo."

"Thank you, dear. Now I won't take up any more of your precious time."

Jason watched her leave—wondering if he had made a mistake. Then he turned back to the problem of Kate. *How to keep track of her now that she'd left the hospital? That's it, the friend. She was still in a coma and Kate saw her every day!* He knew that, that's when he'd catch her in the hall. Sifting through his address book he found the number he was seeking.

"This is Jason Mueller. We need to meet. Six will work fine. Same place." Satisfied with the call Jason returned to the files on his desk.

The look on the receptionist's face was priceless when Nick and Kate entered that morning. Nick made the introductions although he didn't have to, she recognized him from the news and both of them were in Mr. Coleman's family photo his wife put on his desk.

"I'm Nick Coleman, this is my sister, Kate. Due to my father's demise we will be seeing to the company's files until we appoint a new president. We need all of the Coleman Oil Distributing financial files and shipping invoices for the last two years. Please bring them to the board room immediately."

"We need you to show us exactly where the files are kept, and we'll be needing the administrator's password for the computer network."

Nick cocked an eyebrow. "I think that covers everything for now. Would you please direct me to Mr. Hansen's office?"

"Down the hall on the right, sir."

"Great, I'll be informing him of our 'invasion'."

Nick prowled down the hall, knocking sharply on the door.

"Come in."

"Mr. Hansen, I'm Nick Coleman. My sister, Kate, and I have

come to supervise the business and check into its holdings and shipping history."

"Thank God! Your father, unpleasant as he was, knew how to run this business. I'm only the accountant, thrown into this position because no one else wanted it. Frankly, it never was a job I wanted. Have at it young man!"

Pleasantly surprised, Nick filled the man in on what they wanted and Hansen diligently stepped out to help the receptionist and Kate.

The files began to pile into towers on the conference room table until the last two year's of documents filled one side of the work space. Hansen gave them what information he had and helped them sort through the shipping files, categorizing them into foreign and domestic. After considering what they were searching for they agreed to start on the foreign shipping manifests. They each took a pile and began scanning individual items for information. Meanwhile, Hansen went to find the accounts for the last two years to compare with the invoices contained in the files.

"What exactly are we looking for?" Kate questioned.

"You'll know it when you see it," was Nick's reply. "Think of it as looking for fraud on an insurance claim. Something that appears out of the normal, or the same thing one too many times. Just because it's in shipping instead of insurance shouldn't throw your nose off—follow your nose!"

Paint can in one hand and blade in the other, the masked figure stood back to survey the car. *BITCH* had been sprayed in red across the sides and all four tires were flat.

At noon they took a break and ordered in. Hansen tried to help, but Nick finally sent him back to his job—the less people involved, the better.

"By the way, did you think to let Connery or Bell know that you're not working at the hospital anymore?" From the look on her face, Nick knew she hadn't. "I don't know Kate, you better call."

"You know they are going to say that this is too dangerous."

"Well, they might be right."

"If someone is trying to warn me I'd like to know who and

why. You're not keeping me out of this Nick, besides, it was my idea."

Nick glanced at Kate.

"Don't even go there!" she warned.

Sighing in frustration Kate dialed the police station. Connery and Bell were out. It must be her lucky day. She left a message with dispatch before calling in Dirk.

"Dirk, why don't you call your boss and see about stepping up the security here at the office? I have a feeling we're going to be spending a lot of time here."

By nine p.m. they were shot. The type was beginning to swim in front of Nick's eyes.

Kate flung down a sheet of paper. "That's it! I've read the same page forty times, I swear! Let's call it a day."

Quickly they stacked the files into piles for the following day and locking the room they exited with a box of what Kate was into when they stopped. She was tired, but in case she couldn't sleep, she wanted to pick up where she left off.

As the elevator door opened to the garage, Nick took the box from Kate so she could dig out her keys.

"SHIT!"

Kate looked up to see her car. Bright red paint and the word "BITCH" adorned the entire side of the Escort. Pancake tires completed the makeover. "What's next?" she murmured.

"Back in the elevator—NOW!" Nick hissed furiously. They backed into the elevator's still-open doors. Nick furiously jabbed the buttons, ducking inside as the doors whispered shut. He had his phone in his left hand ready to make a call to Connery and Bell.

"I'm fucking tired of this shit!" Nick snarled. "These guys are really pissing me off!" He took a look at Kate's pale face and dropped the box on the floor and took her by the arms. "Come on, Kate, snap out of it! Anger is a better emotion to deal with this. Get pissed off for a change!"

Once out of the elevator and back in the lobby, Nick steered her to a bench where Kate dropped onto the seat. Would her life ever get back to normal? Would she even know normal if she had it?

Connery picked them up in the parking garage at Coleman Oil at nine thirty.

"I can not believe this! You're both out of your minds!" Connery lashed verbally at the two and threw up his hands in token surrender before running his fingers through his hair. Glaring at the two he commanded, "Talk!"

Kate began, "We knew our father had to be involved. And no one else has the authority—or the desire to look. No offense but we'd like to find out what he was into before someone else does. And, even if you two wanted to, you don't have the time. It seems perfectly reasonable for us to take over the business now that our father is gone. If we're looking for something else no one will know. Have some faith Connery. We've already had Dirk call his office to beef up the security. We didn't think we were in any danger, I thought you had settled things with Ligria. Or was I wrong?"

Connery looked at Kate. *My God, she challenges me but I love her,* he thought—surprising himself. He never thought he'd experience that emotion again after his first disastrous marriage and divorce. The lecherous woman had left him broken. Thank God, she was out of his life! Kate had brought emotion and fear back into it—not fear for himself, but fear of something happening to her. Maybe concern was a better word, just that he even cared about anything or anyone again was monumental.

Back at the estate Connery sat on the patio with Kate snuggled next to him. This protective feeling warmed his soul, but it also scared him. Life was so fragile—especially for a cop. He admired her for stepping forward with her father's business. She had a great point. The two of them working on the paperwork would keep the detectives free to pursue the leads they had been narrowing in on. But three generations of Irish rooted in law enforcement had shown him the dangers and broken hearts that were caused by the job. Getting involved with someone on a case would be a double heartbreak. But he was only now learning to live again. It seemed the deck was stacked against them. Leads on the case were few, and far between—with dead ends, twists, and turns, forever popping up. He didn't for a moment believe Ligria was finished.

After listening to the Colemans he had to admit they had a point. They might be able to dig something up while providing the innocent front of taking over the family business. Kate's comment had struck him, 'If someone is trying to warn me I'd like to know who and why.' He felt the same desire. Had her old man double-crossed someone in the organization? Had he been a part of a cover-up and then wanted out? Or, had he stumbled onto illegal operations in his company and been killed for it?

Nick and Kate said they believed their father had been involved, that nothing was beyond him, including child abuse. A father who felt it was his right and children were worthless and a mother too concerned with keeping up appearances—no wonder relationships scared Kate. The only normal person she had was her brother—or was it? He admitted to having blackouts—how much damage had their father actually done that he didn't know about? He shuddered and Kate turned in his arms to ask what was wrong.

"Kate, I'm sorry to intrude but Nick has one of those migraines again." Dirk's concerned look was all Connery needed to know that these weren't normal migraines. Gently he drew Kate to her feet and followed her back into the house.

Nick was lying on the sofa; sweat was running in rivulets from his brow and the muscles at his temples were visibly tensed. Kate quickly went to his side, "Nick, can you hear me?"

"Get it out! Get it out Kate. Help me!" he was pleading intensely before his lids fluttered and he went into a convulsion.

Kate quickly took control. "Flynn, in the refrigerator door there is a bottle of medicine with a purple label and syringes. Get them for me please?"

"Got it, Kate."

"Dirk hold him down while I give him the sedative."

"Kate, are you sure about this? I could call 911."

"It's okay. His doctor showed me how. It doesn't happen often—but they're so bad when they do occur the sooner we sedate him the more we spare him pain. I'll call the doctor after I give him the injection."

Connery handed her the bottle as she stood waiting with the syringe in her hand. Deftly, Kate drew the liquid from the bottle and expertly tapped a vein—injecting Nick with smooth efficiency.

"Looks like you've done that before," Connery noted.

"A few times. We'll give it a few minutes and see if it's going to work before I call his doctor. Sometimes we have to hospitalize him when they get really bad."

"Kate, what's the story here?" Connery asked.

Kate looked at him and Dirk and realized, that for the first time in her life, she was surrounded by friends who honestly cared. Drawing a deep breath she began, "Our father was a mean bastard. He beat us and terrorized us for as far back as I can remember. Nick always tried to protect me. One night when he got in the way, Father threw him down the steps. Nick was twelve. His doctor thinks the headaches stem from that fall, although, he has never been able to find any specific brain damage in Nick's tests. Stress and fatigue can bring them on."

As she watched her brother, Kate was the first to see the visible signs of relief. Muscles began to relax and his brow unfurled. Limp and peaceful after five minutes, Kate jotted notes for Nick's doctor after covering him with a blanket and lowering the lights.

"Are you going to leave him there?" Connery inquired.

"It's best. I'll check on him during the night. Usually he sleeps through the night after an injection. If not, I'll know in a couple of hours."

"Geez, Kate, how do you handle all of this?" Connery asked, concerned.

"He's my brother and I love him. He was my protector when we were children. Now it's my turn. I don't know how he handles these when I am not around. He must have stopped taking the pills."

"And who's going to protect you?"

Soft topaz eyes met steel blue. "I was hoping you would."

His strong arms gathered her close—enveloping her in warmth and security. Gently, Connery pulled her to a large easy chair in the corner of the room. They had a perfect view of Nick while hidden in the soft shadows of the night.

At first they sat quietly, watching. Flynn snuggled her close, breathing in the essence of her hair and body. Kate rubbed her cheek back and forth across the strong chest—*this feels so right.*

Shivers began to curl around her spine at the light nibbles and tongue exploring her neck and shoulders.

"Where did Dirk go?" she whispered—breathless.

"Don't know—don't care," rumbled from his chest before he continued his foray.

Senses burning, Kate allowed herself to drift in the pleasure of his nearness. He slipped his shirt off over his head and she did the same. They fell to the floor and landed with Kate on top. She slowly kissed him all over, then slid her tongue from each nipple to his groin where she slowly slid her hand down his pants. She could barely get her hand around him.

She slipped her wet panties off as he watched her and she helped him with his, exposing his excitement. She practically ripped his underwear off. She would get excited and loose control, then bring herself back, slowing down. It was driving him crazy with passion.

She straddled him and stroked herself with him. He thought he was going to loose it right here before even feeling her inside, then she guided him in. Moving slowly as he entered her, she rocked back and forth on top of him as she felt herself moistening even more. She began to tense as she tried to gain control and slow down but she couldn't stop. She felt in control on top of this huge beautiful man and she loved it. She squeezed as she watched him cringe. He was taking in her beauty as his hands slid along her body. He'd reach up to cup a breast into his mouth and she pushed him back down not wanting him to delay her gratification as she road him toward pleasure. *A little of the rough stuff eh? Two can play that game.* In one smooth move Flynn flipped her over and held both of her hands over her head with one of his great big paws. She didn't like that as she fought for control. He slid the other hand back down where he could guide himself in again. She felt herself wanting him deeper within her darkest recesses and was worried for a moment he wouldn't be able to hit that spot. She felt herself getting close to what felt like an explosion. She tried to gain control and back off again. He felt her resistance and dove deeper, not so afraid to hurt her this time. She tried to regain control, thinking of anything, something that wasn't exciting. Feeding geese, work, detectives ... what the hell ... what was she afraid of? She stifled a scream as he found a spot inside her she didn't know existed. Her nails dug into his back as she tried to stop herself. She didn't want to do anything embarrassing. *I'm gonna let go*, she thought. She felt herself swell and then, teetering on the edge, she exploded. He held her for a moment, feeling her pulsing slow. Then and only then, after her, would it be his turn.

THE BEAST WAS IN A PLAYFUL MOOD.

IT BATTED AT THE SHADOWS
SWIRLING CLOSE BY.

ONE OF THE MISTY, DARK WHISPS
CAUGHT ON A CLAWED TOE.

DEFTLY THE BEAST PULLED THE
SHADOW IN.

TOYING WITH THE WHISP AND
GRINNING, IT REVEALED A DEADLY
SET OF POINTED TEETH.

IT WAS SO HAPPY TO BE FREE.

SOMEWHERE A LION ROARED.

THIRTY ONE

Okay Casey. Girl, you can do this. She was feeling wide awake now despite the dark silence that had become her reality. Still unable to move, she was trying to get some answers by going back over her memories once more. *This time I'll get further than the supply room. I am awake, right? This is not a dream. Where am I? Oh yes, I was getting more red pens in the dark closet. No, I was with my friends Kate, Vic, and Tracy, that meant we were back at the at our favorite pub, The Cellar. We were celebrating.* Casey just got the job in the Claims Department. It was a springboard for her as she had her sites set on Administration. There was someone new there being introduced. Okay, Casey was getting it now, it was the night she met Kate's brother Nick.

"Whoa, who's the cutie?" Casey was smitten with her friend's new acquaintance.

"Hi, I'm Nick, I assume you are talking about me." His smirk was so endearing. He knew it, too.

"Casey this is Nick Coleman."

"Are you two married?" Casey was faking disappointment.

"No, he's my brother. Casey you dork, you've met Nick before."

"Oh yeah, a while ago, that was at our high school graduation—years and years ago. We have a lot of lost time to make up for brother."

"He was away on assignment. I told you that. God, Casey, do you ever listen to me?"

"I'm back from Paris for a while," Nick said.

Casey raised an eyebrow, "How you say, Voo lay booo boo shay avec moi?" she totally butchered that line and knew it.

Everyone was laughing. Kate was trying to get Casey to commit to her. Her parents bought her a condo, not far from the hospital, Kate had to pay them rent. Her father gave her two months to find a job and he wanted her out of the house. Kate was trying to get Casey to move in with her.

"If this is your brother I only have one question ..."

Kate wasn't sure she wanted a roommate who was so interested in her brother and replied, "What's that?"

"When do I move in?" Everyone laughed again.

Kate decided to nip this in the bud, "Me or my brother, you can't have both, Casey. I need the roommate and he doesn't need another girlfriend. Plus I lived with him once, he's a pig." This time Kate cracked everyone up.

Still not looking in Kate's direction she kept her eyes trained on Nick. Casey patted the seat next to her and said "Well, you come sit right over here next to me. I promise I won't bite ... hard!"

The table roared.

It was eight o'clock in the morning. Kate picked up the coffee and a newspaper to read to Casey. Kate sat next to Casey and held her hand. Casey's third day back. Kate knew she wasn't really back, but she was counting on the two to three days the doctor predicted it would take for her to wean off the meds. So far, they had seen positive changes in Casey that indicated she was right where they expected her to be. Her heart rate was nice and strong and sped up when exposed to stimuli. While her body was showing signs of response she still didn't open her eyes. The doctors explained that she was deep in REM sleep while her body mended itself, working from the inside out. Kate could only imagine what was going through her mind. *Did she see the killer? Would she remember what happened, would she remember her? Could she put an end to all of this madness that was following her?*

Kate stared at the posters she tacked up for Casey of a French countryside, the field red with poppies. Casey always talked about taking a trip, just the two of them. It was their five-year plan. Actually, they had been planning it for so long, it was more like a ten-year plan. It helped them both—planning an escape from ordinary life—from themselves. It helped with the monotony of the job and since their vacation days rolled over they were just saving them up for the day. They had even taken CDs out from the library on learning to speak French, a couple times a year. They never listened to them, they meant to. Life took over again with the humdrum. Their hearts were there, though. They would do it. Neither one of them had the heart to admit they wouldn't.

What were they waiting for? They both had alternating reasons to talk themselves out of planning it. For Casey it was the day she lost weight and gained her bikini figure back. For Kate it was the day ... the day, honestly, she didn't know what she was waiting for, maybe she felt guilty because they would leave the claims department two people short. She laughed out loud at that, she didn't have to worry about that anymore. She would see if Casey wanted to go as soon as they could talk.

Pain in her hand brought her back to Casey. "Ouch, your squeeZING ME TOO TIGHT! CASEY!! DOCTOR!"

The nurse came running and then another ran in and then out again to get the doctor.

Flynn reflected on the events from last night while absently stroking Sam. The tom was growly this morning after having spent the night alone and he wanted attention.

"You old rebate. I don't scold you when you spend the night out with the ladies." Flynn tousled the cat's head. "I promise to come home tonight, unfortunately. Maybe we can get Kate to make us lasagna again—what do you think?"

Once again, the night's events played through his mind. Nick's migraine had been debilitating. Flynn had never seen one that bad. According to Kate he'd suffered them since he was twelve. While they had lived at home they had been too afraid to see a doctor. Once they were in college, though, Nick had been diagnosed. The specialist he saw in the city was one of the best. Unfortunately, the doctor wasn't going to talk to Connery or Bell—patient confidentiality. Flynn had counted on Nick to be another buffer for Kate. But now that sense of security was gone, in a tight spot maybe Nick couldn't be counted on—maybe Dirk needed more help with security. The phone rang breaking his train of thought.

"Connery."

"I'm back from seeing Casey."

"Already? How is she?"

"God, Flynn, I thought she was back. She squeezed my hand

and …" She had to stop. Her voice was failing her. Everything she was holding in back at the hospital was about to blow.

"That's good though, right?"

"Yes, the doctor said it was a very positive sign. Then I had to leave while they ran more tests. You know, I can't do anything …"

"Shhh baby, I know. And Casey knows you're there, I'm sure."

Then Sam meowed on Flynn's lap almost into the phone.

"Poor kitty."

"Oh yeah, Sam is feeling put out since he slept alone last night."

"Hmm, I bet. If you'd rather stay home with your cat, I'd understand."

"Actually, he is demanding lasagna for supper tonight."

"Is he? That could be arranged. Will you be home at seven?"

"Should be—if not I'll call."

"I'm taking Nick in to see his specialist this afternoon. Then we'll be heading over to the office."

"Kate, be careful."

"Always." As they hung up Flynn turned to Sam, "Lasagna tonight, boy—so relax a little, huh?" He gently removed the cat from the counter, giving him a final rub he headed out the door to the precinct.

"Dirk, are you sure you want to come with us? There could be quite a wait."

"My plan is to abandon both of you at the doctor's office and drive off to get coffee and doughnuts. That way we can all be civil back at the office."

"Sounds like a plan to me," Nick stated.

"How are you feeling this morning?" The concern in Kate's voice was apparent.

"Other than feeling as if I've been clubbed, fine. The headache is gone. Come on let's go and get this over with."

The three were silent as Dirk drove to the freeway and merged swiftly into the flowing traffic. Following Kate's directions they arrived at the doctor's office in time to see Nick's specialist exiting his own car.

"Morning, Dr. Peterson."

"Good morning, Nick, Miss Coleman."

The doctor preceded them into the office, giving his receptionist instructions as Nick and Kate were ushered to a patient room. After listening to Nick and Kate's account of the past few weeks he turned to them stating, "Nick I'm ordering an MRI and a CAT scan. From what you say, the episodes have shortened in intervals this week, but gathered intensity. After the tests we'll see how to proceed."

The nurse took Nick off for the tests and Kate returned to the waiting room and started flipping through the magazines. One with an article on the rising cost of international shipping caught her eye and she picked it up. As she finished the article a nagging tug started at the back of her brain. She was familiar with the signs. When working in insurance her tug often led to uncovering fraud, or misfiling. She flipped back to the beginning of the article and started to read again from the beginning. There was something here that was important, she knew it. Feeling foolish she tore the article from the magazine, folded it, and stuck it into her purse.

"Nick there are some other tests I'd like to do based upon our findings from today's tests. Until then I'm sending along some new medication for you to try. Since this week seems to be a starting point for the migraines, I want you to take two capsules a day, as a precaution, until Friday. Then back off to one. The instructions are on the label. If a bad migraine occurs use the regular medication. Hopefully, this will help. If you have any questions, please call. I will contact you when I have the test results. Now, go enjoy that sunny day!"

Once in the car Kate asked, "Well?"

"Same old—same old," Nick replied. "It's all in my head!"

"Funny man. I'd slap you across the side of the head, but it might knock loose what brain you have left," Kate replied disgusted.

"Look on the bright side, lady, there's no cancer, no brain tumor, no aneurism. What more could a man want—besides a hot dame, hot coffee, and a fast car?" Nick teased Dirk all the time.

"Well, it looks like you're only one for three there, Nicky boy!" Dirk chortled.

"Yeah, yeah. Now cease your prattle and let a man enjoy his coffee."

"Yes, oh holy one!" Dirk was comfortable with the Colemans.

Kate smiled at the good-natured ribbing between the two. But Nick was right. Things could be a lot worse.

The ride to the company headquarters was quiet as each was lost in their own thoughts. After locating a parking spot they made their way inside to resume the scrutiny of the company records.

Kate dug out the article from her purse and handed it to Nick. "Give this a read, will you? It's tugging at my brain but I can't make a connection—you try."

Nick took the article and began reading as Kate resumed the search through the files. Dirk sat outside the door. He couldn't afford any type of distraction but he wished he could be of more help. He was dying to catch the bad guy.

Binoculars focused on the office. The man continued to watch. So far he hadn't much to report. But this was only the first day. He had found a comfortable vantage point and was in no hurry to push matters. He'd just kick back and see what would happen. Notebook open, he noted the stop at the medical center and the time a delivery man brought lunch. As closing time came he observed the three leaving the office and driving off toward the freeway. He gathered his things and started his car—following at a discreet distance. Odd, why would they stop at a grocery store way out here? Twenty minutes later they returned to the car and drove off. The rest of the trip was uneventful. They reached the estate and went inside. But at 6:30 p.m. the sister pulled her car out of the garage and left. Again, he followed.

Interesting, he thought—his employer would find this interesting. The address where the sister stopped and went inside was the one for Detective Flynn Connery.

THE BEAST ROSE, OUTSIDE ITS CAGE.

WHISKERS TWITCHING HE LAY DOWN WATCHING, WAITING.

THE HOST WAS ENJOYING ITS NEW SURROUNDINGS.

CONTROL WITH THE BEAST COULD REALLY MAKE THINGS HAPPEN.

THIRTY TWO

Life seemed complete, yet for Kate, there was a feeling that something big was going to happen to her soon. She was trying not to fear the worst. Flynn gazed at Kate. She rested with her head on his shoulder unable to sleep. The morning light painted her hair with warm highlights. He held an open palm out and she placed her hand in it making him feel complete.

The cat jumped out of nowhere and landed on Flynn's chest. Eye to eye, the two males gazed at each other. A silent communication passed between them. Then, with a delicate feather touch, Sam patted Kate's cheek. A smile spread over her face.

"Good morning, Sam." Then directing her gaze to the other male, she whispered, "Good morning Flynn."

He smiled. "Good morning, my love. I do love you, Kate."

She gazed into his eyes, "I believe you, Flynn."

"I think Sam does, too."

She laughed. "He loves me for my lasagna! What time is it?"

"Early," his smile warmed her heart.

"Good! Let's play." She lifted the covers and dove under them.

"No, let's talk." He straightened his arms tightly at his sides to tighten the covers and protect himself from her roaming hands.

Kate peeked over the sheets and frowned. "A man who wants to talk instead of make love? Be still my beating heart!"

He tugged her hair. "Seriously Kate. Our time alone is sacred. I need to talk."

Sitting up wrapped in sheets, she gave him her full attention. "Okay."

"There is a lot going on in our lives right now so we need to be honest. I never want to hurt you, Kate."

"Good, 'cause I don't want to get hurt." Kate was still kidding around.

"Really, Kate, I love you. I never thought I'd say it again. I've only said it to one other woman and it turned out to be the biggest mistake I ever made. I don't trust easily. So, when I tell you 'I love you' it's for real."

"You're not still married, are you?"

"Good God, no! I've been divorced for three years."

"Okay, so at least I'm not sleeping with a married man." Her jaunty smile told him she was trying to lighten the mood.

"Just understand, Kate, I can't deny the way I feel. I know you're vulnerable right now and I don't want you to think I would ever take advantage of you that way."

"I don't think you're taking advantage of me Flynn. You have enough info about my childhood to know this is not an easy step for me, either. We'll take it slow. You need to know, right now, that I really care about you, too." She wiggled her eyebrows, "Now are we done talking?"

Sam batted at the door and meowed loudly wanting out.

"Get dressed, woman. We need breakfast. Besides, Bell's picking me up today."

"Last one to the kitchen makes breakfast," she challenged.

The cat scooted out like a streak for the kitchen, forcing both of them to laugh at his antics.

"I'm taking a shower first."

"Me, too. Let's save water!"

"Woman, you are insatiable."

"Don't you know it! I'll wash your back, if you wash mine."

Flynn scooped her up, taking long strides to the bathroom.

Kate saw Flynn's backside in the mirror as he dropped his drawers. She had left deep scratches in his muscular back. "Sorry."

"My God, woman! What did you do to me?"

"It's your own fault, I guess you could say you bring out the beast in me." She smiled shyly and started the shower.

Bell arrived as Connery was kissing Kate goodbye in her car. Bell winked at Kate—who turned red.

Connery got into the car and Bell asked, "Aren't we driving her to work anymore?"

"She's just going home to pick up Nick and Dirk. They are finishing what's left at Coleman Oil."

As she headed off Kate had the sensation of being watched. Glancing around nothing seemed out of place, but mentally she made a note of the cars parked on the street. Over the years she had learned not to disregard the sixth sense. More than once it had been right. She glanced in her rearview mirror and saw Bell's blue Camaro head off toward the precinct. No one thought to look toward the apartment garage, where Connery's brown sedan sat with broken windows gaping.

Kate read through the files one more time. She knew in her heart there was something here she was missing—she could feel it. "I'm going to enter this data into the computer. Maybe then I can figure out why this is bothering me."

"Go for it, Sis." Nick continued to pour over the cargo transcripts. Then, he turned to match up the billing invoice of the shipments. Every ninth shipment the finances weren't agreeing with the cargo slips. Sometimes the payment was over. He retraced his steps again. He had it figured out.

"Kate, I've got something here. Every ninth load the payment doesn't agree with the cargo slip. The first time it's correct, then the next eight slips—it's over. The amounts aren't really enough to catch if you weren't specifically looking for it—but over the last five years it could add up to several million dollars. I think the old man was getting paid a kickback. Do you think these payments would coincide with the shipping weight variances that lead to the slavery bust? I hope to God it wasn't for shipping children. Leaving a paper trail in the books like this is just asking to get caught."

"You're right on," Kate replied from the computer. "Every ninth voyage stops at Volsonvad, where most of the children were from."

Nick looked at Kate. "That's where my contact is, that is where I got my info on the Russian Mafia."

"They probably found out you were asking questions Nick, and that is why Ligria has been after you. He knows you are on to him. The shipment got busted here and here you are, again!"

"Shit!" Faces flashed through Nick's mind as he tried to make connections. "I can't recall seeing or realizing I saw a Mob Boss. I don't think I actually know what he looks like to identify him."

"I'm calling Flynn," Kate reached for the phone. "They need to know how this all comes together. Geez Nick, the Russian Mafia is after you and our father was involved in shipping children for the slavery ring you were about to expose!"

Nick nodded, he was aware of his father's possible involvement. He was trying to find to what extent he was involved before continuing his investigation on the records. He was still trying to pull up faces from that trip, which seemed so long ago now.

Connery scowled as Kate told him what they had found. Bell was deep in conversation on his cell.

"Bring the paperwork and get in here, Kate. If this is true, you aren't safe there—anywhere. You two are lucky to be alive."

Connery tapped his toe, waiting impatiently for Bell to finish his conversation. When he hung up he had the same fierce look in his eye as Connery.

"Kate thinks Ligria found out Nick was asking questions about him in Volsonvad and can identify him. He is probably the one after Nick."

"Perfect," said Bell. "That was the DA, some of the kids started talking after several of their families were murdered in Russia last week. She is sending over the mug shots in case Nick can identify Ligria. They think they've narrowed it down. Nick can help verify it." Bell's eyes were cold.

"Hopefully Nick can identify this creep and we can put an end to this case. We have to end this before someone else gets hurt."

Bell ushered Nick and Kate into a private room and Dirk guarded the door. Connery had printed out the mug shots from the DEA and silently laid them on the table. Nick peered intently at the faces. Each person had his full attention as he concentrated. An hour later he had narrowed it down to the same three possibilities the children did. "I need a break."

"Let's go get you some coffee, Nick."

Connery and Nick sauntered out of the room leaving Bell and Kate behind.

"Are you okay?" Connery queried as they walked.

"Yeah. It's a lot to wrap my head around. You know, investigating this slavery stuff, I knew children were disappearing off the streets, but I never dreamt they were being shipped here by my father's ships. The terrorism was making me think my old man had a lot more to do with it than I cared to accept. I thought they were after us for something he did. I told myself it was a coincidence, small world, that sorta' thing. Now, I realize, I am the one they are after. They actually found out about me before I found out about them. Connery, I've seen all three of those men in the last year. If I could put the faces to the places—I can tell you where to find them."

"Can you trust your memory for answers?" Connery replied.

Nick smiled. "It can be a blessing—or a curse."

"What do you mean?"

"My short-term memory is shot. There are periods of time I can't always account for."

"Do you have blackouts too or just loose time to the migraines?"

"Yeah, when they hit it's like living in a black hole. Losing a day here and there. It can be downright scary."

Back after a few minutes Nick seated himself and focused on the faces again. Kate came over to rub his shoulders, seeing the photos for the first time.

"I've seen that man!" she was pointing to a photo.

"Where?" Connery asked.

"That's the man who threatened me in the garage."

Kate sat down next to Nick and looked at the photo as Nick turned it toward her. "That's him. I saw him for a second!"

Nick pushed the photo aside still concentrating on the other two. Pointing a finger at the one on the right he said, "This guy was following me at the airport in France." He continued to stare at the other photo. Finally, "This man was on the train I took across to Leningrad. But this man," he pointed to the photo Kate had identified, "I have no memory of him. Sorry."

"No reason to be sorry. He's the man."

"Why?"

"You don't remember him, but he thinks you do. So he's been watching you, and threatening those closest to you, and nearly kicking your ass to death. Russian mob bosses like to make their own threats in person but this guy has a lot of people working for him. Maybe even look-a-likes. I bet if Casey could talk, she'd finger this bastard! That's our criminal."

His name was Victor Sabarro, but they were sure, if they asked Trovoishek, he would verify that Victor Sabarro was actually his boss, Ligria. By offering witness protection and a new life, they were able to help a few loyal mob members sing. Hopefully they'd be able to make Trovoishek tell all. Now that they knew who they were looking for, the chase was on!

Kate leaned back in her chair. *Wow,* she thought, *that was amazing. I am totally confused but as long as they understand it, who am I to say they are just chasing their tails?*

HUMANS.

THE BEAST WAS ABLE TO SEND PEOPLE IN ANY DIRECTION.

AH, LOVE COULD BE SO BLIND.

THIRTY THREE

Casey opened her eyes to see three people in white lab coats standing over her.

"Well, hello there. Do you remember us?"

Casey tried, but she could not make a sound come out. Her mouth was dry.

"I am Dr. Lyle, this is Dr. Johnson, and nurse Mary, who has been taking very good care of you."

"Do you know where you are?" Again, she tried, but nothing. The doctor watched her intently, and continued, "You are in Mercy Hospital."

"You may find it difficult to talk, take a deep breath and try to relax," the nurse tried to calm her.

Her eyes showed panic as she looked from one to the next. Helping her slow her breathing the doctor tried to get her to relax a little. He went on with the information, they would test her later.

"The date is February 19th and the year is 2008. You were in an accident and suffered a traumatic head injury. You have been in this hospital for five days. While you were in a coma, your body worked hard to fix its injuries. We'll be running tests now to see how you are recovering. Do you remember your name?"

Casey opened her mouth but nothing came out. She tried again, this time she pushed hard and expected a scream as she realized what was happening.

"Gaaaa."

The doctors were quick to calm her as her monitor beeped quicker and her heart rate soared. "It's okay, Casey, let's not rush things. We are going to take our time. Relax."

She couldn't relax, her eyes darted around the room. She was breathing too quickly and was starting to hyperventilate. Another machine started beeping and a nurse injected something into her IV.

Peace came quickly.

"Call for you Connery," the desk sergeant hollered, "line 2."

Connery picked up, listening intently. Then a muffled, "Shit!" escaped.

"Okay, thanks. I'll send the forensics' team."

"What gives?" Bell inquired.

"Some asshole doesn't like my car. The windows were broken out sometime last night."

"Remind me never to park next to you—or let you borrow my car."

"I think I'll just have the department tow it in. They can see if they can get any prints off it."

"You don't suppose this could be the same person that slashed your tires at the ball?"

"Anything's possible." Connery left the room.

Bell watched the worried look on Kate's face. "Hey, Kate, it's more than likely this incident doesn't have anything to do with this case. Connery has put away a lot of bad guys. Some scumbag is venting now that he's outa the joint. We'll find him, don't worry."

"That's easy for you to say, Bell." She turned her attention back to the files—looking for more clues.

Watching from across the street, he pulled the cell phone out of his jacket pocket. Punching in the number, he waited patiently for the other end to be picked up. "They're all at the police station. Took a bunch of boxes in." He listened to the other speaker. "It's your money." The phone was snapped shut. Diligently, the man made his way to the newsstand and purchased several papers. A cup of coffee in hand, he settled down to watch the door.

"So you think this is your man, Connery?"

"Makes sense, Captain."

"I'll give DEA and Interpol the information and we'll see if we can locate him—be careful, Connery, this guy's not your normal street thug." Connery found the warning amusing. He was right but it was a little late for that now.

Meanwhile, back in the conference room files were stacking up in organized piles as Bell and several other detectives began to match up information with Kate. Stretching lazily, Nick rose from the table.

"I'm going to go stretch my legs and get some coffee. Anyone else?"

Dirk made a move to follow but Nick waved him back.

"Come on—I'm in a cop shop. What could possibly happen?"

Connery nodded and Dirk took a seat, watching Nick as he left the room. Connery started to say something but Nick interrupted with, "I know—stay in the building and look both ways before crossing any hallways."

It was thirty minutes later before Kate realized Nick hadn't come back. "Flynn, Nick's been gone a long time."

Connery checked his watch and rose from the table. "I'll take a look around. He's probably talking to the new lab tech—she's a looker."

"Nice," Kate said as she shot him a look.

His smile warmed her heart—but didn't lessen her worry.

Trying to seem nonchalant, Connery steered toward the vending machines—there was no sign of Nick down the hallway. The mens' rest room was also empty. *Maybe he stepped out for smoke?* Connery thought. He asked Dirk, but he hadn't followed Nick around the corner. That left the rear entrance, or the garage. The garage would have personnel on duty. No unauthorized personnel would be allowed to enter. It didn't seem likely Nick would be there so Connery turned to the back entrance. Nick might have gotten out unseen, but he wouldn't be able to get back in that way without a key. Maybe he was stranded after finishing his smoke. Connery hoped that was all. Exiting the rear door he scoped out the parking area—no one there. He continued scanning the lot. A vibrating in his pocket had him flipping out his cell phone.

"Connery."

"Nick's back," said Bell. "Thought you'd want to know."

"Thanks, I'll be right in."

Once he returned, he sat across from Nick, watching them pour over the files. "You all right, Nick?"

"Sure, why?"

"Seems like you were gone a long time."

Nick grinned foolishly. "Got locked out—I was a bad boy and snuck out for a smoke. Had to go around and come back in the front. Next time I'll know to take you with me Connery."

"Nah—quit instead."

"Tried that—didn't work. Were you concerned, too?"

"You've got to be more careful. We don't know where they might try something next—even here. Use some sense man, your sister was worried."

Nick nodded and turned back to the files.

Connery continued to watch Nick and Kate puzzle over the files. His cop's intuition was buzzing—something wasn't right.

The afternoon sun was sinking in the room's only window when the group decided to call it quits for the day. The files were gathered up and locked away in the evidence room. Bell and Connery watched as Kate and Nick headed out of the building.

"Shall we see what's up with your car, partner?"

"Might as well. I'm going to have to call the insurance company again. I can just see my rates going up."

But before they could get to the garage they were called back to the front desk. Nick was in a rage, while Kate was quiet and pale.

"What happened now?" Bell demanded.

"Go take a look yourself," Nick offered. "Check out Kate's car."

Connery and Bell held their breath anticipating the vandalism as they sprinted across the street to the car. What they found was disturbing. A naked doll was strapped to the grill and cat's eyes were drawn on the windshield with "I'm watching you" written underneath in red paint that dripped down the car like blood.

Connery muttered under his breath. Looking up and down the street for anyone seeming suspicious, he wondered if anyone on the street had seen anything. Just strides from the station you wouldn't think anyone would be so bold in plain daylight—but as they had found, Ligria dared anything!

Bell was already on the phone, "Bring the kit and dust it for prints. Trace the paint—anything!" Bell snapped the phone shut. "Forensics is on the way."

Nick was muttering under his breath and soon began to rub

his forehead. He fumbled in his pants pocket, finding the bottle of pills and popped two into his mouth. "Not now!" Connery heard him mutter.

The CSI team arrived and the two detectives ushered everyone inside.

"Nick, I'll get you a coffee. Sit tight and try to relax," Connery urged as he saw the signs of the impending migraine. Kate looked at him worriedly and Connery shook his head.

In Casey's dream she was playing with a kitten. The kitten was licking her finger with its sandpaper tongue. Casey looked away toward the clouds and the kitten bit her finger. She frowned and looked down at the kitten. It wasn't a kitten anymore. The beast had grown, and it was covered in blood. Not just her blood from her finger, old dried-up caked-on blood. She squinted and looked into its eyes. They were topaz, totally familiar, the eyes brought her comfort and she felt safe, then again she blinked and was face to face with a ferocious lion. She looked at her finger and it was missing. Blood squirted out of it with her heartbeats and was getting faster and faster as the scene started to become a reality. The clouds started to rain, small tender drops at first, then huge water drops that hurt, turning to hail. The lion glared at her and roared, shattering her eardrums she saw pieces fly from her head. She had no where to run. No where to hide.

THIRTY FOUR

"What's bothering you, dear?" Abigail asked Jason. They were seated at the long, formal dining table. Zoia was helping to translate a recent acquisition from the Historical Society. Jason and Abigail addressed thank you's for recent donations. Jason wasn't quite sure how his mother had roped him into this chore, he had only stopped by to pick up Zoia.

"Just contemplating the future, Mother. Zoia are you about finished? The concert starts at eight o'clock."

"We can go as soon as I finish this sentence."

"How are things going at the hospital, dear? Have you heard from the Governor? Sounds like a wonderful offer."

Sometimes Jason wondered if his mother hired someone to watch him. How had she known of the Governor's offer? He didn't think he had told her about it. The hospital was a dead end after his bout with the African sleeping sickness. The board would never trust him to work in the operating room again—on the chance he might have a reoccurrence. The state capital offered new possibilities. He knew the Governor was offering him the position because Jason came with the power of his father's successful law firm hopefully in his pocket. Jason knew, that unlike his mother, his father couldn't be bought—but the Governor didn't know that. It was time for him to move on and up. His mother would certainly be ecstatic with his move to Sacramento. But how was he going to get Kate to make the move to the capitol? He was still determined to have her, and as soon as the detective was out of the picture—she would come around. Although, she would have to pay for spending the night with that low-life cop. He shuddered at the thought. As much as he wanted to know her every move, he was wishing he hadn't found out about that. It was driving him insane. But, he wouldn't let her folly with another change his mind. She was the first thing he thought of when he woke up in the morning, and the last thing in his head when he finally fell asleep.

Perhaps the way to Kate was through her brother. If he could arrange for Nick to get the opportunity to work in the capital on the cutting edge, Kate would surely follow. Then he would be able to continue with his plans to have her, as well as the sultry Zoia. The Governor was already taken with Zoia. The woman knew how to play the game and was skilled at it. She would certainly be an asset to him. Yes, Zoia deserved to be upfront, Kate, he would keep in the background. The thought lifted his mood.

Abigail watched intently as Jason and Zoia left for the evening. She had diligently held her tongue, knowing about the Governor's offer, hoping Jason would seek her advice. But Jason had always been a difficult child—always wanting to go his own way. She had learned, over the years, to hold her council for then she had a better chance of steering him in the direction she wished him to go. Zoia was of the same council—a smart young woman. Abigail could see Zoia planned to hold onto her son. Over time she and Zoia would clash, it was inevitable that two such strong women would. In the long run they were both headed toward the same goal. Success for Jason with Zoia as his wife. *Hopefully, now that I have dealt with that little twit, Kate, Jason will get back on track. Out of sight and out of mind* she always said.

Zoia waited impatiently for Jason to exit the bedroom. The man hated to be late, or to be kept waiting. Zoia had made sure the evening would not start off on the wrong foot, she was ready early. Finally, unable to understand what was taking so long she entered the bedroom—only to find it empty! The bathroom door was shut. Cautiously, she made her way to the door. "Jason?"

A low guttural noise was all she heard.

"Jason!" She spoke louder and then opened the door a crack.

He lay scrunched against the shower stall, arms wrapped around his legs—head tucked. The low muttering was more distinguishable now. "The lions are roaring! The lions are roaring!"

Zoia quietly made her way over to him. Putting her hand on his shoulder she spoke to him softly. "Jason, the lions are gone. They aren't here. Listen to my voice. Do you hear your favorite jazz? Smell the candle in the bedroom? Feel me—I'm here and you are safe."

Slowly he returned. Focusing on her face he grabbed his head with both hands, hiding his face with his arms. "Get away from me!"

"Jason ..."

Quickly Zoia blocked his arm in midair with her left hand and slapped him with her right.

"Don't pull that crap with me Jason! I know exactly what's going on here. It's not the first time I've pulled you back and it won't be the last. Now stop acting like a spoiled child and act like the man you are! I'm not leaving you—so get yourself together! We have a concert to attend—and we'll be late if you don't pull it together this instant." With that she strolled out of the room to wait in the living room.

How dare she, he thought to himself. *How dare she speak to me in that tone of voice!* But then he realized she was responding just as he would have. *Suck it up and get on with it.* A small seed of respect formed for Zoia. She was more like him than any other woman he'd ever met. Get past the adversity and move on to the next event. They would make a solidified pair and as soon as he returned home tonight he was going to clue her in on what it was going to take to be Mrs. Jason Mueller. Kate was another world away. Anything was possible as long as he and Zoia were a team. *Forget Kate.*

Casey was focusing on her last memory when her mind would stop. She was in the supply room with the lights out. Her heart was pounding so loudly she was sure someone walking by would hear it and rescue her from the closet. Then, she heard steps getting closer, "Help me, I am stuck in the supply room closet and it's not funny anymore!" She yelled.

Then, the steps paused at the door. "Casey?"

"Gibson?"

"What the hell did you do now?"

"Gibson, get me outa here!"

Whack, thud.

"Gibson? Not funny at all!"

The door opened, light slivered into the darkness. She squinted, then recognized a friendly face. "Am I ever glad to see you, would you believe I have been in this closet for what seems like forever, while lazy old Gibson took a long break! Where did he go?" She looked down to see him on the floor in a pool of blood. She looked up into a face she didn't recognize anymore, a beastly grimace distorted uncharacteristically. Stepping aside for a second, Casey thought if she kept walking she could just get to the hallway and run. Her lights went out for good.

After the last box they all agreed they found all they could. Connery and Bell packed the Coleman Oil boxes. Just as they were ready to move on the Captain called them into his office.

"DEA called. Their pigeon is starting to sing. Trovoishek positively identified Victor Nabarro as Ligria and says they're planning a welcome home at the Coleman residence tonight. Get SWAT to cover the house. I want you there ASAP. Call PRIME. Nobody enters that house till we clear it first. Set the trap Connery and make sure it springs on this rat."

"Already rolling, Captain."

He didn't like the setup. Mostly because Kate was involved. The house was dark and quiet but full of police officers and a SWAT team hiding both inside and out. Connery listened intently. He heard a noise in the foyer. They shipped off the geese and hoped to trap Ligria and his men before Kate or Nick got home from the movies and then dinner. But they were ready and waiting much longer than they planned. They had baited the trap with a couple of undercover cops as stand-ins for Kate and Nick—if this didn't work, or if Kate got hurt, he didn't know what he'd do. Bell and Dirk had meticulously gone over every aspect of this setup with everyone involved except Nick and Kate. But they knew they were taking a huge gamble by not telling Nick and Kate. Judging by how he wanted to be involved last time, they thought it would be better this way. So now, they watched the clock. It was getting close.

Come on, come on, he thought. Usually he was patient—but tonight was different. A noise, again, from the hallway. Someone was here. Connery hoped Ligria or his men didn't trip over anyone as they were hidden everywhere.

His phone vibrated in his pocket, signaling the rat smelled

the cheese and a car was pulling in. Car doors slammed shut and moments later Nick and Kate made their entrance. They were early! The lights came on in the room and Connery cracked the closet door to verify that it was them and not the undercovers. Where were the decoys? What the hell were they doing here early? Connery's heart soared. He couldn't get them out of here now. The police had been watching the house all evening and on the other side of town someone constantly kept track of the mob. He realized the Mafia was right behind them with the second set of vibrations from his phone. All he could do now, was trust and pray that everyone's aim was dead on.

"Want a nightcap, Sis?"

"Sure? That was a great movie, Nick. I miss Casey though."

"Yeah, but it was great to go just the two of us—like old times."

Nick turned back to the wet bar, bending over to get ice out of the fridge.

A tall, handsome man entered from the hallway. Speaking with a heavy Russian accent he instructed them, "Please to raise up your hands."

Nick stood to see the man pointing an eight millimeter at his sister. Kate screamed.

"Miss Coleman, stay where you are."

"Ligria?" Nick questioned.

"Ah, so you do recognize me. Very unfortunate for you, Nicholas." He pointed the gun at Nick.

"Actually, I've never seen you before. If you'd just left us alone you never would have reached this level of attention."

"A pity. In my business one does not take chances. I am sorry this has to be, Miss Coleman. You are quite lovely."

Kate fixed her stare on the man threatening them.

Then Dirk was flying through the air, dropping her to the ground as Nick dropped and rolled behind the open door of the fridge. Connery burst out of the closet, gun in hand and aiming it at Ligria.

"Drop it Ligria. The game's over."

Scuffles were heard in the hallway, then shouts of DEA. "Drop the weapon!"

An ironic smile twisted Ligria's face before he dropped the

gun to the floor.

Bell entered from the library. Pointing at the floor with his gun he directed Ligria to drop and put his hands behind him. After cuffing Ligria, Bell jerked him to his feet, "DEA and Interpol are waiting for you. Hope you like bright lights."

"Ha! I will be back in Russia in a week! You Americans are so simple! Your justice system will set me free for lack of evidence once again."

"I don't think so," Connery retaliated. "Russian police are quite interested in wrapping up several killings back in Russia. And, oh yeah, your slavery ring operating out of Volsonvad. Our government has already made a deal with them but they want you first. You ticked off the wrong people, Ligria."

The Russian's eyes turned cold, but said nothing as the DEA agents hurried him out of the house and into custody. Ligria's men were split up and ushered into the paddy wagon, leaving the San Francisco police to gather up their gear.

Kate ran to Flynn. He enveloped her in his arms, not wanting to let go.

Nick cast a glance at the two and muttered, "I gotta get a girl."

Dirk chuckled, "Come on, I'll buy you a beer."

Bell left his partner, heading for the hospital to see Casey.

Finally, things were going to get back to normal.

THIRTY FIVE

The concert had been dismal. The soprano began off key, leaving the rest of the event to come crashing down. Jason's mood had turned vicious. He had ranted on the way out—brow beating the manager about the lack of talent. The valet hadn't escaped his wrath, either. Zoia sat quietly in the passenger seat reluctant to focus any attention on herself. She had never seen Jason in such a rage before. His cool demeanor had vanished—the tension rising to an unbearable level by the time they reached the condo.

His guiding grip on her elbow was painful and his angry strides were impossible for her to match in her strappy heels. Front door thrown open, he thrust her into the wall, breaking the fastenings down the back of her gown. Her cry of surprise only spurred him on. Her hands swept up to his, trying to loosen the hold on her hair. He growled menacingly at her.

He dropped down using his body to force hers more tightly into the wall. She heard the rasp of a zipper, moments before her dress was ripped from her. His only impediment was the tiny thong that barely hid her assets.

"Jason, you're hurting me." Her breath came out feather light.
"Shut up!"

Once again, he rammed her up against the wall flattening her breasts against the textured paint. Before she could recover he was inside her. Her breath came in gasps at the painful sensations. He spun her to face him. He tweaked her nipple with his left hand while the other twisted in her hair even tighter. He lowered his mouth to her delicate collarbone and bit her! At the same moment he rammed himself up into her. She couldn't suppress the scream that escaped.

Against her will her body moistened. His dominant demands

brought a thrill to her blood. Zoia tried to ease his way by moving with him, but was stopped as he tightened his biceps on either side of her keeping her arms at her side. "You're mine you slut!" Just then he pulled out of her, dragging her toward the bathroom.

"No Jason. Stop, I don't want this, not this way!"

"Shut up!" He tangled her hair around the copper handrail along the whirlpool before pulling her hands behind her back and binding them with something soft. Zoia balanced carefully on her knees, bent over and bound. With both of his hands free he used them to roam freely over her body.

She was ready this time. Steadying herself while leaning back against him, Zoia tightened her internal muscles, bringing curses from her partner. His pounding continued until she felt the first pulse of his relief. Her body began to warm. He withdrew. He walked out, leaving her bound.

Zoia fumed as she tried to disengage her bound hands. Her position was uncomfortable to say the least. With a deft twist of one wrist one loop fell free. Soon she was loose, trying to untangle her hair. As she turned she found Jason watching her with lowered eyes. His dark face scowled. Striding to within striking distance Zoia was past being careful.

"Don't you EVER leave me tied up like that again!"

"Or what, Zoia? I could tell you liked it."

"Leave me bound again Jason—and the next time your lions come calling I'll let them have you." With that she stormed out.

He watched her go, but off in the distance he heard a lion coughing. He turned to look—but Zoia's banging in the kitchen had driven it off. He'd have to be careful—she was the only one who could hold them at bay.

The tapes arrived from the hospital security cameras. Connery and Bell hunched in front of the computer diligently watching people come and go from the elevator to the supply room.

"Well, that's it Connery. Gibson, Casey, Kate, Nick, two employees from floors 4 and 6, and maintenance. That's the only time frame close to Gibson's time of death. What are we missing?"

"Okay, so our guy didn't come down the elevator. Who has access to the stairs with a key?"

Bell shuffled papers. "Department heads, maintenance, and doctors."

Scanning the list of people on the videos made available by human resources they wanted to delete small or old people and most females, because the detectives felt there was no way they could have drug Casey to the incinerator shaft. But it could have been anyone—anyone with the knowledge of what one well-placed blow to the head could do to someone as large and strong as Gibson. When they were finished the list contained fifteen names they would need to check out, Dr. Jason Mueller's name was at the top of the list. They popped in the surveillance tapes from the stairway.

Rolling through the streets toward the hospital Connery played the pieces of their puzzle through his head. He found himself relaxing as Bell maneuvered the Camaro through the traffic. A glance at his partner showed him to be a man of determination and honor. Connery realized with a jolt that his partner was someone he'd be honored to call his friend.

"Thanks, Bell."

"What?" Bell answered, puzzled. Keeping his eyes on the road.

"Just thanks."

"Okay."

"How are you holding up with Casey's situation?"

"I don't know. This job and finding a killer are keeping me busy. But there is not one minute that she isn't on my mind. When she pulls through I am not wasting any time with her."

"Been there. A word of advice. If she's the one—hang on to her for all you're worth."

"Like Kate?"

"Yep."

"Want coffee?"

"Sure, I'll buy."

The Camaro rolled to a stop. "What the hell?!" Bell looked at his partner, puzzled.

"What's Richie doing here?" The snitch was loitering near the entrance of the coffee shop.

Bell motioned to Connery as he exited the car.

"What are you doing here, Richie?"

"I called the station, Connery. They said you were on your

way to the hospital—figured if you didn't stop here first, I'd catch you there," he laughed oily.

Connery's eyes narrowed. "What's up?"

"Got something fer ya. The 411 on the street is that your friend has an invisible tail."

Connery's eyes were menacing and Richie took an involuntary step backward.

"What are you talking about?"

"Word is that somebody hired a PI to follow your girl around. 'Bout a week ago," Richie constantly fidgeted, looking left, then right. Connery had no patience for crack heads, but finding out someone was following Kate was priceless.

"Got a name?" Connery's voice was steel-edged.

"No, not yet. Come on Connery, you know I wouldn't cross you. Word is he's just keeping tabs on her. This is good, right? Right?"

Connery took a deep breath. "Yeah, Richie. Keep me posted." Connery stuffed a bill in the man's hand before turning to Bell. His partner was already on the phone to Dirk.

"You gotta tail. A real pro."

"No—don't know. Call Donovan—get somebody to watch your back. We'll be at the hospital if you need us."

"Yeah, you too."

Bell eyed his partner's stance. Connery looked like he was ready for a war.

"Let's get coffee. Dirk will take care of it." Before Connery could interrupt Bell added, "If we go rushing out there we'll tip them off. Let Dirk handle it—this is why he's so highly recommended."

Connery took a breath, nodding to his partner before stepping into the coffee shop. It didn't look like things were going to settle down after all.

Jason's cell phone was ringing. Zoia watched as he screened the call, walked out of the room and then closed the study door behind him. Strange. He'd never done that before. She let her gaze drift around the room before rising to walk over to the windows with their fantastic view of the city.

She'd played her hand after his selfish act. Now Jason knows she is aware of his delusions and she knows how to handle them. Zoia didn't mind the rough sex—it excited her. Would Jason be comfortable with her knowledge of his secret? Their relationship had changed since that night. Zoia wasn't sure if it was for the good.

Even before the concert he had seemed more standoffish. Something was definitely different and she didn't like it. Zoia knew what she wanted. She didn't foresee giving up her goals. And these phone calls—what was going on? Was the Governor finalizing plans with Jason? She didn't think so. Abigail was always one step ahead in that department.

She made her way to the kitchen, filling the teapot. Should she pick his favorite tea? Zoia reflected on the past few days and decided against patronizing Jason. If she started now she'd never regain equal ground.

Her tea was steeping when Jason entered the room—a frown on his face. He watched the delicate movements of her hands as she removed the tea ball from the china pot.

Things weren't going as Jason had planned. Connery wasn't getting the message about leaving Kate, and Kate—well, that wasn't falling into place, either. His PI had been spotted somehow. PRIME had increased their vigilance. His dog was being dogged. The PI recommended backing off—allowing things to settle down. Jason had raged—but the PI was probably right. He called the man off for now. He'd spring later—when it was least expected. Meanwhile, how to deal with Zoia?

He hated that she knew his weakness, even if she was adept at dealing with its manifestation. Better Zoia than his mother! Jason didn't want to have to fall back on her! As much as he hated the idea of sharing his secret with anyone—he grudgingly admired Zoia's attitude. She was tough and driven—like him.

"Is there enough for two, Zoia?"

"Of course, Jason." She gathered another cup and saucer from the shelf.

Cup filled, Jason took what she offered—noting it was the tea she liked, although not the Herbal Lime, which he detested. Cagey girl. They would make a deadly pair in Sacramento, and he would much rather have her scheming at his side. And Kate? *Well—who needed her?!*

"I've been offered a position on the Governor's cabinet, Zoia."

"Are you going to take it?"

"Yes, although it will be much more enjoyable if you come along."

"I can't imagine that the Governor will approve of us sharing living quarters."

"Perhaps not." He watched her intently, but Zoia's face gave nothing away. "Although, if my engagement ring is on your hand that should smooth his feathers."

She hadn't expected Jason to be romantic—but every girl hoped for more than this! A business arrangement.

"Do you love me, Jason?"

"We both know that love doesn't have anything to do with this Zoia. I want you, and I won't give you up." A furious glint came into his eye. "We both want what we can get from each other."

"I won't sign a prenuptial, Jason."

"I'll set up an account of your own."

Zoia nodded, "All right."

"I'll call Grayson's. We'll go pick out your ring."

"Jason—it's eight o'clock."

"Power does have its privileges, Zoia. Grayson is a family friend. A private showing is in order."

Twenty minutes later the owner and goldsmith watched as Zoia perused their collection. The quality and size of the stones Jason had requested astonished Zoia. As much as she appreciated the stones this was not what she had in mind.

"Could I have a paper and pen, please, Mr. Grayson?" The man complied and when Zoia was finished an appreciative look covered his face. The sketch was an elegant classical Greek design. The band looked woven from the etching lines. Three stones nestled in the woven lines.

"Can you find a perfect diamond, understated, maybe a karat, to nestle in the center? Then I would like blue sapphires on each side and rich royal blue not the lower grade navy blue. Make the band out of platinum. Can you do that?"

"Of course, Miss Zartoni. I will check the vault for the stones immediately."

Once again Jason was impressed. Zoia's creation was tasteful and expensive. The stones would be perfect, a small fortune on her finger without being gaudy like so many women were after today. Her choices were impressive indeed.

Abigail was ecstatic! Jason and Zoia were visiting to announce their news! Jason had accepted the Governor's offer to join his cabinet. She would continue on to an even "higher society". William scoffed at her idea of moving to Sacramento along with her son. "Stop hovering over the man, Abigail. My God, he's thirty-two! He's perfectly capable of running his own life." She hadn't appreciated his lecture. For now, she would stay in San Francisco.

And engaged? Oh my, how life does go on! She was surprised by the exquisitely understated ring on Zoia's hand. Of course, she favored Zoia as Jason's wife—but she hadn't expected Jason to reach the same frame of mind so quickly. She respected Jason's decision to marry for appearances if nothing more. She didn't want them living together. What if the Governor found out? *With them moving to Sacramento next month, Kate Coleman would be out of the picture! That girl had no desire to be a part of Jason's life, or travel in political circles. My God, look at her now, with that, that detective ... well, she'd be safely out of Jason's life anyway.* It was time for Abigail to cut her ties, too. She'd call off her dog and let things calm down before Jason and Zoia left. That way no one would be the wiser. She turned her attention back to the conversation at hand. William was directing a question toward her.

"Abigail, Jason wants to hold the wedding ceremony at the estate. Is next month even a possibility?"

"My goodness you're in a hurry, son!"

Jason eyed his mother. "I want Zoia with me in Sacramento, Mother. I see no reason to wait. I must keep up appearances. What would it look like if we didn't?" She smiled, that was her boy!

"Of course dear. I'll do my best to make this event everything you and Zoia desire. Zoia and I will pull it all together, dear," ... *in a month*, she thought.

"I don't want this made into a big production, Mother." Jason's warning was clear.

"Of course, dear. I'm sure Zoia has some wonderful ideas." Turning in her chair to face Zoia, Abigail began, "Shall we move to the drawing room, Zoia? We can start jotting down some possibilities."

"After you, Abigail."

When they reached the drawing room Abigail firmly closed the door behind them. She focused her frown on Zoia.

"What's bothering you, Abigail?"

"Kate Coleman. We need to distance ourselves. Do you understand?"

Zoia cocked her head jauntily. "Of course, I don't believe that will be a problem for me—but will you be able to cut your ties?"

"Certainly. We'll let things settle down before you two leave. Agreed?"

"Agreed."

"Jason, what will the hospital think if you give up your practice like this? Politics can be fickle. If you give up surgery you might never be able to return."

"My God, Father! Have you not listened to anything going on here since my return? The hospital banned me from surgery! Some nonsense about the sleeping sickness re-occurring—they're worried about malpractice! I've become a glorified consultant—going nowhere! At least with the Governor I'll have some sway with the medical field."

William viewed his son for the first time noticing the resemblance in stature and actions to his mother. *God help Zoia! To be saddled with a male Abigail would be hell.* But who was he to interfere? "If that's what you really want, Son, go for it."

Jason calmed himself. His father—the most sought after lawyer in the state—never had any interest in him, or his dreams. No wonder his mother was so domineering! Someone in the family had to make things happen. Watching his father return to his paper, Jason rose and stalked off to gather Zoia. He couldn't stay there another moment.

After meeting with the hospital board several days later, and turning in his resignation, Jason began to pack his few personal items in his office. As he emptied the last drawer his fingers encountered a small framed photograph. He gazed at it intently—feeling the rage within him rise.

Framed by a gorgeous orange sunset the photo had captured him and Kate at a hospital gathering over a year ago. She was ethereal in her soft, flowing, peach-colored dress. What a couple they had made! Looking closer Jason examined her tense stance. No smile brightened her face, her body leaned away from his. *That bitch! Even then she had been patronizing me!* He couldn't recall her laughing and animated with him like she was with that detective. *How pathetic was it that the only time I see her look with adoring eyes is when I see her looking at another guy?!* The anger burned bright—flashing to wildfire as he raged out of the room, bent on a mission.

THIRTY SIX

The security cameras were still and the bodyguard was gone. Even the pesky geese had been removed. The arrest of Ligria had given everyone a false sense of security.

Jason watched from a dark corner of the yard—waiting for her to get home. Kate Coleman had rejected his advances for those of a policeman! He would never understand that, NEVER! She spent the night in his sleezy apartment and had him at her parents' estate! She had always rejected his advances. How she had fallen! Now it was time to pay! He'd make her his again, and she'd like it, like Zoia did.

The sound of her car reached his ears. His predatory stare followed Kate from the garage to the house. Lights illuminated the house. Finally, as she had every night, she unlocked the French doors and made her way outside. Silently, he crept along the rock fence gradually making his way to the terrace within striking distance. He stepped out of the bushes—just as he was about to grab her, she turned.

"Jason! What are you doing here?" Kate took in the feral look of his eyes and began backing away. Calming her voice she asked again, "Jason, what are you doing here?"

"I've come for you, Kate. You were meant to be mine. All those days in Africa, it was you who kept me hanging onto sanity. You're the only one who can keep the lions away. Zoia tries, but I can hear the roar over her voice. The lions always run from you."

"What are you talking about?" Kate crafted her backward steps to take her inside the house as Jason continued to hunt her.

"I've got to have you, Kate."

"Jason, I don't love you."

His eyes took on a fiendish gleam. "That cop!" he spat out angrily. "It's that cop! I tried to warn you, Kate. He's not for you." He looked around, then in a hushed, heated voice he continued, "AND you slept with him! You always said you were saving yourself for our wedding day. But you slept with him! You are to have no other lover!" He was quicker than Kate thought he'd be.

She pivoted on one heel forcing him to miss her giving her time to run. She sped into the house frantically thinking of her options. Instinct kicked in and she was running through this old house for her life, again. Instantly she was running from her father. Nick's voice was heard trailing off, telling her to run and hide. Then Flynn's face flashed through her thoughts. *Flynn! What should I do?* As if from afar she heard his voice, *Get out of the house!* She altered her course, Jason fast on her heels, circling around to dive into the hall closet. It smelled the same, hell, it probably had the same coats hanging in it. As she scrambled on her knees Jason grabbed her ankle. Inches from freedom she went crashing to the floor as he pulled her legs out from under her and dragged her out into the hall.

He crossed her legs to flip her over. She was lying on her back looking up at him. "You're all mine now, Kate!"

She caught her breath.

He tried to shove her knees apart but she held them together tightly. Kate wasn't giving up. She drove her head into his face. His blood splattered all over her and she could taste the saltiness on her lips. She felt his nose crunch. Now she wasn't scared. She was pissed off.

"You bitch!" Grabbing her hair he pulled her head into the floor, then started ripping at her slacks.

Stars danced across her eyes. The sound of his zipper created new adrenaline throughout her body. She jerked one knee up into his groin, causing him to grunt and loosen his grip. She struggled against his legs with hers. Then his immobilizing weight was gone! She gathered herself to run, but froze as Nick pummeled Jason with a terrifying ferocity. The sound of fists pounding flesh made her think of raw meat being slapped. She had no idea where that image came from. Nick was silent, yet it sounded like he was growling. He was possessed. She realized that if she didn't stop Nick he would kill Jason. Grabbing Nick's right fist she tried to restrain him.

"Stop Nick, you're going to kill him!"

"Good fuckin' riddance!" followed another punch as he

pulled his fist free from her. Jason's head was being bashed into the floor as she screamed, "Stop Nick! Stop it! I don't want you to go to prison for killing him!"

His next punch faltered as Nick looked into her eyes. A protective gleam focused on her face.

"I need you here, Nick. Please don't do this."

With a deep shudder, Nick restrained Jason's hands, hogtying him with the phone cable like some cowboy from the old west.

"Call Connery," Nick forced out between clenched teeth.

Connery and Bell arrived leaving rubber on the drive as they screeched to a halt. Kate met them at the door and collapsed into Connery's arms. His heart started beating again when he realized she was okay and the blood she was covered in was mostly Jason's. She quickly filled them in. Bell had to hold Connery back from finishing the job Nick started. They stood over the bloody pulp that was hardly recognizable as Doctor Jason Mueller.

"You're lucky I don't … " Connery was at a loss. *Who the fuck did he think he was? Kate was with him, they were in love. What a fucked-up asshole. African sleeping sickness my ass. This guy is certifiable.*

Bell interrupted his thoughts, "You are lucky you stopped when you did Nick. But we still have to take you in."

"What do you mean?" Nick inquired.

"You almost beat the man to death. And Doctor Mueller, you are wanted for questioning, attempted rape and/or murder, and trespassing."

"Murder?" Kate's eyes were huge.

"We thought we had our guy with Ligria, but it seems he was only part of the problem. You are lucky to be alive Kate. Jason you better hope you can account for your whereabouts the day Gibson was found murdered and Casey was almost killed. You may not be the force behind the shipping and slavery—but Ligria swears neither he, nor his men, had anything to do with the death of the Colemans, the editor, Gibson, or the attempt on Casey's life. Nick, Ligria's got alibis and witnesses to vouch for his whereabouts."

"But why would Jason want to kill my editor? That seems a little far-fetched."

"We're not through yet." Connery's gaze rested on Kate who

was in the other room giving her statement to a police officer.

"O'Reilly, take Mr. Mueller to the car and make sure you read him his rights and allow him his one phone call. We will not have any setbacks with this arrest."

"Don't think I am not pressing charges!" Jason gurgled.

"Let's go Doctor Mueller. You have the right to remain silent, if you give up that right, any and all statements may be used against you in …" The voices trailed off as the officers and the assailant left the house and headed for the squad car.

"I just can't seem to keep you safe, Kate."

"I'm fine, Flynn. It was you who gave me the will to fight and keep going. Thank God, Nick arrived when he did."

"Yes, thanks, Nick. Seems you are the hero!"

"I'll always be Kate's rescue hero," Nick announced.

Connery thought that was an odd comment, but then, he knew the past that had twined this brother and sister together. *Probably just making up for times he couldn't protect her,* Connery thought as he considered the beating Nick Coleman had given Jason Mueller.

"Kate, do you think you and Nick should get checked out at the hospital before we take him in for questioning?"

She shook her head. "I am okay, just sore. Nick you okay?"

Flynn pulled her close to him and looked past the blood into her topaz eyes. He loved her and he didn't care who saw it.

"I'm okay," Nick had a scowl on his face and glared at Connery. Connery caught it when he looked up from Kate but wasn't quite sure why. *Oh well, he is still worried about his sister's protection.* It had been a tough day and emotions were still running wild.

"Kate, I probably won't be home tonight with everything that's going on down at the station. Could you do me a favor and stop by to feed Sam?"

Kate's face relaxed. "Sure, I will take care of Sam for you."

"I want my son released immediately, Detective Connery! You have no idea of the trouble this is going to get you!"

"Mrs. Mueller, please sit down. Your son has been charged with aggravated assault, breaking and entering, stalking, and attempted rape. With that list of charges what makes you think we are going to release him?"

The wind seemed to finally leave the older woman's sails. She sat heavily in the chair before replying, "Jason isn't well."

"Men who rape aren't!"

"You don't understand, Detective." Looking around the room she continued, "Jason contracted a sleeping sickness while he was in Africa. Do you know anything about the disease, Detective?"

"Not really, madam. Sounds like he shouldn't be out on the streets."

"Then I'll have you talk to his doctor. Precisely the strain Jason developed leads to disillusion and paranoia. The treatment can compound the symptoms. Lately, his disillusionment has been accelerating. Here is his doctor's number. I'm sure he will be able to explain it all to you simply, in small words, so that you can understand. Jason shouldn't be behind bars—he should be recuperating in a private hospital where those who love him can see to his recovery."

"I'll make sure to look into this Mrs. Mueller. That still doesn't excuse what he did."

"No, it doesn't, Detective, but it does help to explain it. Now, I'd like to visit my son."

Connery signaled to the officer outside the suspect room. "If you'll follow the Sergeant, please ma'am."

Several days passed without incident. Connery and Bell diligently pursued any lead relating to the Coleman case, going over the files and evidence, sure they were missing something but hoping it was all over. Nick's editor's murder was still a mystery. Interpol had ruled out Ligria and Mueller had been out of town. That left someone still on the loose.

"Okay, we've got three unsolved murders here. The Colemans' parents, the murder at the hospital, and Nick's editor. And, of course, the attempt on Casey's life. What do they have in common?"

"Besides Nick?" Bell said accusingly.

"Could their murders be retaliation against Nick?"

Bell shrugged. "I'm not ruling out anything or anyone at this point."

"Where's that list of people who had access to the stairs by the supply room?" Connery shuffled papers until he unearthed the one he was looking for. "And, here's the one for access to the editor's computer. Anybody match up?"

"Besides Nick?" Bell asked again.

"Besides Nick."

"Nope."

Bell looked at his partner, he wanted to scream at him YOU'RE TOO CLOSE!

"I hate to have to say this Connery, but you have to back up. It could be this obvious. It could be Nick. You keep looking past the evidence that's staring you in the face."

"No, no, no—no. Where's Nick's itinerary? Here—Nick was on assignment in Europe when his parents were killed, and here at the house when the editor was killed. You know, Bell, after the hellacious childhood they had, I could see Nick going after his own parents. And I am not too involved that I am not considering him. But the supply room clerk? Casey? His editor?" To hear himself say it out loud he realized it was possible. "That still leaves us with those graphic computer messages though. I just can't see Nick doing any of this to Kate."

Bell shook his head. There wasn't anyone else that made any more sense. "Come on Connery. Who doesn't have a reason for wanting to "off" their boss? And Nick is more computer literate than I am!"

"Okay, let's go at it from the other angle."

"WHY? Do you hear yourself? You are totally tap dancing around it. You would have the guy collared, if you weren't in love with his sister, based on what we have."

"Hold on, Bell. Give me a minute. We keep thinking the murders have to be connected. Maybe they're not. George Coleman had plenty of enemies and Nick's paper certainly exposed enough bad guys. Nick is one hell of a reporter, he has made plenty of enemies too. Maybe someone went after the editor for publishing his stories." Connery rubbed the back of his neck, afraid that what Bell was saying could be true. "Then—we're back to square one." To hear himself say it he knew Bell was right. He vaguely remembered Nick admitting to blackouts. *My God, could it be? Anyone, but Nick ... how am I going to do this without loosing Kate?*

Bell stood up resolutely, "I'll go back and look at the editor's computer again. While I'm at it I'll look at Nick's laptop, too. I still have the feeling the answer is in those computers, but you may not like the answer. I've known you for a long time Connery, and I know you will do what is right. While I am gone, you can figure it out for yourself."

Several hours later Bell came looking for his partner. "Connery," he said quietly.

Connery didn't like the look in his partner's eyes. This was not going to be good news. "Spill it."

"The computers are linked," Bell started.

"Layman's terms, please, Bell."

"E-mails were created on Nick's and set to be released at certain times from Wells' e-mail address. Through the link he could relay an e-mail at any specific time and day. Like setting an alarm clock."

"Shit!"

"It gets worse, Connery. Nick's laptop is the alpha computer. Messages have been sent through Wells' from Nick's."

"So—if Nick wanted it to look like he was in Paris on the 29th ... "

"His e-mails to the editor would say so—leaving him the freedom to be anywhere in the world."

"But why?"

"I think I found the answer to that, too. Nick's been doing a lot of research on the Internet on multiple personalities and syndromes that manifest from child abuse into adulthood. From what I've been reading, even though it's Nick, it's not really Nick." That should help face the facts and ease up on his guilt trip.

"We need to confirm some of this information."

"We also need to make sure the girls are safe."

"Do you honestly think Nick would hurt them, Bell?"

"Nick wouldn't, but his alter ego might."

Grimly, Connery agreed. It was then the heart-wrenching warning he had learned not to ignore, kicked in, waking him up from the denial he was in. "I think we better find Kate."

Bell took one look at Connery and simultaneously started for the door. Their thoughts were in sync.

"I'll get the car," Bell said as he dashed out.

Connery reached for his cell phone as he sprinted out of the precinct. After several rings Kate picked up. "Hello?"

"Kate don't say anything. Just listen and follow directions. Okay?"

"Yes."

"Are you at the house?"

"Yes."

"Is Nick with you?"

"Yes."

"I will tell you everything when I get there. Don't let him know that Bell and I are on our way."

"I'm sorry, we'll have to complete this survey at another time. My brother isn't feeling well and I can't stay on the phone too long."

"Migraine?"

"Yes."

"We're on our way."

Kate hung up the phone and glanced at Nick. She wondered what Connery knew.

"Nick, do you have your meds? Can I get them for you?"

"No, Kate. I don't need them. I just have to get through this."

"Nick? Do you trust me? I am going to take care of everything," Kate whispered.

"Kate, no, I can take care of it, all of it!"

"I've protected us before. You didn't know that did you?"

"A doctor can help you, Kate. It's too late for me, let me handle this."

"I don't need a doctor!" she shouted angrily. Calming, she took a deep breath. "I just have to let it out. It took care of Mother and Father for us and now it will take care of us. We'll be safe and together, forever."

"Kate, you're scaring me!" His migraine was killing him and he thought she was absolutely loosing it. "I know what you have done and I will keep them off your trail ..."

"It would never hurt you, Nick. It just wants out. Now that I understand that, the headaches have gone away and no one will ever hurt us again."

"Kate, what is this thing—where is it?"

Kate tapped her head. "It's right here, Nick. It always has been. It only came out to protect me when we were small, but it's been locked up for so long—it's lonely and hungry. It needs to come out. You thought you were the strong one, Nick, you sacrificed yourself for me before. This is the last time you will have to. I promise." Nick's head hurt so bad he was ready to pass out.

"You were gone for a long time Nick. I tried to stay in control like you do. I really did. But you know what I found out? The pain stops when I let it take me over."

"Here," Kate said, "take your pill."

Connery entered the front door of the estate. His heart quaked. He had finally put two and two together to get the answer—Nick—it was Nick. And, of course, now that he was ready to accept it, it was so obvious. He drove numbly to the estate without even telling Bell. He didn't know why or what he was going to do—he just drove. And here he was, in the face of truth. It was Nick who killed his parents, his editor, and even tried to kill Casey! Nick sent the computer images, and Nick was probably even the killer from Paris. How long had he suffered with this split personality? What was he capable of—what had he done?

He found Kate in the living room. She looked lost and frightened. She didn't hear Connery enter. She stared at Nick. This was her brother—but everything that made him her brother had vanished. Nick was acting like a possessed angry, wildcat on the prowl, pacing back and forth. He only took his eyes off Kate once, her eyes followed to see Connery in the doorway. The arched back, curled fingers, and spitting mouth no longer belonged to anything remotely human. Still human, yet acting insane.

Nick roared, "Kate, what did you do?!" His mouth was foaming and he started to gag.

Connery was lost in this virtual scene beyond his comprehension. Right now his only goal was to see Kate safe. He pulled his gun on the beast that he had called his friend. The friend he came to accuse of murder. Nick held his gaze as he crouched, ready to pounce. He looked from Kate to Connery.

Connery knew not to, but glanced at Kate, her frightened eyes begged for his mercy on her brother. Connery realized then that the beast's stance was protective. Nick kept himself between Connery and Kate, protecting her. He was both a threat and the protector of his prey.

The beast rose off its haunches and pushed itself into the air toward Kate but was stopped by a single bullet in midair. His eyes widened in disbelief. He hung suspended in time, for only a split second. He collapsed onto the floor, convulsing.

Flynn turned his gun sideways as he lowered his palms towards the floor. He just wanted to get her away from this insane beast that was once her brother. It was so unreal. As if on cue Nick spit blood and released a low guttural growl. Nick's focus remained intent on Kate.

Kate's frightened eyes begged him for help.

Could Kate forgive me if I killed her brother?

"Sorry about that, Nick. How about I back up a few steps and give you some space?" Slowly Connery retreated, and backed against the bar making his way along it toward Kate, his hands held low and palms down.

Nick, or whatever possessed him, visibly eased his muscles. He moaned.

"Nick, I just want to know that Kate is alright. Kate, honey?"

A spit and a growl came from Nick's mouth, then more blood.

"I'm okay, Flynn," her voice shook with fear.

"Nick, you're really terrorizing your sister. You need to come on out and let her know you're still in there."

Connery watched his face and saw emotion and the internal struggle that was taking place. He was afraid his bullet was to close to be called a warning shot.

Nick raised a hand to his head—as if to steady himself. The look of horror that moved across his face would never be forgotten. He would not take his eyes off Kate. Incapable of speech, he seemed to be pleading with her. "Kill it Connery, before it kills you. Oh, my God! The things it has done!"

"Go Kate—NOW!" Connery made it a command.

"NO!" Nick bellowed.

Taking one last look at her brother she ran.

His shoulders dropped and the hunting growl returned.

Connery raised his revolver, hoping this wouldn't be Nick's end. The feral mask dropped from the face that Connery knew to be Nick. Eyes stared unblinkingly at Connery. He lowered his revolver, hoping he hadn't killed him, only wounded him. Connery rarely missed a shot and this shot was to the heart. He was afraid to admit to himself that if it weren't for Kate's safety at risk, the shot would only have been to the leg. He fired emotionally. Nick had pounced toward her though. His gun was fired on instinct. He defended the woman he loved. He looked desperately for Bell. Bell had never let him down. He had to trust his partner would show up any second.

Keeping his attention on the cat, Connery caught the minute motion of the patio door handle turning. Focusing his attention back on Nick, Connery tried to get the man back from the feline. Nick's lips were drawn back exposing teeth. His shoulders dropped lower as his body tensed with pain.

"Come on, Nick. Don't leave Kate like this."

A muted growl escaped from Nick's throat.

"Nick, come on man. There's no reason for this anymore. Kate's safe, you're safe."

The rumbling growl was barely recognizable as Nick questioned, "Why?!"

"No one is taking Kate away from you."

More spitting and then Nick began to gag. A slight tensing on his muscles was the final movement before the cat's last breath escaped.

Connery realized he had been holding his breath and took a breath of fresh air deep into his diaphragm.

He straddled Nick's lifeless body, trying to bring the man back to life he started CPR. "I am so sorry, come on, breath. You can get through this, you'll be okay. We'll get you help."

Bell finally arrived in an army crawl through the patio doors with a large net that they had used on the geese.

Connery lowered his head. "We won't be needing that."

"Unbelievable." Bell did not know what to say.

"Where's Kate?" Connery asked without turning around.

"She's waiting with an officer from the medical team."

"Where the hell were you?"

"Going through the garage for a freakin' net. I was hoping to spare Nick his life. What the hell was that? God, I can't imagine the crap they lived through to cause something like this to manifest in Nick! How do you function on a day-to-day basis?"

"Hell on earth from the little bit Kate has told me. Nick was always protecting her. He sacrificed a lot for a long time. It's all so hard to believe or understand. They used to play King of the Jungle and take on the characteristics of lions in a childlike effort to gain control over their predators. Their fantasy must have become his reality. Split personality alter ego facade stuff."

"So, you think it was Nick all along?"

"I don't want to know—I don't know if we'll ever know for sure, if a victim could talk. I'd like to think that Nick isn't a killer, but this thing ..."

"A predator, for sure. Killing is part of its nature."

"Yeah."

"Detectives?" A voice was calling from the patio.

"In here O'Reilly."

The officer made his way in—looked at the body on the floor and muttered a hushed, "Dear God!"

Connery turned and scowled at him.

"Uh, the ambulance is here," O'Reilly slowly managed in shock.

The ambulance siren was deafening and it stopped suddenly.

The men rushed in. "He's gone." Connery announced. "The man was a friend. Please respect his body."

The EMTs strapped Nick to the gurney before wheeling him out to the ambulance.

Kate re-entered the room. Silent rivers of tears made trails down her face as she watched her brother. Connery silently made his way to her side, enclosing her in the warmth of his arms. The quakes of her grief vibrated to his very soul.

Kate's sobs grew louder and she latched onto Nick as they passed her. Connery tried to disengage him from her grip. "Nick! Let me go with him! No," she sobbed, "he's my brother. I need to go with him!" Great gulps of air punctuated her sobs.

"Kate, honey. Let him go."

"No! He's my brother! What am I supposed to do? Where am

I supposed to be? HE'S MINE!"

Connery disengaged from her fists and passed her to Bell. "No Kate, you're not going. You can't help Nick right now and you don't need to see him like this. Bell …"

"I'll follow you over, Connery. Kate and I will be right behind you."

"Thanks, Bell."

THIRTY SEVEN

Connery glanced up at the commotion in the hallway to see Abigail Mueller, lawyer in tow, making a b-line for his desk. Connery took a deep breath and readied himself for a confrontation.

Rising to meet her he said, "Mrs. Mueller—how can I help you?"

"I want my son released!"

"I'm sorry, Mrs. Mueller, but charges have been filed and a psychiatric evaluation has been ordered. There is no way your son is leaving. He is a criminal."

Connery was a bit surprised to find the lawyer representing Jason Mueller wasn't his father. Connery eyed up the other man before introductions started their verbal fencing.

"Detective Connery, Andrew Balsm. I'm Jason Mueller's attorney. We contend that Mr. Mueller was only at the Coleman residence to protect Miss Coleman after discovering her brother's alter ego. He simply went to warn her and escort her to a friend's residence when a misunderstanding took place. I will be filing with the judge in the morning regarding these circumstances."

"File away, Balsm. I believe our evidence will stand up to the actual actions of your client."

The lawyer smiled smugly. "If your evidence includes any statement from Nick Coleman we'll be out tomorrow. Testimony from the dead doesn't hold much ground."

Bell sauntered over, resting against Connery's desk. "How about testimony from a trusted Private Investigator?"

"I have no idea where you are going with this, Detective."

"Seems Mr. Mueller hired one of our local PIs to keep tabs on Miss Coleman. In fact, the man called Mr. Mueller's phone for instructions yesterday—since he hadn't been given instructions lately. Seems to me our stalking charge is getting stronger by the minute."

Balsm turned to speak in a whisper with Mrs. Mueller before turning back to the detectives. "I'd like to see my client now."

Bell stood, escorting Balsm toward an interrogation room, giving Connery a prime chance to challenge Abigail Mueller.

"I suggest you leave well enough alone, Mrs. Mueller."

"I'm sure I have no idea to what you are referring, Detective."

"We know you're involved, it's only a matter of time Mrs. Mueller. When you hire off the street they can always turn on you for a better paying client and around here everyone knows not to cross me—they're funny that way."

"Detective, you are surely out of your mind to think I would lower myself to deal with street scum!"

"Mrs. Mueller, you don't want to know what I think." Connery took private satisfaction in the astonished look on Abigail Mueller's face. "I believe we are finished here. Good day, Mrs. Mueller."

Connery turned and walked away from the rarely speechless woman.

Paperwork covered the surface of Connery's desk. With a sigh, he settled into his chair and picked up the top file. The hospital supply room clerk's name jumped to his attention. The case remained unsolved. He added notes to the typed report. His suspicions were that "the beast" within Nick had been responsible—but Jason Mueller's madness couldn't be ruled out, either. Connery made a note to add the evidence within the file to a box of unsolved cases.

Next was the murder file of Nick's editor. Connery leaned over and dropped it on Bell's desk.

"You take this one. That computer jargon doesn't make much sense to me and I am too close, like you said."

"Sure. Hey, Connery, have you heard from Kate?"

"No, not really. We've been playing phone tag."

"Go see her, Connery. She's having a really rough time. The hospital called about Casey and they said Kate won't leave her side."

"Thanks, partner. I'll do that."

Turning back to the files, Connery fought his way through the remaining paperwork which had accumulated over the last several days.

By the time their shift was over he was looking forward to some fresh air. Outside, Connery unlocked his battered sedan. Now on its third set of tires, with new glass as well, the car was finally fit to drive.

"You really need to upgrade your ride, partner," Bell stepped out of the building.

"Come on, Bell! She's an old friend—she knows me!"

"You're just too stubborn to change. I'm going to see Casey, want a ride?"

"I need to go home for a little bit, see that Sam gets fed before I go. He's been moping around—I think he misses Kate."

The key stuck in the lock as Connery opened the apartment door. "Yo! Sam, man!"

"Yeow!" The cat appeared as if out of thin air to twine around Flynn's legs.

"Hey, fella. How you doin' today?" Flynn bent to smooth his hand over the fight-tattered ears of the tomcat.

Sam arched his back, eyeing the man, then began to purr.

"Let's see what's in the fridge." Carefully stepping over the cat, Flynn made his way to the kitchen.

"Well—this looks interesting." Digging further, Flynn pulled out another container. Popping the cover his heart skipped a beat—there was no mistaking the aroma of Kate's lasagna.

Sam growled at the scent, digging claws into Flynn's pants.

"Okay, okay, Sam—lasagna it is."

The cat paced demandingly along the floor as Flynn warmed the leftovers in the microwave. Dividing the portions, Flynn set Sam's on the floor. He watched the tom dig into it with gentle gusto. When it was gone he looked at Flynn as Flynn finished his last bite.

"Sorry, buddy, that's all there is."

A rumbling growl was the cat's rebuttal.

Flynn showed the cat his plate. "That's it!"

Sam jumped on the counter and Flynn didn't reprimand him. Running his hand over the cat's back he spoke out loud.

"I'm going to go see Kate tonight. We need her back in our

life—don't we, old man?"

Picking up his keys, Flynn tossed on his jacket. Time to talk to Kate.

Sam stood in front of the door, talking to Flynn in his growly voice.

"Come on, Sam," Flynn spoke soothingly—then reached to pick him up.

The cat crawled up his arm, looking him square in the eye.

"What's wrong buddy?"

"Yeowowllll!"

"Sam?" Flynn asked worried at the strange noise from the cat.

The cat growled. His body started to convulse, then gag. He dropped the cat to the floor.

"Sam!"

Then it hit Flynn. He bent over as sharp pains ran from his stomach to his heart.

The cat was vomiting blood and he went limp. Blood ran from the tom's rear end. Connery watched in horror. Then he began to sputter and cough up blood clots.

"What the fu …" He collapsed—convulsing and vomiting. His head landed next to his lifeless cat's. *Poisoned!* He thought, as he felt his bowels loose control.

Jason fumed. His career was ruined. The Governor's offer was out the window with his committal to Green Lawn Sanitarium. The court order stated a minimum of two years, after which his condition would be re-evaluated. In the meantime, Zoia was living in his condo! Spending his money! Granted, she faithfully visited when allowed. If nothing more than to rub it in that it was his obsession for Kate that got him here. *What was Mother up to?* He often wondered.

"Dr. Mueller it's time for your session." They just loved to call him doctor in such condescending tones.

Jason calmed his features before turning in the nurse's direction. Part of his rehabilitation was anger management. What a joke! Anger kept the lions away.

Kate's cab pulled up to the hospital entrance which she walked through almost every day. Even after loosing her job, she still came here faithfully to see Casey. Well, okay, she might have missed a couple of days. It's not like she hadn't been busy. But she did help Casey with her therapy and she still read her the paper. Well, not the whole paper, just what they would read together over breakfast at the condo or at Starbucks, the funnies, fashion, only the feel good stuff to start their day right. The last few days, the paper had Nick plastered all over it. Kate would toss the front page in the garbage before she got to Casey's room. She passed Bell as he was leaving and quickly looked the other way since he hadn't noticed her. She really didn't have time to talk to him. Not now.

Some of Casey's motor skills were coming back slowly, but she would not be regaining her speech. Well, Kate was pretty sure that's what the doctors were trying not say. She wouldn't talk and she wouldn't be able to write or hold a pencil since her fine motor skills were unrecoverable. And she kept asking but never got a solid answer about if Casey would be able to remember what happened.

Kate thought to herself, My *that was certainly… what did they call it? Oh yeah, that was certainly "one well-placed blow"*.

Kate leaned over Casey. "Casey honey, are you sure you can't talk to me today?"

Casey's heart raced. She shook her head. Therapy was still not ready to give up. And she was hanging on to that. She would do whatever she could to talk again.

"Casey I miss you," Kate pouted like a little girl. "You know, I promised we'd take that trip to France. I have a ticket here. I really hate that you are letting me go all alone."

Casey just laid frozen, unable to move and scared stiff.

Kate felt like talking since she had someone to listen to her. "You know, Casey, I did love Nick. Poor sweet Nick. He would protect me from Daddy. I only did what I had to then, and I did what I had to now. There was just the one thing I had to do before I left for Paris. And with that done, there's this …" She opened a small brown vile and tapped it over her coffee, taking just enough of the poison to make her vomit most of it up and not get so sick that the ER couldn't save her.

The emergency room staff circled around her as she vomited uncontrollably. Once on a gurney they wheeled her into a room and pulled the curtain shut. The nurse talked calmly to her and let her know she would be okay. "We are going to have you drink this charcoal, it will taste a little sweet and chalky. Then we will pump your stomach to be sure we get what is making you sick out of there. It was very smart of you to bring the food with you." The nurse pried her fingers off the small tuperware bowl with the leftover lasagna that had been in her bag.

Kate told her this was the last thing she'd eaten and that this wasn't all of it. Her boyfriend, Detective Flynn Connery, had the other half.

"We will call him right away and let him know it may be bad. You were smart to have brought this with you. Were you going to eat if for lunch? Don't worry, you'll be home soon."

Home. Kate hated that word. *She wanted to be anywhere but home.* She smiled again thinking of what Jason was going through at Green Lawn. *What a bonus.* She couldn't have planned that. But Connery, well, that was a shame. *The man killed my brother! My dear, sweet, Nicky-Nick. My rescue hero! How ironic, this life. To find love that falls into a plan. Talk about denial. He totally overlooked me but couldn't keep his eyes off me?*

What was it Nick had said? 'They'd never find another to love them but they would always have each other'? 'Damaged goods', he called her. How ironic. Poor Nick. He rushed home to take care of me again. He knew that I killed our lousy parents. I didn't even have to tell him. He knew all along. His little scare tactics were to direct the others away from me and toward his Russian mobsters. And Casey, how many times have I told you to stay away from my brother? Damn, you are going to miss Paris!

Ah, Paris. It had been so long since she'd been there. But this time was different. This time it was business. Her homework done, she could take her father's place. Now she had to replace Ligria. And of course, she had a shipment to take care of. *This will be a lot easier without Nick snooping around.* Kate rolled on her side as she felt another wave of nausea coming back and smiled to herself. *Who's the King of the Jungle now?*

Casey's head was screaming. She knew Kate was the killer and she couldn't do anything about it. That crazy bitch! What the hell happened to her friend?

When they tried to get Casey to hold a pencil and write, it

was all she wanted to write. She could feel her hand forming the letters to make the words with the pencil but what she'd actually written was only chicken scratch. She even tried spelling the words with the only thing she could control, her eyes and eyelids. She realized that not many people would look her in the eye. Once she made herself so dizzy she gagged. And no one picked up on it.

When she tried to spell with her eyes for the doctor, he thought she was going into convulsions. That started a whole new series of treatments. She was surrounded by idiots.

She would get it all back. And she would find Kate Coleman. All she had to do was tell Connery and Bell. She would find her in France if she had to go alone in a wheelchair. She would find her and if not, she'd spend the rest of her silent days fantasizing about it.

THE WOMAN SCRUNCHED IN A DARK CORNER, TREMBLING. SHE PEERED OUT TOWARD THE SPECK OF LIGHT, LISTENING INTENTLY. A SMALL SLIVER OF WARMTH STREAKED THROUGH HER HEART. THEN . . . NOTHING! SHE WAS ALL ALONE.

FOOTSTEPS! THE BEAST WAS COMING! SHE MADE HERSELF SMALLER, TRYING TO BECOME INVISIBLE.

HOT BREATH REACHED HER THROUGH THE BARS. SHE COULD SMELL THE RANCID BREATH OF THE BEAST. EVENTUALLY, THE BEAST PADDED OFF.

SLOWLY, WATCHING AND LISTENING INTENTLY, SHE CREPT FORWARD TO TEST THE BARS OF HER CAGE. STRAINING WITH EVERY MUSCLE SHE PUSHED, THEN PULLED, NOTHING! THE BEAST WAS STRONGER THAN SHE WAS.

SOMEDAY, THE BARS WOULD FAIL AND SHE WOULD CHALLENGE THE BEAST ONCE MORE.

EVERYONE SHE LOVED WAS GONE AND THE BEAST WAS IN CHARGE.

About the Author, Rachel Gies

Rachel Gies presents her third book, *The Darkness Within*, a murder mystery. Previously self published books include *Captured Pearl* and *One Size Fits Most*.

Rachel is currently a columnist for *The Examiner Newspapers* in Bartlett, Illinois.

Rachel builds suspense as well as she builds characters in this thriller. Enjoy a suspenseful read of intrigue with a little passion thrown in for good measure.

Future projects for Rachel include a children's book that takes place in historic St. Charles, Illinois, and a novel based on a family's incredible true story taking place during WWII.

To order books e-mail: fairburn22@aol.com or call Fairburn Publishing Corporation: (630) 513-6070.